Shadows in the Golden City

THE CHRONICLES OF AMBROSE BOOK ONE

JENNIFER KAY

Content Warning

This book contains the following elements that may be sensitive for certain readers:

- Alcohol Consumption

- Anxiety/Panic Attack

- Drug Use, Forced Drug Use, Drug-Related Deaths/Overdose

- Explicit Language

- Explicit Sexual Content

- Violence

- This list includes but is not limited to all triggers, if you see something that should have been mentioned, please email: authorjenniferkay@gmail.com

Dedication

For every reader who longs for more magic in their lives.

Contents

Chapter 1

Aurum was the most beautiful city in Ambrose, but if I had to choose another one, it would be Circe's Cove. Unlike Aurum, which was a desert, Circe's Cove had green trees and flowers growing around white buildings. Even on the most brilliant days, Circe's Cove was full of shadows, so naturally it was one of my favorite places to *play*.

I wove through the winding roads amidst the buildings to reach the cove's highest point. Green tropical trees towered over me and sprinkled the ground with spotted sunlight. I wondered what would happen if I stayed in Circe, enjoying the comfort of salt on the breeze and the easy humidity that enveloped me.

The mountain top offered breathtaking views and was an easy trek. The green pressed against a vast, never-ending blue sea, and clouds flew high above with billowing white peaks. Nature drowned out sounds from the city, and it was glorious.

"It took you long enough." A gruff voice came from behind a boulder as an older man stepped toward me. He was short and grey in his hair, with a potbelly sticking over his belt.

"It's barely mid-day, Jasper," I pouted.

"And you're not my only priority today." He huffed his annoyance with a permanent frown on his face.

"You won't be complaining when I line your pockets," I laughed. Jasper scowled at me and shoved a small parchment into my hands. I loved Circe's Cove, but Jasper reminded me I didn't love the people. Despite the fantastic views, the people who lived here were rather unsavory.

"If anyone asks where you got this, it wasn't me." He rammed his shoulder into mine as he passed; not enough to hurt, but enough to annoy me.

"Pleasure doing business!" I called back before letting out a groan. At least I could enjoy the view before I had to work. I stretched out, enjoying the warm breeze on my skin, before plopping on the ground and letting the soft grass below lull me into an afternoon nap.

The tall, white building Jasper had directed me to was home to the victims of tonight's crime. I leaned against a column, listening for any lingering noises. The sun had set a while ago, and I had watched as the occupants—a wealthy couple—basked in the sunset on their outdoor dining area until it grew later and later, and they retired inside.

I called for my magic and smiled as it sunk over my skin, covering me in shadows from head to toe. The familiar light buzzing sensation drifted over my skin as my physical appearance shimmered out of existence. I willed it over me as it embraced and covered my figure, and I relished in the pleasurable comfort. My body was still here physically, of course.

I could touch things, grab things, and pull them into my magic. People could still hear me if I spoke out loud, but if someone were to look at me directly, they wouldn't see me at all. I was completely invisible thanks to the gift that the gods had given me when I was fifteen. It was an unexpected and valuable gift that I could never thank them enough for.

The couple inside seemed young and brimming with wealth. The home itself was large and opulent, with large open balconies that gave way to the rolling hills of Circe, offering them an unobstructed view of the forests and valleys below. Vines of beautiful greenery and flowers wrapped around the columns that held the house up. It fit in perfectly with the scene of Circe, rich and thriving, simple in architecture but extraordinary just the same.

I wasn't interested in their identities. There was only one thing I cared about—their belongings. The woman apparently liked to flaunt her husband's deep pockets, even wearing large pieces of jewelry embedded with diamonds, rubies, and emeralds in her own home. It was clear they thought they were untouchable. Most people probably groveled before them or avoided them completely. I was practically drooling thinking about getting my hands on their riches.

I waited until they went back into the house before peering through a window, pressing my ear against the glass pane to listen for them to go to bed and fall asleep. Eventually, they clamored into another room, and I expelled my impatience with a sigh of relief. Listening carefully as they said their goodnights, I pried the window open and waited to move until they started snoring. My eagerness grew, and my fingers tingled with anticipation, but I waited until I knew the couple was fast asleep.

The front door was tall and made of polished wood. I approached it with caution, double-checking that no lingering souls were wandering the streets, and pried the door open with my trusty lock pick. The door swung open, revealing creamy marble floors and stone archways.

I tiptoed through the house and found myself in the primary bedroom. Two figures shrouded in blankets breathed evenly. It was fortunate for them that it was just a simple robbery. Anyone else could have sought to kill them in their sleep.

I tiptoed through the room, but it was only an extra precaution since the rugs beneath my feet silenced my steps. I searched the dark room until my eyes landed on a vanity. Necklaces and earrings sat strewn about on top of the small table, and next to it was a polished wooden box.

I kept my eyes on the sleeping couple as I made my way there and grinned. Riches lay about, and I had to restrain a nervous giggle. This would definitely make Captain Devland's night, his whole year even. More precious gems and priceless ornate jewels were revealed when I pried the box open, and I silently gasped in delight.

There was enough wealth in the box for me to leave the rest, but fuck it. I wanted all of it. My fingers tingled as I scooped as much jewelry and trinkets from the vanity that would fit inside the box before stuffing it in my cloak and making it disappear. I stifled a laugh, thinking about the woman waking up in the morning, screaming about her missing jewels. Seeing the rich have meltdowns over shit that didn't matter was one of my favorite past-times. It's too bad I would be long gone by then.

My hands flitted through the loot when my fingers brushed against a bottle of perfume, knocking it on the teetering edge of the vanity. I reined in a hiss as I watched it topple, and I was too slow to catch it as it tumbled to the ground. The small bottle made a loud sound as it fell from the vanity onto the wooden floor.

"Mmm dear, did you hear that?" the woman muttered, her voice thick with sleep. She shook her husband awake, and I bit back a curse.

The door was on the other side of the room, making it risky to run through without making any noise.

I took one enormous step toward my exit, hoping not to cause any excess sound. The man sat up in bed, clearly half asleep and confused. I stood right in front of them, but they couldn't see me. It didn't stop my heart from pounding in my ears, and I stood as still as a statue, knowing that if they glanced at the vanity, they would see that all of their most expensive jewels were missing.

After rubbing his eyes, the man glanced around the room. Not seeing anything out of place, he settled back into bed and I thanked the gods for unobservant men.

"It's alright, dear," he said, his eyes fluttering closed, "must have been an animal outside."

The lady hummed in agreement, and I waited until their breaths steadied before I moved my feet.

Getting out of the home was simple, and I took a deep breath in the calm night air. It was quiet as I peered around, and I flipped the box open, grinning until my cheeks hurt. My heart quickened as my eagerness to discover the value became more prominent. I only needed to take the box to Devland.

The moon was still relatively low as I traversed the winding cobblestone roads through quiet neighborhoods. The night was still young, and I agreed to meet Devland at The Rumbling Lion, a coastal tavern at the base of Circe. Once I ensured no one was around, I removed my magic, letting the moonlight bathe me in a milky glow. The humidity in Circe wrapped around me like a blanket, and I raised my hands in the air, letting my muscles stretch and release in the quiet night. Circe was as peaceful at night as it was during the day, which was probably fitting since it was the supposed birthplace of the gods.

I could have sworn that my magic swelled whenever I was here, too. Like the ground itself had magic embedded into it. I wondered if mortals felt the pulse of power in the rolling green lands of Circe.

With how popular it seemed, I guessed they did, even if they didn't know what it was. I meandered through the city, letting myself enjoy the humidity and quiet nature before I left with Captain Devland's ship, sailing back to the dry desert of Aurum.

The newly acquired treasure jingled softly in the bag that I strapped to my hip, and I couldn't help the grin that slid over my face. Once again, I took what I wanted—what I needed—without detection. I bit my lip as I turned the corner into The Rumbling Lion. It was always a party wherever Devland's crew drank, and tonight was no different. The tavern stank of salt and sweat as pirates cheered and hollered, slamming their tankards against tables, their faces red with the alcohol they drank. I wrinkled my nose, still not used to the pirate stench despite spending a lot of time around it.

Pirates huddled around a table, and I had a hunch who was at the center. I snagged a tankard of ale from the bar and pushed through the horde of men.

Captain Devland was the most attractive of the group. Unlike other pirates, Devland took great care of his physical appearance. His dark cropped hair was usually windswept from sailing the seas, but tonight he pushed it back, accentuating his sharp jawline with a delicately groomed line of stubble. He held playing cards in his hand, leaning back in his chair. The devilish grin that he wore told me he would win the bets with his hand. Confident and cocky, as usual, and damn it if I didn't find it attractive.

I stood across from him, peering into the hand that the man in front of me held. I held back a laugh as I realized that the man was bluffing. Devland would win either way, and I gave him a slight nod of encouragement.

Devland's kohl-lined eyes flicked up to me, and his grin pulled into a wide smile as he glanced at the obviously full bag on my hip.

"Gentlemen," he drawled, "it has been of the utmost pleasure, but I'm afraid there are more pressing matters to attend to."

He laid down his cards, and the surrounding men groaned as he swept the coins that lay on the table into his own pile. The silver rings adorning long, lithe fingers glinted in the low light of the tavern as he scooped up his winnings. The men vacated the table, and the crowd followed. I took up the seat next to Devland and gave him a knowing smile as I sipped my ale.

"You got the jewels?" He counted his coins meticulously as he spoke to me. I shrugged.

"And then some."

"Run into any trouble?"

I barked a laugh. "Trouble? Please, Dev, it was easy as pie."

Devland narrowed his eyes. "Let me see it."

I pulled the bag off of my person and held it out for him to take. He peeled back the leather, peered in, and smiled. His eyes gleamed like they were reflecting the riches within. He sifted through the jewels with his hands.

"Now, what do we have here?" He gave me a sideways glance and laughed. I frowned, not understanding what he was talking about. I just snagged some rich lady's necklaces and earrings. Albeit a lot of them, but it was still random jewelry.

"What?" I asked.

He clipped the bag closed and stood from his chair. "Not here. Let's go somewhere more private."

Through the crowd, Devland led me to the back of the tavern. He entered a vacant room with a desk and two chairs. The tavern's workroom was for the owner, most likely. It was dusty and unkempt, with parchment strewn about haphazardly.

Devland turned my bag over, and all the contents spilled onto the old wooden desk with a clang. He sifted through the pieces and lifted the delicate gold chain with a massive sapphire and emerald pendant. He held it in front of me, and I watched with curiosity as it swung back and forth in his hands.

"Do you even know what you stole?" He was laughing with his chest and watched the pendant with a predatory grin.

I shook my head. "I don't have a clue." My foot tapped harder while my patience grew thinner. Devland bit his lip with a grin, waiting for me to ask. "Can you enlighten me?"

"These gems have perfect purity. Practically priceless in their worth. Do you even know whose house you robbed?"

I raised my hands and gave him a look of innocence. "Jasper didn't divulge that information."

"It's going to be a bitch to sell," he muttered, a frown tugging at his lips.

"I trust you know the right people," I said while I knocked my shoulder into his, and he chuckled.

"I might." Devland scratched his chin along his short stubble. "You'll owe me one, Leoni."

This time, I was the one laughing.

"After you sell it, I don't think I'll owe you anything." I stepped into his personal space, but Devland made no effort to back away. He only looked down at me with a small smile pulling at his lips. I reached my hand up to his face, letting myself feel the warmth of his skin on my fingertips. I grasped his chin a little tighter and squeezed. His kohl-lined eyes lit up with lust. "But if you sell it for what it's actually worth, then I can think of a few ways to reward you."

He leaned into me, his gaze resting on my lips as I returned the sentiment and pressed my breasts up against him. I relaxed my grip and tilted his head toward mine. Devland slid his hand behind the small of my back, pulling me into his chest.

The door swung open, and Jasper rushed in, scowling. We locked eyes with him, neither of us backing down.

Jasper scoffed. "Well, at least I know why you work with the bitch now."

Devland struck with speed. He moved away from me and slammed Jasper to the wall, making the wood groan and dust fall from the ceiling.

I crossed my arms and leaned on the wall opposite them, trying to distance myself from the violence yet intrigued enough to see Devland lash out.

Devland towered over Jasper. The muscles in his back grew taut as he wrapped his hand around Jasper's neck and lifted him. It was a strength I knew he worked for. Devland may have been a pirate lord, but he was never below doing physical labor. He often worked alongside his pirates, pulling ropes and carrying crates. He was always willing to get his hands dirty, which I admired.

Jasper sputtered, and his face turned a deep shade of red. I watched with a small smile as his hands scraped fruitlessly against Devland's arms.

"This *bitch* is about to make you lifetimes richer. For a mere mortal, it seems like you've forgotten who holds the true power. Do you really expect to barge in here and tell me how to conduct my business?"

Jasper's red face was slowly turning purple as he shook it the best he could, tears welling in his eyes. Devland dropped him. Jasper fell to the ground with a large thud. He lay pathetically on his side, gasping for air. He stared up at me and glared. I sneered at him in response. He disgusted me. I didn't know the man well, but I watched how he conversed with Devland and his contrasting disdain for me. He was the kind of bastard that never fought his own battles and only clung to the more powerful with pretty words and shallow promises.

Jasper wasn't the first to doubt my abilities, and it wouldn't be the last time someone voiced their distrust about my relationship with Devland and his crew, but Devland made sure that it was never the same person who expressed those doubts twice. I winced when he stomped on Jasper's hand with his boot, the bones in his hand crunching underneath. Jasper wailed out in pain.

"It's a shame," Devland shot me a wicked smile. "Mortals don't heal like us Magi. With their short lifespans, it's like the gods had forsaken the lot of them."

I scoffed, "They've forsaken us all, Dev." Devland glanced back at me and I shrugged back at him.

Devland grunted as he bent down over Jasper's still-sputtering body. "I wouldn't say that's entirely true." He pinched the man's face between his fingers; his pudgy cheeks squished in Devland's grasp.

I watched Devland as he focused his magic. His pupils dilated as he gazed down at Jasper.

"Do you enjoy the benefits of working with me?" The words spilled out of his mouth with his power—compulsion. He was so strong that even I felt the power rolling from his voice. Thick magic washed over the room, making me shiver. The gods may have disappeared, but our magic still remained. We possessed an advantage over mortals, but I usually refrained from using it against them when they were powerless. I had to pick my battles, though, and Jasper wasn't worth fighting over.

"Yes." Jasper's voice was flat under the influence of Devland's magic, compelling him to tell the truth.

"Then you won't have any problems respecting me."

"No."

"And if you disrespect me again, you will throw yourself into the ocean and sit at the bottom until you can't breathe. Do you understand?" Poor Jasper. Devland's words were now solidified in his mind, and his body would obey Devland's order no matter what.

"Yes," Jasper sputtered. Spit flew out of his mouth in Devland's harsh grip.

"Very well. You'll live, for now. Now get out." Devland released his hold on Jasper and stood up. Jasper knew he was getting off easy as he climbed out of the room and back into the tavern. The door swung closed behind him, and Devland and I sighed in relief.

Dusting his hands, Devland turned to the treasure. He placed the pieces back into my bag before strapping it to himself.

"Maybe you should have just killed him," I muttered. Devland paused, his lips upturned for a moment. Jasper set off all of the alarm bells in my head; I didn't enjoy working with him, and I definitely didn't appreciate how he made fast judgments about me. It was satisfying to see Devland exert his power over him.

"That's unlike you, Leoni," he chuckled. "You're not usually one for bloodshed."

"Exceptions can be made," I said, shrugging, even though I didn't really mean it. The guy pissed me off, but it didn't mean I actually wanted him dead—just incapacitated. I stared at the door, now eager to get back to the ship.

"I'll take care of this and meet you back at the ship," Devland told me as he slung the bag over his shoulder. I nodded while he opened the door and the tavern sounds filled the small space. More people seemed to occupy the tavern now that the night grew later, and it was nearly suffocating as I squeezed in between sweaty, burly bodies.

The night air was pleasant and welcoming as I exited the tavern. I inhaled deeply, enjoying the salt and briny smell of the docks as I approached *The Devil's Serpent*—a medium-sized vessel with white sails.

Some of Devland's pirates were already on board; adjusting ropes and sails, shouting orders at each other. The quartermaster, Langley, stood on the ship's port side, barking orders and nitpicking other pirates' work. He was a surly man with brutal, ugly scars that ran across the side of his head. I gave him a small wave, to which he only inclined his head a fraction before directing his attention to his work.

Someone had strewn the ropes that held sails to the ship around the deck, leaving potential traps for anyone who wasn't careful with their steps. I weaved through them on agile feet and stopped at the bow of the ship. The ocean was breathtaking from this point of view. It was vast and never-ending, full of life and danger.

It reminded me of infinite possibilities, and how I embraced those possibilities to improve my family's lives. Spending so much time away from them was a bitter feeling, but seeing my family grow and watching the children gain the tools necessary to make their lives easier was worth every second.

Two months each year, aboard *The Devil's Serpent*, was how long it would take for me to earn enough and start feeling the pang of missing them. Two months, and I was ready to return to my home: Aurum. This year, the two months passed by quickly, but even so, I was more than eager to get back home.

Glancing toward the horizon, I noted the seas were smooth, and the night clear. It would be perfect for sailing back, and hopefully, it would be quick. If I closed my eyes, I could almost smell the sand and desert of Aurum and could taste Tala's bread on my tongue. I let myself imagine her face when I handed over the coins I made this summer. She would wear a bright smile, and there would be gratefulness in her eyes. I couldn't wait to get my hands on the money myself, but I wouldn't get that until whenever Devland decided to show up.

A loud screech overhead had me blinking away my thoughts, and my heart skipped a beat as a massive silver being with expansive wings flew above the ship. The men aboard started shouting worried orders.

"Dragon above! Take cover!"

They moved around the deck, taking refuge in any place they could find from the dragon that circled high above. I called my magic, shadows shrouding me from view, and I turned back with a calm breath to watch the beast.

Silver scales reflected over the smooth sea, and if the dragon flew high enough, it could easily be mistaken as a star itself. I gazed at the creature with awe. It circled over the ocean and snapped its wings shut before dropping toward the water with impossible speed. I grasped the guardrail in front of me, nearly leaning over the bow as I held my breath.

It dived into the water, disappearing with a small ripple in its wake. I squinted, trying to discern the large body underneath. A blast exploded from the water, and the dragon emerged with a large fish in its mouth.

The silver dragon beat its wings and rose higher and higher. It swallowed the fish whole and dove back into the water, letting out a satisfied roar. Its spray was massive, specks of water reaching up to the night sky.

The dragon, satisfied with its meal, floated on the smooth surface of the sea. It shook off the rivulets of water from its long neck, tucking back its wings close to its body while swimming peacefully on the surface.

"How did I know you would be out here?" Devland smiled and stared at the dragon beyond. I removed my magic and stepped up next to him as he draped his arms over the edge of the ship.

"How *did* you know I was out here?"

He chuckled. His smile was lined with satisfaction. More pleasant than I had seen it this whole summer. "How long has it been since you joined my summer crew?"

"Ten years," I shrugged. I brushed a loose copper curl out of my face. I hadn't tied it back up since I got back on the ship, the wind knocking my hair out of its braid.

"Plenty of time for me to know where you would be during a dragon sighting." He nodded toward the creature that was slowly disappearing along the horizon.

"There's so few of them now. I wonder what it would be like to work with them, like the Dragon Riders do?" I asked as I chewed the bottom of my lip, allowing myself to daydream about riding a dragon myself one day.

"I wouldn't know. By the time I was born, the mortals already claimed most of the dragons, and the ones that remained here were nearly extinct." He shrugged, and I nodded back.

Magi lived a few hundred years longer than the mortals, but the dragons lived whole centuries, and it was a well-known history that the fallout between Ambrose and the mortal lands—Tantal—resulted in the near extinction of dragons. Magi considered me young at a mere thirty-five, even if that was fully into adulthood for mortals. I never asked Devland how old he was, but I knew he wasn't old enough to remember the Golden Age of the gods. Even Magi didn't live that long.

"Seems like their numbers are growing. That's the second time we've seen a dragon on this ship. That's good, isn't it?" I asked.

Devland only shrugged. "Who knows? We may not see another for a hundred years."

"I heard about a new Dragon Rider in Ambrose. Maybe the gods are waking up?" I laughed at the absurdity of my question. The gods were long dead.

"Have you ever seen the Dragon Rider yourself?" Devland gave me a quizzical look like he doubted that a Magi Dragon Rider could even exist.

"No, but Ambrose is large and widespread."

"Myths and fairytales," he muttered. There had been no record of Magi Dragon Riders since the gods disappeared, so I couldn't exactly blame Devland for that conclusion.

"Mortals could say the same about us in Tantal," I argued.

"They have real Dragon Riders. They have seen magic, whether or not they want to villainize it."

"I wonder how living like that is. Seeing the magic between mortals and dragons and yet declaring that a Magi's blood is evil." I shivered at the thought. There was a reason I kept to the east coast. The west was far too dangerous, and I had mouths to feed.

"Who knows?" Devland mused. "No one enters or exits Tantal; if you see a Dragon Rider, you're likely dead." A slight glimmer met his eye as he spoke, but he said no more and reached for the pack on his hip. "You ready for your portion before I give the rest to the crew?"

I held out my palm to him and grinned widely. "I'm only here for the money."

He handed me my satchel back, now heavy with the coins inside. Without looking, I knew it held more money than expected. More money than I should have made from the entire trip.

"I never thanked you." I smiled up at Devland.

His eyes glittered in the moonlight as he raised an eyebrow. "For what?"

"For taking me in, giving me a chance when I needed it the most." I gazed out at the starry sky. Wisps of clouds drifted over the moon. It wasn't like me to get sentimental, but something about seeing that dragon made my chest lurch with gratitude. Devland tipped his head toward me and smirked.

"You don't need to thank me. Thank my soft heart."

I scoffed. "Devland, if there's anything I know about you, it's that your heart is as cold as ice."

"It's soft for little red-headed Magi that was too skinny and dressed in rags." He picked up a curl in his fingers and flicked it away, laughing.

"I am not little," I protested, crossing my arms over my chest.

"Not little for a mortal."

I tsked at him. "Mortals and Magi look the same. The only difference is the magic that runs through our veins."

"And our lifespans. And our superiority," he countered.

"Devland," I groaned, "how many times do I need to remind you that there is no value on mortal or Magi lives?"

"At least one more," he chuckled, and his eyes glinted with mirth.

"Well, regardless, thank you. If you hadn't taken me in, trained me—" my voice cracked and I quickly cleared my throat. "I'm not exactly sure where I would be. Probably dead in the gutter somewhere."

I remembered the night I met Devland like it was yesterday. In my early adulthood, I stole from anyone I could. Devland's ship had docked earlier that day, and I watched as they unloaded crates of food and teas. Exotic goods that I had never seen before. I remembered how my mouth watered and my fingers twitched. When I struck, I tripped over a crate and got caught.

But when I met his dark eyes, he only smiled and handed me a piece of fruit I had never seen before. It was the most delicious thing I ever tasted. Sweet juices filled my mouth, and I licked every single finger by the time I was done. Thinking back, it was embarrassing. I was like a wild animal, devouring everything in sight.

He tried to convince me to join his crew that night, but I held back, afraid to leave my family. It took him three years of asking every time he docked in town before I finally conceded. It was the best decision I ever made. Our work together was flawless, and I turned the money into a hospitable home for the orphaned children of Aurum. Children like me.

Devland pursed his lips. "You? Dead in the gutter? No way. You're a survivor. Your will and strength enable you to thrive. It's not in your blood to cower in life."

I smirked at him. "I suppose you're right. But I wouldn't be as flush with money without you."

"Now that is true," he laughed. It was contagious, and I laughed right alongside him.

Chapter 2

COINS SPILLED ONTO THE deck of *The Devil's Serpent*. The metal shifted on the wood, clinging against the greedy hands of the pirates that Captain Devland currently employed. We sailed away from the port of Circe's Cove, going faster with a cutting wind that whipped through the white sails.

The seas grew rougher after leaving Circe, but I was accustomed to the ship's motion. I laughed at the inexperienced pirates that would fumble through rough seas.

When I first joined Captain Devland, the pirates were wary about me boarding the ship. Some of them spouted nonsense about how it was bad luck to keep a woman on board, but I cut those words short when I brought them riches. Now, when *The Devil's Serpent* made its way to Aurum, they greeted me excitedly, eager to get to the next destination.

I stood next to the captain, picking at my nails with my dagger with a smug smile while I watched his pirates scrounge for any riches they could get their hands on. The dagger was my favorite theft, which I loved so much that I kept it instead of selling. Black diamonds lined the hilt.

The stones gleamed clearly in both sun and moonlight. It was also the only treasure that I consistently kept on my person. I didn't know why I felt an affinity for it. I didn't like to entice violence—especially since I worked better under the guise of my shadows, but I thought it was better safe than sorry, and carried it with me, anyway. Devland had always harped on me about carrying a weapon, and I only ever used it twice or thrice, but I never killed with it. I left that up to him.

Devland clasped my shoulder, grinning, his brown eyes glinting with pride and satisfaction.

"This calls for celebration." He turned, beckoning me to follow him to the captain's cabin.

A desk sat towards the back, stacked with maps and compasses. I walked around the desk, taking in all the locations he had marked with various symbols. He had once called himself "a man of cartography and treasure". It was impressive, each line and pen sweep indicating lands I had never traveled. The world was wide, and if I was honest with myself, it frightened me. I loved traveling through the summers, but I was always meant to be in Aurum—my home.

Devland rummaged through a cabinet, grabbing two crystal glasses and a decanter of red wine. The wine was aged, thick and dark, looking close to blood. My mouth watered at the sight. I loved a good wine. I loved good food, too. Devland introduced me to cuisines I didn't know existed. It was almost worth the homesickness that I felt when I was gone.

"You aren't holding back, Devland. That's the good stuff." I smirked and rounded on him, taking one of the glasses before lifting it to my lips.

"Of course," he lifted his glass to mine, tapping it with a light clink, "we deserve it."

"What are you going to do with your portion?" I asked. I leaned on the desk, picking up one of the small ship replicas and turning it in my hand.

"Investments. Transporting product. More of the same." He waved away the question as if he didn't just get a year's worth of loot. Placing the tiny ship down, I headed to the other side of the cabin to view Devland's priceless collection. I picked up a round vase with portrayals of people and dragons coexisting. Back when they ruled with the gods. The dragons were flying, and a few had Magi riding their backs. The clay bore evidence of blues and golds, now faded. I wondered what it would look like if Devland polished it and had someone repaint it.

"Careful with that," Devland spoke into my ear, making me shiver. "What you're holding is three thousand years old."

"Three thousand?" I fought to breathe as my fingers hovered over the paint, and my hands got clammy as I realized that I probably shouldn't have even been touching it at all.

"Why do you have this sitting out on your ship?" I asked incredulously.

Devland shrugged like he didn't have a single care for this ancient piece of history. "I like the precedent it sets. It causes people to think twice about my nature."

I lifted the vase and observed the cracks that had developed over time. "This should be studied. It should be somewhere safe."

Devland took the vase from me gently, his fingers brushing against my own.

"I highly doubt that the original owners of this vase cared whether it lasted three thousand years, and I don't think they care now. The dead can't speak."

He placed the vase back on the small table before turning back toward me, but I kept my gaze on the vase. I laughed and shook my head.

"I guess if it has to be in any scoundrel's hands, it might as well be yours."

Devland moved closer to me, his shoulder brushing up against my own.

"What about you? What are you spending your earnings on?"

I moved back to the desk, rubbing my palms on my pants, trying to remove the sweat that appeared when I realized I was holding a piece of history. I grabbed my glass and sipped the wine, tossing my long red curls over my shoulder. It was smooth against my tongue, rolling down my throat and warming my insides.

"Giving it to my family, of course."

"The orphanage?" he asked, and I nodded with a smile. They deserved it all, and then some. I could always steal more tomorrow, but Tala, and the children that she cared for, deserved to feel loved as if they had a real family. I would be their family, because I never had one.

My satchel held the same weight as my relieved burden. Their education could lead to a better life. One that I never got to have. A relief that Tala—the orphanage matron, and the closest thing I had to a mother—could sleep knowing that the children were provided for.

Devland grabbed my wrist and pulled me toward him. His brown eyes were heated with a hunger, and he licked his lips as his gaze dropped down, leaving scorching goosebumps on my body wherever his eyes roamed. He ran his hand along my chin, and I leaned into his touch. His breath rolled over my skin as he leaned in, placing his lips along my neck.

The adrenaline from my heist and the wine set my body on fire. Intimacy with Devland had been unplanned, but not unpleasant. The first time it happened was due to heightened adrenaline and lots of wine, but then it became a regular occurrence. Now, it was almost expected. It was easy, and since neither one of us wanted to fall in love or be in a relationship, it wasn't something led by emotions. Just two people fulfilling our physical needs.

"I'm going to miss you when you're gone." Devland's voice was low and husky. Devland's ruggedness was a bonus, and sex with the pirate captain felt daring, even though my life was already filled with such experiences.

"I'm sure you'll manage like you do every year." I breathed back. I meant to lace my words with sarcasm, but it was gone with the flush that settled over my body. Devland's brown eyes stared into mine.

"I'm going to miss seeing these eyes, as grey as the stormy seas in the rainy season. Whenever it rains, I'll think of you." His hand skated up my ribs and roamed over my breast. Even through my shirt, I felt a current from his touch. I bit my lip and looked at him through my eyelashes. He pressed his lips against my neck.

"Get on the desk." His low voice against my skin sent shivers through my body. I wasted no time in doing exactly as he demanded. He pressed his hand under my tunic, grasping for my breast, making slow circles over my peaked nipple. I shuddered and arched my back, letting out an involuntary moan.

"We should move before we ruin all of your maps—"

"Fuck the papers," he chuckled, his warm breath skittering over my skin. He smelled of soap, salt, and tobacco. The only light we had were the candles that flickered in rhythm with the ship's movement. Not even the moon filtered through the port-hole windows. He lifted me further on the desk, swiftly untying the laces on my boots and removing my trousers. His brown eyes never left mine. I laughed and downed the rest of the wine in my glass.

"I love watching you on your knees for me, Devland," I muttered over the rim of my glass. Mischief glinted in Devland's eye.

"Watch what you say to me, Leoni." My name rolled off of his tongue thick with lust. "Or I will have to find a way to shut that pretty mouth of yours." I laughed as he slid his fingers into my wet center, my back arching in response.

"Yes," I moaned, all sarcasm leaving my body. He pumped two fingers into me, slow and firm. Slowly, he licked up my center, lingering on my clit, toying with it as I shuddered against him. I didn't love Devland, never spent time pining over him for the rest of the year, but I did enjoy his company. And even though I hated to admit it, I sometimes missed his touch when I was alone.

Devland's dark eyes took all of me in, his gaze hungry and eager. My heart picked up its beat as he looked at me and feasted on my core. I knew he would bring me to the precipice and then leave me hanging for however long he desired, sometimes leaving me unsatisfied altogether.

It was a game to me. Would I be able to reach my own pleasure before he reached his? I was determined to win tonight. I clasped my thighs around his head, grinding further into his mouth.

I grasped his black cropped hair, holding him until I felt my climax rising, rising, rising. I held on to that feeling, urging the dam of pleasure to pour over. I shuddered, and a loud moan escaped my mouth.

Devland leaned back and pushed my thighs wide. He pulled away from me, his absence leaving me empty and utterly frustrated. I groaned. Perspiration gathered along my forehead, and my chest heaved with heavy breaths. He only laughed at my untethered expression. He unbuckled his pants, releasing his cock, hard and proud.

"Bend over."

I let out a huff in frustration, but did as he said. I gave him a little teasing wiggle as I leaned against the desk. Papers pressed into my breasts. I looked back at Devland. His expression was dark, and he wore a stupid smirk that I couldn't help but roll my eyes at as I bent over further.

A large wave hit the ship, causing the room to sway. Loose change and trinkets fell off the desk and rolled along the floor. I braced against the desk, keeping still, while Devland placed a hand above my head to stabilize himself.

"It seems like we might be running into bad weather." His voice was anything but concerned.

"I guess we will just have to roll with it." I pressed myself against his hard length, and he let out a hiss.

"Better hold on." His lips brushed the back of my neck as he pressed into me. I gasped as he filled me, wet desire dripping down my thighs. He took me slowly, his hands splayed against my lower back. I let out a haggard breath. The ship rocked once again, and he shoved into me completely. My legs buckled, and my heart hammered.

The sound of crashing waves and breathy moans filled the air. I could feel every inch of him inside, pressing against me. My climax built faster this time, aching for sudden release. Sensations changed with every wave crash and shift from the ship.

He moved his free arm around my waist, bracing me against his hard body as he pinched my clit, rolling it around in his fingers. My moans were escalating higher and higher as I returned to the height of my pleasure. I was reaching for it, and my legs shook from the incessant teasing Devland had done. I ached for the release, burned for it.

I was gasping, and my legs nearly gave out from under me, trying to chase the wave of pleasure that my body called for. But it wasn't fast enough. Devland tensed behind me. The rise of my climax suddenly lost. I slumped on the desk in frustration, papers and small implements pressing hard against my skin. He breathed my name before letting out a guttural groan, clearly pleased by his performance. We stayed in that position for a few moments. His cock still twitched inside as he rested his head on my back.

"Stay with me tonight." He practically begged, clearly planning our last night to go without a lot of sleep. I pushed him off of me and reached for my pants.

"No," I snapped. I wanted to stay, but the lack of climax made me irritable and I wanted some privacy. I pushed my legs through the pants and ensured all my buttons were in place. Devland sighed and poured himself another glass of wine.

"Why not?"

I sighed, trying to rein in my frustration. It wasn't his fault. In my experience, men struggled to give women pleasure, and Devland and I haven't had enough time to learn about each other's bodies, anyway.

"It's been a long day. I'm tired," I lied. A dark expression flashed over Devland's features, but it was gone so quickly I thought I imagined it. He smiled at me.

"Come on, Leoni. It's our last night together. Let's make it a memorable one."

I laughed, placing my hand on my hip, and as frustrated as I was, I couldn't stay mad at Devland.

"I'll be back next year." I dismissed his proposal with a wave, but he stalked toward me, the hunger still lingering in his gaze.

"And it won't be soon enough," Devland whispered in my ear, making me shiver. He smirked down at me, knowing he'd get what he wanted. I bit my lip. I could attempt to sleep in my small bedchamber while listening to other pirates snore. Or I could stay with Devland

and hope he gets tired by dawn, and quite possibly find my own release.

"Fine. But only because it's our last night," I relented, and he gave me a wicked grin full of dark promise and a sleepless night.

It was far too early for the sun to peek through the portholes in Devland's cabin. I peeled my eyes open. My body was heavy with exhaustion, and the feeling of salt on my skin grew irritating as the temperature started rising in the cabin. My mouth was dry, and last night's wine was settling in my head. I groaned. We still had a whole day of sailing before we would be home.

Home. My heart skipped a beat as I thought about it. I would finally see my family again. I would feel the dry sun heating my skin and hear the whispers of sand skirting through the dunes. I shook my head, banishing the thought of home away. I was too close now to get homesick.

I reached out next to me to find empty sheets. Devland must have gotten up earlier, preparing the crew for tonight's anchor. I quickly wiped the sleep away from my eyes and gathered my garments strewn around the cabin room.

I could hear Devland shouting something above, but the wood muffled his voice too much to hear what he was saying. He sounded angry, and I hesitated to venture out and see what was happening. My hands curled up against the cabin door before I pushed it open to see Devland's crew gathered in the center of the deck while he addressed them from the helm above. The wind whipped his hair away from his face, the sharp angles of his jaw more pronounced with the scowl he wore. Langley stood beside him. His face was blank while he watched Devland address the ship.

"It has come to my attention, that there are some members of my crew who are trying to undermine me." Devland's voice boomed over the whipping winds of the sea. I saw fury in his eyes like a violent storm, but what triggered this sudden anger? I didn't know.

A lower murmuring broke out between the men. They wore confused faces, and I took each one in, looking for signs of guilt or apprehension.

"If I have to interrogate every man on this ship, so be it." Devland's eyes were vicious as he swung them around the ship. A few of the men gasped. I couldn't blame them. Devland was infamous across Ambrose for a reason.

I watched with wide eyes as Devland swaggered down to the deck, eyeing the pirates with a deadly gaze. Right now, everyone was in danger of Devland's wrath. He swept his brown eyes over the crew until he zeroed in on a grubby pirate with greasy blond hair tied off behind his neck. The men parted as Devland walked towards the man.

He was newer to the crew. I had never seen him before this summer. If anyone were to betray Devland, it would likely be a new recruit. The man stepped back and encountered a wall of men. He was shaking, and his face paled as Devland leaned toward him. Devland loomed over the man, who cowered from his large body blocking the sun.

"Tell me," Devland's magic washed over the man, and the pirates closest to him shuffled away from his overbearing aura. "Are you stealing from my ship for your own gain?" Devland's voice was cold and monotone, laced with controlled power.

"Yes," the man whispered. Devland made a noise that resembled a growl. The man whimpered. "B-but it's not just me! I was just the hands!"

Devland's lips turned into a chilling smile. "And who were you working with?" The man squirmed under Devland's magic, biting his lips closed. But it was useless. "Tell me." Devland pushed more of his power into him, and the truth spilled from his lips.

"L-Langley made me do it, Sir. He promised to double my wages." The man pointed a shaky finger at Langley, who stood wide-eyed at Devland.

Devland shifted his attention to the pirates on his right. "Hold him down!" He ordered. Two men grabbed the new pirate by his shoulders and forced him to his knees.

Devland turned to his quartermaster with a vicious leer. He stalked toward Langley with his shoulders back, taking firm steps toward his prey. Langley spun in circles, seeking an escape, but we were on the sea. There was no escape from Captain Devland. Langley looked over his shoulder like he was debating whether he would rather jump into the sea below, but his hesitation cost him.

Devland pulled him back from the ledge and swung his fist into Langley's face with a resounding crunch. I flinched as blood sprayed onto the deck, dotting it with red.

Langley wiped the blood away from his face, his nose surely broken, but he didn't back down. I had to give Langley credit. Facing off against Captain Devland took courage, but it was foolish. Devland was absolutely ruthless when he wanted to be.

Devland struck again. Once. Twice. Three times. Each punch was fortified with the rings on his fingers. They left deep gashes on Langley's already scarred skin. Langley fell to the ground. His large body hit the deck with a resounding thump. Devland didn't waste any time pressing his knee into Langley's back, immobilizing him.

Langley balled up his fists, and I sucked in a breath as I recognized his movements. He was trying to summon his magic. His power was being able to manipulate natural materials in his hands, one of the reasons Devland kept him as his quartermaster. The wood groaned underneath his hands, and he attempted to pull the wooden slats beneath him, but Devland was faster. He wrenched Langley's face into his own, and his pupils dilated as he spoke.

"No magic." The simple command had Langley relax his hands, releasing the magic within. "Give me the truth, all of it."

Langley's eyes glazed over, but not before he flicked his eyes to me. I sucked in a breath as I watched Devland grow more rigid, but he didn't say anything, as if he didn't notice Langley's momentary flicker.

"I took some of your...spices and undercut your costs. Made myself three times richer." He looked directly at Devland without an ounce of fear. "I deserve it more than you do."

Devland pulled out his cutlass, and I closed my eyes. The sound of the metal cutting through flesh met my ears, and then the smell of copper hit my nose. I heard Devland cut away at Langley's body, whose screams echoed through the ship. His death would not be quick. I kept my eyes closed, and my face turned while Devland hacked away at Langley.

A squishy thump followed a scream and slash, and I guessed Devland had cut out Langley's tongue. I didn't want to imagine the puddle of blood that Devland was standing in. Devland was relentless. With each slash and hack, the noise grew louder as he pressed on. Devland's blade was the bell toll of death.

When the screaming finally ceased, I turned away from Devland's position and opened my eyes. Pirates tied the man who also betrayed Devland to the center mast of the ship. He faced Devland's carnage, most likely watching the entire slaughter. Tremors wracked his body, and his face was deathly pale.

I almost felt bad for the man, but you didn't join Captain Devland's crew without knowing how terrifying he could be. And you certainly didn't betray him without knowing there would be consequences if he caught you.

Devland sauntered over to him. He was a vicious god of retribution, bathed in the blood of his enemy. He bared his teeth at the man, drawing his cutlass and slashing it through the man's neck. Devland didn't prolong the man's death; his bloodlust clearly satisfied with slaughtering Langley.

"Clean this up!" he barked at no one in particular. Pirates jumped into action, untying the man and dumping pieces of Langley's body into the ocean. Devland tore his tunic off and used the fabric to wipe droplets of blood from his skin. He was still seething, and I decided to leave him alone until he cooled down. Avoiding Devland's rage was my priority.

I knew Devland was dangerous and ruthless. This wasn't the first time I had seen him like this. In moments like these, he even scared me. I always hoped our friendship would mean something, but I still made sure not to betray his trust. I never wanted to find myself on the other end of his sword. So, I would let his mood fizzle and pass time soaking up the sun.

"ALRIGHT." I PACED AROUND Devland's cabin. Devland's sour mood had slowly dissipated, but I made sure to still tread lightly around him. He didn't show his anger, but the betrayal of his second-in-command must have been eating him up. I pointed to the map of Aurum's main estate that lay across Devland's desk.

"The main entrance is here. Guards will switch an hour before midnight. I'll sneak through the servant's entrance." I moved my finger to the other side of the estate, where I had scribbled a poor rendition of a rose garden.

"I'll move to this side of the estate and leave through the gardens after collecting the jewels."

Devland raked his hands through his hair, leaving pieces sticking up at the front.

"Leoni, this is a big robbery, even for you." It was true. Normally, our thefts were lesser noble houses, which meant they generally had less security and an easier way in and out.

I waved my hand, brushing off his comment, "Devland, this is my city, remember? I've watched the gates every night for months. It will be a quick mission. I was able to tour the whole estate during a public event. The layout is straightforward. A servant's tunnel goes straight through the entire place."

He sighed and took a swig of brown liquor straight out of the bottle, "We had a massive win yesterday, and I don't want to push our luck."

"The Lord is gone until the next dark moon, and he took his wife with him. They are all at the Lord's Summit—it's the perfect time to strike."

This could be the robbery that set me free. The orphanage would be funded for years. I could slow down and spend a few days wandering the city. Maybe I would travel outside of the coast.

I splayed my hands open. "Last night's earnings could be doubled or even tripled."

"It could." Devland leaned on the desk, his eyes raking over the diagrams my sketches of the blueprints. "But there's not a guarantee. Failure could end your life. I can't bail you out."

Devland, pirate as he may be, also carried some weight with many of the smaller town's Watchmen. They either didn't want to go through the trouble of messing with him, or he could pay them enough to keep their mouths shut. Aurum was no such city. If I got caught robbing the estate, the city officials wouldn't think twice about throwing myself, Devland, and any accomplices in the cold, wet sewers, leaving us to rot.

"Devland, you have never doubted me before. Why the sudden apprehension?" It took a lot for me to get frustrated, especially with the pirate captain, but I felt it bubbling at the bottom of my stomach. I ground my teeth, waiting for him to answer. He blew out a breath.

"You know I don't doubt your skill. If I'm being blunt, this is a bigger risk than we can take." He set the bottle down and leaned on the desk, crossing his arms. His eyes narrowed on mine.

"Why don't you use the money you made to do something for yourself? Get out of the slums. You could travel to another city. Lie low for a few years. I don't even like that you return to Aurum and live there. You should build a new life. Stay out of trouble." Devland chuckled darkly. He pulled out a sheet of parchment from under the stack of paper. It was a wanted poster. The sketch had no face but instead was a dark silhouette.

WANTED: THE THIEF OF AURUM
DEAD OR ALIVE BY DECREE OF THE AURUM LEGION

"I wonder who this could be for?" He pushed the parchment under my nose. I sighed. I had seen that poster in Aurum before I left, but I wore it like a badge of honor. They would have to catch me to find me, but ever since I joined Devland's crew, I never got caught. Thanks to my shadows, they didn't even know what I looked like.

"If General Riel is behind this, exercise caution. Start a new life. There are countless cities that haven't experienced your thievery yet," he said, and I grimaced.

Riel Valor. The General of Aurum, head of city security, the man of "justice," and Aurum's Executioner. Named for the amount of criminals he put on death row and killed himself. He was supposed to be terrifying, but I didn't fear him. I hated him.

Before I could get in a word, he continued, "Haven't you done enough for your orphanage? They should be taking care of themselves, and so should you."

It took everything in me not to lash out at Devland. He never understood why I had never moved out of Aurum. I wanted to provide. It was what drove me.

"The orphanage is everything to me, Devland. If they don't survive, I don't either. Tala saved my life, and I will never repay that debt." I couldn't imagine what would happen if I ever left them. Would they suffer without me? It was a question I refused to answer.

"I highly doubt Riel is out there stalking the streets for me anyway. They put those posters out for everyone. I'm sure you have one, too."

Devland chuckled. "Oh, I do—and General Riel is absolutely looking for me. Which is why I hire people to keep myself safe." He pointed his finger at me. "Who do you have keeping you safe?"

I ignored his question. I could keep myself safe just fine. General Riel was the boogeyman of Aurum's law enforcement. I, a petty thief, was not on his punishment list.

"I'm doing this, Devland." Snagging the rum off the desk, I took one large swig and slammed it on top of my messy blueprint. "Besides, I have my gift. With everyone gone, it will be a heist that will sail smoother than your ship on glassy seas. It will be done tomorrow night, and I'll meet you back at the docks. I'll even bet you a coin that I'll be there before midnight."

Devland reached for the rum out of my hands and shrugged.

"Well, if anyone can do it, it's you." He raised the bottle in a mock cheer, as his eyes were still skeptical. "But if anything happens, don't say I didn't try to warn you."

"I won't get caught." I hissed at him. And I wouldn't. A wanted poster was not enough to scare me.

"Land, ho!" a shipmate bellowed from the crow's nest of *The Devil's Serpent*. I watched as we approached the city of Aurum. Ambrose's Golden City. We arrived at the perfect time.

The sun was setting over the large rolling sand dunes that surrounded Aurum. Golden light washed across the tall spires that marked the city. Day or night, the buildings gleamed gold. But when the sun lowered against the horizon, the sky went from blue to reds and purples. That was when Aurum truly shined.

Gold sands surrounded the city, and dunes upon dunes served as a backdrop, giving the illusion that Aurum was the only source of life in the entirety of Ambrose. Aurum's spires were like golden fingers reaching into the realm of the gods. Though not made of actual gold, the buildings were filled with riches beyond measure. They held riches in knowledge and technology, and physical riches of precious gems and vast amounts of highly guarded money.

One day, I would get my hands on a handy piece of technology that allowed instant teleportation. But until then, I relied on darkness and my gods-given ability to suppress my presence in the shadows.

I patted myself down as the crew anchored out in the bay. My initial stop would be at the orphanage to drop off yesterday's coin after taking a small boat to the piers.

"You've got everything?" Captain Devland monitored the crew as they lowered the tiny rowboat to the waters.

"I believe so. I'll meet you tomorrow night when the job is done." I clasped Devland on his arm. Departing from Devland was always bittersweet. I never had as much fun when we weren't conspiring together, but the last two moon cycles on his ship left me mentally and physically drained. Honestly, I couldn't wait to sleep without rocking back and forth.

Devland nodded and rocked back on his heels. "Be careful out there, Leoni."

I laughed him off. "I'll be fine, Devland. I promise."

Devland raised his eyebrow, and a slow smirk lifted on his face. "Alright." He tucked his ringed hands into his pockets. "You get this one, and we'll be set for life. I'll meet you at the docks at midnight." He offered his hand and helped me down into the boat.

"Midnight, and not a minute later!" I shouted and waved as I rowed toward my city. My home.

Chapter 3

The way through Aurum into the South District was quieter now that night was settling in. The stars glinted in the cloudless sky, like a smattering of white paint on deep blue canvas. I walked the familiar path from the docks through the city. Coming back into town after being gone for so long was always a little strange. There were slight changes that happened, so small that I could barely put my finger on it, but I still felt it. Like even though the sands looked the same, I could tell they had shifted in the wind while I was gone.

The road changed from cobblestone to dirt, signifying the entrance to the South District. Neglected by the rest of Aurum, we didn't have the same maintenance or money to have upkept roads or buildings. Our buildings were even made of beige mud brick instead of the sturdy material that made the rest of Aurum's buildings shine gold. But I liked it this way. The South District had a distinct grit to it; we were all survivors.

I passed the first few buildings; homes stacked one atop the other. A woman nodded at me in greeting as I passed by, and I gave her a small wave. My heart sank when I realized I had no idea who she was. It felt like I was growing apart from the South District a little more each year. I once knew every person who lived here, but now the South District was growing. There were unfamiliar faces and I knew there were people that left while I was gone, never to be seen again.

I stared at the orphanage, my only true home. It was a small, unmemorable building. Tattered fabric barely hung from the open windows. It wasn't much, but it made me smile. It was the one place I knew I belonged. No matter where I laid my head at night, this would be where my heart remained.

Laughter and high-pitched squeals filled the evening air as children clamored around the house. I could hear dishes clanging together from the street, and my cheeks warmed.

I swished through the fabric that Tala used to barricade the orphanage from the street and made a mental note to tell her to get an actual door with the earnings I would give her tonight. A bundle of children and teenagers squealed as I strode through the entry. They hounded me with questions, but I could only laugh as I passed around hugs and peppered their cheeks with kisses in greeting.

Seth, a small squirrelly boy, grasped me around my middle, nearly toppling me over.

"Leoni!" he shrieked, my ears ringing at his high pitch. "How was the ocean? Did you see any whales?"

I laughed. Seth was always the most curious after my summers away. He wanted to know about all the sea life that I came across, and badgered me to promise to tell him if I ever saw a mermaid. That made me laugh, because mermaids most certainly did not exist.

"No whales, and no mermaids this time." He pouted, and it was so cute I just wanted to squeeze him. "But I saw a dragon!" He widened his eyes in curiosity. More children surrounded me as I recounted the dragon. I may have embellished some details, but I couldn't help the joy that it brought me with their squeals of excitement. They followed my story up with countless questions, and I answered them all with a smile so wide my cheeks hurt. Being back home filled my soul, replenishing any emptiness I found from my time apart. My exhaustion and weariness were momentarily forgotten and replaced with a warmth in my chest.

The brothers and sisters I had grown up with were now long gone. They were off married, traveling, living their own lives, and I couldn't blame them. We all had rough childhoods here, and I knew that a lot of them just wanted to be rid of Aurum as soon as they could. But something kept me here. This weird rotating family just kept me going. The children that lived here now would know nothing of the hardship that we went through, if I had any say about it.

"Calm down, everyone!" Tala's sharp tone had the children quieting. "It's time for you all to go to bed. Leoni will be here in the morning."

Tala shooed them away from my side, and many of them made moaning protests as they filed into their shared bedroom.

Once the children had scattered, Madame Tala spread her arms wide and embraced me. She smelled like freshly baked bread and spice. It was the most comforting smell in the entire world, and I let the scent envelop me as I gave her a hard squeeze. She untangled her arms from around me and braced my shoulders.

"Leoni." Her eyes were brimming with tears. I had to hold back from rolling my own eyes. She did this every year, and I was far too old to have my mother crying over a two-month journey. "It's so good to have you back, dear. The children missed you. I missed you. Would you like some tea?"

"Yes, please." I said, and I accepted the small cup of hot tea she handed me.

We sat down at a small rickety table that had been in the house for decades. Just another thing that needed to be replaced.

I pulled out the sack of coins that I kept in my satchel and slid it across the table to her.

"Thank you so much. You have always been such a blessing for us." She shook her head as she took the bag. Her eye quirked up as she felt the heaviness. She opened the bag and gasped. "How did you get this much?" Tears rimmed her eyes, and she covered her mouth with her hand.

I shrugged. "It was just a good job. Now you can get a new door. And be sure to get some new books."

She smiled at me, her face blushing. No matter how much I brought to the orphanage, she deserved so much more.

"Where are you staying tonight?" she asked.

I shrugged. "If it's not too much of an issue, I figured I would stay here."

Tala reached across the table and squeezed my hand. "It's not an issue at all. I'll go set you up." She quickly got up from the table to search the house for any spare bedding. I would sleep on the floor most likely, but that didn't bother me in the least.

I kept a few of the coins for myself to get a space I could live in the morning. Anywhere in Aurum would be fine, as long as I was near the orphanage. I gazed around the room, noting all the minor details that needed to be fixed. The shelves leaned on a slant. I could fix that tomorrow. The table in front of me wobbled unevenly on the floor as I grasped it, and I frowned. Something could be stuck under the shorter leg, but maybe there would be a way to permanently fix that, too.

Tala came back with her arms full of threadbare blankets and passed them to me. I followed her into the adjoining living space. Tattered pillows were arranged on the floor and I spread the blankets amongst them to create a cozy makeshift bed.

"I put out a bucket next to the spigot in the back. You are free to wait, of course, but I would prefer if you didn't soil the linens." Tala tossed me a raggedy towel and gave me a small smile before turning to head to bed herself. "It's good to have you back, Leoni."

I gave her my thanks and she turned away, quietly humming to herself.

The stars were bright as I made my way behind the orphanage to the well. I removed my clothes, leaving on my undergarments, and pumped the spigot a few times before the water started sputtering out.

The water was ice cold against my scalp as I plunged my head directly underneath the spigot, forgoing the bucket altogether. I moaned deeply as I scrubbed the salt and dirt off my skin. The water was refreshing. The sign of another year yet to be born. A small bit of soap rested next to the spigot and I grabbed it, scrubbing it against my skin. I sat on the ground, easing my muscles with each pass of soap, releasing the tension that had built up over the summer. Despite the chilling breeze from the night air, I was finally beginning to relax. The summers with Devland were always fantastic adventures, but I was ready for some much needed down time.

"I could do that for you, if you want."

I yelped and turned around to see a tall man above me blocking out the moon. I scrambled from the ground and quickly wrapped myself in the towel.

"What are you doing, Seraph?" I hissed. I wrapped my towel tighter around me. Had Seraph gotten taller over the summer? He had lost some muscle mass, but maybe it was the shadows in the moonlight.

A nervous laugh escaped my lips. Seraph was one of the few people in Aurum that I considered a friend.

We grew up together. His mother often left him at the orphanage when she needed to find ways for extra income. He was always evasive when I asked about her, so I didn't push him on his personal life too often.

We bonded through the years, and spent most of our time together as teenagers, coming up with wild stories about what happened to the gods, creating outlandish conspiracies, and making wild plans to flee Aurum. Obviously, neither one of us had left. Seraph was a mortal, left to take care of his mother, who had developed an illness and needed full-time care, and I decided I didn't want to leave behind the people I considered family.

"I saw you when I was taking my walk." He shrugged. "I didn't realize you had gotten back already, and I wanted to welcome you home."

I squinted my eyes at him. "You were spying on me?" My face heated, and I wasn't sure if I was more embarrassed or angry that he would watch me bathe from afar. Of course, it was always a risk bathing outside, but most people had the decency to offer the semblance of privacy.

A sly smile crossed his face. "Not spying, just noticing."

I bent down and picked up the soap that I had dropped amid my shock. "Well, I would appreciate it if you didn't 'notice' so quietly next time."

He laughed. "Well, now that you're back, do you want to get out of here?" I didn't miss how he didn't apologize for spying on me, or scaring me, but Seraph was easy to forgive. He was my longest friend.

"Not tonight," I replied easily. My body was tired, and I could feel the tug of sleep beckoning me.

"Oh, come on! We always have such a good time together." He laced his tone with innuendo. I gave him a pointed look that said "no".

I leaned toward him, trying to get a better look at his face.

"Are you okay?" I asked. I took notice of the dark circles under his eyes, and the wan look of his hollow cheeks. The Seraph I remembered was handsome, but now he looked haggard. Seraph's eyes widened in excitement, and I took a step back. An unsettling smile stretched across his lips.

"I'm fucking fantastic!" Seraph outstretched his arm toward me. "Come on, Leoni! Let's go somewhere! I'll show you a really good time." Seraph, who was usually reserved and level-headed, was anything but right now. He looked crazed and completely unhinged. I recoiled from his hand, the uneasy feeling of wrongness settled in my belly.

"I just got in this evening. I'm exhausted and I just want to sleep. Maybe tomorrow?" I was basically naked. How could he possibly think I would want to go anywhere like this?

Seraph dropped his smile into a scowl and he took two wide steps toward me. Anger seemed to pulse from him, and I instinctively called on my magic to envelop me. I ran past him, uncaring if he heard me or saw the steps in the surrounding sand.

I backed myself against the wall of the orphanage, watching Seraph carefully. He let out a frustrated shout. My heart began racing. I trusted Seraph. He was never physically violent or prone to outbursts, but I couldn't deny what I was seeing in front of me, no matter how many times I blinked.

"What the fuck, Leoni!" he yelled in the opposite direction from where I currently stood. He took a muslin bag out of his pocket and dipped his hand in. I watched with raptly with wide eyes. He coated his finger in light-blue powder, and he placed it in his mouth, rubbing it along his teeth. What was he doing?

My heart skipped a beat. Drugs weren't uncommon in the South District, but Seraph had shown no interest before. And I had never seen a drug that looked like that.

What kind of trouble did you get yourself into, Seraph?

Seraph shivered as the drug settled in, and I couldn't tear my eyes from him as he started howling with laughter. He sauntered away, wearing another smile, his eyes glazed over. My heart broke. My friend was gone, and in his place was someone I didn't even recognize. It seemed like he completely forgot I had just given him the slip as he disappeared around the corner of the orphanage back into the street. I let out a sigh of relief, but my heart was heavy with worry.

SMALL FINGERS PRODDING MY face and soft giggles roused me from the deep slumber I fell into. I peered out under my eyes to find the big brown eyes of Seth staring down at me while he was clearly trying to hold back his laughter. Katerina was beside him, her face red with laughter. I swept my arms out, snatching the two of them and rolling them onto the pile of pillows next to me. I pinned them down and poked their ribs with my fingers. They howled with laughter as I tickled them until they became breathless.

"Stop!" Seth squealed in between screaming laughs.

I released them and pulled them up as I stood. They wrapped their arms around my middle, and I let out an *oof* as their grip tightened around me. Katerina pulled back and swept her long black hair out of her face.

"Guess what, Leoni!"

"What?" I asked with excitement.

"Madame Tala says that our new teacher is coming this morning!"

"Then you better get ready!" I pinched her cheek, and Katerina nodded with excitement, and pulled Seth from me. A tight knot in my chest loosened as they ran off. I felt relieved knowing they would get an education I never had.

One of the older orphans, Helen, strode into the living space. Her nose was in a book and she plopped down onto a pillow, making herself comfortable. She was old enough that if she had any magical ability, she would start showing it soon. Unfortunately, since many of us didn't know our parental history, it was a gamble on whether we would be mortal or Magi. Since she wasn't giddy with power, I guessed her powers hadn't awakened yet, if she had any.

"What are you reading?" I asked.

"The book that Tala brought in this morning. *Insight to the Great Divine*." Helen shrugged. "It talks about the gods. What life was like before they disappeared."

Intrigued, I leaned over her, reading the words on the page.

"It says here that when the gods were alive, they would bestow blessings to the Magi. One blessing was a Soulmate. Apparently, every Magi is born with a piece of their soul that resides in someone else, and when they find that other person, it's like two halves become whole."

I wrinkled my nose and snorted. "What a bunch of bullshit. Who is willing to wander the world to find their other half? Sounds boring."

Helen sighed. "It sounds romantic." She flipped the page. "I wonder if mortals have Soulmates, too."

"You don't need someone else to make you complete, Helen." She tore her gaze from the page and looked up at me. Her eyes were full of questions and a bit of sadness. "No magic, yet?"

Helen shook her head.

"No." She flexed her hands, balling them up in fists and then extending her fingers. "I keep trying. Been working on the breathing exercises you taught me and waiting for something, anything." Desperation laced her words, and I wrapped my arms around her and squeezed.

"If you have Magi blood, it will happen. But if you don't, that's okay, too. Being a mortal doesn't make you any less than a Magi."

She huffed in my arms but didn't push me away. "What was it like? When your powers awakened?"

"Terrifying," I admitted. "But also exhilarating. I wasn't expecting it." Shadows wrapped around my hands and I watched as they swirled around my fingers, making them disappear. "I almost scared Tala to death. She went to wake me up and thought my bed was empty. I was panicking because she couldn't see my body, and I thought I was a ghost." I laughed a little at the memory. "When I started talking, Tala screamed so loud it woke the whole house up."

Helen's arms tightened around me. I knew she fiercely wanted her powers to come in, and if she were mortal, it would break her heart. I chewed on my lip and looked down at her.

"No matter what happens, if you get your powers or not, I'm here for you. Tala is here for you. Perhaps there is a Soulmate for you as well."

Helen gave me a small smile and turned back to her book, releasing herself from my arms.

"Yeah, maybe my Soulmate is out there."

"But you don't need them."

"Right." She smiled and turned back to her book. The rest of the world may as well have been nonexistent.

I left the pillows and checked the kitchen for bread. I found a small loaf and began cutting it as I thought through all the tasks I needed to complete before I attempted to steal from the estate this evening.

The first few days back from traveling with Devland were always the most stressful. Finding a place to stay was difficult due to limited options in the South District and my desire to stay close to home.

The street filled with shouts and screams, causing me to drop my bread. I swept the fabric away from the doorway and peered out into the street.

My heart skipped a beat. A lifeless body lay on the ground while people shouted for help. I ran to the body and sucked in a breath. Seraph was still as stone. His face was grey and his eyes were open, unseeing at the sky above.

"Help him! Please!" the unknown woman who greeted me earlier shouted, her face full of tears.

"What happened?!" I demanded. I grabbed Seraph's hand. It was cold and limp. My blood ran cold, and my magic started flickering inside me in panic.

"Move aside!" A large man shoved me away from Seraph. I bit back a curse from the rocks that dug into my hands from catching myself. The man picked up Seraph and began running with him in his arms toward one of the South District houses. I followed behind him, shouting to beg him to stop. He flung open the door of a house close by and set Seraph on a long table inside.

I watched, panting, my heart hammered in my chest.

"What is going on?" I demanded.

The man turned toward me. Another woman was bustling around the room. She tutted to herself, checking Seraph's body. I allowed myself to pay more attention to them. The man had a bushy beard, and I barely recognized him.

"L-Lucien—" I stammered. He was the "doctor" of the South District. He wasn't a doctor, not really. But he and his wife knew enough about basic remedies that people in the South District flocked to him when they needed.

"Leoni, you need to leave." He pushed me out of the house, slamming the door in my face.

I raked my hands through my hair. My curls got caught in my fingers, and they snagged against my scalp. The pain was enough to ground me.

I ran to the other side of the house, looking for another way inside. An open window sat beckoning me to scale myself inside. I pulled on my shadows and jumped up. I slid into a bedroom, and quietly snuck through to the front where Seraph lay, cold and unmoving, on the table.

Lucien grunted as he prodded Seraph.

"That's the fourth one this week," he muttered. I stood in the back of the room as tears streamed down my cheeks.

Lucien and his wife were completely unaware of my presence and they scurried around, checking for any signs of life. But Seraph was dead.

"I found this in his pocket." Lucien took a small muslin bag from his wife's hands. It was the same small bag I had seen him use the night before. Lucien peered inside, confirming there were drugs in it before crushing it in his large palm. He roared, and I flinched. He tossed the bag onto the table next to Seraph.

"These damn drugs." Lucien began pacing, dragging his hands over his face. "Where are they even coming from?" Lucien's wife wrapped her arms around him, muttering things in his ear that I couldn't hear. I retreated through the house and leaped back out the window. My magic was useless in the sun, so I disbanded it and sank to the ground.

How could this have happened? Seraph was bright. He was always ready to help others. He was nothing like he showed last night, and he was alive. Seraph didn't deserve to die. And these drugs—four others had died this week because of them? Where did they come from? What could I do to protect my family from Seraph's fate?

THE REST OF THE day passed in a blur. I secured a small room in the South District that wasn't too far from the orphanage. The owners accommodated me with glee once I shoved a couple of gold coins in their hands.

I set up a small space in my new living quarters, retrieving the plans I had shown Devland and going over my route several more times until I was sure I had it memorized. Seraph lingered in between my thoughts, and I caught myself clenching my jaw whenever I thought of him.

I tried to nap, but every time I closed my eyes, I kept seeing his lifeless body in the street. And then I would see his face become someone else's. Helen, Katerina, Seth. The fourth this week? How many deaths were caused by these drugs? My vision blurred with unshed tears, and I sucked in a deep breath as if I could banish the tightening of my throat.

I stilled my shaking hands as I looked over the parchment once more. Every crooked line committed to memory. The moon was rising; it was almost time for me to go. I shoved Seraph's death to the back of my mind. I couldn't allow this to distract me.

Mourn tomorrow. Feed your family tonight.

Chapter 4

THE NEAR SILENCE OF the West District set me on edge. My ears were open, and I kept my eyes peeled while I snuck through the shadows of the buildings lining the streets. I knew the people who lived here were safely tucked away in their homes. I realized some people lived without fear, but it still left a bitter taste in my mouth.

Reinforced wooden doors and glass paned windows decorated these homes that sat next to each other. Although I wasn't usually jealous, I coveted the security that these walls and windows provided. The streets were empty, and the only sound was the occasional wind that sent sand particles skittering across the cobblestone avenue. Using the cover of buildings and various awnings made my trek through the West District easy. I could have covered myself with shadows, but Seraph's death drained me. Every ounce of energy was crucial so I could expel my magic later. Using it on the street seemed like a waste.

Two guards manned the estate's front gate. They were at ease and discussing something that made one of them laugh. I narrowed my eyes at them, but I kept my body relaxed. The Lord specifically trained them to keep watch for an intruder, someone like me, but it didn't seem like they were all that worried. Hah. This would be a lot easier than I expected.

The gate itself was tall and wide open. The Lord never closed his gate. It was open for easy access for servants and late-night shipments. Crime was at an all-time low in Aurum, but poverty still riddled the Southern District. It felt like a sham. He was sending the message that the rest of Aurum didn't need to worry, because he didn't worry. The South District could never even imagine this way of life. Tonight, the Lord would learn that things in Aurum weren't what they seemed. It wasn't even about the money anymore. No, this was about the challenge.

In the distance, a loud clanging bell chimed. It was eleven. On schedule, the two men entered through the open gate. It was now or never.

I BLEW OUT A bated breath and jumped between shadows. The moon was high, and I had ample cover from the gate and the estate. The trees were sparse, but I could make do. Breathing in, I focused on my magic. A warm trickle flowed over my skin, drawing its source from the center of my soul.

My magic was as much a part of me as my arms and legs. I pulled at it, and it bled over my skin. As warmth flowed through my limbs, they became encased in shadow, completely invisible.

Sidling along the gate, I kept the two guards in my vision until I reached the side of the estate that led to the servant's entrance.

I scoffed at my surroundings. Terraces and mezzanines sat above with dangling ivy and flowers that had no business growing in Aurum.

Columns lined the building, giving it an imposing feeling, but they provided more nooks and crannies for me to weave through. The Lord had paid unmentionable amounts of money to keep the greenery alive around the building. He had fresh water shipped in daily, since Aurum's climate only provided so much. The lush plants and opulent architecture were much to my advantage, but the priority and money that got poured into maintaining it made me feel sick.

Passing security had been easy. Easier than expected, but I counted my blessings. I clung to the wall. The lack of torches on this side of the estate made things much simpler to navigate. I made my way to the servant's entrance nestled between two columns, hidden from the view.

Gently, with soft hands, I tested the door. The handle jiggled, but didn't budge. I silently cursed and fished out my lock pick. The pick was relatively new, and it slid into the lock like cutting through soft butter.

Every click and tug on my hand registered against my deft fingers. A slight left shift and small right rotation made the door open easily. I grinned, happy that this lock was a simple one, and moved through the threshold.

A dimly lit stone tunnel revealed itself. I stood in a cold, dark corner, listening and watching as my eyes adjusted to the tunnel light. Seemingly, the staff was also mostly out of the manor, along with the family. No voices or footsteps could be heard. Adrenaline and eagerness started to pump through my veins, and I had to remind myself not to let impatience distract me from my goal. Mistakes happened when things were rushed, and I refused to allow any missteps on this robbery.

Crouched low, and taking light, slow footsteps, I listened for any signs of servants passing through the tunnel. If I had done my research correctly, and I knew I did, this tunnel would lead straight into the kitchens. I could locate the estate's various rooms from there.

My breath was shallow and fast as I tiptoed on swift feet. My fingers tingled with a hunger for the riches that lie in this mansion. I hurried through the tunnel and discovered another door.

I hugged the wall and grasped at a small knife I had strapped to my thigh. The kitchens, while still possibly empty, had a higher chance of someone lingering. I pressed my ear to the door and listened through the wood.

There was no noise, no indication that there might be someone waiting for me on the other side, but I held my dagger as I nudged the door open anyway, the black diamonds feeling warm in my palm. After exhaling, I peeked through the small door crack. The brick oven had no glowing embers, and the countertops were free of debris. Completely clean.

I smirked. No one to cook for, no need for a chef. I smiled at my luck and the heavy fortune I planned on walking away with. A small door was located by the stove, unlike the wide arch on the opposite end of the kitchen. Another entrance to another servant's hall. On swift feet, I moved through and shut the door quietly behind me. Half the battle was over.

Not a soul passed my senses as I snuck through the building. I peeked through each doorway, revealing bedroom after bedroom. I nearly cursed out loud when I opened my fifth bedroom. How many gods-forsaken bedrooms did one family need?

Finally, I cracked a door, and in it I spied a wall of books. Jackpot. The room was dark. No candles or torches lit within. My feet met the soft plush carpet, silencing my footsteps completely. Bookshelves lined the walls on either side, while a large balcony with closed double doors looked out to the front of the manor property.

I moved through the shadows around a desk and chair on the side of the room. The desk was simple and contained no cabinets, so I quickly focused elsewhere. From what I could see, there wasn't a book or paper out of place.

No dust settled through the moonlight that streamed through the glass doors. The books were packed together on each shelf, except...

One shelf was different from the others. Between a stack of texts was a small box. Surely this wasn't the treasure. It was too easy. I glanced around the pristine room. Nothing else looked like it might contain anything expensive, and I groaned. If I had to sift through every room in this manor to find it, I would. I grimaced at the prospect of delaying my time.

I ran my hands along the spines, feeling for any false books that might contain a treasure of their own, but none of the books my fingers brushed against registered as abnormal.

I straightened my back and tiptoed to the box. It was made of dark wood, nearly black, with a small clasp adorning the side. The box called to me. I reached out, shaking off the tremor that pulsed through my fingers.

This had to be it: Aurum's Diadem. I opened the box with unsteady hands. A gold circlet sat inside on a black pillow. Diamonds and rubies gleamed on the gold finish, reflecting the moonlight that streamed through the windows.

It was said that it held gems so perfectly that the gods themselves forged them. I breathed in a shaky breath, willing myself not to tear up at the sight. The design was delicate and ancient. It had to have been hundreds, if not thousands, of years old. I bit my lip and snapped the box shut.

I placed the box in the satchel on my side and quickly returned to the servant's passage. I couldn't stop myself from jogging to the other side of the estate. No one passed by or even breathed in my direction.

The exit came quickly, torches blurring in my vision as I rushed through. It was a risk, going through the estate this quickly, but my pounding heart didn't let me stop.

I flung the door to the gardens open and quickly shut it behind me. I could feel the blood pumping through my veins, and my body was heated from the rush. I leaned my back against the door, breathing in the fresh air. I tried to steady myself and cease the shaking that was currently wracking through my arms. The diadem was still on my side, confirmed by a quick pat on the satchel.

I needed to think clearly. Move from gardens to docks. The moon hadn't quite reached its apex yet, and the chance of me getting to the docks before Devland was high. I couldn't wait to watch his eyes light up as he opened the box to see Aurum's most coveted possession in my hands.

Roses and spindly vines grew in groves on this side of the estate, giving me ample cover. I avoided considering the high expenses of maintaining the non-native plants. As much as it pained me to fathom the wealth that went into the estate's frivolous decor, I had just stolen Aurum's sacred diadem. I would be able to fund the orphanage for decades.

It would also be a direct hit to the Aurum's government. Their most prized relic was stolen from under their noses. The realness that the actual diadem sat on my hip made my heart race. I grinned. This was my most exciting robbery. My biggest success.

I moved stealthily through the garden and saw just two different guards at the front gate. I thanked the gods as I navigated through easily. I returned to the gate near the property's end where the guards were stationed. The shadows were thinner here, so I needed to create a distraction to get out.

Praying that my shaking arms were still useful, I pulled two stones out of my satchel. I aimed for a distant window. I pitched it, but it landed short and made a thud on the ground. Shit.

"What was that?" one of the men muttered.

"Hmm?" The other guard's hearing wasn't quite as keen.

"I guess it's nothing. I thought I heard a sound."

I waited until their suspicions had diminished and their postures relaxed before aiming again. This was my only chance. I threw the stone.

Glass shattered. Perfect.

"There's someone there!" The guard turned towards the noise.

Please go, please go, please go, I repeated to myself. After exchanging a look, they investigated.

I trotted through the shadows and pulsed more magic through my veins. The twinge of exhaustion rattled my brain, but I shrugged it off, darting through the gate. I made my way into the street, keeping in the shadows.

I only spared a single glance back. One last look to make sure I wasn't followed. I slowed my feet and regained a steady rhythm of breath before releasing my magic. If anyone were to see me now, I would look completely innocent.

THE ADRENALINE THAT WRACKED through my limbs made me want to bark out a hysterical laugh. I almost couldn't believe that I stole the gods-damned diadem. My feet wanted to sprint to the docks, but I refused to let them lest I gain any unnecessary attention. Instead, I pressed my palm to my lips and pulled my hooded cloak further over my face.

My feet thudded against the wooden docks as a loud clock tower rang. Midnight. Damn, I said a minute early, but I was exactly on time. I chuckled, imagining Devland using this to negotiate a larger cut. It wasn't going to happen. In my satchel sat the most renowned artifact in all of Ambrose. He can take his negotiations and shove them up his ass.

I looked over the dock, brushing my hair off of my sticky forehead. I breathed the scent of sea and sand and perched myself on a wooden crate. A few lingering souls meandered in the moonlight. Where was Devland?

Heavy footsteps thudded behind me, and I smiled.

"Captain," I drawled, "you're late—"

"Put your hands up and stand slowly," a voice that I didn't recognize spoke into my ear. It was low and firm. I flinched as a point was pushed into my lower back. I didn't dare look behind me or make a sudden movement other than the slow rise of my body.

My hands shook above me, and I slowly turned.

"Good evening, Watchman." I added a sultry note to my voice. Surely, whoever they were looking for, it wasn't just a lonely girl alone on the docks. "I think there's some kind of misunderstanding."

I willed my hands not to shake. Willed the tremor out of my voice. Willed my heartbeat to slow. Willed the weight of the diadem to disappear off of my side. I didn't dare glance down. I didn't dare bring any attention to my side.

In front of me stood three Watchmen. My eyes narrowed. Two men, one woman. The man holding the knife under my chin was the tallest and broadest. He wore a hooded cloak with a golden rose embroidered on the left. Four stars sat under the rose, and my brow rose. "Not just any Watchman, I see. You must be a general."

Even under the guise of his hood, his teeth gleamed in the moonlight as he snarled, "I am *The* General. General Riel."

I sucked in a breath. The two behind General Riel stepped forward. He lifted his hand to signal a halt. His name rang in my ears. General Riel was the fiercest general in Aurum. Known for relentlessly hunting down criminals and delivering gore-filled and vile justices. Why was he here?

My stomach rolled, recalling Devland's warning about staying safe. I mentally berated myself for not taking him more seriously, not taking that damned warrant more seriously. It took everything in me not to glance down at the pouch on my hip.

"We were told that Aurum's Thief would be down here tonight. Female, with hair the color of flames, short, and bronzed skin. I believe you fit that bill." He gestured his knife to all of me. My heart raced, and my magic roiled under my skin, but it was minimal. I used most of my magic in the estate and barely had any left.

Devland's warnings rang over in my mind. Why did Riel want me? Surely, there must be bigger, badder criminals that he should have been focused on. Despite it making no sense, he stood in front of me.

"You must be mistaken." I schooled my face, trying to convey surprise. I didn't need to try hard. How did they gather so much information about me? I had kept myself under wraps for years. Shit. I knew about the warrant, but their ability to locate me here was a mystery.

"Where were you tonight? Before you came to the docks." he asked, each word clipped.

"In the South District. Visiting family. I came up here for some fresh air." A half-truth, but one where it wouldn't appear like I was lying.

"Interesting," he drawled the word out, emphasizing each syllable. "Because we got reports of you in the West District, oh," he looked back at one of his companion soldiers, "fifteen minutes ago?"

I swallowed thickly. I must have released my magic too soon. Too eager to get to the docks and rub my success in the captain's face.

"And so you came rushing over to find me? I'm flattered, General Riel." I gave him a smirk, but I knew the expression didn't meet my eyes. With my confidence wavering, and the diadem weighing heavy on my hip, I only had one option.

I ran.

I twisted around. My feet pounded against the wooden docks, splinters flying up from underneath me. Maybe I was stupid. Maybe I had a death wish. Or maybe, just maybe, I could get away. A glance behind me confirmed I was being chased, but I only needed to find a place to hide for the smallest amount of time. I just needed to find a dark enough alcove to call my magic. I cursed at the fact that I needed focus and couldn't call it on a whim.

A series of low buildings were on my left. Just a few more paces. I pumped my legs, heat building in them like I had never run before. I fumbled with my satchel, my desperate fingers not working as they should with the ties. With a grunt, I pried it off.

I threw it between two buildings with expired food and waste, far from the General's position. I cringed as it landed in a sack of rotten food. But better the diadem in the garbage than my head on a stake.

I slid next to a building shrouded in shadow—my perfect hiding spot—and forced myself to stabilize my breathing. I called on my magic, but it was just a speck in my soul. The magic was desperate for a slumber, exhausted from my earlier usage. I closed my eyes and pinched the bridge of my nose, reaching for the dregs of my magic. Scraping for each and every piece of energy that could settle over my body.

Strong hands grasped my shoulder and pulled me back into the street. I screamed and kicked and punched, but I couldn't escape the vice-like grip on my arms.

"You're lucky I don't gut you here in the street, thief," The General's low voice growled in my ear. Metal clasped over my wrists. Cuffs. Cuffs embedded with a magic of their own to negate mine. At least I had ditched the diadem. They had no proof of anything.

"We found it, sir. Lying on top of a rotten bag of potatoes."

Fuck.

Chapter 5

The poor excuse of a cot squeaked as I sat on it. General Riel and his crew threw me into a dungeon so deep underground that I was sure any screams, or the smell, never reached the golden sands of Aurum. I crinkled my nose. It reeked of rot and waste. I thudded the back of my head against the stone wall behind me over and over. I wouldn't let myself spiral. There was always a way out of things. Sometimes, a situation just needed a creative solution.

Running had been stupid. Honestly, I was lucky that Riel hadn't painted the streets red with my blood. In fact, after they had placed the cuffs on me, Riel and his men hadn't even touched me. They only shuffled around me in a tight triangle formation. But I had heard of the legends of Riel and his powers.

Truthfully, I shouldn't have been able to run from him at all. His magic was notoriously powerful, but equally mysterious. I heard stories, though. Some said he could teleport, others said he had speed, and I even heard he had some sort of healing gift.

The rumors were no doubt exaggerated, but one thing was certain: he could destroy a person in the blink of an eye. He could pop in front of someone at a moment's notice and kill them before they even knew his sword had struck. I shivered. My life had been that close to its end, but he *chose* to keep me alive. I wasn't sure if that scared or comforted me.

"Fuck." I muttered, processing the dire situation I had gotten myself into. I tried to calm the increasing panic that crept through me, and I took in my surroundings. I wiped the sweat off my palms on my pants, peering through the metal bars that held me.

They put me in a single-cell dungeon. They kept prisoners who were to be tortured in places like this. A door stood on the far side. It was definitely guarded.

I patted myself down, remembering that I had lock picks with me. I cursed. They were in the satchel with the diadem. The satchel that I hastily threw into the garbage. And even if they were on my person, I wouldn't have had them on me, anyway. The General patted me down and removed all of my belongings. His hands brushed roughly over my clothes, his palms shocking everywhere he touched, until he found my black diamond dagger. I grimaced. I needed to get that back. My heart started picking up its pace again, and I blinked back tears. Now was not the time to panic.

When they dragged me into the cell, I claimed the package wasn't mine. I had spat at Riel to prove that I was the one that had thrown it there. He only gave me a cold, calculating look and turned on his foot. He motioned for his guards to lock me in here before leaving me in this gods-forsaken dungeon.

My ears perked when I heard muffled voices from the other side of the door, and I made my way over to my cot. I reclined back, placing my hands behind my head, attempting to give the illusion of easy confidence. Only the pounding of my heart betrayed me.

The door swung open, and General Riel strode in. His hood was removed, revealing his brown eyes, sharp nose, and short brown hair that curled at the ends. Shadows from the flickering torchlight ran across his deep brown skin, sharpening his features. His presence was powerful and intimidating, and I hated to admit it, but he was devastatingly handsome. I eased my face into an expression of calm and smirked. Only my big toe, tapping against the inside of my boots, was any outward indication of my panic.

"Coming to let me out?" My lips curled into a grin, betraying every horrible thought in my head. "I'm innocent until proven guilty." The lie formed easily on my tongue. The General only pinched his lips. I tried not to let my face falter. My chances of being released were clearly slim to none.

"Lying will not win you any favors." General Riel paced down the length of the cell, stopping in front of the cot. He held out his hand, and a hooded watchman handed him a small pile of papers. "Leoni of No One. Grew up in a small orphanage in the South District."

His lip curled in disgust. I had to keep myself from rolling my eyes.

"Interestingly enough, until twenty years ago, that orphanage was all but destitute. Children were starving and sick. Now it appears the children there are well-fed and even educated. I wonder how that happened." He pointed his stony gaze at me.

"Beats me," I told him.

"Poor orphaned child, subjected to a life of poverty and crime. It's no wonder you ended up the way you are," he sneered, "criminal scum."

My face heated. He didn't know what I did for the community. He had no right to call me names. I leaped up from the cot with a snarl.

"You can think what you want," I spat at his feet, "but the scum in this room is not me. I'm not the one parading down golden streets in the name of justice while I leave people to rot. You are just some pig-headed, pretentious piece of—"

"Enough!" He shoved the papers back at the hooded Watchman. "There have been relics that are mysteriously disappearing, and you just so happen to be caught with one tonight."

I stopped breathing.

"Well, I didn't steal those relics, and I didn't steal that one. I haven't even been in the city for the last two months. You have nothing on me," I said and crossed my arms.

He leaned toward the bars, his piercing brown eyes meeting mine. "Stop. Lying."

I threw my hands wide. "I'm not lying. You can go ask that little poor orphanage if I have been out of the city and they will confirm. I only arrived back yesterday."

The General stepped back. He looked between the two other watchmen beside him and nodded, seemingly able to have a private conversation without words. I stared at them. Just who were these people, and what sort of magic did they wield? General Riel glared down at me.

"You have two choices, so you better listen closely." He bent down, leveling his face with mine. "You can help Aurum with a small task. You will ask no questions, make no sudden decisions to run, and no sneaking and stealing. Or I will execute you and burn the orphanage down myself. If you think they have it bad now, just wait until they face my wrath. My wrath for using stolen goods to fund their little 'lives'."

He stood back up and looked at me over his nose. His broad shoulders blocked out the light from the torch.

"If you don't want to help, I have a public execution prepared for Aurum's Thief eight hours from now. And don't be remiss that I won't take back what the orphanage owes us after." I watched as he turned away, blood rushing through my ears, my hands clenched into fists so tight that my nails bit into my skin.

"Your choice," he called back as he ascended, slamming the door behind him.

I SCREAMED AND YELLED until my throat turned raw. The General deserved to burn. My hands bled from hitting the cell bars with my fists. It was one thing to make me pay for my crimes, but my family was innocent. I refused to let General Riel tear them apart without a fight.

Resigning to the fact that I was stuck in this impossible situation, I bid my time until the bastard returned to retrieve me. I used the time plotting. I sat in the cell thinking of all the ways I would kill Riel myself and make him suffer. I wasn't a murderer, and I had never even killed before, but I could—just for him. Making me pay for my crimes was one thing. Threatening the orphanage was a whole different story.

I wanted him to feel the desperation that so many of us in the South District felt. Rage heated my body and fueled my desire for bloodshed. General Riel and the whole of Aurum should thank me for putting money into the community. Their community. It was only because of their shortcomings that I had to steal in the first place.

I lost track of time in the cell. There were no windows for light, so I had no way of telling how much time had passed. I ran my hands down my face, smearing blood along my cheeks. With the Magi blood that pumped through my veins, my wounds usually healed quickly.

Thanks to my shackles, all of my powers had been negated. No summoning the darkness to hide, no quick healing, and exhaustion took over a tenfold. I gritted my teeth, determined to keep my eyes open, and waited.

I started awake after accidentally falling asleep when The General and his Watchmen came back, strolling through the door. The General had apparently refreshed himself. Scruff that lined his jaw was now shorter and neatly trimmed. His jaw ticked, and he stared at me. I refrained from the yawn that was inching its way out, but he only glared at me. For eyes that held the warm color of honey, they had a very distinct way of making ice sink into my bones.

"Have you made your decision?"

I said nothing, only crossing my arms in defiance.

"Death it is." He waved his hand, and the Watchmen opened the cell and grabbed my shoulders. One had a burlap sack. I once again attempted to fight, kicking and shoving my shoulders, but my strength was no match for the Watchmen's sheer size. The one with the sack went to put it on me, opening it wide and raising it above my head.

"Wait!" I shouted. I slumped in their grips. I wasn't afraid of death, but I was afraid of what would happen if I died. That stupid burlap sack shook out all of my defiance. Even if the threat to the orphanage was a bluff, I couldn't allow my family to be displaced or let them starve because they lost their primary source of income. I met The General's brown eyes with false confidence.

"I'll do it. I'll work with you."

"Great." General Riel's tone was flat and cold. "Bring her to my office."

The Watchmen kept their firm grips on my shoulders. I tried to shrug them off three separate times, but it was futile. We followed

General Riel, his cape billowing behind him through a series of halls and stairwells.

They shoved me into the threshold of a small office with a desk and a modest bookshelf. It was clean and organized without a single speck of dust out of place. The General whipped off his cloak and placed it on the back of a chair before sitting and gesturing me to follow suit across from him. His tunic was tight over his broad shoulders, and I pointedly looked in another direction, taking in the too-clean office.

"When are you going to take these off?" I shook my cuffed hands in General Riel's face. He only nodded, and the Watchman removed them. I rubbed my wrists, shocked that it was that easy. He dismissed them with a wave of his hand, and it was just the two of us. Silence filled the room, but he never took his gaze off me. Like he was studying me, my every action, every slight movement.

"Take that as a peace offering. For your cooperation." He scowled at me. My magic flooded back into my veins. But I wouldn't use it now. That would have been even more foolish than when I had originally tried to run from him.

I looked around the small room. A window looked out into Aurum. We were in one of the spires of the city. The buildings below shimmered against the clear blue sky of morning.

"So, what sort of work do you need me to do? Surely you wouldn't want some lowly peasant to manage your books." I gave him my best sarcastic smile. "Since I'm uneducated." He didn't even so much shift his eyes at my cynicism.

Finally, he broke his gaze and looked out the window, relaxing back in his chair. He sifted through a cabinet under his desk and pulled out a liquor decanter and a small glass. He poured two fingers into the glass before lifting it to his lips.

"Aren't you going to offer me some?" I raised my brows at him. This was a man of stone, and gods knew if I had to work with him, I needed a drink.

He only met my stare and drank fully while maintaining eye contact. He swallowed and kept his eyes on me over the rim of his glass. I scoffed at his intimidation tactic. I worked with pirates and the Black Market. It would take a lot more than a look to scare me.

"You are going to help us catch some thieves. It takes one to know one, and these thieves have been evading us for weeks. It's a payment for your crime."

I scoffed. "You can't even prove that I stole the diadem."

"If you didn't, how did you know it was a diadem?" His eyebrow raised. Shit. They had never said outright that it was the diadem. He sighed, sipping from his glass. "You didn't steal the diadem, anyway."

"Excuse me?"

"The diadem you stole was a fake." My face felt hot as he continued. "We knew there was a skilled thief that lived in Aurum. One who was rumored to be stealing from nearby cities, coves, and towns. Reports said it was a red-headed woman, and I had watchmen keep an eye out for you. You set yourself up. They saw you at the estate during the public tour. Watched as you mentally mapped out the manor, watched even closer when you memorized the schedules of the inhabitants.

"Honestly, I was impressed with how thorough you are. But not thorough enough. Not enough to not get caught stealing a diadem dupe."

He pulled out the circlet and tossed it to me.

"Getting the Lord's house empty and getting you interested in the diadem took a lot of work, but it paid off."

I scrutinized it and cursed. With better lighting and adrenaline no longer clouding my thoughts, I could see the imperfections. It was, admittedly, a good replica, but it definitely wasn't "made by the gods". I threw the diadem back at him in irritation. Irritation that I had been deceived and caught. I crossed my arms over my chest.

He placed it back in the black box and stowed it in a drawer.

"So, it was all a ruse?" I asked with acid in my voice.

Riel smiled wickedly. "Exactly."

"How do you know that I'm not the other thief?"

The General exhaled and set his glass on the desk. "You were on the top of our suspect list. But, like you said, you haven't been anywhere in the last two moon cycles. We don't need to confirm that. I have eyewitness accounts of you leaving the city." I stopped breathing. Just how long had they been tracking me? Suddenly, my mouth was dryer than Aurum during the wind season.

"We originally set tonight's plan in motion to capture you, but when the robberies continued to happen, you were gone. I pivoted my strategy. I saw you as an opportunity." He gave me a grin with a dark gleam. I wanted to shrink back into my chair, but I refused to cower in front of him.

"So, what do you need me to do?" I asked as a rolled my shoulders back. Riel passed over a stack of papers and scrolls.

"This is the current information we have on the thieves. Where and what they have stolen, and any eyewitness accounts." He paused and tapped his finger along the rim of his glass. "If you help us track and arrest the culprits, I will remove the bounty on your head, and you will be a free woman."

I blinked. He had no idea what being free meant. Freedom required money. It required security. I had none of those things. The poverty that rested with my family still shackled me. I would never be free. I didn't want to be free. Not until everyone I loved would be free with me.

"Now, if we hear of any more mysterious robberies afterward, you will, of course, be the top suspect. If you don't step out of line, we will never cross paths again." He said the terms with such conviction and finality that my heart raced. I needed to steal. It was my whole life. But, if I needed to go elsewhere to do it, I guessed it was reasonable. It was certainly better than some public execution.

"So, once we find these people and get them into the dungeons," I glared at the General, "I will never have to see you or your watchmen again?"

He nodded. "That's correct."

I blew out a breath. Suddenly I had a much higher value in finding these mysterious thieves. I looked down at the stack of papers The General had handed me.

I couldn't stop myself from asking, "Any particular patterns worth mentioning?" A thief had their tells. Did they prefer to slip in quietly and unnoticed? Or did they like to leave a message behind?

"The only pattern that we have been able to identify is that they are getting more confident, and yet, the robberies seem at random. No schedule, no sign of premeditation. It's as though the thieves wait until someone else tells them where and when to strike. We can't seem to find the loopholes." The General sighed. It was heavy, and I noticed faint lines of tiredness that sat below his eyes.

"Look through the files tonight. I'll show you your room, and someone will collect you tomorrow."

"I get my own room." I sat stunned. There would be no dungeon with a pile of feces next to my head?

He turned, his cold stare sending icicles down my throat.

"You'll be staying at The General's House, my house, in the guest room. Don't think there won't be someone guarding it at all times. If you try to escape or run, you will be back on death row."

"Got it." I waved him off and turned to the notes. I was getting familiar with The General's threats, and they only made me more irritated. The General's Watchmen reappeared and shoved the cuffs back on my wrists. I held in my protests, knowing my "freedom" was too good to be true. But, I got to sleep in an actual bed, rather than some dilapidated cot, so I counted my blessings where I could.

Chapter 6

The General's House, or the General's Quarters, as General Riel had called it, wasn't far from his office. I trailed behind The General, still flanked by hooded Watchmen. I took in the neighborhood. The houses were large, but they weren't overly excessive, like the Lord's estate.

The Quarters, made of the same golden stone as the rest of wealthy Aurum, stood out from the other homes in the neighborhood with its fence. We made our way through, and I noticed the property was simple but beautifully maintained. Whoever had designed the house clearly did so with Aurum's climate in mind. Desert plants and succulents lined the pathway to the front door.

The foyer I stepped in felt inviting. The complete opposite of Riel. Whoever he inherited this house from had good taste. Metal lanterns hung from the ceiling, glowing against the plush rugs and carpets that silenced our footsteps. Each textile looked to be handcrafted and colorful. Plants hung from walls, which kept the air fresh.

I followed him upstairs, where he opened the door to a small bedroom. It was...cozy. Decorated like the rest of the house with a splash of greens and yellows.

"You'll stay here." The Watchmen filed out and left me alone with the General. I took a deep breath and refused to meet his gaze.

"You will not leave unless prompted, and there will always be guards outside the door, so don't even think about trying anything," he said. I nodded, and he left, snapping the door shut behind him. I honestly had no desire to try to flee. The bed in front of me looked entirely too inviting.

I fell asleep almost as quickly as Riel had left me and ended up sleeping all day. I woke up in the middle of the night and spent most of the time poring over Riel's notes or dozing back off in the soft bed. When I went through the notes, I caught myself scoffing. They hadn't been caught or identified yet, but they weren't very intelligent. I could tell they were becoming greedy. My thoughts sobered when I supposed that I hadn't been very smart, either, since I was so easily caught myself.

A series of impatient knocks shocked me awake. Papers slipped off of my chest, scattering all over the floor.

"Come in!" I called while hastily collecting the papers on my knees. Large boots entered my vision, and I looked up. General Riel towered above me with a scowl.

"You didn't bother to bathe?" he scoffed.

I hadn't even bothered to change, too tired to care, and too curious about these thieves. Even though I was helping The General find them, I needed to find out who they were for myself. I was going to be back on the streets eventually, so I needed them gone. My competition needed to be eliminated.

I looked down at myself. Dried blood was still caked in my fingers, dirt and grime layered in my hair, and I was sure smeared blood was still on my face. I gave Riel a winning smile.

"Go clean yourself. I'll go get you some new clothes." He turned to leave and then stopped in the doorway. "And make it quick. We are already wasting time." The door slammed on his way out, and I laughed myself into the bathroom.

For a temporary prison, I couldn't complain. The bedroom had a wide—and locked—window, the bed was soft, and there was even a dresser and desk. Even having a private bathroom was, truthfully, something I hadn't ever had before. I wrapped a towel around myself after scrubbing off all the salt and grime I had accumulated in the last two days. I still felt like I needed another bath to get the last layer of dirt off, but it would have to wait.

General Riel was still in the bedroom, standing with his arms behind his back and a pile of clothes stacked on the bed.

"Your uniform. You will wear this when working, and you can get new clothes in the city another time. Now change."

When he didn't try to leave, I raised my eyebrow. "Are you waiting for a show?"

He gritted his teeth. "Go change," he pointed behind me, "in the bathroom."

I grabbed the clothes and turned, flipping my wet hair over my shoulder. I glanced behind me as I shut the door and smirked when I saw Riel deliberately turn in the other direction.

GENERAL RIEL LED ME down the stairs and through the halls of the General's House. The sun was high in the sky; light poured through glass windows.

We passed a living room with plush, low-seated cushions, presumably for entertainment. On the left was the kitchen and the dining room with a large wooden table that seated at least ten. Someone scattered green succulents around the house, giving it a natural feeling. At least these were native plants and didn't require excess for upkeep. We turned and walked by an outdoor seating area with a fire pit in the center. Colorful awnings covered a few chairs, protecting the would-be patrons from the desert heat. It was still more rich than I was comfortable with, but it was no comparison to the Lord's estate, who showed off gaudy, exuberant wealth for no reason.

The General cleared his throat, calling my attention to the open door in front of him. I stepped into what I assumed was his personal office. Books neatly lined the walls. I took a closer look: tactical books—and they were all in alphabetical order. I ran my hand across the shelf. Not a speck of dust in sight.

"You're so..." I turned to him, "clean."

"Sit." He pointed at a chair across from him.

"And demanding." I dropped my weight in the chair and swung one of my legs over the arm.

"You are here to do a job. I have put up with your smart comments, but need I remind you that if you make any effort to betray—"

"Yes, yes, you'll chop off my head and hold it up for all of Aurum to see." I gave him a pointed stare. "I don't need you to keep reminding me of my impending doom, General."

His eyes narrowed, clearly irritated that I kept talking out of turn. I wasn't one of his minions, and I refused to act like one.

The office door behind me swung open, and a man and a woman walked in. I assumed these were the other guards from my arrest. They both wore similar uniforms to the one I was wearing. Official-looking black pants and shirts with the Aurum insignia. Where Riel's had four stars, ours had three.

The woman stepped ahead, her dark hair tied in a tight braid along her back. She gave me a look up and down. "I see my clothes fit you well enough."

I threw her a smirk. "A little tight in the bottom, but they will do." I winked at the bearded man behind her, who was clearly trying not to laugh.

"Enough." General Riel stood, and they sat in the open chairs across from his desk.

"Did you look through the files I gave you?" Riel's stern eyes met my own, his gaze not quite as icy as before.

"I did, General." I hissed back at him.

The Watchman that had just walked in snickered. I shot him a quizzical look.

General Riel sighed. "You can call me by my name. Riel. I am not one for formalities."

I smirked, seriously doubting that he didn't appreciate the decorum. But what the General wants, the General gets. "Well, *Riel*, I did look over the files. Poured through them most of the day and night, in fact."

"Did you notice anything?" His question was clipped, but not laced with irritation.

"Nothing other than what you already told me. It seems like they are getting bolder with each theft. It's only a matter of time before they bite off more than they can chew." The others nodded. "Who are you all, anyway?"

The woman responded first, "I'm Masika. Riel's second." I raised my brow. Her stern face, with a slight pinch in between her eyebrows, gave me the impression she didn't tolerate a lot of misconduct.

"A woman as a second to the General?"

"We hire on skill, Leoni." Riel cut in and pointed to the bearded man who wore an easy lopsided grin, "That's Chefren. Now the introductions are out of the way," Riel gritted his teeth, "let's get back to work."

Chefren leaned forward to face me. His golden-brown skin shimmered in the sunlight that streamed through the office window. "What's your magic, Leoni?" He was completely unconcerned about the glare that Riel was giving him for his interruption. I had to admire his boldness.

"It's impolite to ask others what their magic is." Masika gave Chefren a side-long glance before pinning me under her gaze. "Although you may as well tell us what it is." Her amber eyes bored into me.

I looked at Riel. He rested his chin on his hands on his desk and raised his eyebrow. Fuck. If they knew what I could do, I might never get away from them. I grimaced.

"I can hide."

"How?" Chefren spoke up. His voice was gravelly and low.

I ground my teeth. "I don't recall me telling you my personal information was a part of this bargain."

Riel reclined in his seat. "Lest you forget, Leoni." My name rolled off his tongue, and I hated how much I liked the sound of it. "You are not just some hired consultant. We found you guilty of a crime, and you are paying for it. So tell us," the corners of his lips turned up, "how do you hide?"

I spoke through clenched teeth, "I can manipulate shadows. Depending on my surroundings, I'm practically impossible to see."

Chefren grinned, his green eyes boring into me and the mischief in it slightly unnerving. "Show us."

"Absolutely not," I retorted instantly. "Besides the fact that I have these," I raised my arms high to jingle the shackles on me, "it doesn't work with this much light, anyway." I lifted my head to the window that was streaming in the bright morning light.

Riel sat up straight. "You will not be showing us your magic." I blew out a relieved breath. "Nor will you be using it at all."

I held back a grimace. Riel, of course, wouldn't want me to use my magic. He could lose track of me, and I could escape.

"How do you expect her to help us if she can't use her magic?" Chefren leaned forward, elbows propped on his lap. I didn't miss the edge of sarcasm that lined his question.

I shot him a saccharine grin. "Just because I can't use my magic doesn't mean I'm useless." Gods, did they think I was a complete moron? I was starting to wonder why I was here.

Masika gave me an appraising glance. Where Riel's gaze did nothing to scare me, Masika's stare gave me a shiver down my spine. It was like her presence was physically pressing in on me. I steeled myself and forced my gaze to her brown eyes staring daggers at me. If she thought she could try to intimidate me, I would meet her every step of the way. She only smirked as she reclined back into her chair.

I rolled my shoulders back. When Masika looked away, her overbearing aura moved with it.

"What we know," Riel shifted through papers, copies of what I had, "is that they seem to go for relics and ancient artifacts. Sacred paintings, historical tomes. They stole the statue of Himera from the

Sun Temple. As far as we can tell, the thefts started as far back as two seasons ago."

"Why are you just looking into it now?" I asked. Two seasons without investigation was an incredibly long time for continued high-profile thefts. Especially for thefts that seemed to happen one after another in the same vicinity. Masika turned back to me, and I braced myself for the overbearing power she expelled, but it never came.

"There were reports of the thefts as far back as two seasons ago, but they were petty thefts. It started out in the slum districts. Petty goods. Then it expanded into someone's jewelry, a sacred book from the library, and small pieces of technology. We didn't start looking until they started becoming more opulent."

I bit my lip, attempting to keep my scathing thoughts to myself. Instead of biting out insults that would get me nowhere, I clenched my fists. These people had been stealing from the less fortunate for moon cycles, and only when they started stealing high-profile items is when Riel stepped in? Typical. That was how Aurum ran, how it thrived—only caring about the needs of the rich. I cracked my neck, releasing the pent-up tension. "Do we know anything about where the artifacts ended up?"

Chefren chuckled. "If we knew that, we wouldn't be asking for help from criminals."

Riel went through his notes, telling me about the ways they had already tried to discover the thieves, his voice low and rigid with recited professionalism. I had to admit I was losing focus as I got caught up in staring at the sunlight that reflected in his dark hair, making some pieces shine with a reddish hue. I was getting lost in the way Riel's sharp jawline flexed when he spoke, the passion for finding the thieves coming out with a rising voice, when he swung his brownish-gold eyes in my direction.

"The problem is that the robberies are inconsistent. They seem to happen at random, and the location of the robberies varies. We had one robbery happen at one temple in the City Center, so we bolstered security around any potential marks, but then another robbery happened within someone's home. It just doesn't make sense, and I only have finite resources as it is. The temples are public, but how would a thief know what was in someone's home without going inside first?"

"Information is just as big of a commodity as anything else," I said. "For a price, you can know whatever you want, about anyone." I felt six eyes on me as I spoke, but I didn't feel threatened. They were taking my words seriously, even if none of them seemed surprised. "What are the connections to the relics?"

"We don't know. Other than that they are old and priceless, there isn't much more to go on. And I've sent my people to recover them, but the relics are missing completely." Riel sat back in his chair and tapped his fingers on the armrest.

"Whoever is stealing them isn't recirculating them through Aurum. It's a possibility that they are no longer here at all." Riel's eyes met mine, and as I peered into them I saw his frustration, his life's work as a keeper of law and order being put to the test. "Bargaining with you is our last resort, something I fought hard against. But we need an insider's mind."

I blew out a breath in thought.

"If the thieves are for hire, there's a chance there's been an influx of money from unknown sources, and that's where we need to look." I leaned back in my chair, and Riel raised his eyebrow at me. "It could be spent as gambling, someone who doesn't have money buying rounds of drinks at the taverns, anyone spending money they shouldn't otherwise have." I shrugged my shoulders. "If you looked into the orphanage and the fact that it has a newly hired tutor, you might have found me a lot sooner. We need to find the thieves, and if there are consistent robberies but nothing to show for it, there is something bigger at play."

Chefren let out a low whistle. He rubbed his hand through his beard, twisting it at the end. "She's not wrong, Riel. Maybe we've been missing something. I'll send some men to watch for any unusual activity in the city."

"Go to the City Center of Aurum," I advised. "The poorer regions are too wrought with destitution. It's depressing, and the chances that a beggar would try to take advantage of someone with money are too high. Anywhere in the West or North Districts is too wealthy. It would raise suspicion."

Chefren nodded, his eyes twinkling in consideration. I didn't particularly care about the way he looked at me. Like he knew something I didn't. But I supposed I wasn't exactly a welcome addition to their little crew.

I sat back and contemplated. I knew that the best source of information on the items would be the Black Market. Since the thefts were happening close together, it seemed unlikely they were taking the relics outside of Aurum. That would require transport either by ship or over the dunes by foot or horse.

Dragons could be another way of transport, but dragons were rare, and even rarer was a dragon that willingly worked with a companion. But the Black Market was full of my allies. I couldn't risk mentioning it now, especially if I expected to resume to normal life. Eventually.

"It's a good start," Riel clasped his hands in front of him. "Chefren, start monitoring the City Center. Masika, see if you can find anything about where the relics may be now. If Leoni is correct, the thieves could still be in the city." I chewed the inside of my mouth.

"Chefren, did you bring the bracelet?" Riel asked.

Chefren nodded and pulled a solid gold bangle and key out of a bag strapped to his side and handed it to Riel.

"Give me your hand, Leoni." I hesitated, then slowly raised my arm towards him. "If we will be working together, I can't have you in those bulky cuffs all the time. This bracelet will negate your magic. If you even try to pry it off," I grimaced at him, and his grip around my arm tightened; it was almost painful, "I will cut both of your hands off and throw them into the sea." I glared at Riel with such conviction that I hoped he would turn to stone.

He placed the bracelet on my wrist and removed the shackles. I rubbed the skin that had become irritated from the cuffs, rotating them to increase circulation.

"Will I be able to heal?" I look at Riel through hooded eyes. My energy was fading, and I guessed that the bracelet had something to do with it. Either that or the successively long days I had endured. Maybe both.

It was Chefren who answered, an amused look on his face. "Your healing and agility will remain, but your magic is no longer accessible. You'll need to get used to living as a human does—magic-less."

I didn't even have the energy to summon a retort. Living as a human was exhausting. Fuck this Aurum technology.

Riel and Chefren escorted me back to my room. The room was pleasant, but the walls felt like cell bars when I moved inside and Chefren placed himself outside my door. He stood tall and rigid, and I knew he would be there until Riel told him otherwise. The door shut with a click once I was inside, and I trudged toward the bed and sank into the soft mattress with a sigh.

Wariness settled into my bones. The day had barely begun, but I was too tired to care. Sunlight was bright through my window, but my body paid no mind. I didn't even have the chance to fully process everything that had happened before I succumbed to the call of sleep.

Chapter 7

Moonlight filtered through the window in the bedroom. I finally felt well-rested, and I thanked the gods that Riel hadn't bothered me while I slept the day away. I looked at the new bracelet on my left wrist. It was a solid gold band with a small, intricate clasp. Designs were etched on the band with weaving letters and symbols.

It looked like a complicated lock that only Riel had the key to, and I doubted any pick would be able to unlock it. Other than the fact that it took away my powers, it was actually very pretty. The golden glint on it complimented my terra-cotta skin nicely, and it was a large improvement from the metal shackles I had on before. I always did like the way gold looked on me. I preferred it to silver because whenever I saw gold, I was reminded of my home. But looking at the bracelet now, it just reminded me of a job that I didn't complete, and a home that I didn't know when I would get back to.

I rolled over, tugging the soft blankets over me, cocooning myself in their warmth. As much as I hated being captured and caught, I had to admit that at least I was sleeping in a nice bed.

My mind drifted back to Seraph, and I twisted the covers in my fists until they were tight enough to start cutting off circulation. He didn't deserve to die, even if he was addicted to whatever substance was going around now. My heart squeezed, and I shed a tear as my thoughts reeled with the what-ifs.

What if those drugs became a bigger problem? What if someone at the orphanage got a hold of them? Why was it always us who was targeted first?

I bit my lip. Would Riel know anything about the drugs? Even if he did, would he care? I shook my head. There would be no way that he would. Aurum cared more about finding thieves than making sure their poorest citizens were healthy. There had been four deaths in the South District. In the last week. There shouldn't have even been one. I pinched my eyes closed, trying to banish the thoughts away. I couldn't worry about that right now. It was time to buckle down and earn my freedom back.

Slowly, I peeled back the covers and rubbed the sleep out of my eyes. It was still dark, and I couldn't tell how far into the night it was. I crept through my bedroom, reaching for a small candle on a side table.

Footsteps shuffling past my door made me freeze. Hushed voices filtered through the door and I crept closer, trying to hear what they said.

"She still sleeping?"

"There's been no change."

"That's good." I heard Masika let out a sigh. "Are you really going to stand out here all night? I'm sure Riel would give you a break if you just asked."

"You know I can't. He will let me go in the morning."

"I know," Masika sounded tired, and she lowered her voice into a whisper. "I was just hoping we could go out together tonight."

Chefren chuckled. "I wish that too. If neither of us works tomorrow, let's go then."

"Do you think this is going to work?" she asked. "I trust Riel, but bringing in a criminal into his own home? I wonder if he's lost his mind."

"Riel knows what he's doing." Chefren's voice was stern. "I would keep your opinions on the matter outside of this house."

Masika sighed. "You're right. I better get home anyway."

I listened closely for her footsteps, but I heard them get closer instead of farther away. My ear was pressed to the door, hard enough that I could feel the wood biting into my skin. Clothes ruffled on the other side, and then I heard Masika walk away.

A loud thump hit the door, and I fell backwards. My ears rang from the loud noise.

"Go back to sleep, prisoner!" Chefren called.

I scrambled back to the bed. How the hell did he know I was awake? I let out an audible *hmph* and Chefren chuckled under his breath.

"You're not the only one with magic, so I would be more careful if I were you. Next time you decide to snoop, it might not be me out here. And if Riel catches you, he would be a lot less forgiving."

I crawled back into the covers with a scowl. He was right, but I would sooner cut my arms off before I let my curiosity go.

MY SLEEP PATTERN WAS officially ruined when my door was hit twice. I groaned as Riel swung the door open. I was sweaty and chilled from waking up from nightmares. Whatever fatigue I had was gone; in its stead were constant visions of Seraph's death.

"No such thing as privacy, I guess," I muttered. He gave me one of his best glares.

"Criminals don't get privacy. This room is more than you deserve."

I rubbed the sleep out of my eyes. "Noted."

I blinked up at him, realizing that he was wearing casual clothes. Black pants and a deep green tunic, complementing his dark skin and topaz eyes. He paced the room, examining the desk with the scattered notes he had given me. I couldn't help the heat rising to my cheeks as he stared at the desk, no doubt judging me for my disorganization. He turned to me, his back rigid with his hands clasped behind him.

"While you are still a prisoner, you are working with us, so I expect you to do your due diligence."

Chefren strolled in, carrying a handful of folded laundry. He put them on the desk by the wall. "Your clothes. Washed and ready." He gave me a wink and walked back out.

Riel glanced at me over his shoulder. A strand of dark hair fell over his eye. "Get changed and Chefren will escort you to my office."

I reached for my clothes, pulling them into my arms. Riel walked out and shut the door behind him.

I sighed and stepped into the fully equipped the bathroom adjacent to my room. Warm water poured through my fingers as I turned on the taps to the bathtub. I grimaced. Bathing in the elements was normal for me. I couldn't say I wasn't grateful for the change, but I was also starkly aware of how differently the people of Aurum lived in the South District. I had to spend a lot of money on baths like this, and even they had little privacy. Meanwhile, Riel's unused room had warm water access. What a waste.

I sat in the warm water, letting my muscles relax as well as I could. I should have been enjoying this bath. Gods knew I should have been in that cell full of rot. But I couldn't relax. I got out of the tub, the water sloshing and dripping onto the floor. My fingers sifted through my wet hair and I scanned the vanity for any kind of oil. Of course, there was none. My hair would be a frizzy poof without it, so I resorted to binding my hair in a braid.

Looking in the mirror, I saw the last few days etched on my face. Darkness lined my eyes, and it was like Seraph's death was visible. I smoothed out the crease between my eyebrows, like I had been pinching them through the night. My skin had darkened through the summer, giving me a dark, sun-kissed hue, but it looked pallid in the reflection.

I pulled on my clothes. My clothes were always worn and flexible, but now they were clean and I finally started feeling a little more like myself, even though I didn't have access to my magic. Not having magic left my soul empty. Every time I tried to dig for it, there was nothing. A magic-less void. Despite focusing and deep breathing, I felt nothing. Like a piece of myself had just vanished, my body felt like an empty shell with nothing to hold inside.

My hand paused over the doorknob to the bedroom. Despite my unwillingness, I worked for the government of Aurum now and it made my stomach flutter. I closed my eyes and took a deep breath. Chefren was right outside, waiting for me.

"Ready to go, prisoner?" His smile was friendly despite his taunt.

"I have a name. Feel free to use it," I muttered. He started walking down the stairs and I followed.

He laughed. "Of course, Leoni. Guard habits die hard. How did you sleep?"

I narrowed my eyes at him. "Fitfully," I answered honestly. He knew I had been spying on him. Lying was pointless.

"I'm sure this is an adjustment," he said while glancing back at me.

"You could say that."

I fidgeted with my bracelet as I followed him through the house. The sun was shining through the open windows. It illuminated all the beautiful textiles that made the house feel comfortable and welcoming. I breathed in the fresh air that moved through the house. I willed the tension out of my back as I followed, but my stomach flipped as we got closer to the office.

"If you need anything at all, just ask."

I stopped in my tracks.

"Why?" I placed my hands on my hips. Chefren had no reason to give me anything. I definitely hadn't forgotten my place in this situation.

Chefren sighed and ran his hand through his beard. His emerald eyes were soft as he regarded me. I scrutinized him for any kind of animosity, but I found none there.

"Working together would be better on good terms, yes? Riel and Masika, they are both ruthless and won't be kind. But I think we'll both find it a much more pleasant experience if we can be cordial." Chefren resumed his path, and I continued to follow. His words were polite, but they set me on edge. No one was kind for the sake of it, especially toward someone like me.

"I'll let you know if I require anything." There was no chance of that. I would rather my hair be a giant nest for birds to lay their eggs in before I asked for anything from the people who kept me away from my true duty.

RIEL KEPT HIS OFFICE as clean as the day before, but he had piled books and parchment on his desk. I sat in the same chair from yesterday and looked at the book spines.

The History of Ambrose

Gods, Magi, Mortals

Living in the Dragon Age

I sucked in a breath as I noticed titles describing our country's history stacked amongst larger, unlabeled books. What is the historical value of this room? I ached to reach for a book, eager to read more about the dragons and their origins. The history I knew was just through spoken tales, but these were reliable recounts. My fingers itched with the desire to dive in and learn more. I reached for the book that sat on the top of the pile. It was heavy and thick, bound together with leather.

The pages were thin and blocks of text swam in front of my eyes. All of my eagerness evaporated. The texts were dense, and I was a slow reader as it was. Chefren stood by the door, keeping watch as I took it all in.

I was thumbing through pages when Riel strode in. His broad frame took up space as he made his way around his desk. Masika followed him, her back straight and shoulders back.

The presence of all three made me more vigilant, recalling how they were able to arrest me easily. Despite Chefren's attempts to be amicable, the room remained tense. Riel handed us each a piece of parchment with a long list of seemingly random items.

"All missing artifacts from Aurum are listed. We need to determine the relationship between them. Right now, we don't have a way to link them by the thefts alone." He slapped his hand on the pile of books. "Analyze these artifacts for any clues about the thieves' motivations."

I swallowed thickly. Between the long list and the giant pile of text, I wasn't sure how I could even get started on this task. This was so entirely outside of my realm that I might as well have been in the mortal lands. In fact, Riel should have just shipped me there. I would certainly have more in common in a world without magic than I would with these books.

Masika nodded, taking the order in stride, and I marveled at her confidence in the face of something so daunting. Riel must have seen the trepidation on my face, because he turned to me, his lips lifting ever so slightly.

"Masika will be here during the day to aid you in the research. It's important that you are thorough. The sooner we find the thieves, the better," he said.

I held the book in my hands a bit tighter and gritted my teeth. There was so much to go through, and I was quickly losing confidence that I would ever gain my freedom back. I should be out in the streets, listening for whispers, not reading thick books for a piece of a puzzle that may not even exist. A calming sensation swept over me, and I steeled myself in resolve.

"If this is what it takes, then I'll do my best," I said. Riel tipped his head to me.

"Good." He gave Masika a knowing glance. "Take her to the living room and get started. Chefren, you're dismissed. I'll need you on night duties for the foreseeable future."

I glanced at Chefren, whose amiable smile was completely gone, and his jaw feathered at the order. Masika pressed her lips into a firm line. I felt a pang of guilt. They clearly wanted to spend time together, but had to work opposite hours because of me. I quickly disregarded that feeling. Why should I feel guilty if some General's righthand people didn't get to spend time together? This was temporary, after all.

"I need to go to the Spires and implement new security protocols. Leoni, if you put one toe out of line, the deal is off. I can arrange your execution in no time flat." He narrowed his eyes at me, his strong jawline set, and as much as I hated his constant reminder that I was straddling life and death, the fire in his eyes set something alight within me.

"You won't be disappointed," I ground out, meeting his harsh tones in kind.

MASIKA AND I SAT in the living room with books and papers surrounding us. My head swam in confusion with where to start, and I watched Masika as she picked up her list of stolen relics. I mimicked her and read through mine as well. The list had each name of the artifact, followed by the estimated year it was created.

"How do they know when these were made?" I asked. Masika sighed, narrowing her eyes at me.

Her tone was clipped as she answered, "Aurum uses technology paired with magic to decipher when ancient relics were made."

She said no more on the subject, and I sat squirming in the uncomfortable silence. I pulled one book into my lap, blowing out a breath. I flipped it open to a random page, and a sigh of relief left me as I realized that each entry had a date on them. It wasn't exactly what I needed, but it was a step in the right direction.

I peered down at my list, noting the date on the first artifact and thumbing through to find the corresponding date in the book. Blank parchments were on the table, and I quickly started jotting down notes. I included the general history of what was happening during that time and continued looking for any links that it could have to the artifact.

Pages started blurring together as I fell into a smooth groove. My movements were near mechanical as I copied relevant information onto parchment. My eyes blurred as I barely registered anything I was reading. I would pour through the details later.

I didn't even notice that the sun had started to set until Chefren cleared his throat. He stood, leaning on the doorway, his mouth tugged into a soft smile as his green eyes shifted to Masika.

"I hate to break up the riveting party, but Riel said your shift is over."

Masika sighed and collected her notes together. She held out her hand to me. "Give me your notes. I'll go through them tonight and make copies." I handed them over wordlessly. She took them and placed them on top of her own.

Chefren slid his hands in the pockets of his dark uniform.

"Let's share a dinner before you head home for the evening. All of that research must have worked up an appetite. Leoni, you'll be joining us, of course." He grinned, and that was the moment my stomach decided to make everyone aware of how hungry I was. I glanced at the small platter of fruit we had been snacking on through the day, but it wasn't nearly enough to satiate me.

My legs were stiff from sitting all day, and I groaned as I stretched them out. I didn't know how scholars managed. Being sedentary wasn't in my blood. The urge to expel some energy itched under my skin, and I sighed. I needed to find these thieves so I could run around the city in the dark again.

We made our way to the kitchen, where the large table already had dinner on it. Steaming rice and curried meat made my stomach growl even louder, and Chefren laughed while Masika shot me a glare.

"Did you find anything interesting?" Chefren asked as he tucked in to his meal.

"Nothing of importance so far, just hours of mind-numbing history." Masika went into the kitchen and emerged with a bottle of wine. She poured two glasses and slid one to Chefren. He shook his head.

"Not tonight, I'm working." He shot me a wink and slid the glass over to me. Masika tutted, but Chefren only laughed. "What? She's not going anywhere."

"You're too lenient with your prisoner."

Chefren leaned back in his chair as I gently sipped the wine.

"Prisoner or not, we are a team now. Maybe we should start acting like one."

Masika pursed her lips. But she didn't refute him, and she didn't take the wine away from me.

"Enjoy that for now." She gave me a vicious smile. "But don't think this current lapse in my judgment means that I trust you at all."

Her sharp cheekbones only enhanced the piercing threat that lay underneath her amber eyes. I swallowed down the wine in my mouth and put the glass down slowly.

"What happened to you to make you so cold, Masika?" I was prodding the beast within her, but I didn't care. All day her tone had been short with me, I was constantly treading lightly to keep her from retaliating against my questions; and I was done with it. I hadn't done anything to her specifically. Honestly, she should have probably thanked the gods she got me as a prisoner.

If Devland were in my place, it would have been a much more dreadful experience. Besides, she couldn't do anything without Riel's permission—at least that was what I hoped.

Masika's eyes widened and she snarled at me, but before she could rip into me, Riel strode in and placed himself in the chair next to mine. He glanced between us and narrowed his eyes at me.

"I don't know what I just walked into, but drop it, Masika." His eyes cut into mine. "What did I tell you this morning?"

Shards of ice sank into my gut, as I realized I should have just kept my mouth shut.

"Apologies," I relented, not wanting to cause more problems for myself. It wasn't in me to back down from a verbal fight, but in this moment I knew it would be more hassle to argue.

"Good." Riel grabbed food for himself and let out a little grunt of satisfaction as he ate. I allowed myself to smirk. It didn't matter where anyone came from. Good food was always something people could appreciate together.

"How were the security briefs, sir?" Chefren asked around a mouthful of rice. Riel sighed and scratched his chin.

"New security protocols will be in place tomorrow, but Lord Eduard is insistent that it's unneeded. He thinks we are spending our time and money unwisely, but the council insists that we look into these thefts."

"Where would he rather spend it?" I asked. Curious that the Lord didn't care about precious Aurum history disappearing from sight.

"Research and development," Riel answered, surprising easily.

Masika scoffed, and Chefren just averted his eyes.

"What does that mean?" I asked.

"It means that he would rather use government funds to make his life easier than keep criminals off the streets." Masika spoke through clenched teeth.

I took a bite of my food and chewed slowly, but I tasted nothing. I was glad for the food in front of me, because if I had opened my mouth, I would no doubt start spewing vitriol about the government and their corrupt ways when people were actively dying in the South District.

"Well, it's too late for the Lord to make his demands now," Chefren cut in. He nodded toward me. "We are already investigating the robberies, and we should have some new information soon."

I grimaced; that meant more time flipping pages for me.

Chefren cleared his throat. "I actually have some good news on that front as well." Riel leaned forward, eager to hear what Chefren had to say. "I had some of our men patrolling to be on the lookout for any new spenders, and we got a hit. Some strangers gambling every few days or so. No one there seems to recognize them. I have been tracking them, but we need to investigate before we can interrogate."

Masika's scowl softened into intrigue, and Riel's lips curled up into a damned almost smile. I had never seen anything other than hardness in his face before, and I found myself wanting to see more. I wanted to crack him open and see what a genuine smile would look like. The idea captivated me, and I wasn't sure why.

"Report to me the next time the guards see him." Riel commanded, and Chefren nodded. Riel turned to me. "How do you feel about a brief field trip?" His gaze bore into mine, and I gave him an honest to gods smile. Leaving the General's Quarters was far too appealing for me to argue.

"I'll be ready whenever you are." They wouldn't be able to keep me in this house if they tried.

Chapter 8

THE NEXT THREE DAYS were the same routine. Riel would come in and offer me his best threats, and I would take them in stride. I had to admit, his threats became less severe, and it felt like teasing. Sometimes. Then I would read until my eyes felt like they would bleed.

Masika wasn't unkind to me while we researched, but she mostly ignored me like I wasn't there at all. Riel was in and out due to his duties at the Spires. He was most likely trying to find another low-stakes criminal to ruin before holding himself accountable for Aurum's problems.

Chefren would return with no news, leaving me to spend more restless nights in my room plagued by nightmares. As far as prison sentences went, I was positive this was ideal, but I wasn't content. Each day brought the possibility of a death in the South District, and I felt helpless to prevent it from being someone I knew.

I sat in the main living space on one of the dark blue cushions with a large book in my hand and a pile of other books next to me. The list of stolen items was long and tedious, with no apparent connections except their value. Masika sat across from me, her own nose in a book, jotting down notes on a piece of parchment.

The main door clicked opened and shut. I perked up and gave Masika a questioning look, to which she shrugged. She placed the book on the table between us and stood rigidly with her hands behind her back. She looked fierce when she was expecting to be around Riel. Well, she looked fierce all the time, but when it was just us, she was quieter and more relaxed. But now, there was nothing but oppressive formality.

Riel stepped into the living room followed by a tall golden-haired man who had such an aura of entitlement I could practically taste it. His hazel eyes met mine, and he sneered in my direction.

This was Lord Eduard Magnus. Aurum's latest Lord, elected by the people in Aurum who were blinded by his dazzling smile and charisma.

He held none of the friendliness that he often donned in front of large crowds, instead making his disdain for me well-known to this small group in Riel's living room.

"So this is the thief that attempted to rob me blind." His scowl deepened as he regarded me. Each line in his face showed his true nature, and I gave him a glare back.

"Sir," Riel cut in. His face was a mask of emotion. "This is Leoni. She has been evading our grasp for years, and we believe that with her help, we can find the missing relics along with whoever is stealing them."

Eduard's gaze lingered on me, piercing me with a cold prickling sensation before he turned to Riel.

"You had better be right. If she's as useless here as she is in the South District, I want her head on a spike by the end of the moon cycle."

Riel's eyes flicked over to me and his lips dipped into a frown for a fraction of a second before he nodded.

"Yes, sir."

He turned to Masika, who was still standing straight as an arrow, her gaze pinned on the wall behind Lord Eduard and Riel.

"What have you been able to find regarding the stolen artifacts?" the Lord demanded.

"Nothing yet, sir." Masika's voice was rigid and emotionless. "We are still parsing through the items and their related histories."

The Lord scoffed and turned his back on us. He walked with an authoritative stride.

"I had better have more information the next time I arrive. There is no room for error. The council is breathing down my back on this issue. They want their items back. We have already spent too much time and money."

"Yes, sir." Both Riel and Masika answered simultaneously. We watched as the Lord left and the click of the front door signaled his leave. Masika let out a sigh of relief, her posture relaxing. A flood of calming energy filled the room as though the Lord had taken his superiority with him.

Riel sank into the cushions and threw his head back. He looked exhausted.

"Do I need to be worried about my future?" I asked in a whisper, knowing that the Lord's threat wasn't idle.

Riel looked at me from the sides of his eyes, too worn from whatever day he had to give me his full attention. He sighed and collected himself before sitting up and placing his elbows on his knees.

"If we can't figure this out, we all need to worry about our future." The silence after was deafening.

"Riel!" Chefren's voice called from the front entrance as he let himself inside. He stormed into the living room, shattering our somber ambiance. "We are observing the men in the City Center. I have someone trailing them, but we need to leave soon." A bright grin lit his face, and I didn't resist the smile that pushed across mine.

"Excellent," Riel said as he shot up, reinvigorated with the good news. "Go get ready, Leoni. Change out of the uniform and wear your own clothes."

I jumped up from my seat, a heavy book thudding from my lap. I mumbled a quick apology and picked it up before bounding to the stairs. Chefren was on my tail and laughed at my excitement.

"Eager to get out of here?" he asked.

"More than you even know." I couldn't help but grin back at him.

I ran into the room, snapping the door shut behind me. I stripped off the uniform I was wearing and filled the tub with water. A small bottle of oil sat next to the soap, and I grabbed it greedily. I unstoppered it and dropped a few drops in my palm while grinning.

The smell was incredible, and the oil was clearly of high quality. My hair would have never looked so good after I finished using it. Riel must have noticed my fly away strands and wanted me to look more tolerable. I checked my cleanliness, fixed my curls, and got dressed. Chefren was waiting for me at the door with a smile.

"Your hair looks good tonight," Chefren said, and I shot him a quizzical look. I thought Riel had given it to me, but instead it was Chefren?

"Did you get me the hair oil? What for?" I toyed with the ends of my hair, now sleek and maintained. Had they really looked that awful that a stranger would sneak hair oil into my bathroom? I frowned. I hadn't given much thought to my appearance in these quarters, but I supposed I had looked downright haggard.

Chefren chuckled and shrugged. "Let's just say it's a token of good faith, since we're working together now."

I chewed on the inside of my cheek as I followed him. Gifts were for people who cared about each other or were bribery. If it was a bribery, then what did he want? If it really was a token of good faith, well, I had to admit that I was starting to like the guy.

I opened my mouth to ask when Riel and Masika met us at the bottom of the stairs. Riel ushered us out into the street, his body rigid with urgency, while Masika moved up to walk by Chefren's side.

WE MADE OUR WAY to the City Center in silence. Chefren and Masika had taken an alternate route, not wanting to draw too much attention to our little group. Riel decided that he would be my escort tonight, and while I was expecting the walk to be filled with threats of my potential demise, he had kept his thoughts to himself.

I wondered if the Lord coming in to threaten all our positions had subdued him, and I wasn't sure how I felt about that. I expected the little ruthless quips from Riel. They were certainly better than this awkward silence. I toyed with the golden bracelet around my wrist, watching how it glinted in the moonlight.

I sighed in the night air, breathing in the crisp breeze that scattered sands along the cobblestone road. Though my magic was gone, I felt more like myself than I had in days. I reveled in this small slice of freedom. Chatter filled the streets, and a new hope bloomed in my chest. Tonight we would find these thieves, and I would be free.

The City Center was Aurum's soul and spirit. The place was always bustling with people from different backgrounds. Even in the dead of night, the streets were lined with the wealthy and the poor, both looking for escapism.

Brothels and taverns were open to anyone and everyone. It was where most exchanges in trades, goods, and services happened. The Black Market lived in the City Center, if you knew where to look. I pulled my hood over my head a little further as we neared, covering my copper hair.

"Riel," I mumbled. I gently placed a hand on his arm. He turned abruptly, with a vicious gleam in his eye, and veered his arm away from my touch. I ignored him. "Some people might recognize me. It might be best if we keep our distance."

He scowled, and for a second, I thought I heard a growl emit from his mouth. "You will not leave my sight."

I shrugged. "Just thought you might want to know if somebody...interesting comes up to me. At least try not to mention that you are Aurum's Executioner."

"I know how to be discrete, Leoni." His voice was low and harsh. I didn't really care to be seen in public and certainly not with Riel. I didn't voice my trepidation though, since Riel's mood was already foul.

"Fine," I retorted, "just...try to keep a low profile."

He snorted, and I glared at him from under my hood. We strode through the city, torchlight and music spilling into the street. Riel kept by my side, and surprisingly he kept a mask of casualness as we sifted through the night crowds.

He was a natural at keeping his eyes peeled and sidestepping around the stumbling groups of Aurum's citizens enjoying a night out. There was always illegal activity happening in the City Center—bar fights, drug deals, a handful of wanted criminals.

It didn't seem like Riel cared much about that tonight, and I wondered how much he cared about that at all. Was he a pawn for the Lord? Only doing his bidding? I shuddered. The Lord was clearly out for himself and didn't care as much for his citizens as he said he did.

I followed Riel when he turned into a dimly lit tavern where Chefren and Masika were already lounging at a table. They looked at ease, like we weren't currently trying to chase down mysterious criminals.

Chefren laughed loudly at something Masika had said, his voice bellowing over the chatter. Riel pulled two chairs to the table and motioned for me to sit before plopping down himself.

"We are supposed to be working," Riel gritted out, gesturing at the ales in front of his second and third.

Chefren smiled. "We are working." He took his ale and sipped. "We're blending in," he mock-whispered with a mischievous grin on his lips. Masika leaned back. Her relaxing demeanor shocked me more than Chefren's.

She smirked at Riel. "It's just a recon mission. All we need is more information and we leave. Might as well enjoy it." She shrugged.

Riel frowned at his companions and scanned his surroundings. I followed his gaze to a suspiciously placed hall with an equally suspicious man standing in front of it.

Riel leaned into me, his words whispering against the shell of my ear.

"It's an underground gaming den. They aren't legal, but we let them slide as long as there's no trouble."

I scoffed. "So, you conveniently look the other way for illegal gambling, but when I get caught for one robbery, you want to string me up on the streets?"

Riel turned to me, the planes of his face hard and sharp. A slight upturn formed on his lips, but it wasn't a comforting sight.

"You were attempting to steal a timeless artifact that pre-dates Aurum as we know it. That is hardly petty thievery."

I bit my lip, holding back a scowl. Riel's face was close enough to see freckles on his cheeks. I resisted the urge to take notice of them despite not noticing them before. His brown eyes burned into mine, and they dropped to my lips before looking back at me. My heart skipped a beat, and heat rose in my cheeks. I pulled myself away, huffing out an irritated breath, and pointedly looked anywhere else.

His one brief look made my skin hot. What was wrong with me? He was very handsome—in a vicious, assertive kind of way—but he was my prison guard for gods' sake. I needed to keep my guard up, but I couldn't help but spare a second glance. I smirked as I noticed how his throat bobbed, and he cleared his throat as he veered his gaze across the tavern.

I coldly reminded myself that this man wasn't Devland. He was a man of the law, but laws were made by the corrupt. My body might betray me, but I locked my mind with steel. I needed to keep my eyes on the prize: freedom.

I refocused on the gaming den. If the thieves were there, I needed to get inside. Just one step closer to freedom. If only I had my magic...

"Leoni?" Riel's voice jolted my thoughts back to the table.

"I'm sorry. What were you saying?" I asked. Riel gritted his teeth at my aloofness, but Chefren placed his elbows on the table, leaning in.

His smile faltered as he spoke. "There are three young men—mortal by the sounds of them—spending an awful lot of money. No one seems to know who they are."

I let the fact that they were mortal mull in my head. It was interesting, but not surprising. Mortals had no magic but often fell prey to promises of prosperity. Some clung to the Magi for power, money, sex, or other things. They were easy to manipulate, especially if they were desperate.

I let out a long breath. I looked around with exasperation. It could be several people in this tavern. Mortals and Magi intermingled, so seeing a group of them here wouldn't mean they were our thieves, and I refused to accuse the wrong person. I chewed on the bottom of my lip, narrowing my eyes at the gaming den entrance.

As though Riel could track my train of thought, he leaned towards me. "Remember, this is for information only. Do not make a scene." He regarded the other two as well. "We watch and wait until we get solid evidence."

We all nodded at his instruction.

WE DESCENDED STAIRS HIDDEN by a discrete curtain in the tavern. I tugged my hood a little tighter, my knuckles white against the dark fabric. The room was dim and smoky. Tobacco filled the enclosed space, and I refrained from constantly waving the haze away from my face.

"Keep your eyes peeled. If there is anyone that you think seems suspicious, you will tell me immediately," Riel muttered in my ear, his breath caressing my earlobe.

I nodded, but my heart raced with trepidation. People, both mortals and Magi, were crammed into the room. It was too dim for me to make out any faces without being right in front of them. Most people were wearing hoods, and kept their heads bent over the games they played.

I gritted my teeth, frustrated that it would be impossible for me to recognize anyone even if I wanted to.

I could feel Riel glaring at me as I scanned the room. He was surely watching me for the moment I saw anything familiar. His scrutiny bored into the side of my head and didn't waver when I blew out a breath.

"I don't recognize anyone here."

He glanced at Chefren and nodded. I raised an eyebrow in question, but he didn't say a single word. His head swiveled around before spotting an opening at a card game table and making his way toward it.

I followed, sliding between bodies crowding the room. It was unbearably hot under my hood, but I refused to remove it. Just because I didn't see anyone didn't mean that they wouldn't see me.

"Leoni?" A rough hand grabbed my shoulder, and I spun around. My hood slipped off and cool air hit the nape of my neck. I cursed and slipped my hood back up, shoving out of the grip forcefully.

"What are you doing here, Leoni?" a deep and familiar voice asked. I turned, meeting the face of Jyran. An older Magi with hair streaked with silver. Crinkled skin adorned his eyes and lips. I schooled my features.

"Jyran, it's nice to see you." I tried to offer him a warm smile, but I was sure it looked like a grimace instead. Jyran was a merchant who lived on the south side. He sold an array of goods, from fine cloth to trinkets. He was well-known and well-liked in the South District.

His normally kind brown eyes were now pegged on me with apprehension and concern. His face was wan, and he had dark circles lining his eyes. He was thinner than the last time I saw him. Concern weighed on my chest. It looked like he needed help, but my current disposition didn't give me the ability to do anything.

"Why are you here?" he repeated.

"Just visiting some friends," I replied and gestured to Riel, who was merely pretending to be focused on the game in front of him. I caught him peering out of the side of his eye with a frown. He shifted in his seat to keep a better watch on me.

"You're not in any trouble, are you?"

I laughed, a little too boisterously.

"Of course not." I quickly sucked in a breath. The irony wasn't lost on me. "Just having a fun night out." I tapped my chin in mock curiosity. "What about you, Jyran? Is there a reason you're out here and not at home with your wife?"

His face became red. "I—she's fine." I clicked my tongue. Jyran was in trouble. This old man would never have otherwise ventured into this sleazy gaming den.

"Did you need more medicine? Is that why you're here?"

"N-no." He ran his hands through his unkempt hair. "Well, yes. What you gave us will last until the end of the moon cycle, but she will need more. I didn't want to ask you again, so I thought I might—"

My shoulders curved in, and a chewed my lip. I laid a soft hand on his shoulder. Out of the corner of my eye, I saw Riel tense.

"I'm sorry. I don't have a way to help you right now."

He nodded, and I saw the tears welling in his eyes. I could tell that when he saw me, it raised his hopes. All for those to come crashing back down.

He wouldn't have to gamble his livelihood if I could get what he needed. And I currently couldn't give him anything. All the more reason to find these damned thieves and be free.

Riel stood up from the table. "It's time to go."

I spared a glance at Masika and Chefren, who each nodded at each other and Riel in their wordless communication. Jyran gave me a weary look. Even if Jyran didn't know who Riel truly was, he was an intimidating man, and there wasn't a doubt in my mind that Jyran knew I was in over my head. I stepped forward and gathered Jyran into a tight hug.

"I'm so sorry. If I can help, I will." I leaned closer to his ear. "Tell no one you saw me here tonight. It isn't worth the trouble." I squeezed him tighter and then turned on my heel before following Riel back into the tavern.

"Who was that?" Riel questioned as we walked down the dusty streets of Aurum's technology district. Chefren and Masika had both parted ways, and I trailed next to Riel, breathing in the night air. It was quiet, now that the night grew later.

This is where the tallest spires were located. Some of the smartest people in the world collaborated within those towering buildings. They created items, like my bracelet, that would make life easier for whoever could afford it. I could only imagine the copious amount of technology they contained.

It was quiet in this part of town at the late hour. Riel and I walked alone. We only passed by a handful of people before turning onto a deserted path toward Riel's house.

"He's nobody," I replied as I pursed my lips. A rare wisp of clouds moved through the sky. It shadowed the streets, and I sighed. It was the perfect condition for my magic.

Riel placed his hands in his pockets. I could feel his gaze on me, curious but not demanding for more information. Fatigue weighed my feet down, and whether it was because of Jyran or the calming cool breeze, I sighed.

"Jyran is a man I helped a few moons ago. His wife is ill and needs constant medical intervention. I've given them what I could, but it appears their luck has run out."

It was serene, with no sound but the gravel under our feet. It was on silent nights like these, with no noise to block out my thoughts, that my purpose weighed on me the heaviest. I had assumed the role of caretaker in unconventional ways, which left me independent and often alone. Not that it ever bothered me, to be alone. I liked the solitude.

I had to admit, though; I liked the quiet company of Riel. He had dropped his typical rigor as we continued through the city. I wondered if he was more pleasant behind closed doors, and of all the masks he wore, why he chose one of closed off brutality.

But why did anyone choose to present themselves the way they did? I was alone because I needed to be. Others needed me to be. I wondered if I hadn't become a thief at such a young age, would I have been able to provide for others differently? A way that didn't involve me getting arrested and taken prisoner in Aurum? I shook off my questions of what-ifs with a shiver down my spine. It was far too late for that.

"I will help them." Riel said it so quietly I thought I misheard him. I stopped in my tracks and stood with my jaw dropped.

"Riel, you don't have to do that." I didn't know why Riel was suddenly feeling charitable, and the last thing I needed was to be indebted to Aurum's fiercest law keeper. He shrugged. The moonlight reflected on the curls of his dark hair. He turned and waited for me to catch up, shifting his hands in his pockets.

"If you were still out there"—he meant if I was still free—"would you get the medicine for her?"

"In an instant." My response came out in a whisper. My heart beat unevenly as I looked at him, his sharp features looking softer in the moonlight, and it felt like he was staring right into my soul. Riel's brown eyes flicked over my face, filled with understanding. I could feel the walls around my heart cracking. For the first time, it felt like Riel saw me as something other than a criminal.

"Then I believe it's my fault that family won't get their medicine, so I will give it to them in your stead," he said matter-of-factly. I blinked, not believing the words that came out of his mouth. I wanted to pinch myself to make sure I wasn't dreaming.

"Riel," his name barely was audible in my breathiness, "that is extremely generous." I lifted my eyebrow at him. "What do you want in return?"

Riel looked at me with a tender expression, as if he understood. I could see his hard exterior fade away as he looked at me, and my breath got stuck in my throat. I desired to know him wholly, aching for him to reveal himself to me.

"Contrary to what you may believe, I care about the citizens of Aurum." He slid me a wry smile.

"What makes you think I believe you don't care?" I asked, and his jaw feathered. I could tell he was trying his hardest not to put his walls back up.

"You make it known every time you lay eyes on me. Not to mention you called me a 'pig-headed, pretentious piece of shit' when I threatened your orphanage." He eyed me like he was looking for confirmation, and I chewed on the inside of my cheek, fighting off a smile. I certainly hadn't tried to hide my hatred for the General or his personnel.

"I don't think I finished that full insult, but I think it would have ended more eloquently than 'shit'." I shrugged and held back a laugh.

Riel's cheeks darkened for a moment and I thought I saw a smile play on his lips, but he looked away, raking his hair between his fingers.

"In all seriousness, I did some digging into your past. I haven't been to the South District in a long time, but I had to inquire about you," he told me with a glint in his eye.

My breath got stuck in my throat. Who did he talk to? Did he threaten Tala?

"I hope you didn't scare them," I said in a flat voice. If he hurt my family, I would happily die for the murder of the General.

Riel threw me a malicious grin, but his eyes were playful, and he laughed. A genuine laugh that sparked something in my chest. It was musical and if I closed my eyes, I could practically see the stars dancing at the pure sound of it. I brushed off the lightness in my chest and I narrowed my gaze at him.

"Of course I didn't scare them, Leoni." He placed his hand on my shoulder, and then, as if he realized what he was doing, removed it, and quickly stuck it in his pocket.

"No, I was just checking your background. I..." his voice trailed off, and he cleared his throat. "Your efforts for those people surprised me. They were all loyal to you; they didn't reveal anything. That kind of loyalty can't be bought."

"What if I did buy that loyalty?" I hedged. Devland had taught me that fear was a great motivator for loyalty. Fear and power. Did he think I wasn't capable of instilling fear in the people of the South District?

Riel shook his head. "No. People with no consequences will easily sell information, and unless you have overpowered every Magi in the district, then they truly are loyal to you."

I scoffed. "Are you saying I couldn't?" I was a little offended that he didn't think I was strong enough to do so.

Riel scowled. "That's not what I meant."

I threw him a grin. "I know." He shook his head.

"I must admit you have done great work with the orphanage," he said reluctantly.

My cheeks heated. The orphanage was still a dilapidated building and needed countless improvements. I was embarrassed by the state it was in now. I had many plans to improve it, and the orphanage in my mind was the one I wanted him to visit. To show him I was capable, to show that I was useful, and more than a petty thief.

"From what I saw, the children are well-behaved and eager to learn. Maybe the South District has hope after all?" Riel smiled, but my blood ran cold. There was no hope for the South District, not when death lied on its doorstep. Seraph's still body flashed in my mind, and Lucien's words echoed in my ears. *That was the fourth death this week.*

Hope was a pipe dream for those of us in the South District. I learned a long time ago that nothing was ever given freely, and we had to fight until we bled for the things we wanted—for the things we needed. And the drug problem was another hurdle to add to the long list of problems that I needed to fix.

"Leoni?" Riel's voice jerked me out of picturing Seraph lying on that kitchen table, and I sucked in a breath that didn't quite meet the bottom of my lungs.

My fingertips tingled and my head buzzed, and it had nothing to do with my magic, because I didn't have any. I had no magic, no way to help the people I loved. My breaths were shallow, and an incessant ringing in my ears was buzzing louder and louder.

I needed to find my way out of Riel's grasp, and quickly. But I kept going over all the small details that didn't add up yet. We were too far from figuring out who our thieves were, and tonight had been no use. I placed my hand over my quickening heart.

If we didn't find these thieves, not only would I not be free, but I would be dead, and then what? The reality of my situation settled into my stomach like a boulder. Forget about the thieves. The drugs were killing my people, and how much longer would the South District survive without me?

Riel was kneeled on the ground front of me, his hands clasping my shoulders tightly.

"Take a deep breath, Leoni." I shuddered in a breath, but it wasn't deep enough. My chest tightened, and I couldn't get enough air. I tried blinking back tears that I desperately didn't want to fall, but it was no use. I sucked in more air, to the best of my ability, but my lungs were too small. My city, my people, they had nothing, but they had me. And they were loyal to me. What would happen if I were to die? What if I couldn't provide for them anymore?

"Leoni, look at me," Riel demanded. I found his eyes, not realizing I hadn't been paying much attention to him at all. His rich brown eyes, with infinite depths of color, were flecked with yellows and golds. His grip tightened, not enough to hurt, but just enough to ground me. I blew out another shaky breath, and Riel coaxed me through a few more breaths before the buzzing in my ears quieted, and my hands warmed.

"I'm sorry," I muttered while wiping the tears off my face with my sleeve. Riel's brows pinched in what looked like worry. That wasn't right, though. He wouldn't worry about me.

"Where did you go?" he asked with a gentle prod.

I shook my hands, trying to get the last numbness out of my fingers. Riel watched me with intensity, and I squirmed under his gaze.

"It doesn't matter," I mumbled.

"Leoni." Command filled his voice, but there was no hostility. "Tell me what you were thinking about. I had just complimented you—"

"My friend died!" I shouted even though I didn't mean to, but my emotions were haywire. I couldn't hold it in anymore. "He died in the streets, and there was nothing I could do about it!" Riel's face contorted into confusion, and I shoved myself out of his grasp, turning away so he wouldn't see more tears fall.

I hadn't cried over Seraph, never getting a chance to mourn him, and I cursed my body for making me cry over him now. My tears dried as I wiped my cheeks once again, and I steeled my resolve.

"Let's go." I demanded and walked past Riel toward the General's Quarters.

Riel watchful eyes bored into me as I strutted to the house entrance, but he stayed silent. I could only guess that he was making wild assumptions about me. My boots stomped up the stairs, and I paid him no mind as I walked into my room, snapping the door shut.

A ball of unwanted energy sat heavy in my chest, and I couldn't let it out. I had the sudden urge to scream. Instead, I sucked it back in and took a deep breath until the feeling in my chest subsided. I sank onto the bed and wrapped myself in the blankets, where I finally allowed my tears to fall.

Chapter 9

RIEL'S CLAIM TO HELP Jyran was still gnawing against my mind the next morning. His offer seemed genuine, but I couldn't help but ask what he wanted in return. When Riel had gently knocked on my door and requested I meet him for breakfast, I jolted out of bed. I had fallen asleep at some point, and my face was puffy and sticky from crying.

I barely paid attention while I dressed, thinking about the fact that I had made a complete fool of myself in front of Riel. I didn't like to cry, especially in front of others. The last thing I wanted was for Riel to think of me as weak. I didn't care what he thought of me on a personal level—whether he hated me or not—but I wanted him to be confident that I could finish this job, and that my emotions weren't going to get in the way.

I was lost in my thoughts as Chefren escorted me into the kitchen, where Riel was eating his breakfast. He wore his black Aurum uniform with his sleeves rolled up to his elbow, and I watched his arm muscles flex as he made notes against a piece of parchment.

I braced myself as I approached on soft feet. He was engrossed in his work, and it allowed me the chance to take in his dignified features. The sun streamed in from the open windows, and it bathed Riel's skin in a golden glow. His hair curled slightly above his brow, which pinched in concentration. Light stubble lined his defined jaw, and Riel in the sun was a sight I wanted to memorize.

I shook my head and blinked my gaze away. I tried to clear the rising heat that pooled in my core, pushing away the flutters I felt in my belly. The way he had looked at me last night, with his face full of worry, came flooding back into my mind. Surely he didn't care for me; he just wanted to get the crazy person he was walking with off the street.

He didn't even look up as I approached the table and helped myself to a cup of tea. I sat next to Riel, inhaling the floral notes of the tea that drifted into my nostrils.

"Good morning, Leoni." Even though he didn't spare me a glance, it was the first time he said my name without disdain dripping off his tongue, and I blinked in surprise.

"I'll have a witch sent over to Jyran's home this afternoon. Please write down where I can find him and his wife." He handed me a small piece of parchment and a quill. I jotted the location and quickly handed it to him. Our fingers brushed, and a spark went through me.

I muttered a quiet thanks, shocked that he kept true to his word. His gaze roved over me, and I felt my body flush, but I couldn't look away. His face was still pinched, but his eyes seemed to soften when they met mine.

My stomach fluttered. And if he was true to his word, Jyran's wife would survive. I could have wept from Riel's generosity if I still wasn't sure of his intentions. It was all I could do to stand still and stare. I wanted to say something, anything, but I couldn't form a coherent thought, much less a sentence.

"I will be gone until this evening. Masika will be over later to keep you company. I know you need clothes, so she will take you to the shops." He narrowed his eyes and sat taller, crossing his arms over his chest.

"If you cause trouble, you will find out exactly why Masika is my second in command. And if you try to run, there will be nowhere you can hide." His threat sent shivers down my spine. His reputation preceded him, after all. He relaxed in posture and sighed. He placed a hand on my shoulder and removed it quickly. Warmth seeped through my clothes, his touch nearly burning through me at the brief contact.

"Although," his eyes settled over my bracelet and lingered over the symbols that were carved into the gold band. "I don't think I have much reason to worry."

I had to remind myself to breathe. He stood abruptly and left the dining room without another word.

I stared at the empty space where he stood, placing my hands over my cheeks, trying to cool them down from the unexpected heat that I didn't know how to process.

Light footsteps approached the kitchen not long after Riel had left, and my pulse increased, but it was only Masika.

A new excitement lit inside of me. I was finally going to get out of the house, and I was finally going to wear something that didn't have Aurum's seal embroidered on it. Masika strode into the dining area, her black hair tied into a tight braid over her shoulder. She looked me up and down and pinched her brows.

"Let's go get you some new clothes." Her voice was flat, and I got the feeling that this was more than a minor inconvenience for her.

Masika and I walked alongside each other through the shopping district in the City Center in silence. Stalls of various sizes and heights were clustered together. Each one was topped with colorful awnings that offered refuge from the desert heat.

Any imaginable product that one could need was offered in the Main Market, for a price, of course. People milled about, flitting from stall to stall. They stocked up on anything from spices to fabrics, and I took in the familiar layout of the stalls.

My instincts had me peering for easy hiding spots and back-alley routes. Memories from when I was younger flooded my mind. The City Center was the first place I mastered my skills. My gut tightened, remembering the ways I struggled to survive.

Masika didn't speak. She only gave me sidelong glances, making sure I was keeping up and that I wasn't, as Riel had called it, causing trouble. I trailed behind her and watched as she sifted through ornate garments and jewelry.

Handmade necklaces sat on a table in front of me. They were made with delicate chains and gems that I knew fetched a pretty coin. I eyed the jewelry, but taking it now would be pointless.

There was no reason to steal it, and no way to sell it if I did. I moved through the stall, my fingers fanning across folded garments and fabrics that felt soft and luxurious under my skin. I cleared my throat and turned to Masika.

"I have no way to pay for anything..." I let my voice trail off into the wind. Masika turned and gave me an appraising stare. Her lip turned up, and it was almost mischievous. I hadn't seen that look from her before, but I liked it. It was a nice change from the constant unfriendly attitude she normally pushed my way.

"Riel gave us credits. Pick out what you want, and the charge will go to him." She turned back to the necklace she had been inspecting, her fingers drifting over the intricate folds and bends of wire over a blue stone.

I blew out a breath and paced around the stall. I drifted over to a set of garments with sheer blue fabric. It held subtle inlays of gold threads, and it felt soft and light in my hands.

It was perfect for Aurum's climate, but I felt an uncomfortable twinge in my gut at the excess of it all. I guessed the price for those clothes was more than what Riel would have been willing to pay; and in truth, it was more than what I was comfortable wearing.

"You should try it on." Masika snatched the garments out of my hand and held it up against the sunlight. The cloth shimmered in the sun like a blue night sky against the golden sands.

I shook my head. "It's too much."

"Nonsense." She shoved the clothes in my hands. Masika seemed to detect my apprehension.

She leaned in close to me and whispered, "Someone worked very hard on these clothes." She nodded to the shopkeeper, a stout older woman, her hands tanned and wrinkled, who was currently speaking with a paying customer.

"Whatever the cost, it doesn't matter. The money we spend today will go to the hard-working people of Aurum. Our purchases feed families."

Masika nudged me in the direction of a closed-off portion of the stall. Tall black panels of fabric draped down from the awning, making for a small, private changing area. Behind the curtains, I removed my clothes and set them aside. I held the blue clothes up and studied them.

Masika was right. Whoever made this provided for their livelihoods, and they did it without breaking the law. My heart sank. How many families had I stolen from? Did my actions cause someone else to go hungry at the expense of my own stomach?

I sighed. The last time I had stolen from businesses like this was ages ago. Ever since I started teaming up with Devland, I only ever robbed the rich. Deciding that dwelling on the past would get me nowhere, I put on the clothes.

It was two pieces. My midriff was exposed by the loose-fitting top, a gold band cinched at my ribs. The pants were also loose, cuffed with matching gold bands around my ankles. I swished in the light and breathable fabric. It was absolutely stunning. Each golden thread shimmered into different colors with my movements.

I had worn nothing so delicate or excessive as these clothes. I simply had no use for them. While I felt spectacular, I also felt...exposed. It made me want to retreat to my shadows. The gold band on my wrist weighed heavier as I stared at it. If I could use my magic, I wouldn't have to step out of the black panels, but there was no hiding—not anymore.

As if my magic was calling to me, the gold bangle itched against my skin, and I tried once again to pry it off. But it was no use. It refused to budge. I would have to break my hand to remove it.

"Come out here and let me see," Masika called from the other side.

I peered around the black curtain and tiptoed my way to Masika. I could feel my face heating, and Masika's eyes lit up. She had her hands on her hips and nodded her head.

"You'll get that. Now go change, and we can go."

I stood stunned.

"Why do you want me to get this so bad? I don't have anywhere to wear it, and I can't pay Riel back. Not even mentioning," I lowered my voice, "that I am a prisoner."

Masika hardened her lips into a line. "Yes, but if you are parading yourself as an Aurum official, you need to dress like us. There are many reasons for decent civilian clothes."

I couldn't argue with her logic, even if it made me queasy. Would I have to mingle with other high-ranking citizens, too? I changed into my clothes, embracing the familiar texture against my skin. I held the blue fabric in my hands, letting the silky textile sift through my fingers. It made me feel like an imposter. It didn't matter what type of clothes I put on; I was still a thief.

Masika was smiling as she spoke to the shop owner. I didn't think I had ever seen Masika smile before, and I wondered what she was like outside of the stern environment of her job. She came across as unforgiving, but there was a tenderness about her at this moment. Riel had shown me similar vulnerabilities, and it made my stomach drop.

I didn't want to see them as people. They were part of a cruel system that had no grace for the people I cared for. Even Chefren, who had shown me nothing but kindness, I kept locked behind the visage of corruption. I had no room, no grace for the fools that worked for the Lord, no matter how they were as people.

I followed behind Masika, both of our hands full of bags filled to the brim with new apparel. Masika had not only picked out a select few items for me, but she also purchased a haul of her own. I admired the deviousness since she knew that Riel would be paying.

When she had seen me eyeballing a simple yet elegant necklace, she had urged me to get it, saying, "When Riel is paying, you don't need to look at the price tag." I almost felt bad for him, but when I had complained about his reaction, she only waved me off.

I even had to admit, allowing Riel to pay for my clothes after he had cruelly thrown me into a dungeon felt good. Like he at least owed it to me. I grinned and looked into the bag, watching the sunlight glint over the shining jewelry inside.

Masika veered off to a small food stall where a delectable smell of fresh bread and meat perfumed the street. We set our bags down at a small table. A short man came over to take our order, where Masika had requested a pot of tea and some meat pies with potatoes and peas—their specialty. My mouth watered from the smell of coriander and spices. It had been a while since I ate a good, rich meal, and the scent alone made my stomach rumble.

The same short man came back to deposit two pies in front of us. My eyes rolled to the back of my head when the smell wafted toward me. We sat and ate in silence, and I opened my mouth and closed it again several times to start a conversation.

Masika didn't seem keen on speaking, though, and the awkward silence was gnawing on my insides. Instead of trying to force conversation, I took a bite of the pie, relishing the rich taste. The tender meat melted in my mouth. Earthy spices exploded on my tastebuds. Flavors of Aurum coated my mouth, and I wondered how I had never stopped by this stall before.

I peered at Masika as she tucked in to her own meal. She looked relaxed, and she genuinely seemed to enjoy herself. It made me even more curious about what she was like beneath her hardened exterior. No. I shouldn't be wondering about anything. She was Aurum's Watchman, and I was nothing. I was her sworn enemy, and she was mine. And so was Riel. And Chefren. I steeled the walls around my heart, pushing my curious thoughts to the back of my mind.

I cleared my throat. "Were you able to find anything about our thieves?"

She looked at me with skeptical eyes, but responded just the same. "The gaming den wasn't a complete waste of time." She swallowed her food and placed her fork on the table. "Chefren had spied some mortals that fit our profiles, and he left to follow them after we made our way out of the building." That explained the urgent rush that Riel was in this morning. "He's got his people watching them all hours of the day. If they make a move, we will know about it."

I nodded. The sound of mortals and Magi chatting and laughing in the street filled up the growing silence between us. I watched as Masika lost herself in her thoughts. Her eyes glazed over, and she tugged on a piece of bread before nibbling on it with the corner of her mouth.

"I saw you with that man in the gaming den." Masika's tone was sharp, nearly accusatory. "I followed him after you and Riel left. He went straight to his home—in the South District."

"Yes, and?" I clenched my jaw. The last thing I wanted was to get my people, my community, involved.

"He didn't end up gambling that night. He left and went home."

I sighed. It was a relief to know that he didn't lose his entire life's savings.

"Riel seemed to think your explanation was good enough, but I don't buy it. Anyone who knows a thief like you is trouble in my book. I want to hear it for myself." A pressure surrounded my chest. It wasn't pleasant, but it didn't hurt either. Suddenly, I felt an urge to tell her the truth. Biting my lip, I looked away from Masika, focusing on a tall spire in the distance.

"Not that it's any of your business," I said, "but that man and his wife are some of the best people that live in the South District. He has never stepped a toe outside of the law. He sells the meager teas and herbs that he can grow himself. On the rare occasion that the gods bless them with good sales, they use the extra money to feed and clothe those of us who aren't so fortunate. I admire him—the both of them." Masika cocked her head, taking in every one of my words. "Lucinda, Jyran's wife, has an illness."

I paused, unexpected emotions bubbling up, my cheeks getting hot. "Her memory is fading and her body is deteriorating. There's a witch that sells medicine to ease her pain and help her keep her memories, but it's expensive. She has to import the herbs from the northern mountain regions.

"I provided funds to get the medicine, but that was many moon cycles ago, and she needs more. Jyran never told me the supply was running low. Otherwise, I would have given it to them when I dropped off my last donation to the orphanage." My palms were rough as I rubbed them against my cheeks. "I just wish I knew."

Masika propped her elbows on the table and studied me. "You count yourself as one of them—someone who can't afford to put food on the table or clothes on your back." It was a statement, not a question.

"Whether I have food or clothes doesn't matter." My face grew hot, and I tried to blame it on the relentless sun. "The people in the South District are my family. We all help each other. If my neighbor is hungry, then I feed them. It's not about how much I can get back—it's about the value of life and what we put into the soul of our city. It's about respect. Not just for people of blood, I have never had blood relatives, not that you would know anything about that—"

I cut myself off with my chest heaving. Masika would never understand. None of them would.

"He is an innocent man, Masika. So you can call your hounds off." I bit out those last words with pure acid. Masika only lifted her brow in response and that made my blood boil more than if she had spat vile words back at me.

"If Riel trusts my word, then why can't you? He's your leader." I pointed my finger in her face before instantly withdrawing it and blowing out a heavy breath. She was getting under my skin, and I didn't want her to have that kind of power over me.

I needed my freedom, but why did it have to be so damn hard? Shaking my head, I focused back on my pie, but I was no longer hungry.

"Even if he had gambled his life away, it's not your responsibility," she said matter-of-factly. I scoffed. Her comment, no doubt she thought it harmless, made my teeth clench.

"Of course it's my responsibility. No one cares for us down there except each other. We are all we have."

Masika narrowed her sharp eyes on me, making me feel like my entire insides were exposed. I couldn't help the words from coming out of my mouth. They were filled with years of repressed resentment that was now bubbling over.

"We help each other. You may think of the South District as low-life scum, and there are certainly people there that fit that profile, but everyone there struggles. The only hope for survival is to rely on each other." I lowered my voice to a whisper. "We are all we have. They were all I had."

A tear leaked from my eye, and I quickly wiped it away with my hand. None of what Masika said was anything I hadn't heard before, but it made me emotional to have this conversation with her. To finally tell someone who worked for Aurum how they had left us in the dark and in the dust.

I sat back and blinked up at the clear blue sky above. My family, Tala, the children, my elders; would they be lost without me? Had I made a mistake in giving them so much with no way for them to fend on their own? If I was gone tomorrow, what would become of the South District?

"And now with the drug problem..." I barely realized I had muttered the words.

"What drug problem?" Masika asked sharply.

I glared at her.

"The drugs. In the South District. The ones that are killing people. Are you telling me you haven't heard of it?" I gritted my teeth so hard I thought they might crack. Aurum's officials were negligent, but I honestly didn't think they had turned their backs on us so fully.

"I'm afraid not." Masika answered, pressing her tongue to her cheek. How could they not know? Did the Aurum officials pay so little attention to us? The small amount of respect I had for them—which was none—fell even lower.

I leaned over the table. I laced my words with all the venom and hatred I had for her.

"There have been four deaths in the last week. Probably—no, definitely—more while I was gone, and who knows how many since. It's a godsdamned epidemic, and you and Riel are too busy making sure you appease your precious Lord to see the strife that the citizens of Aurum are suffering. That is why the South District is my responsibility." I held her gaze for several moments before I leaned back in my chair.

A sense of calming came over me. I was still fuming on the inside, but letting those words out had lifted a weight off of my shoulders.

"I'll have to inform The General about this." Masika blinked, and I swore her face softened before she fixed her face into the harshness that I was used to.

Unsure if I was supposed to laugh at the absurdity, I held her in a stare.

"What good will telling him do? It's not like you or Riel, or anyone else, has cared about us before." I balled my hands into fists. "As usual, we have to take care of the problem ourselves." I was muttering more to myself, unable to wrap my mind around the reality that the South District was so far removed from the rest of Aurum.

"How could any of this be news to you?" I blurted, my cheeks hot. She didn't answer right away, as if she was deliberately trying to find the right words.

"It's possible that we have been oblivious to the needs of our people." Masika's gaze was unfocused as she spoke. "Maybe if we had been better about caring not only about what was right in front of us, we would find Aurum a much better place."

We ate the rest of our meal quietly. Unsaid words settled with heaviness between us. I fidgeted in my seat, barely picking at the food in front of me.

Chapter 10

After Masika and I had returned from our trip, Riel knocked on my door and told me he would be holding a meeting this evening. He didn't barge into my room that time, and I wasn't sure if I should feel relieved or apprehensive. He was polite as he spoke to me. It felt he was trying to play mind games with me, and if he was, it worked. Chefren escorted me down to the office, where we took up our normal chairs, but one chair remained empty.

"Where's Masika?" I asked, noting the empty chair on my right.

Riel sat at his desk, shifting his notes around mindlessly.

"She's in the South District," he said and I widened my eyes. "She's looking into the lead you gave her on the drug appearances."

"That is…" Words escaped me. I couldn't believe my ears. The Aurum government hadn't looked into the South District's problems in decades, probably centuries. "Thank you."

Riel pointedly glared at me and sighed. Exasperation flashed across his features. "You don't need to thank me. It's our job, Leoni. We work for all of Aurum."

I held back a retort. Until this afternoon, it hadn't been practiced for centuries, as far as I knew. Everyone in the South District knew that the government would rather watch us rot.

"Chefren," Riel's voice was commanding and his face serious. "What's the status on the men you have been tracking?"

Chefren's face was stone as he nodded. He looked past Riel, no hint of his regular humor when he spoke. "I had them followed to a tea shop in the City Center. It looks like it could be a front."

If I was expecting Chefren to say anywhere in Aurum, that was not it. I knew exactly which tea shop Chefren referred to. I willed my heart to slow and my face to keep from reddening.

Riel nodded. "A front? To the Black Market?"

Chefren stroked his beard and gave me a side-long glance. "Could be." He shrugged. But I knew. It was the Black Market. Neither of them seemed to realize this for certain, and for that, I was grateful. If Riel got his hands on the Black Market, so many people and underground businesses would cease to exist. Most of my contacts and trades were formed at that location.

Captain Devland had even invested his money in that section to keep it afloat—and away from prying eyes. It was hidden and warded by magic and mundane. It had gone undetected for centuries, and those two thieves had just led a fox to the rabbit hole. I wiped the palms of my hands on my pants, hoping that neither Riel nor Chefren could feel the tension that was radiating off my body.

"We need to investigate. Do you think we can get in?" Riel asked. I was surprised at how easily he sought Chefren for advice. I was used to the pirate's way of life. You either listen to the captain or you get off the ship.

Chefren shrugged. He lounged in his chair casually. "Should be easy enough. You'll have to give me some time, though."

Riel's gaze drifted to the back of the room as he thought out loud. "While our goal is to capture the culprits"—he paused, still mulling over the new information—"if it is a front for the Black Market, perhaps we should change tactics. We could catch the thieves and shut it down at the same time."

I gulped and hoped that Riel didn't take any notice of my nerves or my rapid heartbeat that they could surely hear in the quiet of the room. I glanced at Chefren, who only shook his head.

"No, if we try to go for both we will thin out our resources too much. We need to focus our efforts one at a time. The Black Market will still be there when we are done."

Riel leaned back in his chair and I could practically see the cogs turning in his mind as he weighed his options. His gaze trailed to the empty seat next to me. I figured he was wishing he could get the thoughts of his second in command before making his final decision. She wasn't here right now, though, and time was of the essence. He needed to make a decision to put Chefren's plans into action.

Riel clicked his tongue. His mind was made up, and I sat on the edge of my seat hanging onto every breath, every word, that came out of Riel's mouth as if my life depended on it—because it did.

"Alright," he replied. "We go after the thieves and deal with the Black Market another day. I'll relay our discussion with Masika, and she will know that we aren't to touch anyone else for now." I reeled in the urge to sigh in relief.

Riel and Chefren continued to converse strategies with each other, but I tuned them out. I tried to regulate my breathing while releasing the building pressure in my chest. Neither one of them asked for my input about anything or even looked in my direction.

But even as I tried to dismiss my panic, I could only think about what would happen when I gained my freedom. One day they would go after the Black Market, and this discussion would return to haunt me. I hadn't given them any information that they didn't already know, but no one would believe it. At that point, I wouldn't need Riel to gut me. The other thieves and criminals in Aurum would do it themselves. Neither Riel nor the gods above could save me then.

Riel stood up from his desk with his eyes cast down as he shuffled the parchment in front of him. "Keep trailing the suspects, and when the time is right, we will make our move. Dismissed."

Chefren stood and made his way out the door. But as I went to follow him, Riel's demanding voice stopped me in my tracks.

"Not you, Leoni," Riel said, and I glanced at Chefren, who shrugged and gave me a look that said "good luck" before snapping the door shut behind him. Turning to face Riel, I tried not to cringe. I would have given anything to have my shadows at this moment.

His face was taught, but I kept my chin up. I would not show him my increasing panic. Riel strode around his desk until he was directly in front of me. Riel was between me and the door, as if he knew I wanted to rush out and lock myself in the room upstairs.

The walls of the room suddenly seemed too small, and my chest squeezed as my head filled with a light buzzing sound. There was still a small distance between us, but his lips slightly upturned as if he could read my discomfort.

He took a step toward me, and then another, until I felt the desk hit my thighs behind me. His hands were in his pockets, and I gulped as he leaned on the back of his feet.

"You've been unusually quiet tonight." I didn't realize he had been observing me so closely.

"Just not used to all of this"—I wracked my brain trying to come up with something, anything that would move this conversation on—"business." I grimaced. Business?

He scoffed, but it sounded like it could have been a laugh. "And here I was, thinking that you were some sort of thief mastermind. Hm."

I ground my teeth together. "Just because I don't feel comfortable in your little government planning sessions doesn't mean that I'm incapable."

"I didn't say that." Any evidence of a grin was gone now, and instead his eyes looked me up and down. He let out a frustrated breath. "We are getting off topic." He shook his head, refocusing himself. "I want you to come with us when we scope out the tea shop. Your intel will be invaluable—"

I raised my hand to cut him off. "I am not going. And to be quite honest, you shouldn't be going either."

"It's not an option." In one step, his long legs invaded my space. Our chests were once more practically touching and I could smell faint traces of incense from his clothes.

I swallowed, ignoring my suddenly dry mouth. I didn't want to be anywhere near that tea shop, especially without my magic.

"It will be dangerous." It was all I could say without spilling the secrets of the Black Market.

Riel looked down at me, our eyes meeting, and my body broke out in gooseflesh at the searing heat that came from Riel's honeyed gaze. I grasped the edge of the desk, knowing that if my hands were free, I would drag them through his dark hair. I would not—could not—allow myself to get lost in this strange attraction.

He didn't smile, but I felt heat rise to my cheeks when he said, "I will protect you." He did a sharp intake of breath and stepped back. The air was suddenly cold between us. I got the impression that he hadn't meant those words to escape his lips. Riel cleared his throat and strode to the door, where he opened it wide.

"What I meant to say was, that you have nothing to fear." I could practically see him building walls in his mind. "Now, get back to researching."

My feet carried me through the door automatically. I looked at him as I passed, but he refused to meet my gaze. He followed me through the house as I made my way back to the living room.

I sighed as I sat in my usual spot, the parchment and pages open from where I had previously left off. Chefren was already there, in his chair on the far side of the room. He had his own stacks of books that he was flipping through.

I looked through the list once again, searching my notes with as much of an open mind as I could. There should be something linking them together, but what?

The Statue of Himera - Himera is the goddess of the sunrise, often depicted with a great white dragon bringing the rays of dawn into the world. No longer magical. The statue was said to have Himera's blessing imbedded in the gold inlay.

The Chalice of Offering - Golden chalice that was used in ancient rituals to invoke the power of dragons when filled with a worthy sacrifice. No longer magical.

The Eye of the Divine - A stone basin that was used to scry messages from the gods. No longer magical, used by priests.

I sat up, scanning over my notes again, checking every item. I inhaled sharply.

"What is it?" Riel asked.

I looked between Chefren and Riel, both who stared at me with interest.

"These items...they hold some sort of historical magical property, dating back to before the gods' disappearances."

Chefren sifted through his own notes, and Riel stood to look over my shoulder.

"Look," I said, pointing to the entry of each item across several books. "All the items lost their magic when the gods disappeared. It's like someone wants these for their magic or to grow closer to the gods?" I guessed, and Chefren shrugged. I looked over my shoulder at Riel, who had inched closer to me, his eyes glimmering with excitement on my find, a small smile playing on his lips.

Chefren sifted through his notes. "I can confirm that my items are the same, but why would someone want relics that can't be confirmed with magic or not? Aurum has plenty of magical items."

My brow furrowed. Chefren was right. Why did someone want these magical pieces that no longer worked? The gods had been gone for ages. What was the point?

I sighed, looking at Riel. "Does it even matter why they want them? The fact is we found the missing piece, and that should help us find the culprit, right?"

Riel smirked at me. "Even better, if we can pinpoint all the relics that haven't been stolen that meet the same criteria, we could potentially catch them in the act. Good job, Leoni."

Riel clapped his hand on my shoulder. I bit my lip and tried to look away from his eyes that shone with what looked like pride. My heart swelled, finally able to prove that I was useful. Maybe my imprisonment would be a quick sentence after all.

Riel made his way to the hallway.

"Chefren, tomorrow I need you to meet with the archeologists of Aurum and see if they know where we might find the other relics. I'm relieving you of duties tonight."

Riel's eyes met mine, and my breath caught. I wouldn't have a guard tonight?

"Leoni, Masika is still looking into the drug problem in the South District. If you want help and answers, you need to stick to our current plan. I am placing my trust in you not to run this evening. Can I count on you for that?"

"Yes," I stammered. My freedom was so close I could taste it, but if I wanted actual answers to the South District's urgent problems, I would need to stay. I would sacrifice my freedom for them. I would do anything for the people I loved, even if that meant no magic and solitude.

Riel and Chefren moved our little group into the dining room, where they had placed cured meats and cheeses for dinner. I thought it was interesting that night after night, even though they were all peers, they shared meals together.

I watched as Riel and Chefren shared smiles over the food, noticing how Riel's mask was slipping easier around me. The only thing that was missing was Masika. Even she had eased around me, not being quite so bitter in her responses to me.

As if my thoughts summoned her, Masika strode in, taking a seat next to Chefren. She gave him a tight smile before she sighed and greeted me and Riel.

"I have good news and bad news," she said while reaching for the pitcher of water on the table and pouring herself a glass. It looked like she had just come directly from the South District. Grains of sand were latched into her dark braid that must have come slightly undone with the wind. "The good news," she continued, "is that the drugs seem to be isolated for now."

I swallowed thickly. How was that good news? If it was isolated, it seemed like it was targeted. Who would want to target the South District?

"The bad news?" Riel asked.

"The bad news," she glanced over to me, hesitating, "two others have since passed since we have captured Leoni."

I let out an aggravated scoff and clenched my fists. Burning tears threatened to let loose out of my eyes and I blinked them back rapidly. I knew it was a possibility. I had hoped it wouldn't happen, and yet I knew that it would. Was it selfish of me to hope that it wasn't someone I cared about?

Riel leaned slightly toward me, his shoulder brushing mine, but he made no other move.

Masika bit her lip. "It's Dragon's Breath, Riel," she whispered.

"What's Dragon's Breath?" I asked. Chefren's face paled.

Riel dragged his hands over his face. He let the tiredness show, as though he couldn't handle putting an extra weight on his shoulders.

"Dragon's Breath is a powerful opiate. We heard of the drug being used overseas a few moon cycles ago, and there are whispers of it showing up in cities around the Ambrose continent. We haven't seen it here, though."

"Until now," I said wearily.

Riel nodded. He looked around at all of us.

"The sooner we find the thieves, the sooner we can address the drug problem. Chefren, as soon as you get confirmation on the tea house, let me know."

Chefren was unnaturally quiet as he nodded at Riel's command.

"How will we get the approval to look into the drugs in the South District, Riel?" Masika asked. "Lord Eduard hardly wants us to look into the robberies, and those are happening to the people who gave him his seat. He won't care about the drugs."

She gave me a pitying look, and a lump formed in my throat. She was right. The Lord wouldn't want them to help us. It was even more reason for my service to be done so I could help on my own terms.

I would find whoever was poisoning my city and poison them right back. Riel slammed his fist on the table, making me jump.

"I don't care what the Lord thinks," Riel hissed. His face was stony with determination. He gave me a sidelong glance. "All the people are Aurum's people, and if there is a drug problem in the South District, then we will find it and eradicate it." The lump eased as I felt the truth in his words.

Masika threw her hands up, placating Riel's anger. "We will figure something out then."

Chefren said nothing as he cleaned off his seat at the table, moving into the kitchen. Riel buried his head in his hands and took a deep breath. He looked up, reaffirming his mask of indifference.

"You both are dismissed. I'll see Leoni to her room."

Chefren leaned in the doorway while he waited for Masika to grab a loaf of bread and make her way out of the dining room. They left with a quick nod toward us, and Masika gave me a sorrowful last look as they left the house.

THE METAL BAND AROUND my wrist felt like it was binding tighter with each passing day. I needed this thing off of me. I needed to get back to the South District. Prying on the bracelet had been useless. I tried so many times that the tips of my fingers bled. There was a small drop that formed on my middle finger, and I cursed as I sucked the blood away.

I paced around my room. Anxiety and eagerness tore through me. We were close to catching the thieves, but I still had many unanswered questions. Why were the thieves targeting these ancient relics? How much were they getting compensated for them? How was I not informed of it? As the thief of Aurum, I figured whoever wanted these relics would try to hire the best, and I was the best. So why were they using mortals?

I blew out a breath of frustration and turned my head to my door. Riel left me in the room and I questioned if he left the door unlocked. I didn't want to run, but I hadn't explored the house all that much since I was always accompanied or watched, and my instincts urged me to find out the house's secrets.

The knob turned with ease, and I smiled mischievously. I glanced down at myself, wearing my nightgown that I had bought with Masika—a dark green slip that hit my thighs with small straps. Breathable for the desert night air of Aurum, and an absolutely stunning contrast against my copper hair and bronzed skin. I decided not to change since I would be back soon and was too eager to sneak around to pause and change.

I stepped into the hallway and peered around the corner. There was no sign of anyone, but I waited, listening for sounds of movement. With a smirk, I pondered how much snooping I could do before getting caught. I silenced my doubts, closed the door, and took the risk.

A door to another bedroom stood ajar, with a flickering light streaming out across the hall. Curiosity piqued my interest, and I tiptoed across the hall. I was silent as I nudged the door open a little wider.

Slowly and carefully, I stuck my head in and breathed a sigh of relief when I found the room empty. A massive bed sat next to a desk riddled with papers. A candelabra lit the entire room in warm, flickering light. I let out a low whistle. Everything in this room screamed wealth and knowledge.

Books lined one wall, while beautiful paintings of Aurum's desert and ocean decorated the rest. The bed had some of the plushest blankets and pillows I had ever seen. And it was a crumpled mess. It was a juxtaposed setting compared to Riel's neat and clean offices. Despite the wealth, the room felt lived in and cozy. It was clearly a place of refuge and relaxation.

"What are you doing in here?" A low, husky voice had me spinning on my heels. Standing in the arched frame between the bedroom and a bathroom was Riel.

A towel was slung over his hips, not hiding his broad, chiseled body from my view. I swallowed. How did the gods allow one man to have so many muscles? Water dripped down his chest, catching in the crevices of his carved body.

The low light flickered against his dark skin, which made the shadows dancing against him look fierce and outright captivating. I snapped my eyes up and mouth closed before stammering out a response.

"You let yourself into my room all the time. This only seemed fair." I let a small smile play on my lips. My heart raced, and I tried to rein in my betraying eyes, tried not to notice how his forearm flexed when he formed a fist.

I tried not to imagine what his chest would feel like under my hands. I had to remind myself that he was still my captor and my enemy. A chiseled, wet enemy.

He stepped toward me, his body close to mine, and I swallowed. He towered over me. His face was harsh and angry, but there was a definite heat playing in his eyes.

He slipped his gaze down, and I silently cursed myself for not changing. Everywhere his eyes touched, my skin pebbled. My nightgown was entirely too provocative, and a rush of heat pulsed through me. I squeezed my legs tighter, willing my core to stop mixing signals with my mind.

"I have given you many liberties, Leoni," the way he said my name was practically a purr, "I don't reprimand you for your smart tongue." He took a small step closer. Our chests nearly touched.

"I let you enjoy the sunlight when you should be in a dungeon." He looped his finger through a copper curl and my breath hitched. "I have given you a comfortable place to sleep."

He was so close I could smell soap and incense rolling off of his skin, and he leaned closer. Hesitation flashed through his eyes as he quickly dropped my hair, realizing that he was so close to touching me. My breasts pebbled under his gaze, my thin nightgown hiding nothing, and I was sure he noticed as his eyes widened as he glanced down my body. "I allow you to enjoy the fresh air of the city." His voice was nearly breathless.

"Under guard, of course." My retort came out breathy and strained, with none of the attitude I intended.

"Of course," he replied.

I stepped back, my face burning, and Riel stood taller at my retreat. His face hardened, The General making his appearance in the man before me.

"I think you are losing sight of your role in this arrangement," he said.

Hoping that he wouldn't notice how my body was reacting to him, I closed my eyes and tried not to let him see me shiver.

I was definitely losing sight, alright. Losing sight of my conviction. But who could blame me when he stood so close I could practically taste the remnants of the bathwater dripping onto the floor? And damn it, wasn't he losing sight, too? I didn't miss the heat in his eyes that he was so desperately trying to hide.

Riel grabbed my shoulder with a calloused hand and spun me around. I gasped, but then he shoved me out of his door.

"Don't come into my room again, Leoni." He pushed me out the door, slamming it behind me. Maybe he wasn't losing sight, and Riel had just played me.

"Don't leave your door open next time! Some would take that as an invitation!" I shouted through the door. Surprisingly, it cracked open, and Riel's head popped out, his dark hair beginning to curl as it dried.

"Oh, Leoni." His tongue popped in a small tsk. "My invitations are not nearly as subtle, and as much as you may like an invitation from me," he smirked, and heat radiated through my body, "I'm not sure that you could handle it."

He scowled at me, but it didn't match the heat I saw in his eyes, the temptation that I saw floating through them. I backed up a step, positive that my heart had stopped completely. He masked himself back into his stiff demeanor.

"Oh, and if you stole even a single item from this room, I will find out."

"I didn't steal anything," I snapped.

He slammed the door once again. I reared my foot back and hit the door with a swift kick, but it only left me with sore toes and a bruised ego. I wasn't sure how to process his hot and cold attitude, and I cursed at myself. Of course, he would think I was trying something nefarious.

No doubt, his flirtatious attitude was a ploy to catch me in the act, and I was a complete fool for falling for it. I muttered obscenities directed at Riel as I made my way back to my room. My desire to explore vanished, and I went into the bathroom and splashed cold water on my face. Riel's image was seared into my mind. Why did The General have to be so attractive?

Now that I had seen him almost naked, filthy thoughts kept filtering through my mind. I tried to focus those thoughts toward my memories with Devland, but Devland's face kept changing into Riel's and I shook my head.

I laid in bed, staring at the ceiling above me. One candle remained lit, flickering against the walls, and I squeezed my legs together, trying to banish these feelings that I knew were only a reaction to seeing Riel's physique in a towel. I thumped my head against the pillow.

What if I just touched myself? It's not like Riel would know. I glanced at the door. It was late enough, and I had a feeling that Riel wouldn't try to barge in tonight. Or maybe he would. That could be fun...

Stop it.

I didn't want to know what an invitation from Riel would look like. I didn't want to know what his lips would feel like against mine, or his hands digging into my hips. I certainly didn't want to know what his body would feel like pressed against me.

My fingers trailed down my stomach, pulling up the night gown far enough to reach into my undergarments. I spread my legs wider, granting myself access and finding that I was coated in wet desire. My body's response was completely unwarranted. I shouldn't be feeling this way toward Riel, but I yearned for release more urgently than I did with Devland on our last night. And it wasn't like Riel could read my mind. What harm was there in fantasizing about the man across the hall for one night?

I dipped my fingers inside of myself as I pictured Riel in his towel, but instead of a scowl, I saw his smirk and the scouring gaze that felt like he could see me underneath my clothes. I pictured him pulling the straps off my shoulder with his teeth, his hands roaming across my body before finding my core soaking wet like I was now. Would he murmur filthy words in my ear or shower me with praises?

I bit my lip as I dipped a second finger in, gasping in the pleasant intrusion, and I bucked my hips up, wishing that Riel was on top of me, licking his way down my neck and across my breasts. What would his teeth feel like biting against my nipples? I wanted to know. I needed to know. I pinched my nipple with my free hand at the thought. An involuntary moan left my lips, and my eyes slammed open.

I glanced at the closed door and hoped Riel didn't just hear that, but what if he did? My body grew more needy at the thought, and I pictured him making his way down my body, his lips pressed against my skin, his tongue flicking further down.

I circled my clit slowly, and my legs began to shake as I thought about him tearing my undergarments away with needy fingers, his powerful arms lifting me as his lips met my core. I imagined his tongue flicking against me, dipping inside of me, and my body froze. Pleasure poured from me, and I couldn't breathe as I came undone completely from the thought of Riel working me with his mouth.

I made a nearly inhuman sound, pent up energy cresting and over-flowing through my body wracking me from the inside out. New wetness coated my thighs, and I heaved in air in deep gulping breaths. My body shuddered with the aftershocks. I hadn't experienced such a climax in a long time. For the first time in weeks, my body fully relaxed, and I laughed softly as I blew out the candle.

But as darkness settled in, so did the anxiety.

I should not have done that. Pleasuring myself in Riel's home already felt like an intrusion, but imagining Riel's face and body while doing so? Absolutely unforgivable. But it was too late now, and guilt creeped up as I laid there, hoping that Riel hadn't heard me cry out his name. An unusual mix of embarrassment and satisfaction flushed through me, and I bit my lip as I tried to focus on the fact that Riel was probably asleep. At least I hoped he couldn't hear my sounds through the thick walls of the house.

ANOTHER NIGHTMARE JOLTED ME awake, my skin sticky with sweat, my hair plastered against my forehead. My heart raced as I tried to shake away the images of Seraph screaming and dying in the street as the Lord towered over him, laughing. The dream wasn't real, but reality haunted me more.

My family and friends were dying, and there was nothing I could do about it. Each time I closed my eyes, Seraph's crazed, drugged-out face appeared on different people, making my hands tingle and my stomach drop. I imagined their bodies lying cold on the streets while the other people in Aurum walked right past. I rubbed the last of the sleep out of my eyes, hoping Riel would be out of the house again and I could try to nap through the day. If Masika needed to watch me sleep, so be it.

I wasn't so fortunate. I heard the footsteps before a quick knock sounded on my door. It swung open, and Riel strode in, as he usually did, with his stern face. His eyes looked golden in the sunlight that streamed into the bedroom. His jaw clenched, but that only sharpened his features. There was no sign on his face that he had heard me last night, and I tried not to let the heat rise to my cheeks as I recalled the earth-shattering orgasm I had given myself as I thought about his face between my legs. He took a seat on the bed next to me. He was close to me, and I scooted further away, trying to run from my made-up images of him.

"We need to discuss plans." He was firm and convicted with his words.

"What plans?"

"Chefren thinks he found our thieves. We'll check out the tea shop soon, a few days, if we're lucky. See if we can find anything ourselves," he said.

My stomach plummeted. Riel wanted Chefren to work fast, but I wasn't expecting it to be so soon. I needed more time. Every single worst-case scenario ran through my head. They could kill me on sight for even showing my face. My disappearance was no doubt known by now. It was uncertain if my arrest was common knowledge, but I didn't like the chances.

"We can't, Riel. The tea shop, it's the Black Market. It's too dangerous." His jaw flexed at my admission and refusal. "The Black Market has eyes everywhere. If anyone recognizes me—us—it could end in disaster." I glared into his eyes to make my point. "For everyone involved."

I rubbed my face, hoping it would wake up the parts of my body that demanded rest. He mulled over my words, a pinch forming in between his eyebrows. At least he wasn't threatening me with death, or worse. A part of me—a twisted, depraved part of me—wanted to reach out and rub out the tension he held in his shoulders. Wanted to smooth the lines on his forehead. I shook my head, the lack of sleep clearly getting to me.

"I am Aurum's General, Leoni." His gaze bore into me. "We have our own security protocols, and even then we are not weak individuals. You don't become a part of my team without intensive training and our own fair share of battles."

I met his hard gaze with my own and stared him down for several moments. Finally, I broke free of our stare-down and sighed.

"Alright, fine. Don't mistake my actions for approval of this idea. I know these people. I know how ruthless they are—they won't hesitate to fight dirty to save themselves."

"Your approval has no sway in the investigations of Aurum."

His voice was steely, but his features held no hostility. We sat for a few moments, his gaze still pinned on me. Riel sighed and lifted his head, staring at the ceiling.

"There is something else I wanted to ask you."

My breath hitched. "Well, go ahead."

He took a deep sigh and flexed his fingers. Riel's tough exterior softened as he looked at me. He seemed interested in breaking down barriers between us, but unsure if it was wise.

"How are you? I know it must be hard knowing about everything going on, and being here can't be easy." Of all the questions Riel could have asked me, that was not even close to what I thought he was going to ask.

"I'm fine." I wasn't fine, but I was dealing.

Riel gave me a pointed look. "You had a panic attack on the street the other night. Masika's information about the drugs isn't exactly easy to digest." He exhaled a long breath through his nose. "I just want to make sure you're alright."

"I'm fine, Riel." The smile I gave him was too wide, and I knew didn't meet my eyes. Part of me wanted to tell him I was drowning, that I couldn't close my eyes without seeing death. "Why are you asking?"

Riel pinched his brows together. He looked away from me, and I wasn't sure if he was going to answer. Rolling his shoulders back, I watched him try to rebuild those walls, but I saw them shatter in his eyes.

"I'm not going to lie. Finding Dragon's Breath in Aurum is alarming."

He hesitated before he shook his head. I couldn't help but notice the circles under his eyes.

"I thought we were airtight with security checkpoints at every city entrance. You might not believe this, but I worked very hard to keep those drugs out of our city. Checkpoints for each package and shipment from the outside. Each crate and barrel searched." Riel sank onto the edge of my bed. His shoulders sagged as he sat down.

I tucked my feet underneath me and took a closer look at Riel's face. His frown was loose and his expression was softer than I had ever seen it. It was an unusual expression for him, different from his usual General persona. I toyed with the bracelet on my wrist before I spoke, choosing my words carefully.

"Usually, there's someone from the inside willing to compromise," I said.

He whipped his head at me, and I raised my hands up and said, "I don't know any information about who. I rarely take goods in and out of Aurum. I prefer to travel with gold."

He eyed me wearily, but he didn't object, so I went on, "But there's always someone desperate enough. Desperate for money, for excitement, for purpose—even if that purpose is to rebel." My teeth gnashed together. "Whoever is behind these thefts excluded me, and it's driving me insane. I'm the best thief in Aurum. It's been killing me, sitting here and wondering why I wouldn't be involved, and I'm coming up short.

Riel's gaze was unfocused as he thought. I was sure he was replaying every order he had given, every check he had made to keep the city secure. It was like he was bearing the entire weight of Aurum's security on his shoulders.

I had seen the same type of betrayers with my own eyes. Humans and Magi who yearned for more and sought it in the wrong places. I had to bite back a laugh, because I was that person. Desperate enough to steal and rob, and as a result, I helped Devland sneak an insurmountable illegal goods through Aurum. His ship in the bay indicated he had bribed security guards.

I got up from the bed, and Riel watched as I strode toward the dresser and pulled out a clean Aurum official uniform. His eyes followed me around the room, and I couldn't help by feel a little squirmy under his gaze.

"Listen." I gently squeezed the clothes in my hand. "Things happen. You can't control every single person in the city. It's not your fault some people choose to spread rot wherever they please."

He straightened his posture. "And yet, you hold me responsible for the South District's rot. You believe that I am the reason the people there suffer." His jaw ticked, and his brown eyes filled with guilt and apology. I guess I couldn't blame him for that conclusion. It wasn't far from the truth. I gave him a small smile. I spoke my heart's truths instinctively.

"It's not you specifically. It's how Aurum runs. The entire nation of Ambrose knows we are the wealthiest city, and yet people die daily because they can't get food or medicine."

I leaned against the dresser, the dark wood digging into my hip. I clenched my fists as I held back my anger.

"It's the fact that we have a Lord, who presumably does nothing but whine when he doesn't get what he wants. The same Lord of Ambrose, who has enough money to import enough water to keep his precious rose garden alive in the desert. He does nothing when people in his city are suffering, starving, becoming drug addicts. I hate the government of Aurum, and you, as their General, represent that."

My face was becoming heated. Anger that wasn't directed at Riel rose in every word I spoke.

"You know," I took a shaky breath and softened my voice, "it's not like I wanted to become a thief. It just happened. Out of necessity. Just like the fact that I'm stuck working with you is out of necessity." Riel narrowed his eyes at my words, but he didn't cut in. "It's not your fault that I became a thief or that the only way my brothers and sisters can survive is by crime. But it is Aurum's fault. The city has failed."

And with that, I turned to the bathroom.

Riel stared at me while I swung the door to the bathroom open. His eyes were guarded, and his lips turned into a frown. I stomped into the bathroom and groaned. The door slammed behind me, and I slid down to the cold floor.

The lines with Riel were blurring, but I didn't want to see him as a person of authority who actually cared. But, despite what I originally thought, he truly did care about Aurum. It was his approach that was geared towards the success of the rich and elite that irritated me.

I needed to keep Riel in my mind as the calculated and fearsome general, otherwise I could feel my resolve shattering. But the fact remained that where I had previously seen a cold-hearted enemy, I now saw a genuine Magi, trying to do right by his own resources.

Chapter 11

Darkness spilled into my room, but the sky was slowly turning a paler blue with the oncoming day. For the last four days, I had woken up before the sunrise. My thoughts were always warring with each other, and knowing I would be going to the Black Market weighed me down.

I crawled out of my bed. My chest constantly felt like it was caving in, driving me mad. I rolled my shoulders, attempting to release my stress as I dressed. I pulled my new clothes on and smirked. They fit perfectly over my hips, the tunic hugging my torso. As practical as they were, they complimented my figure, and I couldn't help the smile that pulled at my lips.

I grasped the handle of my door. My heart raced though there was nothing to fear. Riel hadn't placed any more guards outside of my door, and it remained unlocked. That was enough for me to feel comfortable leaving my room's confines. Regardless, I listened closely for any shifting movements before nudging the door open.

The hall was silent. I let out a relieved breath. Tiptoeing around the house, I committed the layout to memory. There were areas that I hadn't seen previously, and even though I couldn't access my magic, there was a comforting familiarity about slinking between the flickering shadows cast from the metal lanterns above.

I went through the kitchen to an unfamiliar hall. Pantries and storage lined the walls, but I didn't bother to snoop. Truthfully, I had no urge to try. Flitting through the darkness was enough to appease me. I still wasn't used to my lack of magic, and I probably never would be, but the shadows that I walked between were a wonderful substitute.

There was a door at the end of the hall unlike the others. It looked old—older than the rest of the house. Most of the homes in Aurum were rebuilt, but this door looked ancient. The wood was thick, with a tarnished iron handle. Decorative carvings were etched into the woodgrain. Symbols that I didn't recognize, and I traced them with my finger, wondering what they meant.

Slowly, I grasped the handle and turned it. I knew I shouldn't try to open it, but my fingers tingled with anticipation. I forced open the heavy door and discovered a small courtyard, which appeared to be a training area.

The sun was making its crest, bathing the yard in cool pale light. It illuminated a wide area of sand with a rack of weapons on one side. I turned around, taking the space in, and I startled when I saw Riel standing off to one side, rolling up his sleeves.

His back was to me, not noticing that I had accidentally stumbled into his alone time. His shirt was tight against his solid frame, and I took a step back, attempting to retreat before he noticed I was there.

I grasped the handle to shut the door behind me, but Riel turned before I made it back inside. He stood still as he saw me, and I tried to muster the best 'I promise I'm not up to anything' smile. It definitely looked more like a grimace.

"What are you doing here?" he growled.

I shrugged. "I couldn't sleep."

"You shouldn't be sneaking around."

"The door was unlocked." Silence filled the courtyard, and I took that as my queue to leave. I made it halfway through the threshold before Riel called out.

"Wait."

That one word rang through the quiet of the early morning. Riel raked his hands through his hair and studied me, his eyes roving from the top of my head all the way to my feet. His gaze scorched every inch of my body.

"Since you're already here, we might as well see what you're capable of."

I glanced over at the courtyard. This was clearly a training area for fighters, and I was anything but. I must not have been hiding my trepidation very well, because Riel only huffed in impatience before I pried my feet off the ground to make my way toward him.

"Erm—" I stammered, unsure of what I should do or where to go. I met him in the middle of the sanded yard, pinching my eyebrows together.

"What am I supposed to do?"

Riel crossed his arms over his shoulders, making his biceps looking even larger, stretching the fabric taught.

"Since you don't have access to your magic, let me see what you can do physically," he said.

The sand shifted under my feet as I paced around the miniature arena. I fidgeted with my bracelet. The mention of my magic missing felt like a burning in my chest. I would get it back. I just needed to find these thieves and finish serving my sentence. The bracelet negating my magic made me feel like I had a bottomless pit inside of me, like a limb had been severed. And I hated every moment. I inhaled deeply and looked at Riel for further instruction.

He led me through a circuit of exercises, testing and measuring my capabilities. They started off easy, getting harder and harder with each new round of movements. I kept going, and Riel never relented in his tasks—mostly running and jumping, seeing how hard I could push myself before expiring.

I had decent stamina; I had to, in case I needed to make a fast exit. It felt refreshing to move, my blood pumping through my body. Finally, after jumping through a course Riel had laid out in the sand, he stopped me.

"How is your hand-to-hand combat?" he asked, removing his shirt and exposing his dark skin. My cheeks blushed as he revealed his toned body cut by the gods themselves. I cleared my throat, forcing myself to answer his question.

"I'm lousy at a fight, even with my powers." I shrugged. Riel's gaze was skeptical.

"Let's find out then," he commanded. I looked at him with hesitation as I paced around him, but he only held his hands up in fists in encouragement.

"No magic?" I asked. The last thing I needed was to be caught in the snares of Riel's magical ability with nothing to defend myself. He nodded in confirmation. I planted my feet on the ground, mentally running through the handful of times I had sparred with others. It wasn't much.

My shadows could protect me from fights, so combat wasn't a skill I had ever honed. I didn't need to. But what I lacked in raw combat skills, I made up for in tenacity. I wouldn't give up for anything.

Keeping my hands close to my face, I waited for Riel to make his first move. He watched me with a voracious gaze, ready to pounce at any sudden movement. It both thrilled and scared me. My heart was practically beating out of my chest. I wasn't afraid that he would hurt me, I was afraid of disappointing him. The realization struck through my core, and I scowled.

Breathing out my trepidation, I rolled my shoulders back and shifted my weight forward. My hand cut through the air, aiming for a small opening below Riel's ribs. But he was fast. He batted my hand away with ease. My scowl deepened when I caught Riel with a small smirk on the edge of his lips.

"Again." His voice was thick with authority, and I felt the command pulse straight through me. I backed up, honing in on his stance, and adjusting myself to mimic him. I threw more punches, but he blocked each hit and batted my hands away. My chest heaved with heavy breaths. Riel never made a move to hit me, and instead, he took stock of my movements, gauging my strengths and weaknesses. My arms shook. Sweat dripped into my eyes, but Riel was unrelenting, constantly beckoning me to keep going.

Every missed strike dragged my already wavering confidence lower. It didn't even seem like Riel was working all that hard, and here I was, shaking and drawing in ragged breaths, trying to land a single hit. I threw punch after punch, my lungs screamed, my arms like wet sand, but I refused to show how tired I felt. If I couldn't hit him, I would rather die trying than admit defeat.

I threw my body at him, all my frustration boiling over into a shout that echoed through the courtyard. Riel's hands wrapped around my wrists. I nearly toppled over from the forced momentum, but he held strong, and I stumbled into his chest. I stood still, his firm hands still binding me, and the proximity had me panting in his scent. My heart hammered in my chest, which had nothing to do with my excessive workout, when I looked up into his face.

A fine sheen of sweat had broken out over his forehead, curling the ends of his hair, and I sucked in a breath.

"You can't fight." he said simply.

"I told you that." Frustration laced my tone, but some of it faded when I saw the gold shimmering in his brown eyes in the full sunlight of the morning. He tipped toward me a fraction of an inch and I held my breath. His lips turned up, just slightly, and for a moment, the world dropped away.

"But even still, you won't back down from the challenge." Riel's eyes glimmered with mirth, and the walls he kept up around me fell away. Standing before me was the true Riel. Not the General of Aurum, but a man who knew understood the fight I had to go through to survive.

"Never."

His lips popped open as though he wanted to ask me something but couldn't find the words.

I leaned into him, feeling the hard planes of his chest against my breasts. Each point of contact sent sparks of desire through me. Nothing existed except for our mingling breaths.

I ignored the voice in the back of my head whispering *this is wrong* as we leaned closer. His hands grasped my shoulders, but he didn't push away, even though I could feel his hesitation, the war in his mind on whether we should be this close.

It should have felt wrong. He was the general of a city that failed me. He failed the people I loved. But at this moment, being pressed up against each other, it felt right. So right that I didn't think this should have felt possible. Even being in the arms of Devland, or anyone else, had never felt like this before. The world never fell away, the heat pulsing between my legs never reached the depths of my soul the way being with Riel did.

I tilted my head toward him, and he trailed over my arms tentatively before wrapping them over my wrists, pulling me closer. Each touch sent a blazing trail of fire through me, and I leaned in further.

Riel hesitated, second-guessing himself, as though his thoughts mirrored mine, but I thought I heard him curse as he leaned in and pressed his lips to mine. His kiss was feather light, a manifestation of his own apprehensions, but it was nothing compared to the fluttering in my stomach. I felt as though I could fly away.

My hands met skin as I pressed them to Riel's chest, unsure if I should push him away or draw him in closer. He clasped the back of my neck, making the decision for me, pulling me into him. A tidal wave crashed through me. I opened for him, our tongues meshing and dancing with fervor.

I couldn't deny my want for him. A small part of me worried about the cold nature that was sure to rear its ugly head, but I didn't care. I wanted him, and if that was the price for this life-altering kiss, the heat between my legs, I would gladly pay it. Or would I?

Fear prickled through my desire, and I tore myself away from him. The General was kissing me, and this was wrong. I shoved at his chest and we stared at each other with hooded eyes and panting breaths. I wanted Riel, and it terrified me. The urge to leave suddenly overcame any lust-filled desires.

Riel dropped his hands instantly, but the warmth that remained was seared into my skin. We stared at each other in silence, both stunned and unable to articulate anything. I turned my back and shot into the house before I decided to make any more poor decisions. I didn't even look behind me as I left, not wanting to see the regret on his face.

I sat in the bath, soaking until the water went cold, but I stayed in even longer until my skin wrinkled and pruned. Despite feeling battered, I felt better from the surge in activity.

My mind was clearer than it had been in days, and the muscle burn was a welcome one. I scrubbed my skin roughly. Part of it was to get the sweat and grime off, but I was also trying to scrub away my feelings for Riel.

I touched my fingers to my lips. The sear Riel had left on them had yet to fade. The imprint he left on me burned hotter than the sun on the summer equinox.

I took apart and analyzed the pieces of him—his stiff demeanor and the actions that contradicted it. His gift to Jyran, the anguish he revealed when he found out about the drug problem. I wanted to hate him, just as I had hated him when he dragged me into the dungeons. He stood for everything I had ever fought against, but there was a constant pull to him I couldn't seem to shake.

The cold, calculated Riel I knew how to navigate around. This new version of Riel, with a bleeding heart and a softness underneath the stone demeanor, I knew nothing about. And that kiss, gods, that kiss. I certainly didn't know how to feel about that.

I stood abruptly from the bathtub. Cold water sloshed over the basin, as twisted and tumultuous as my warring thoughts. Feelings were for the weak, and I was not weak. Once this job was done, everything with Riel would be done, too.

There would be no more heated glances, no more palpable tension, and no more lips locked around each other. Even if they were soft and delectable and tasted like the sweetest wine. I shook my head.

Stop it, I told myself again.

When I emerged from the bathroom fully dressed, Riel was sitting in my bedroom with his leg propped on his knee. He narrowed his eyes at me, and I flushed at the scrutiny. I bit my lip.

"If you were waiting for me to come out in only a towel, I'm sorry to say you must be disappointed." I flashed him a smile, and his eyes widened before he scowled.

The Riel that kissed me softly in the morning sunlight was gone, replaced by a masked version who concealed his true self and emotions. Riel stood up and flung the bedroom door open.

"I apologize for my behavior this morning. It will not happen again." He gestured to me, my normal black attire. "We are going to the teahouse tonight. Be sure to wear something presentable."

I stood, shocked by his abrupt apology and that he changed the topic so quickly. I was getting Riel whiplash.

"Tonight?" I stopped in my tracks. "Riel, I'm not going."

He turned, his brown eyes fiery. "Yes. You are."

"You're going to get us killed. I've been missing for days on end. They will know something is off if I show up to have tea."

Captain James Devland would have spread the word that I was missing by now. If he knew I was locked up, he would have spread a warning. In the Black Market, they quickly communicated news about who could and couldn't be trusted.

"You are going. We are going. And that is final."

I threw my hands up in surrender.

"Fine. Your funeral." And mine.

WE WERE TO GO to the tea shop an hour after sundown, and the sun was currently casting its setting glow on the city. Golden rays reflected into my room through the window, refracting rainbows on the walls.

If I wasn't so nervous, I might have taken the time to appreciate the colors that painted the room. Instead, I paced in circles, shaking out the tingling in my hands. I blew out several haggard breaths while I changed into the outfit I tried on at the shops.

Masika had paired the blue set with cream-colored slippers, and I had to admit she had a good eye. In an attempt to hide in my very identifiable red curls, I twisted and tucked my hair into a braided crown.

This was a terrible plan, and I tried once more to break the lock on the bracelet. It was no use. If I tried anymore, I would risk snapping my wrist in two. It almost seemed worth it.

I patted myself down, more so to try to release anxiety than check that I had what I needed. I wasn't allowed any weapons, and it made me feel naked. There was no way of protecting myself other than relying on Riel.

Riel seemed confident that he could protect me well enough, but I had my doubts. I had seen what the kind of people in the Black Market could do, and regardless of Riel's power, we would be outnumbered.

Seething and anxious, I opened the door to make my way downstairs. Riel was standing at my door with his hand raised as though he was about to knock. At least he would offer that courtesy this time.

He looked devastating. His dark hair was pushed to the side, and a single strand fell on his forehead, curling right above his eyebrow. His muscular frame was flexed against the dark blue shirt with a low-cut neckline, and I suppressed a groan.

I wondered if Masika had bought him his clothes as well, intentionally making us match. Screw her if she did, that shirt was unforgivable. It was hard to hate someone who looked so delicious.

I plastered on a saccharine smile.

"I'm ready whenever you are." He stood in front of me silently, but his eyes trailed down my body, sending a zing of awareness through me. My cheeks heated at his gaze.

"You look..."

His words trailed off, and I gave him a dramatic spin while batting my eyes.

"Beautiful? Exquisite? Like the girl of your dreams?" Sarcasm dripped from my inflection, but I secretly hoped he did think that.

His gaze under darkened his eyelashes, and his lips impulsively upturned. My forced smile wavered at his heated inspection, but when he caught himself lingering, he closed himself off, and his mouth formed a thin line.

"Presentable."

I let out a bellowing laugh and assessed him with my hand on my chin. "You look presentable yourself." That was a severe understatement.

He turned on his heel and walked towards the front door, assuming I would follow. I did follow, but not before I noticed the way his tight-fitting pants hugged his thighs. I sighed at the view. It was not the time or place—or person—to be appreciating, but it wasn't my fault if my jailer was so overwhelmingly attractive.

THE TEAHOUSE LOOKED LIKE a completely average upscale tearoom. Low-sitting square tables filled the space surrounded by plush cushions. Groups of patrons sat at the tables with hookahs and teacups in front of them. Meat and cheese plates were brought to the tables from behind a thick curtain. Though unassuming, I knew the entrance to the Black Market was through the kitchens.

Without even realizing, I crept closer to Riel, weaving my hand into the crook of his arm. I looked up at him and gave him a thin smile, hoping he wouldn't pull away. To my complete shock, he gave me a curt nod in understanding, while his free hand gave mine a tight squeeze.

Could he hear how hard my heart was hammering? Did he feel the trepidation pulsing through my veins? We hadn't really broached the subject of the searing kiss in the courtyard, and while I was content to leave it in the past, I also had questions.

Why did he kiss me? Was he feeling as confused as I was? In the end, it didn't really matter. I would be gone soon, hopefully, and it would all be in the past. Let the kiss sit where it belonged—on the courtyard that I would never venture back to.

I held my head high as we walked to a table close to the kitchen entrance. My insides felt like a tangled mess of anxiety and fear, but I refused to let anyone else see it. Riel spoke to a server, whispering an all-too-average order of tea.

I scanned the room, looking for anyone whose eyes were also wheeling. No one seemed to recognize me yet, even though I recognized one patron.

An assassin from the Seaside Cliffs. There was no mistaking the thick scar that ran down his cheek, even if he wore a hood attempting to cover his long jet-black hair in shadow.

I turned my gaze toward Riel in case the assassin's obsidian eyes decided to meet mine. It was unfortunate that my red hair stood in stark contrast to the rest of the people in Aurum. With my magic, it was never an issue, but being here without magic was a huge risk.

Riel had to know that I stuck out like a sore thumb. And among people who would surely recognize me, a thief, sitting with Aurum's most notorious law enforcement. I wondered if Riel had removed the wanted posters from the city. I didn't even have a hood to place atop my head. It was infuriating. My leg bounced up and down under the table.

I spied Chefren at another table, sitting with Masika. They looked so comfortable together that I could mistake them for a couple. And from my previous observations, I could be right in my assessment.

Masika looked stunning in her purple outfit, the same style as mine. She wore silver instead of gold, with large drop earrings that swished along her collarbone when she moved. Her dark hair was pulled to the side, the length of a braid falling over her breasts.

I watched as heads swiveled in her direction. Men and women both admiring from afar and close. A man even tried to divert her attention from Chefren. I laughed when he was met with a scowl and an angry gesture from Chefren.

"Everyone's focusing on Masika," I spoke in a hushed tone, my lips close to Riel's ear. "She can manipulate their attention?" Riel nodded and leaned into my ear.

"Masika is feeding into their emotions, and Chefren has a form of mind reading." Riel's breath tickled the shell of my ear. My back straightened. Could Chefren have read my mind? If so, how the hell was I still alive?

"He can't sift through people's minds for specific thoughts, but he can tell their most heightened and forefront thoughts. So, for instance, if someone is a drug dealer or an artifact thief, he wouldn't know it unless they were actively trying to sell drugs or steal artifacts." It made sense, and I wondered how much he got from me.

"They work well as a team. She can make people more comfortable and more willing to talk, and Chefren reads their minds. If our artifact dealers are here, we will know soon."

She could make people more comfortable. I rubbed my hand along the center of my chest. So it was her power that she had used, coaxing the truth out of me, making me feel emotional around her that day in the market. I shivered, not realizing at the time that she used her magic on me.

A server dropped off a steaming pot of tea and two cups. Amber liquid steamed from my cup, and I hesitantly reached for the saucer. Regardless that Chefren had captured the minds of the surrounding people, my nerves were still on high alert. The cup and saucer shook in my hands, and I abandoned the tea altogether and placed it back on the table before tucking my hands back into my lap.

"Leoni," Riel's hand gripped mine under the table. He let go after one squeeze and placed his arm behind me. "Lean back and be sure to keep physical contact with me."

I leaned into the muscled arm as he draped his arm around me. His hand gripped tightly on my shoulder, even though his hardened gaze was focused on the surrounding room. I wasn't entirely sure he even knew he was doing it.

"Why?" I asked.

Surprisingly, I wasn't opposed to the contact. I even found his touch comforting, but it was so far from Riel's usual demeanor.

I imagined what it would be like if this wasn't a mission, to be so casual and public. What if we were a couple on a night out? The thought both jarred and entranced me.

Riel spoke through gritted teeth and his hand stilled. "It's the only way I can protect you."

I followed his gaze across the shop to the two men in hooded cloaks. One man had a large bag strapped across his chest, with whatever was held in it looking heavy.

I spied a sword on his hip, his hand hovering over the hilt. His companion passed him a small vial with thick silver liquid. Masika caught the attention of everyone in the shop, including the two men. One of the men tipped a vial of liquid into his mouth. He shook his head, as if he was coming out of a daze.

"Riel..." my voice trembled. If that liquid did what I thought it did and negated mental magic... Riel's hands tensed around my shoulder as if his thoughts were the same as mine. "Riel, get this bracelet off of me right now."

Riel whipped his head to mine, his eyes sharp. "I can't do that, Leoni."

"Do you think I'm trying to trick you?" I hissed. "If I don't cloak myself, we will all be killed." The men were definitely looking at us, whispering to each other. I wanted to crawl into my shadows, my red hair melding with the surrounding stone. "They know my profile. They know who I am. And soon, so will everyone else. Take. It. Off."

"No."

His refusal sank into the pit of my stomach. I closed my eyes and took a deep breath, clearing all my thoughts from my head. I prepared myself mentally, noting all the exits and obstacles I would have to maneuver without magic.

I refused to blink while I watched the two men. They gestured toward our table, and I held my breath. Chefren's eyes widened. He must have realized that he could no longer hear the men's minds. My body froze as one of the men released his sword and barreled toward our table.

I could only sit as he reared back and swung straight for—no, not me, he was swinging for Riel. My hands moved of their own accord as I pushed Riel down, away from the oncoming sword, but it was a poor decision because I shoved myself into Riel's spot, the sword now aiming for my neck. Fear gripped me so wholly that I couldn't move away. I only saw the gleam of metal as it slowly made its descent. The last moments of my life would not come as a quick flurry of metal on bone, but an agonizing slow cut of metal through air.

A hand gripped my wrist and pulled so hard I thought my arm would pop out of its socket. Riel swung me off of the cushions and onto the floor. He lay on top of me, his heart hammering against mine. Looking up, I saw the man with the sword *hovering*.

"What is happening?" I shouted through the adrenaline. My shout rang in silence. Everyone in the shop had stilled unnaturally. They were stuck in a moment. A table that was being overturned hung in the air. Tea and water droplets were suspended and glimmered in the dim light. Time itself stopped.

Riel could stop time.

The rumors—how he could appear in front of someone instantaneously, how he could kill someone without them even knowing—it all clicked into place.

Riel gripped my chin and forced me to look at him.

"Leoni. We have little time. I can only hold this for a few moments." He let out a haggard breath.

Riel hung his head, resting it on my shoulder. "I need you to run. Get out of here and go back to the house."

I glanced at the now-frozen Chefren and Masika. Chefren was in the middle of twisting away from a woman who charged him, while another person stood behind them. His dagger was pointed toward Masika's neck. Three others had joined the commotion, ready to fight. They were barging in through the front of the teahouse, their weapons raised.

"They knew we were coming," my voice trembled, "how did they know?" Panic seized me.

"I don't know." Riel gritted his teeth. "I'm sorry." He laid a hand against my cheek. "I was supposed to protect you," his voice cracked, and he fished out a key from his pocket.

"If I remove your bracelet, will you go to the house? Protect yourself and go back to the house." I nodded, eager to do anything he said. Riel's jaw feathered, and he took the small gold key and unlatched the bracelet. "Don't make me regret this."

Chapter 12

THE BRACELET FELL OFF, and a powerful surge riveted through my body. I screamed. Magic flowed into me, too fast, too much, too hard. My chest tightened, and my heart squeezed as if it had grown weak. Riel gripped my shoulders tightly. His eyes roved over me as the magic settled back into my blood. Everything around us still paused, but I noticed ever so slight movement from the hovering objects and people. Riel's magic was holding. But for how much longer?

"I'm fine," I croaked. I flexed my fingers and sat up. The energy from my magic was overpowering the pain, and I was fine. At least, I thought I was fine. Magic flooded my veins like fire and ice, and it burned. Each passing beat of my heart lessened the pain, and my magic swelled in my soul to the brim. It was like a dam had opened, and I could finally replenish what I was missing. Strength flooded into my limbs, and the power of my magic washed through me like a wave crashing against the hull of a ship.

"I'll meet you at the house," I promised. Riel's eyes met mine, and suddenly I was burning from the inside, my ache for him potent and pulsing through my body. Before I even thought about what I was doing, I kissed him.

I was tired of holding back. Who was the woman who lacked the courage to take what she wanted? Not me. So, I took what I wanted the most.

I grabbed his hair at the nape of his neck and swept my tongue across his lips. If I was the thief of Aurum, I was going to steal Aurum's most precious commodity: Riel's lips against mine. The heat that burned so hot between us. His entire body stiffened before he wrapped his arms around me.

He brought my body closer and tighter to his. His lips were urgent, and his hands grasped my arms with a vice-like grip—as if he didn't want to let me go. As if he couldn't let me go. It was like he believed that releasing the embrace would signify losing me altogether. We broke from the kiss, his golden-brown eyes glinting.

"Do not make me chase you," he growled in my ear, and it wasn't clear if it was a threat or plea, but I knew I needed to get away. We all did.

I crawled under the table next to ours and summoned my magic. The warm sensation poured over my skin as my magic embraced and cloaked my body. I sighed in contentment. I was meant to be in the shadows, using my magic to hide. Riel watched my every move. He watched as my magic settled over me, and I became nothing but a mirage. His eyes widened, and I moved behind the assailants before Riel turned, his face contorting with concentration—holding his magic for as long as he could. I watched as Riel plucked the sword from our attacker, and time reverted back to normal.

The man, now empty-handed, swung and stumbled. He crashed into the table, sending glass and tea flying through the air. Screams pierced the shop, patrons shoving and yelling to make their way out. I should have been among them, but instead, I continued to watch.

Chefren and Masika were now standing at their table. Chefren wielded a sword of his own and dodged his assailant. He made fighting look easy. Chefren's swings were graceful arcs despite his bulk. The sword whistled as it cut through the air. Each slash was within a breath of his attacker, only a hair away from making a connection. I cursed under my breath and cheered him on silently, praying that he would make it to safety.

My gaze turned just in time to see Masika whip out two daggers that she must have sheathed under her outfit. She quickly slashed across the man trying to attack her from behind, and I gasped. Blood splattered along the walls of the tearoom and the man dropped to the floor with a resounding thud. She held no remorse in her face for killing the man. Her only goal was survival.

Chefren and Masika stood back-to-back, inching their way to the front door, parrying and fighting attackers that stood in their path. I sighed in relief. Together, they could make it out of this bloodbath, and I wondered exactly how many people were involved with the mystery of these stolen relics. I noted how none of them seemed to use magic, but they were vicious just the same.

I sank further under the cover of my table and watched as Riel swung the sword he took from our attacker backward, pommeling the hilt toward the man's head. He wanted to take him alive and question him, but his focus was too narrow.

I shouted at Riel, but there was too much noise for my voice to carry to him. Once he took out the man, he blipped through the room, moving through frozen time, helping innocent bystanders out the door.

One of the other attackers disappeared through the kitchen, and I sat under the table, conflicted. Riel wanted me to get to safety, and by remaining here, I was already disobeying his orders.

The answers we had spent so much time looking for were fleeing, and with each passing second, I could feel them slipping away. Pushing myself up, I hoped Riel wouldn't be too upset with me. We needed that man, and I was going to get him myself. The teahouse was thoroughly trashed, and I skirted around puddles of blood and broken glass. Patrons huddled close together, scared and praying that they didn't become the next lifeless body on the ground. Workers of the teashop scrambled to help innocent bystanders or flee for their own lives.

I followed the man, but not before a body blurred in front of me. The scarred assassin. He cut me off, making me lose my footing, and I had to throw myself against the wall as he passed. He rushed by, and a trail of wind that smelled of mist and sage whipped over my face.

I followed that mist and sage scent into the kitchens, down a hidden hatch of stairs, and through a dark tunnel. The Black Market wasn't exactly a market but more of a communal area. From an outsider's perspective, it was just another extension of the teahouse. But I knew everyone sitting at a table was wheeling and dealing in stolen goods and blood contracts. I kept my eyes peeled for the two men in cloaks, but there was not even a sign of disturbances.

They couldn't have gone far, but I still cursed myself for losing sight of them. My magic still flowed generously in my system, with no indication of weakening. Good. I knew there was a small alcove at the back that led outside—if you knew how to open the gate. Figuring it was worth a shot, I hurried in that direction.

I slithered through the small gathering of Aurum's criminals, keeping my eyes peeled to see where they could have gone. My ears were open, listening for whispers of the stolen artifacts, but whomever I passed by didn't speak of it.

A whiff of the mist and sage scent trailed through the dark, and I thanked the gods for my stroke of luck as I followed it. No torchlights illuminated my path. Perfect for my cloaking magic, but unfortunate for my eyesight. I listened carefully as I stepped into the quiet end of the tunnel, hearing two low voices.

One was groveling, his voice watery and whiny, while the other voice was deep and smooth. I turned deeper into the tunnel, and a small light lit the two men. The assassin was bent over the cowering figure, who had his hands raised above his head in a defensive posture.

"You will tell me where he is, or I will cut off your air supply, leaving you to choke down here, and then I will cut your body into pieces and throw them in the ocean so nobody will find you. The only thing that will remain will be your head, which I will take with me—"

The assassin whipped his head toward me, and I quickly checked my magic. Everything was in place. He should not have been able to see me. My heart quickened, and a loud rushing filled my ears. Not rushing from my heart, but a powerful gust of air.

"I know you're here. Make yourself known." He turned toward me, his eyes directly at me, but I knew I could not be seen. I released my magic slowly, cursing myself. I was without weapons, without a way to escape.

"Don't kill him." I felt the magic leave my skin, and the assassin's eyes widened, his scar stretching across his cheek. He smiled sinisterly, like a cat ready to pounce on his prey.

"I know you," he chuckled and moved closer to me. I made to take a step back, but I met a stone wall behind me. No, not a stone wall, a wall of air. "If it isn't Aurum's Thief."

He took his dagger and traced it along my jaw. I braced myself for a pressure that didn't come, but the threat was the same. His finger traced along my neck, leaving cold dread in its wake until he reached a loose curl and tucked it behind my ear.

"The thief with hair of fire." He walked back toward the figure. "You have been the talk of the town. No one has seen or heard from you in a while. Some have assumed your death." He laughed low and slow. My stomach turned in unease. "It seems that isn't the case." He stood straight, pointing his dagger at my heart. "Why are you chasing this lowlife scum? And why are you trying to save his life?"

The assassin's wind magic encompassed me. He pinned my arms at my sides, and my legs wouldn't budge.

"He has information that I need." I gritted my teeth.

The assassin looked back at me with a bored expression. "What information could this mortal scum possibly have that you need?"

"That's Aurum's business," I spat.

He shrugged. The mortal was on his knees, tears, sweat, and snot dripping down his face. He was most likely bound by the wind magic, too. The assassin's voice was icy.

"A thief like you, hunting people down for information in the name of Aurum? Doesn't seem like your wheelhouse."

I grimaced and let out an angry shout. "At least let me have at him before you kill him."

His black eyes met mine with a frown.

"No." He slit the mortal's throat with no warning, blood spraying across the wall. I felt wetness hit my cheek, and I yelled in frustration. Obscenities and streams of curses left my mouth. That mortal was my lead, my freedom. Blood poured from the mortal's neck, his lifeless body only being held up by the assassin's magic. Red streamed down the tunnel into the darkness, and I felt my chance of freedom flowing along with it.

I hoped that the other mortal hadn't gotten away. I hoped that Riel had trailed him, but this was supposed to be my moment. Now I would go back empty-handed and look guilty for running away.

"You ruined everything!" I spat at his shoe. His magic still held me in place, but I didn't care. If he didn't kill me now, Riel would.

The assassin didn't even deign me a look, but he released his magic, my body crumpling on the ground.

"That mortal has ruined much more than whatever you consider 'everything'," he seethed. His face contorted into anger and his scar flamed along his obsidian eyes. He wiped his sword with his cloak, holding it so tightly his knuckles were white. "He had a bounty on his head. Dealing Dragon's Breath in the Seaside Cliffs." The assassin's words echoed in my head.

"He was a relic thief..."

The assassin only laughed. "I assure you, he was a drug dealer. A peddler for Dragon's Breath. But," he shrugged, "who's to say he didn't also steal relics?"

My heart skipped a beat. The artifacts and drugs were linked. But these were mortals. How could these men, with no powers, run a drug ring under the noses of the Magi? It didn't make any sense.

"This is bigger than just him, and you know it." I bared my teeth. "We need to find who is in charge and end it."

He laughed, a cackling, raucous laugh. "*We* don't need to do any-thing. My job was to find and kill this man"—he slammed his sword across the mortal's neck, metal meeting bone and severing his head completely—"and bring back evidence. I have done my job. I have protected my people. Find another way to protect yours."

He strode past me, heels from his boots clicking on the stone floor. The tunnel went dark, and among the smell of blood and impending silence, my world came crashing into me. I pulled for my magic. It was still there, thankfully. But it was as erratic and sputtering as my shaking limbs.

I RAN BACK TO the General's Quarters as fast as my legs could manage. I sent silent prayers to the gods that Riel would and could understand my absence. My feet were swift as I bobbed and weaved through the nightly City Center crowd. As I neared, I felt my magic sputter. Honestly, I was surprised that it lasted as long as it did.

I recalled when Riel removed my bracelet, the emptiness and void suddenly filled and overflowed with raw power. Removing it after so long had released a dam. My magic had overflowed like a torrent, unable to be contained. Now, my power was dwindling, and exhaustion was setting in.

I glanced back, fairly certain I hadn't been followed, and I released the rest of my magic as I stepped onto the property. My chest heaved with labored breaths, and the fatigue dragged my body down.

One foot in front of the other. I just needed to make it back to the house. My thoughts turned to those thieves. If I had any guesses, they were trading artifacts for drugs and then distributing them in the South District. Nausea turned my stomach at the disgusting greed these mortals and whoever they worked for asserted. I needed to find out who their leader was, and fast. My blood boiled, and a new urge pulsed through my veins.

An urge to kill, to hunt down whoever was responsible and tear them limb from limb. But I was a thief; not an assassin, and not a murderer. My bloodthirsty thoughts should have registered a wrongness in me, but they didn't. And I didn't care.

That assassin had done me no favors by killing that mortal. Anger pulsed through me. He should have let me deal with him. I would have brought him to Riel, alive. It could have been my ticket to freedom.

Instead, I had nothing. And Riel...what would he think? Would he kill me for this? I thought we reached a sort of understanding, but I knew I hadn't earned his trust yet. No matter what our bodies craved from each other, he would never trust me. I couldn't trust him either.

My feet stumbled over a batch of loose rocks and I tripped, landing face-first on the dirt and gravel in front of Riel's home. There were no torchlights and no flickering candles inside.

I let out a small whimper. Blood coated the inside of my mouth. Scrapes on my hands and knees stung from the rocks below. My clothes tore against the ground, the beautiful fabric ripped into ribbons around me. As I tried to pry myself from the packed dirt path, my arms gave out.

I let out a humorless laugh. My magic had depleted completely, so I wouldn't even be able to heal quickly. I escaped the fatal situation at the tea shop and the Black Market but couldn't reach the house's threshold.

My head spun and spots filled my vision. At least I was alive. Could an overuse of magic kill someone? I never heard of that happening, but regardless, I thought about Riel's kiss as I lay on the ground. If I *was* dying, then at least I had the memory of Riel's hands on me to keep me company. Kissing him was all-consuming and left me yearning for more.

I brought a hand to my lips and noticed blood from where I had busted it when I fell. Sand and dirt sprinkled over me, pecking at my face with the slight breeze that shifted through the buildings. I felt so, so tired...but I knew I needed to get up.

With a groan, my hands scratched at the ground, attempting to pull me closer to the Quarters. My nails dug into the hard-packed dirt before me, but darkness vignetted my sight. I closed my eyes, hoping the dizziness would dissipate. I would open them in a second. I would get back up and run through those doors. I would barge in...

Chapter 13

Incense smothered my senses. I pried my eyes open. They were caked closed and dried. Dirt coated my tongue, but I wasn't on the ground. I was in a soft bed in a dimly lit room. Bookshelves lined the wall across from me. I squinted at the paintings on the wall, familiar scenes of Aurum's desert and ocean.

This was Riel's room. I tried to lift myself up, but pain lanced through my body. I heard a slight shuffling and a sharp intake of breath from my peripherals.

"Leoni." Riel's voice was not commanding or angry. It was calm, and I thought it sounded like he was worried. Clearly, my head was still addled from the overuse of magic. His large hand grasped mine. I sat up, but winced as my muscles ached in protest.

"Slowly, Leoni." Riel's eyes met mine with a crease between his brows. "I shouldn't have taken the bracelet off like that."

His hair was disheveled, a shadow of a beard stubble along his jaw. I strained my eyes, trying to determine why Riel was acting the way he was. Everything I did went against Riel's orders. I used my magic. I ran away. I came back empty-handed. He handed me a cup of water, and I took it graciously.

"You had it on for so long that the repressed magic blasted through you. I was a fool for taking it off. I should have removed it under supervision. Luckily, overuse of magic isn't fatal, but your body will be weak for a while. With the magic not able to settle, it was released too quickly, causing your nerves to need to readjust to the magic." Well, that explained why every movement prickled with needles. It was a shallow pain, though, when compared to my failure.

"I'm sorry," I croaked out, the words scraped against my dry throat.

Riel cupped my cheek, his thumb tracing along my cheekbone.

"Why are you sorry?"

What *was* I apologizing for? For the fact that I had failed? The fact that I was sorry that I had essentially caused my demise? For the fact that I was arrested at all?

"I followed one man, but the assassin killed him before I could bring him to you," I told him.

I wasn't sure why I was explaining myself. If he didn't know that the human got killed, he was sure to know now, and our end was a dead one. I tried to turn my head away, pain shooting through my neck at the movement.

"The man we were chasing was dealing drugs to the Seaside Cliffs. That's why the assassin was there."

Riel's brown eyes were soft, even as his lips formed into a thin line. A muscle twitched in his neck.

"You chased after the assassin?" I gave him the smallest nod I could manage. Riel's brows knotted. "Why?"

"He had the mortal—I thought I could hide...I thought I could stop him. He caught me with wind magic. Sniffed me out almost immediately."

Riel groaned, "Leoni...that assassin is ruthless. He is outside of our laws. He could have killed you, and there would have been nothing I could have done about it."

"I know..."

Riel shot up to his feet.

"No! You don't know!" I flinched at Riel's abrupt show of emotion. He raked his hands through his hair, pulling at the strands. I couldn't help the shock I felt at his sudden anger. Not at me, but at my mistake.

"If I had known you were going to follow him, I would have never even allowed you to use your magic! I should have dragged you out of the shop as soon as I stopped time." He paced around the bedroom.

"That assassin was Kasiel. He doesn't leave survivors. He doesn't leave witnesses...he only has one loyalty—to the people of the northern region. The thief must be more dangerous than we thought if he came here to track them down. So why did he let you go?" Riel's eyes clouded over with skepticism.

"He told me to protect my people my own way." My voice was small. This was it. This was when he would doubt my intentions and decided I couldn't be trusted. Not that he had a lot of trust in me in the first place, but I was fairly sure that I had just signed my death sentence.

Riel hovered above me. His shadow cast me in darkness, and I could only make out his broad silhouette. I imagined every worst possible situation, and I braced myself for violence. Instead, his large hand grasped mine, his calloused fingers running over my skin, sending shivers down my spine. Riel hovered above me with a frown and crinkle between his brows.

"We will protect our people."

"How?" I croaked. He had pulled himself closer to me, his eyes so close I could see the reds and yellows that made the coloring of his irises so golden in the sunlight.

"Together. I am releasing you of your imprisonment."

I stared at him wide-eyed, and Riel gave my hand a squeeze. He blew out a breath, mingling with my own, and I longed to meet his lips with mine. Slowly, oh so very slowly, I raised my hand to his cheek, ignoring the pins and needles that prodded my nerves. I conveyed my love for my community as I looked at him.

"What changed? Why do you care?" I asked. His eyes flickered, and I saw flashes of frustration in them, but also concern. He took a long moment to study my face. I let all of my emotions show. I wouldn't hide from him. Even if he represented everything I hated about Aurum, I couldn't deny that there was something about Riel that I definitely didn't hate. He wanted to heal Aurum, and so did I.

"Leoni," he breathed my name into me, and my heart fluttered. He chewed on his cheek, his face contemplative.

"Tell me, Riel." I moved through the pain and tried to sit up a little. Riel's hands were around me instantly, propping me up against the pillows, and he tucked me under the covers. His touch was tender.

Riel held me and allowed my body to rest against the plush pillows. He removed his hands slowly, as if he were afraid if he went too fast, I would break.

"When I first joined the Aurum Legion, I had ideas very similar to yours. Aurum was a...much different place back then."

I nodded, recalling stories from Magi older than me. Magi, who still remembered before Aurum, before it became the thriving city of gold today and was instead a desolate land of sand fueled by greed. Aurum's riches attracted people worldwide to come and take them. Tales were told that so much blood spilled it stained the sands, which gave it a burnt-gold hue rather than white.

Those were only stories, but there had been much violence. It was like that for over a thousand years until a small group of Magi ended the violence and used the rich grounds under the sands to create a society.

The first spire was built for Aurum's people to negotiate and communicate. Humans and Magi alike met and debated, making terms to create a new city. Despite the rise of peace, it took a long time for Aurum to become a renowned knowledge and trading hub.

Riel sat in a chair beside the bed. Books were stacked next to it, and a small tray of empty plates and a teacup lay haphazardly on the floor. He sat back and crossed his ankle over his knee. It was in the flickering candlelight that I noticed the dark circles that lined his eyes. How long was I out, and was he next to me the whole time? My heartstrings tugged.

"I joined the Aurum military when I was very young, barely a man. Aurum itself was young. The military was first forming. Laws were in place, but there was hardly a way to enforce them. Criminals ran rampant, but instead of outright bloodshed, they concealed themselves. Made their crimes nearly impossible to track."

He rubbed his finger over the top of his lip. "Many generations of my family lived in Aurum, dating back to before we became a trading city. Despite their efforts to survive, trouble persisted, even during peaceful times. Robberies were common. We never walked alone after dark. I remember watching my family and my friends be so compliant with how life was.

"'It was better than before', they told me. But I couldn't understand why that was the highest standard. I worked at a tavern for extra income, and there I heard stories of other cities. Cities where there was complete peace. Cities where women and children could walk alone at night, and they wouldn't have to worry about their lives. When I asked why we couldn't be the same, elders said it was impossible. That the people here liked their lives. They may have been right, but I believed in improvement. So, I set out to change it."

He blew out a heavy breath. "I joined the incredibly small government with the idea to change Aurum. And I did. I set up the first patrol unit. The idea was to protect the citizens. And it worked."

A small, rueful smile played on his lips. "It took decades, but I worked my way through the ranks, spearheading security and hiring trusted advisors. We tested techniques that were used from different areas of Ambrose—from the high mountains of Neverwind to the deep marshlands of Helos. We invited foreign officers and got their input.

"I was proud of my work. Aurum became a desirable destination for work and leisure due to my efforts. The ocean brought foreign traders, and they brought more money to the city."

Riel looked down, his hands braced on his knees. "I started focusing on building more and more, but I had forgotten one very important piece of myself." He shifted his eyes to mine. They were glassy. His brow knotted. "I had forgotten the very people I swore to protect. Aurum's people include all the people. My obsession with safeguarding our work and its contributors caused me to overlook the individuals who laid the foundation. You reminded me. You reminded me who I was, where I came from."

Riel reached out, his warm hand tenderly gripping my own, his heat seeping into my chilled bones.

I let out a nervous laugh. "Just how old are you, Riel?"

He squeezed my hand. "I'll be eighty-four this year. Young enough by Magi standards, but old enough to have an active hand in changing Aurum." He almost smiled at me, and heat blossomed in my chest.

His next words were slow and thoughtful. "When I saw you on the ground, lying utterly still with blood splattered on your clothes, I thought the worst." His voice cracked, "Everything I had done to protect the citizens of Aurum, it didn't matter if I couldn't protect the one person I thought I could have protected the easiest.

"You were lying so still, and everything you had shouted and sputtered at me came into focus. What was I even doing, if not for the people? What was I doing, if I couldn't protect you?

"You have become wedged in my mind. Your compassion—the way you will stop at nothing to provide for those you love—you have opened my eyes, and I know..." He let out a haggard breath.

"I know that if I hadn't met you—if you had not become such a presence in my life—I would have lost sight of everything that I had once stood for. I can't stop thinking about it, Leoni. If we were reminded of our origins more, what kind of world could we live in? Magi live long lives. Long enough to forget ourselves. Maybe in that way, mortals are blessed, and we are the ones forgotten by the gods."

His fingers slipped through the ends of my curls, and his eyes met mine. His full lips parted slightly, and I stared at him with wide eyes. The General's emotional response to Aurum was surprising. Feelings buried so deep that I, a lowly thief, was able to pull them out of him. For the first time since coming into Riel's home, I felt a spark of confidence that Aurum could be in good hands. Maybe Aurum had hope after all.

"So, I have decided that I am relieving you of your imprisonment. But I still need you here while we find the thieves. I am officially hiring you as a consultant. And as such, you will also be paid for your services."

My cheeks flooded with heat. Riel had no need to protect me. No need to feel the way he did. No need to *set me free*. An involuntary laugh wheezed from my lips.

"I didn't realize you cared so much, Riel. Thank you." Tears lined my eyes, and I gave him a half smile.

He cupped my face and ran his thumb across my cheek. I inhaled as he leaned down and kissed me. His lips were soft against mine—tender and gentle.

Nothing like the passionate kiss we shared in the tea house, but there was a devotion that made my heart skip a beat. His hand shifted to the back of my head, and I wrapped my arms around his neck, threading his hair between my fingers.

He groaned as I touched him, my hands drifting down his neck and over his shoulders. Riel's hands grasped my wrists, firm but gentle.

"This...probably isn't a good idea," he whispered, his voice pained through his words.

I leaned my head back, holding his golden-brown eyes in my gaze. "I rarely do things that are a good idea, Riel."

He flashed me a wary smile. "I don't want to hurt you."

"You won't," I promised. I was still sore and tired from my magic, but it was nothing compared to the need I felt for Riel. He wasn't wrong. This was a terrible idea, but I didn't care. I wanted to actually feel him against me, no longer wondering what his touch would feel like.

We were so close to each other I could feel his heart skip a beat. I felt him shudder around me. He released my hands slowly, and I moved my hands down his stomach, aching to feel him. I reached for the growing bulge in his pants. He hissed as I made contact, and I squeezed his hardening cock through the thin fabric.

Riel lifted my hand off of him and chuckled in my ear. It was low and dangerous, and delicious. His fingers fluttered over my skin as he traced over my collarbone, drifting lower, finding my breast. He grazed his thumb over my nipple and I moaned in relief from the contact. At the same time, his lips caressed my neck, and he flicked his tongue against my skin.

Riel leaned up, his body bent over me, and he removed his hands from me. I felt cold in his absence.

"You aren't well enough," he stated.

"I'm fine," I let out a frustrated growl. "I need you, please."

Riel shifted, and he shook his head.

"Look at me," I demanded. "I want this, I want you. Right now." My body was too cold. I needed the warmth of his palms. I needed him. I needed Riel.

His fingers met my skin again, those drifting, soft fingers, and even just the gentlest touch made me want to arch my back. His lips crashed into mine, and I moaned in his mouth.

Riel pulled my shirt up, revealing a small band around my breasts, and he pushed that up too. My skin pebbled from the cool air. Riel strummed my nipple with his thumb, and I let out a breathy moan. He crawled over me, placing himself by my side and tucking me into his body.

His eyes were molten as he took me in.

"You're so beautiful, Leoni." Riel placed a hand on my chest, the warm weight of it solid against my beating heart. "Not just on the outside, but in your heart, too. I wouldn't have been able to forgive myself if anything happened to you. Aurum doesn't deserve your compassion, and I don't deserve to be in your presence. You make me want to be a better man."

I huffed a laugh. "Imagine that, a criminal convincing a man of the law to be a better man."

Riel smirked down at me, his eyes glazed with lust. His hips leaned into me and I felt his hard cock against my hip.

"Does it make me a criminal, if I'm glad that I arrested you? That I want to spend my time making you scream my name?"

He circled my nipple again, and I moaned.

"The worst kind of criminal," I panted.

He leaned over and took my breast in his mouth, licking and sucking on it, as his hand drifted lower, dancing over the band of my pants.

I ached for his hand to go even lower. I wanted to feel the friction, to feel anything. His finger brushed against my seam and I bucked my hips, moaning at the sudden movement. Riel stilled, but didn't remove himself. He smiled against my mouth, and I only whimpered as his fingers teased my opening and gently circled my clit.

I wanted to writhe, I wanted to move, but Riel shimmied down and placed his arm over me, immobilizing me. He grinned and pressed a finger into me, and I shuddered around him.

He pumped his fingers in and out of me in a slow, steady rhythm, coaxing me to heights I didn't know I could reach. My whole body reacted to his ministrations.

I muttered unintelligible words that all ended with his name. Riel wrang pleasure from me expertly. I was hot, burning from the inside, my legs shook and I let out a cry that echoed through the halls of the house.

Riel finally removed his weight off of me, allowing myself movement in response to the way his hands made me feel. I was left panting and breathless, and I watched Riel grin out of the corner of my eye. He kissed my temple, and then my lips.

"Rest well, Leoni." He gave a smirk as he got up and left me to fall asleep.

THE NEXT MORNING, I padded down the stairs. My limbs ached, and my body was sore, but the biting pain from the magical draining was gone. Clinking dishes and quiet laughter got louder as I neared the kitchen.

Masika and Chefren were sitting at the dining table, helping themselves to plates of roasted meats, cheeses, and breads. Spices wafted past me, and my mouth watered. Memories of the last night with Riel occupied my mind. His touch was divine, and I couldn't stop thinking about how I intended to return the sentiment sometime soon.

"You're finally awake." Chefren was chewing through his words. "Wasn't sure how much longer it was going to be before I would have had to drag you out myself."

Masika shot him a pointed glare. "Don't let Riel hear you joking like that." I stared at her. Did she know what Riel and I had done? Did he confide in her his private ongoings? How much did these two know? My cheeks turned hot.

Chefren only laughed and motioned for me to sit across from them. I smiled awkwardly as I sat, reaching for an empty plate to load. My stomach grumbled from only eating small bits of food in between naps.

"How long was I out, anyway?" I asked. My body felt refreshed but tired. Like I had slept too long the night before. Riel hadn't replaced the bracelet on my wrist, and my magic sat happily contained inside me.

"A day and a half. Is your magic replenished?" Masika asked. Her eyes narrowed onto the empty spot on my wrist where the bracelet used to sit.

I nodded and flexed my wrist. My magic was back, and I felt it like it had completed me. I willed my shadows to my hand and grinned as the control I had was back. Masika watched me with wide eyes as I made my hand disappear and reappear an instant later.

I threw her a grin, to which she only shook her head, trying to hide a grin of her own.

"Did you catch the thieves?" I asked halfheartedly as I bathed in the feel of having my magic back.

A deep voice answered from behind me.

"We caught one, but he wouldn't say who he was working for." Riel entered the room, his posture slightly slouched, his hair disheveled, and I didn't miss the spots of dried blood on his neck. "He couldn't say, actually. He was spelled against saying anything. If I hadn't restrained him, he would have killed himself. I ended up having to do it myself."

Masika let out a low curse, but my face paled. I knew that magic. It sounded a lot like Devland's compulsion. I pinched my brows. Why would Devland have put his magic on the thief that was stealing relics and potentially distributing drugs?

I swallowed the piece of bread that I had bitten off slowly. There was no way I could tell Riel and his group about *The Devil's Serpent*. Loyalties to Devland aside, if he found out I had dropped his ship's name, there would be a death warrant with my face on it.

"What do you know, Leoni?" Masika pointed her fork in my direction.

I shook my head. I couldn't rat Devland out, and there must have been some crossover from someone he used and the artifact thefts. Maybe the thief worked for multiple people. It didn't make any sense.

Riel plopped down in the seat next to mine. He stretched out his legs, his head lolling over the back of the chair as he stared at the ceiling.

"Do you know anyone with that kind of magic?" His honeyed eyes met mine, and I warmed from the softness they held. The night's event replayed in my mind, and I squeezed my thighs together and felt my cheeks getting hot. Veering my gaze away from Riel, I cleared my throat.

"I might have heard of something similar."

"How so?" Riel asked.

"Erm—"

"She doesn't want to tell us," Chefren smirked at me and I could feel my heart picking up pace with the three of them staring me down.

"I don't remember," I lied and kept my eyes on my plate. It tasted grimy and bitter on my tongue. I could feel all three gazes on me. I peered up. Chefren popped his tongue with his lips turned up in a mischievous smile. Masika's brows pinched, her chin resting on steepled hands. Riel's eyebrow lifted at my response, but he showed no other emotion. Masika's narrowed eyes remained pointed at me, and the air grew colder. Tears welled up in my throat, and anxiety pulsed through my chest.

"Enough, Masika." Riel raised his hand and stood from the chair. The air cleared, and I felt like I could breathe again. I shook out my hands.

Damn, Masika's magic scared me more than Chefren's ability to read my thoughts. Chefren—I shot a look at him. From his sly smile, it seemed he knew exactly what ship I was on. He let out a low laugh, and his eyes sparkled with dark humor. My skin heated, no doubt blotching red.

"If you'll excuse me." I shot up from the table, the chair's legs squeaking against the stone floor. Grabbing my plate of food, I turned on my heel and beelined to the guest room. I winced and my stomach dropped, thinking about what Chefren may have seen or heard.

Not only the fact that I harbored the information from Riel, but I was also scared for my life, and I wouldn't—no, I couldn't—let them see that. But if Devland knew that I had been the one to give up his ship's name, that I had brought him into an investigation, well...I shuddered to think what he would do.

I trusted Devland, and he trusted me in return. He was certainly not behind these thefts that somehow put more drugs into our city. I couldn't believe it. He was cleaner than that. He wouldn't stoop so low as to poison his own customers. Surely it was a coincidence.

The door to the guest bedroom opened easily after a swift kick. Sunlight streamed through the window. Fragmented rainbows decorated the walls. I placed my plate of food down on the desk and went to close the door.

A foot lodged between the door frame when I went to close it. Riel's smell of incense prickled my nose. I let the door swing open and strode to my food, my back remaining to Riel.

"He'll have my head, you know." I stared at a piece of bread that had exactly four holes in the center of it. I shoved the plate away. The thought of consuming anything only made my stomach roll. I didn't look behind me, but I heard Riel step towards me.

"Who?"

"Devland." My words were barely a whisper. I braced my hands on the desk, locking my elbows and shoulders. I stared at bread and its holes, wondering how much longer before Devland would find me and kill me. Red curls slipped over my shoulders, blocking the sun from my eyes.

"Devland?" he asked, before recognition flashed over his features. "Ah, *The Devil's Serpent*, Captain James Devland." I refused to look at Riel. If I turned to see the disappointment surely written on his face, I didn't think my heart could bear it.

"I've just signed my death warrant, Riel."

"He would have to find you first."

"And what makes you so sure you can hide me?" I turned to find Riel so close that his chest nearly pressed against mine. He tucked a piece of my hair behind my ear.

"I don't need to. You can hide yourself." He was speaking of my magic, but he was also speaking of my agility, my skill.

"But for how long?" I asked.

Riel took my hand, warmth seeping into it. He raised my hand to his mouth and pressed a soft kiss on the inside of my wrist, where the bracelet no longer sat. I didn't pull away. I found more comfort in that small gesture than I thought possible. My shoulders sagged, and I leaned into Riel as he braced his arms around me.

"Until we find out who is dealing the drugs to Aurum. Devland is just a clue to the mystery. We will negotiate with him, see what he knows, and you will live."

"So you're still going to go after him? And then let him go free? He is a wanted pirate."

Riel grabbed my chin with his fingers and made me look up at him. My heart raced in my veins.

"He is the most famous pirate on the continent. Of course I will go after him. I did not say he would go free. If all goes according to plan, we will have his head." He bent his head towards mine, his breath shifting over the shell of my ear. "Not the other way around."

Riel's lips trailed along my neck, leaving gooseflesh in their wake. I loved this new affectionate Riel. My body trembled at his light touch, but I knew Devland. He mentored me and gave me a chance to become something that truly helped my community.

Guilt dropped low in my stomach. Just being here was an act of betrayal. I would need to talk to him before he was reprimanded by the authorities. Devland may not have been an innocent man, but he didn't deserve an ambush.

I pushed Riel away, letting him sit on the bed, the mattress dipping from his solid frame. Riel's eyes narrowed, and he grabbed my wrist. His fingers swallowed my hand.

"Do you want to help your people?"

"Yes." I tried to pry my hand out of his, wrenching to no avail. "Obviously."

"Then listen to me," Riel pulled on my arm. I lost my balance and fell into his lap. He wrapped his free arm around my waist before trailing his hand up my back and over my shoulder. He stopped at my chin, pulling my face to meet his gaze. My heart beat faster with each sweep of his fingers. His thumb ran along my bottom lip, and I froze. Heat welled in my core, and his incense scent burned through me.

"I told you that I would protect you. Everything I said last night, I meant." A smile played on his lips, "I was"—he hesitated—"hoping you would help me rehabilitate the South District."

I pushed at him. "Are you offering me a job?"

A low laugh rumbled from his chest. "Yes, if you are going to stay, you'll need a legal job. And I can create one for you."

"To watch me." I glared at him from the sides of my eyes.

"To assist you." Riel revealed one of his rare smiles. A coy one, where it was clear he had nothing but bad intentions. I couldn't deny I loved seeing this side of him. He bent his head toward my neck, kissing it, and then dragged his tongue across my skin. I let out an involuntary whimper. Riel laughed into my neck.

"And this," my voice came out breathless, "is this coercion? To go along with your plans? Are you trying to seduce me, so I will promise whatever you need?"

His gaze met mine. There was a hint of humor in them.

"Is it working?"

I shoved my hand into his chest.

"No."

I pulled back from him. The coolness of his absence left goose-bumps on my flesh. I shook my head.

He sighed. "No, this is not coercion."

"I don't understand." He pursed his lips, and I pushed further. "Why do you want to help me, Riel?"

The question left my lips in barely a whisper. I wasn't sure if I wanted to know the answer. Was he using my feelings against me? Could he just want to keep tabs on me as Aurum's Thief?

He sighed low against my neck.

"You've done more to help your people, my people—our people—than I managed to do in all my time since Aurum became a reputable city. My time has long since evolved into a meaningless bureaucracy. I admire that so much, even if you resorted to less admirable ways." He gave me a wry smile.

"You have so much potential, but you were forced by your circumstances to make unfortunate decisions. And every time you were given the option of any easy out, you never took it. You always put your community first. That is admirable beyond belief, Leoni." Tears pricked the back of my eyes. "Imagine the change you can make once you have the actual means to do so. I have forgotten just how vital it is to have someone, anyone, standing in the corners of the less fortunate."

Riel's thumb traced my jaw as he looked at me. True awe and appreciation filled his features, and I blushed at his complimenting words.

"I helped build this city. I want to see it thrive—want to see Aurum's people thrive. You are the key to making those dreams come true."

A choked laugh escaped my throat. "So, you like me because I'm useful. Because you see me as a pawn."

Riel growled and wound his arm around my waist tighter.

"No." His gaze was hard. "I like you because of your resilience. I like you because you are thoughtful and kind. I like you because you don't back down when you stand for what you believe is right.

"When I'm here, it takes everything in my power not to follow your every movement. When I am gone, you are the only thing I think about. You consume me. You challenge me."

Riel broke from my gaze, and my stomach knotted at his words and the outpouring of emotion that lined them.

"You fight so hard for anything good in your life. How do you think I will feel if I send you back with nothing? I want to protect you, and I don't want to cage you. This job is how we achieve that."

I stared at Riel. No one had ever noticed exactly what I do for the community before. My deeds, like my magic, stayed in the shadows. That Riel had not only noticed but voiced and admired my actions brought a lump in my throat and tears in my eyes, but doubt lingered in my soul. Nothing was ever easy, and nothing was ever just handed to me.

"What will the Lord think? I doubt he will let me work under him." No matter Riel's pretty words, I was still a criminal at the end of the day, and I had seen how the Lord had regarded me already. I shivered, thinking about having to work for someone like him.

Riel shrugged. "Let me deal with him. He will eventually listen."

His voice was thick with confidence and a pleasurable shiver went down my spine. The Lord probably wouldn't, but that was a problem for another day, if it ever happened.

I swung my legs over Riel's lap, straddling him. His hard length met my core, and I could feel his need and desire. I couldn't deny this pull any longer. He saw me. Nobody had ever seen and recognized everything I did, and why. I leaned into him, his arms banding around me. Slowly, I splayed my hands along his chest and peeled the fabric away from his skin. His heated gaze penetrated through my skin, and I breathed in his incense scent, relishing in it.

"Leoni," he groaned, my name leaving his mouth like a soft prayer. His hardened muscles and smooth skin met my hands. In one quick motion, Riel lifted me and placed me on the bed. His arms braced around me, caging me in, and I drank in his dark skin.

Up close, I could see the white lines of scars, my fingers tracing the little raised bumps they left. Reminders of fights he's won, and any training that he had conquered. Riel lifted my shirt off, bearing my peaked breasts. His mouth met mine, and he filled me with languid strokes of his tongue, and I moaned into him.

Calloused hands roamed my body, studying every line and every curve as his eyes took in my exposed skin. His brown eyes flashed golden in the sunlight, filled with hunger as he dove into my breast. I moaned, relaxing my entire body as he flicked my nipple with his tongue and tugged with his teeth, leaving a shockwave of pleasure mingled with the lightest pain. It was better than I had imagined, my fantasies not holding a candle to the reality.

I arched my back into him. One hand palmed my other breast while he eagerly unfastened the buttons of my pants. He was rushed, like if he didn't have me right now, I would disappear. Riel's hands on my body felt like they were always meant to be there, strumming against my skin in tandem with my heart. His lips were painting lightning against my skin, like fate itself was embedding across our bodies.

"Leoni, you are the most beautiful creature to roam this world," Riel muttered into my skin, his voice sending ripples of desire flooding through me. He pulled my pants off with ease.

He picked up my leg and placed his lips along my ankle, my calf, my knee, my thigh. Each press of his lips sending heat directly to my core, goosebumps prickling in his wake. Riel stood up, staring at my bare body. Heat flooded my cheeks in a sudden burst of self-consciousness. I went to close my legs, but Riel caught them and pulled me to the edge of the bed.

"I don't think so," he breathed, his warm breath fluttering against my sensitive skin. He forced my legs open, and I shuddered as he grasped a thigh in each hand. Riel knelt down before me, and I loved the image of him on his knees, worshipping my body—worshipping me. He ran his tongue through my center and hummed to himself in satisfaction. His mouth was gone as quickly as it had come, and I groaned in protest.

"More," I begged.

He chuckled over my skin, leaving me breathless while his short stubble scraped against the tender flesh of my thighs. His fingers dug into my skin as he went in for more, and my hips bucked up in response, my body tingling with anticipation.

"Even better than I imagined," he said, although I wasn't sure if he was talking to me or himself. He licked me again, and I let out a moan so loud it had me slamming my hand over my mouth.

Riel was on top of me in an instant. He removed my hand from my mouth.

"Let them hear you." Riel moved back down, still clutching my hand. He kissed my palm, his stubble gently scratching against my skin. "I want them to know who protects you now, and why. I want them to know that if anyone tries to take you from me, there will be no stopping my wrath. Because this…" His tongue circled my clit, and he let go of my hand, placing two fingers inside me. I cried out, my head rushing, my hands clutching the sheets under me. "This is mine. You may not be my prisoner any longer, but I still plan on keeping you. So do as I say, Leoni, and let your voice be heard."

I shuddered at his words. I couldn't deny that Riel made me feel secure. He made me feel wanted for all the right reasons. He wanted me for me. Not someone who was a convenience, not someone who could only value me for my gifts. I grasped the strands of his hair, moaning as his lips latched onto me.

His fingers curled, and pleasure rolled through me as I screamed his name. My legs shook, and my hips bucked. I couldn't breathe. I couldn't think as Riel wrung wave after wave of pleasure from me.

Riel peeled my fingers from his head, my hands shaking as he crawled over me. I reached for him, wrapping my arms around his broad back, willing him to take me completely. He placed a hard kiss on my lips, his tongue sweeping over mine. I wrapped my legs around his waist, urging him to move faster.

He pulled away and removed his pants, shifting back over me. He tucked a curl behind my ear, gazing down.

"I can't explain this connection, but I want you more than anything I have ever wanted before." My heart skipped because I had similar feelings, but I was apparently doing a much better job of hiding it. "Do you want this too?"

His eyes shone with vulnerability and an aching need sank into my core. I did want this. Riel was the one thing I coveted more than anything, and the one thing I could never steal.

I wanted Riel. I wanted him, and I wanted to be his. He offered for me to be his while still providing for my people. It was more than I could have ever dreamed of. I forced myself to push away the niggling self-doubt that crept into my head.

This couldn't last.

He isn't a good fit for you.

You have more important things to worry about right now.

I banished those thoughts and took what I truly desired.

"Yes," I breathed, and his lips crashed into mine. One word was all it took. One word for Riel to give himself to me. He slid into me, filling me and stretching me. He shuddered and moaned. The whole world fell away. Just like our first kiss, nothing existed except us. But this time was more intense. More tangible.

His hips moved slowly against mine, our bodies colliding. He pinned my arms above me. Each thrust was like new stars were born and they shined only for us. I closed my eyes, and he peppered my skin with soft kisses down my neck and across my clavicle. I shivered.

In all the times I had been intimate with someone, nothing compared to the devotion that Riel was showing me. I could feel his intent with each thrust, each kiss, each caress of his hands as they moved down my body. My mind had tried to conjure the feeling of Riel inside of me, but it was nothing compared to the real thing. It was everything I wanted and needed and more.

Pleasure crashed over me and I was long gone from the real world. Riel had me at his mercy and I loved it. I pushed him off of me, flipping him to his back. The new angle made me gasp for my breath. He filled me so much, and I moaned from the fullness. He groaned as I ground on him, and I felt complete with him inside of me.

Riel dug his fingers into my hips and started lifting me up and down at a rapid pace. I could feel my climax edging closer, and I lost myself in Riel's arms as he snaked one around me, and used his other hand to circle my clit. I cried as my pleasure overflowed, my legs shaking around Riel's thighs. He shuddered underneath me, falling to the throes of his own pleasure as he whispered my name repeatedly.

I collapsed on top of his chest, Riel's fingers intertwining with my hair. We lay together, panting and basking in the afterglow. Riel's arms wrapped around me and pulled me closer into his chest, holding me, caring for me. He drifted his hands over my skin and trailed his soft lips along my temple as he held me tight, like he never wanted to let me go again.

Chapter 14

I ROUSED SLEEPILY IN Riel's arms. The sun was cascading through the window in the room, hitting Riel's face, and I took a moment to appreciate the glow of his brown skin, the shape of his full lips. We had napped until late afternoon.

He was warm and comforting, and his smoky scent enveloped me and I didn't want to get up. But I was technically free now, and I wanted to exercise a little of it. I lifted my hand and watched as I coated it in my magic, letting it disappear from my vision, and grinned. My heart leapt, and I was eager to stretch my so-called magical legs.

I shifted in Riel's arms, his muscles flexing in resistance, and I sighed at how peaceful he looked in sleep. His frown was gone, and a small smile played on his lips. I could have watched him sleep forever, but my eagerness to slink around the Quarters won out. I hadn't explored as much as I wanted to, and I was dying to know what sort of secrets Riel kept in his home.

Riel peeked his eyes open as I removed myself from his embrace.

"Where are you going?" he asked languidly. The sunlight shined over his dark skin as he wiped the sleep away from his face. I camouflaged myself and his eyes widened as I disappeared.

Removing my magic, I laughed, and he wrapped his hands around my middle and pulled me onto him before I could escape.

"I was going to sneak around your house and find every dirty little secret you have," I answered honestly.

He chuckled in my ear, sending a shockwave of goosebumps over my skin. "The thief wants to know how I live?"

I buried my face in his neck, enjoying the smell of his skin and the feel of stubble on his cheek. "Mhm. I'm going to find out everything about you."

Riel sat up, taking me with him. "Well, why don't I give you a real tour? Then you can slink around all you like."

I sat up straight over him. "You would let me do that?"

"Did I not tell you that your sentence is over?" He smiled. I got off of him and starting putting my clothes back on.

"Can I go home then? I'd like to say hello to everyone." And if I happened to meet Devland along the way, I could warn him about his accidental involvement...

Riel's smile dropped and his gaze didn't meet my eyes.

"I would prefer if you would stay here for the time being. Until we can find Devland and solve this mystery of the artifacts and drugs, it would be safer for you to stay."

Devland's name made me swallow thickly. It reminded me once again of how right now, our goals were aligned, but my loyalties were still with my family, and Devland too.

I crossed my arms over my chest and bit my lip. "Devland is innocent, I know it."

"You don't know it. And he certainly isn't innocent." Riel shot me a frustrated look while dressing himself and sighed. "Come on, let me show you around."

He took my hand and tugged me into the hallway. He pointed to the door across the way.

"You've already seen my room." He looked down at me, his eyes full of mirth. I allowed myself to release a huff of a laugh. "Maybe you'll see more of it soon?"

"I don't know," I replied with a smirk on my face. "It seems a little stuffy and boring in there. All of those books."

Riel whipped around and dragged me into his arms. He pushed me against the wall, my wrists locked by his hands above my head.

His chest pressed against mine and my breath caught. His eyes darkened down on me with a sideways grin.

"Too stuffy with all the books you say?" His gaze moved down my body like he could see me there now, wearing nothing on his bed before him.

"Too boring?" His touch heated through me and I bit my lip in return, feeling the evidence of his arousal pressed against me. My core tightened, and I took in a ragged breath. "I distinctly remembering hearing some very erotic noises from your room after the last time you ventured into my room."

My face grew hot, and I squirmed under his piercing gaze. He smiled down at me with a playful smirk.

"Y-you heard that?" I stammered. My embarrassment reached an all-time high, and I couldn't help the nervous giggle that escaped my lips.

"Oh, I heard it, Leoni." He pressed his lips to my ear, his breath brushing against my skin. My skin immediately pebbled, and my nipples hardened under the soft tunic I wore.

"I replayed those noises countless times, wishing I could hear you make them with no barriers between us. Stroking myself to my name on your lips."

"Looks like you got what you wanted," I breathed.

"Oh, I did." He smirked at me, but then pulled away. The cool air rushing between us jolting me from my desire.

"But like you said, only stuffy old books in that room." He shrugged, his face in a frown but amusement in his eyes. I cleared my throat, my face no doubt reddening.

"If we go into that room, I'll never get my house tour," I whined. "And as much as I like knowing you in the bed, I would very much like to know you outside of it, too."

"Fine," Riel relented, and I immediately missed his body over mine as he tugged me further down the hall.

"This is my personal study." I lifted an eyebrow at him while he swung the door open, revealing a cozy space that was entirely different from his office downstairs. Warm light trickled through the room as the last rays of the sun settled over Aurum. Personal touches of artwork lined the walls, and worn books sat on shelves. I held in a laugh at just how much this man liked to read. At the back was a couch with soft cushions, and at the center was a table with four chairs.

"Riel, this is a beautiful room." I turned to find him standing with his eyes gleaming and a smile on the corner of his lips.

"Thank you," he said. "I decorated it myself. I decorated the entire house, actually."

Pride emanated from him and I smirked. He had a natural talent. Much like Masika's eye for fashion, he had one in interior design. I held back an impressed laugh and turned to the bookshelf. I brushed the spines with my fingers when I saw a familiar title and pulled it out. *Insights to the Great Divine.*

Helen was reading this book when Seraph died. I flipped through the pages until I saw the familiar words swimming before me.

"Have you read this?" I asked Riel with excitement.

"I've read most of these books," he answered. He put his hands in his pockets and strode behind me, my back meeting his chest.

"You like history?" I peered up at him. He wore a soft smile that made my stomach swoop.

"I like history. And mythology." He pulled the book from my hands and read over the pages himself. He let out a low laugh.

"Soulmates?" he asked with his brow lifted.

I huffed a laugh. "One of my sisters was reading this book. She said that the gods bestowed Magi the gift of Soulmates. That there is a bond that snaps into place when they find each other, but I've never heard anything like that." I shrugged.

I placed the book back on the shelf. Riel was quiet behind me. I turned, giving him a questioning look. "What? Do you believe that nonsense?"

He shrugged and went to sit back on the couch. "It could be possible. Many things disappeared with the gods."

"Like the Dragon Riders in Ambrose."

He nodded his head and beckoned me to sit next to him. Our legs pressed together, and I bathed in the small contact.

"Do you play games?" He picked up a deck of cards that was sitting on the small table next to the couch.

"Depends on the game," I teased with a playful smile.

"Ever played Fox Hunt?" he asked with a gleam in his eye.

I shook my head. Riel shuffled the cards, his deft fingers graceful against the cardstock.

"I'll place a card down, and then tell you what it is, and you have to place the next higher card on top of it. To make your play, you need to put the card of your choosing face down. If you don't have the right card, you will have to lie. If you get caught in a lie, you have to pick up the pile. The first person out wins."

"Sounds simple enough," I laughed. Riel was beaming, and I could tell that he really loved playing these card games.

I reminded him, "Don't forget you're playing against a renowned thief that has lived on a pirate ship. I doubt you'll be able to beat me."

"And don't you forget, Leoni," my name rolled off his tongue, deep and lustful, and I shivered, "that I am the one in charge of finding and delivering justice to thieves and pirates." Riel's threats were no longer fear inducing, and instead I found myself clenching my thighs together.

He dealt us the cards, and I looked at my hand. None of my cards matched. I watched Riel attentively as he plucked out a single card and laid it face down.

"I'll make this easy for you. Two of cups." He smirked and leaned back, pushing his leg to touch mine. It was only a small amount of contact, but desire pulsed through me. I shook my head. Why did Riel affect me so much? I had a burning need for him like never before, and I was ready to throw the cards off the table and let him take me right now.

I bit my lip and put my card on top of his. "Three of coins."

He gave me a scrutinizing look, as if trying to determine if I was lying. He smiled with mischief and laid out another card. "Four of wands."

I glanced down at my hand. He may have been telling the truth, but I needed a five of something and I had nothing. I pulled out a card and placed it down.

"Five of swords." I said with a slight shrug. Riel's hand drifted over mine before gently clasping my wrist.

"You're lying." He moved my hand and flipped over, revealing the seven of swords.

I laughed nervously. "How did you know?"

"You wear everything on that pretty face of yours."

I scoffed. "I do not! I have a great bluffing face, thank you very much."

"No you don't, Leoni." Riel laughed a contagious laugh, and I joined him.

"Okay, fine. How about if I do this?" I released my magic and let it drift over my head so that it was completely invisible, but my body remained.

Riel's face twisted in horror. "That is the most bizarre and terrifying thing I have ever seen." He was right. Perhaps there was a story about a headless person who snuck into homes in the middle of the night.

"You execute people—brutally, I might add—and you can't bear a headless woman in front of you?" My words echoed around the room, and I had to stop myself from laughing. I could only imagine what Riel was thinking. His face paled, revealing his fear for the first time in my experience. I shoved him playfully and his mouth opened, aghast.

"Please, Leoni." He shuddered. "Bring your head back. I can't look at your headless body." He was staring at the place where my head should have been. His eyes blinked rapidly, and he shook his head like he couldn't believe my head was gone.

"What in the Realm of Darkness is going on in here?" Chefren's voice called as he and Masika strolled in. Chefren carried a bag of what looked to be food, looking amused at my headless figure, and Masika shifted her eyes between us in confusion. I lifted my shadows from my face while laughing.

"Riel said I don't have a bluffing face, so I fixed the problem."

"Nearly giving him a heart attack in the process," Chefren chuckled. "What are you playing?" He sat himself down at the round table.

"Fox Hunt. Have you played it before?" I asked, while Riel started gathering the cards. Masika shook her head.

"No. I am not playing Fox Hunt with a mind reader." She pointed to Chefren, and I couldn't help the smile that pulled at my lips. Chefren gasped in mock outrage.

"I would never sour our game nights with my magic powers." He threw me a quick wink, and I laughed, feeling for the first time completely comfortable in their presence. Masika and Chefren started bickering while Riel stood up and beckoned me to join them at the table. Chefren passed out each of us a plate, which he piled high with the delightful food he brought.

I drank in the camaraderie between the three of them. It warmed my heart, but I also felt a pang of jealousy. I never had this kind of relationship with anyone. Devland was sure to keep an arm's length away from anyone getting too close, and he sure didn't appreciate jibes that went against his power. I didn't even feel Masika's magic in the room; we were all relaxed and laughing with each other.

The more I thought about their happiness, the more I felt like an outsider. I wasn't made to work with others. I spent my entire life in the shadows, working by myself for myself. Devland understood that. He gave me my space to figure things out on my own. As much as I felt like I had an innate pull to Riel, in this moment, I saw all of our stark differences.

A foot hit my leg, and I flinched back in my chair. I looked around the table and met Masika's gaze. Her eyes widened and her face turned beet red.

"Sorry," she apologized with a laugh, biting her lip shifting her gaze to Chefren, who stared down at his food, his face reddening as well. I raised my eyebrow and looked at Riel, who was conveniently distracted by pulling out a small box and placing it on the table.

"Let's play some dominoes." Riel poured the contents of the box on the table in front of us. Dominoes clanked against each other as he shuffled them around.

We each took turns picking up dominoes and laying them out. Chefren made snide remarks to Riel, and Masika would reprimand him for cheating. Whether he was cheating or not didn't matter. I found myself smiling so hard my cheeks hurt.

"Your turn, Leoni." Masika pointed at the sprawling dominoes that were forming a weirdly shaped mess of lines on the table. I frowned, looking for any options that I could use to make my next play. I only had one domino left, but I needed its match to win.

Grinning, I spotted the perfect piece and laid my last domino on the table.

"I win!" I laughed as the others grumbled their disappointment. Masika and Chefren stood from the table.

"Good game, Leoni." Riel's eyes glimmered as he regarded me.

Masika yawned, and Chefren ushered her into the hallway.

"I'll walk you home, Masika." Chefren said and then turned to us. "Goodnight, you two. Don't do anything I wouldn't." And with another wink, they were gone.

Riel and I walked through the hall in comfortable silence. He gazed down at me with heat in his eyes.

"That was fun." I hedged as we paused in between our rooms. Riel hummed an agreement.

"So, Masika and Chefren?" I asked, clearly noticing how they looked at each other, and I didn't think Masika's foot against my leg was a complete accident. It just wasn't meant for me.

"I don't know what you're talking about," Riel smirked. He brushed his hand against mine and I grasped it, interlocking our fingers. "They think I haven't noticed, so I just pretend to look the other direction until it either becomes a problem or they decide to make things more official."

"And you really don't care if they know about us?" I asked, knowing that they already knew, especially because who knows what Chefren had seen or heard in our thoughts? Riel took me by the chin and angled my face up to meet his lips. He kissed me tenderly, making my stomach flip.

"I don't care what they think in the slightest." He brushed his lips along my chin and over my collarbone, placing a trail on kisses along my neck, and I arched into his touch.

"Stay with me tonight. I promise the stuffy, boring room would be much more comfortable with you in it." I tried to hide the grimace that moved over my face, wondering if I should just hide my head in shadows again.

Moving into Riel's room felt like a leap and an intrusion. Like, if I slept in his bed, then I really would be beholden to the Aurum government. Maybe it was my pride, but I didn't want that. I was still a girl of the South District, and no amount of words or orgasms would change that.

Riel and I were like fire and ice. Two opposing forces capable of burning. It hadn't been more apparent than it was tonight when he was playing games with his colleagues—his friends.

"I—"

Riel lifted his head from my neck and his brow pinched at my hesitation.

"It's alright, Leoni. You don't have to," he said, and I breathed a sigh of relief. "I'll just stay in your room instead." He laughed.

I went to protest, but he swung the door open behind me, and then his mouth crashed into mine. Our lips and tongues danced with each other, sending sparks of need through me. I fisted his tunic, trying to tear it off of him. If Riel was Dragon's Breath, I was addicted, and no amount of reason could stop me from falling into his brawny arms.

RIEL WAS SLEEPING SOUNDLY with deep, steady breaths. I lay next to him in the guest bedroom with my heart in my throat. My body was still sated from the earth-shattering moments Riel had given me, but my heart was shearing into two.

Despite my fear of being on Devland's list of people to eliminate, my loyalties to him persisted. I felt like I needed to ask him myself how his name got involved with a bunch of drug dealers. He needed to affirm his innocence. More than that, though, I had to tell him he was unintentionally involved in something bigger than his usual exploits.

I slid out of the covers quietly. The black clothes that Masika had gotten me were clean and folded on the desk and I grabbed them with deft hands.

Technically, I was free. If Riel had remained true to his word, I was no longer a prisoner, so I was free to do as I pleased, but a pit still formed in the bottom of my stomach. With one last lingering look at Riel, I mouthed a quiet apology before slipping out the bedroom.

By the time I was halfway out the front door and shoving on a dark cloak, conflicting emotions swirled within me. My gut turned, but it needed to be done. This was the right thing to do.

With a quick check in, I confirmed that my magic was full and pulsing under my skin. I could return before dawn. How often had I snuck into homes with no problem? If luck was on my side tonight,

Riel would be none the wiser. As much as I didn't want to keep secrets from him, it was for the best.

With one heavy breath, I called my magic forward, feeling the familiar rush of the shadows sink over my skin. Having my full power back made me breathe easier. It felt like a well-loved blanket's comfort. I let it trickle out slowly. Less magic meant that I would be more visible, but it would pace my usage for me to access it later.

I jogged across the property, breathed in the night air, sparing one last glance at the house. Letting Devland take the fall was the easy solution. But it was short-sighted. I would have to deal with his consequences later. So, no. I needed to find Devland, warn him, and slip right back into bed. My one last act as a thieving criminal.

Exiting the house was simple. However, my heart started racing as I made my way to the docks.

Running through shadows, that was what I knew, what I thrived on. So why did this feel so wrong?

Stone paths turned into dirt roads, which eventually turned into the wooden planks of the docks. Salt and brine permeated the air, and I breathed in the familiar scent. I willed my magic to flow freely, encapsulating me completely in shadow.

The docks were quiet. A small group of three shared a pipe while only a few others loitered. I walked freely. With my shadows, I was confident that I couldn't be seen. I looked out to the ocean, and sure enough, *The Devil's Serpent*'s white sails sat on the horizon like distant clouds. That meant Devland was most likely visiting his favorite tavern, not far from the docks.

I turned a corner into a dark alley, hoping for a shortcut, when I was stopped short by two masses shrouded in cloaks in front of me. Shrinking against the wall, I was close enough to hear the words being exchanged.

"I can pay you whatever you require. Tell me where the drugs are located." The first figure was tall, and his voice was low and familiar, but I couldn't place where I heard it before.

"I can't tell you," the second figure's voice was a harsh frantic whisper. "But I can show you."

"Even better."

I could hear the sneer that the first figure held. I stood in stunned silence. Devland was probably at the tavern, but finding the drugs with the help of these two would give me more info for Riel and stop the distribution.

I grimaced as I weighed my options. If I could clear Devland's name, then there wouldn't be a need to investigate him, and we would be closer to catching the source. A double victory. The moon wasn't at its apex yet, so I could follow the two, find the drugs, and return home in time.

I followed the figures through the alley and across the docks. They walked to the beach, where golden sands met the deep blue waters of the sea. Moonlight lit the path, and I cursed. The lack of shade weakened my shadows. I called my magic, willing it to coat me further. I would have to follow from a distance. If I got too close, I risked exposing myself.

They left large footsteps in the sand behind them, and I carefully followed their exact path, leaving no trace of my own feet in the sand. The sea breeze moved through the sand, whipping loose pebbles across my face. I followed as they turned around a large boulder. The boulder blocked some of the moonlight, and I crouched behind it and hid among the shadows.

Tied to a rickety post, halfway breached on the sand, was a small dinghy. I peered at the sea beyond it, but no larger vessels were in the area.

"Take this boat to the ship. You'll find...them...there." Small hands darted out from his cloak and wrung themselves, "And now, my payment?"

"Which ship?" The other figure demanded as he wrestled something on his side. The fidgety figure shook his head and pointed. I sucked in a breath. He pointed at the white sails beyond...*The Devil's Serpent*. I stopped breathing, unable to believe it. Pins and needles stung my fingers.

Was Captain Devland behind the drug ring? Would he actually subvert the peace of Aurum and corrupt the oppressed for a hefty payday? I swallowed the rage and disbelief I felt bubbling inside my blood.

An unsheathing of a sword startled me from my thoughts.

"Sir, what is this?" the fidgety one whimpered.

"The payment," he swiped the sword across the man's neck. I clutched my hand over my nose and mouth, bile threatening to come up from the back of my throat. A copper tang filled the air, and the sands sizzled with red blood. "For your crimes, is death."

The man sheathed his sword and removed his hood. Black hair, dark as a raven, fluttered in the sea breeze. Kasiel. I held back a hiss. The assassin that spared my life once stood a stone's throw away from me. He looked as lethal as his reputation, with his sharp features now speckled with blood.

Only a truly mad person would try to follow him, but what choice did I have? I needed to get to *The Devil's Serpent*. I needed to confirm if Devland was responsible for Aurum's chaos. What was the point of turning around now?

I made to move around the boulder, but I was stuck. My ankles wouldn't budge. I tugged until a fine sheen of sweat broke over my forehead, but an invisible shackle held them there. I looked up. The man with black hair, one long, thick scar running down the side of his face, turned to me. The moonlight only made him deadly and ruthless.

"I know you're there. Show yourself."

Chapter 15

I REVEALED MY HOODED face and body. Kasiel ripped the hood off my head and wrapped a loose red curl around his finger. I glared at him through my eyelashes, conveying that I was not afraid of him, even if my racing heart was telling a different story.

"You just couldn't stay away." His lips turned into an amused smile, his eyes predatory in the moonlight.

"I'm going with you." I jutted my chin out. "Let me loose, and I won't cause a scene."

Kasiel's eyes flickered over me, appraising me. "I knew I was going to regret letting you live, but...fine." He waved his hand. His magic unbound me. As soon as it released, wind surrounded my entire body and shoved me towards the dinghy.

My feet splashed in the wet sand and sloshed water against my boots. Kasiel quickly following. I looked back in the direction of the city, making my final decision. Kasiel's magic eased, and he leaned toward me.

"If you go back now, I won't mention this. I rarely let sneaks go, but this job is risky. If you prefer not to get your hands dirty, you can go back to your general."

I hardened my resolve. "No, let's go." I reached for the oar.

"No need." With one wave of his hand, the wind kicked up around us. The boat propelled itself along the water, Kasiel's eyes pinned on *The Devil's Serpent*.

As usual, the night was clear. No clouds drifted past the moon. Stars twinkled brightly next to it. I gazed up, taking in the swathing purple and blue clusters, praying that I would find answers.

We neared the ship, and I let my magic wash over me once again. Kasiel watched me with a bored expression as I became invisible.

"Neat trick," he said. I only scoffed. "What's the plan?"

"Plan?" I laughed. "I didn't have a plan. I was trying to find Captain Devland, but I came across you instead."

"Then stay out of my way. Find what you need, but I work alone." His voice was clipped and sharp.

"Fine, and don't use your wind magic against me." I replied through my teeth. Kasiel only raised his eyebrow and let a sly grin play on his lips. It pulled his scar up, flashing venom in his gaze. I shuddered. He was terrifying.

Anxiety prickled in my neck. My lack of planning left my mind reeling. Once I got onto the ship, I would have to look for the drugs. I would figure out what came next after. I grimaced. One thing was certain: I would have to ensure this rowboat didn't leave without me.

The boat floated up to the ship on silent and still water. Kasiel wasted no time in climbing up, leaving me by myself. I heaved myself up on the deck, keeping my feet soft and my grunts low. I kept myself shrouded in shadows along the cabin walls and under sails.

A few men lingered on the deck, clinking ales, dealing cards. Every one of them was unaware of both Kasiel and myself. I spotted a ladder that would take me below deck. If anything, drug related was on this ship, that's where I would find it.

As I descended, I smelled the familiar scent of sage and followed it. Sure enough, shouts and sounds of brawling reverberated from the lower decks. Maybe Kasiel wasn't trying to hide at all.

I practically leaped over the ladder. Narrow steps slid out from under my feet, but my hands caught on the wall before I fell. I rarely went to the lower decks. It was a storage for Devland's transports, and typically, the less I knew about that, the better. But I also knew how much he usually transported, and this was stocked much, much more full than usual.

I gasped. Boxes and boxes were stacked next to and on top of each other, creating a maze. Grunts and shouting led to where Kasiel was currently sparring with a pirate. The pirate he sparred against looked worse for wear, blood trickling out of cuts and what looked to be a broken nose. I winced when Kasiel blew a final blow to the pirate's ribs. The pirate crumpled onto the ground. Kasiel gave him an extra kick for good measure, sending blood arcing onto one of the nearby crates.

"I thought I told you to stay away," he sneered, wiping the sweat off his brow.

I removed my magic with an easy thought. "It seems our goals align."

I eyed the crates, running my hand over the rough wood. Wedging my fingers into the top of a crate, I tore it apart and sucked in a breath.

"Are all of these crates Dragon's Breath?" I asked. Muslin bags stuffed to the brim with light-blue powder were piled high in the crate. I turned and opened another crate. More drugs. I opened another and another. Bags and bags and bags of blue powder sat inside. I grasped the box with white knuckles. My head spun. How much was this amount of drugs even worth? I couldn't fathom even trying to sell this much of it...but when people were addicted—

Footsteps came closer, but I didn't hear them through the pounding heartbeat in my ears.

"Get down!" Kasiel whispered. He crouched low, listening and watching, while I called my magic back. My heart hammered in my throat and ears. I knew the intruder couldn't see me, but I was still shaking from the discovery.

I should have stayed with Riel, kept ringing in my ear, but it was too late now. Devland wasn't just involved, he was the source. I couldn't even count the number of crates that sat on the lower deck. Flashes of Seraph dead in the street flooded my mind, and I saw red. Rage took over my senses, my magic pulsing with my heartbeat.

"If it isn't the Assassin of the Seaside Cliffs. Tell me, what do I owe the pleasure of having you on my ship?" a husky voice called out. It was a voice that I knew well. Captain James Devland strutted forward. He faced Kasiel, completely at ease and confident. I ground my teeth so hard they threatened to crack. How could he do this? I knew he was greedy, but this was too far.

Kasiel drew his blade with lethal grace. I stood, shrouded by shadow, invisible to everyone but myself. Devland had given me an opportunity. Devland had partnered with me, treated me like an equal. He taught me how to negotiate, how to find the best places to rob. He saved me countless times. He had my back. And now to see him stand in front of me, in front of these drugs—

Rage poured through me. I stepped out of the shadows and let my magic disappear.

"Explain this, Devland." I couldn't stop the tears from streaming down my cheeks. Devland's eyes widened when I revealed myself.

"Leoni." He schooled his face into a cocky smirk. "What are you doing here?"

"What is all of this?" I repeated. Kasiel seemed to be done with the conversation and jumped towards Devland, his blade slicing through the air with an electrifying zing. I watched in horror, but Devland sidestepped him.

Watching Devland fight was always a spectacle. He was graceful and brutal, his fists containing lethal strength. Watching him fight in close quarters was intoxicating. Kasiel was an even match. Swing for swing, they rounded each other, and neither one landed a blow. Kasiel would swing his sword, narrowly missing the crates, and Devland would dodge or use the crates to his advantage. It was a dance of death.

Kasiel swung, his blade nicked on a wooden beam, and he stumbled. A rush of air blew past, attempting to right his mistake, but as though his magic was draining, he faltered. I sucked in a breath. He must have used most of his magic to get the boat to the ship. Devland didn't miss the opportunity and swung his fist, his arm muscles corded and tight, straight into Kasiel's temple.

Kasiel slumped to the ground, his body still. I wasn't close enough to tell if he was breathing. My heart raced, threatening to beat out of my chest. I needed to leave, but Devland stood between me and the only exit.

I called my magic. It trickled over me, and I didn't give it a second thought as I sprinted past Devland. Devland, however, was quicker. His hand shot out, grabbing my half-shrouded wrist, and slapped a piece of metal over it. I felt an instant draining. I looked down. I was completely visible. Weariness and exhaustion settled over my bones.

"Devland? Why?" My voice cracked as I peered up at him, his face grim.

"Wrong place, wrong time, love." My legs gave out, and Devland caught me under my arms. "You never were a good listener, and now you have to pay the price for your stubbornness."

DEVLAND SHOVED ME INTO the ship's holding cell. A layer of dust coated the floors, which shifted with my stumbling steps. I looked at the bracelet Devland slapped on me through heavy eyes. Swaying to stand upright, I lifted the piece of gold in the flickering light of the deck.

It wasn't as intricate as the one that Riel gave me, but the markings were the same. I realized the markings bound the magic to them, and I cursed. How Devland got his hands on these, I had no idea. As far as I knew, the cuffs were only available to Aurum's patrol. I fell to my knees, hissing as I tumbled onto the wooden planks.

I might have been able to negate the magic. I searched for a loose nail or a piece of plywood, but the bracelet weighed on me. My eyes drooped and my head lolled. Much like having a few too many drinks, my body just wanted to succumb to sleep. I couldn't let that happen, no matter what.

The cell door swung open, and someone threw another body next to me. Kasiel's black hair spilled onto the floor like a dark halo. I rolled him over, my muscles protesting, and checked for his pulse.

He was still alive. I sighed a breath of relief. He also had a bracelet on, identical to mine. Godsdammit. We needed to get out and off the ship. I tugged at the roots of my hair hard enough for it to sting.

How long until Devland left Aurum? Would he kill us and then toss our bodies to the sea? Would he make us walk the plank in the middle of the ocean with nowhere left to go?

I shook my head. Those were problems I would have to face later. I gripped Kasiel's arm, anchoring myself. My head was light, and my body was heavy. I could feel the pull of sleep reeling me in. It was inevitable.

Chapter 16

My head was pounding in the same rhythm that a loud metal clank kept ringing over my head. I peeled my eyes open, unsure of my surroundings. Memories came crashing in...I shot up to my feet, stumbling to the wall behind me.

I looked up to only be met with metal bars and Devland's muddy brown eyes. He had a crowbar and was dragging it across the cell bars. Kasiel's body was still slumped on the ground.

"Cut it out, Devland," I snapped at him. He turned his gaze toward me and stalked toward where I stood.

"Leoni." He purred my name like he often did when I pleased him, but now it only taunted me. His hand reached through the bars. I barely had enough room in the small cell to cringe away from him.

"How could you?" I asked. "You're messing with people's lives! You know how dangerous this shit is."

Devland threw the crowbar down with a loud clank. I recoiled from the noise and he clutched the cell bars in front of me. His rings glinted in the low light. His knuckles were white, the only indication of his simmering anger. He shrugged. He motioned to the crates behind him.

"High demand, high prices, and most importantly, loyal repeat customers." He grinned, a grin that I knew well. One that meant he thought he had the upper hand.

"What good are the customers when they wind up dead?" I hissed.

He chuckled. "My dear, that's why I've been cutting it." He opened a bag of Dragon's Breath and sifted his hands through it. The powder filtered through his palms like sand. "I get the pure form and dilute it. It's just enough to get people hooked, but not enough to kill them."

He turned to me, dusting his hands off. "Don't you see? It's perfectly safe. I'm not outright killing anyone." He gave me a small smile, but it felt like goopy oil sliding down my neck. "And if one or two consume too much and die, now that's not my fault." He stretched his arms through the bars again. I pressed myself against the wall, but it wasn't enough.

The cell was too small, the bars too close. His hand grasped my chin, his thumb rolling over my lower lip. Some of the powder had transferred, and I tried not to lick my lips.

Devland clicked his tongue. "Now, why don't you be a good girl and come with me." His gaze slid down to my wrist. The bracelet weighed heavier under his watchful eye. "You don't have any magic, and I would have taken all of your weapons. But you didn't have any...which was a mistake, Leoni. You know better." I glowered at him.

Devland opened the cell and grabbed my arms. He dragged me from the cell, his hands clamped in my hair. His grasp pulled hard enough to bring tears to my eyes. He shoved me across the ship and into his personal cabin.

"You should have left me in the cell, Devland," I sneered. He shoved me further into the small room, and I tripped and fell in front of his desk. I tried to push myself up, but my arms were weak and my body was heavy.

Devland crouched down next to me, and my defiance wavered for one moment. His familiar face now felt so foreign. Gone was my former friend, my former lover, and instead stood the brutal pirate lord. I should have been frightened. I should have been cowering, but I was livid. He killed Seraph. Devland stood and went to his liquor cabinet and poured himself a drink.

I took notice of his cabin. It was filled with precious items—the same items that had been on the list of stolen relics. The worth of these precious artifacts in one place had heart beating in my ears. I should have known. My eyes settled on the vase I held before, and I gasped. He had told me he was collecting these, but why?

"I tried to warn you, Leoni. I really did," he took a long drink, "but you just had to try to steal the diadem. I knew they were looking for you. I knew the whole thing was a setup. So, what did I do?"

Black boots stomped into my vision, and he bent down before me. The smell of whiskey filled my nose.

"I tried to tell you to leave it alone. You should have listened when I told you to leave, but no. You had to stay. For your precious orphans." He laughed low and void of humor. "I thought for sure that The General would kill you. But I guess you fucked your way out of that one, too. Loyalty, my ass. I practically raised you, I gave you endless opportunity, and this is how you repay me? By fucking Aurum's General and turning me in?"

"I didn't turn you in, Devland," I spat.

"Save your fucking breath. I have eyes everywhere." Devland turned to his desk. He rummaged around in a small box before turning back to me. He grabbed my face, pinching the hollows of my cheeks until it hurt. I looked into those brown eyes and tried to discern the James Devland I knew from the man before me now.

Every tender moment, every pleasant memory had been wiped with his rage. His eyes glazed over, the brown glimmering with a reflection of my own.

"Stop fighting," he demanded. His voice was thick with coercion and I felt the magic settle through my limbs. I willed my arms to move, for myself to kick at him, but they were useless. I fought harder until sheering pain tore through my muscles, and I screamed.

"Stop," Devland demanded again. My body limped at his command. Devland's grip loosened, and he wiped my cheek with his thumb. Devland would pay for this. I noticed that his order wasn't that I couldn't fight him, eventually. I would survive this, and I would fight him. My heart hammered in my chest as I pictured Devland dying by my hand. I hated bloodshed, but like I told him once before—there were always exceptions.

"Why?" I hissed out. "Where are the relics going? How are you doing this?"

Devland chuckled with malice.

"The King of the mortal lands has a great need for those relics, and in return, he supplies me with expensive blue powder. Aurum just so happens to be the city that harbors the greatest amount of artifacts. Pieces held in the homes of the rich, the extensive temples and museums. It's easy pickings in Aurum, and convenient enough to get them back to the King." He spared himself a look around at all the old pieces of history. His eyes gleamed with greed. Devland shrugged nonchalantly. "Even the Lord doesn't seem to miss them much. Pity, they are beautiful."

"And Lord Eduard, is he in on this, too?" I asked, with venom lacing each word.

Devland laughed, full of wickedness. "No. He's not, but his own desire to make his life as dull as possible made my endeavor easier. He is a naïve idiot. Artifacts like these mean nothing to him."

He took one last look at the riches that filled his cabin before he turned back to me and scowled.

"Oh, Leoni." He opened the small box, revealing the blue powder. He scooped some on his finger and shoved it in my mouth. I screamed and kicked, but it was no use. The drugs were in my mouth, in my system. My body relaxed instantly.

As the Dragon's Breath made its way into my system, I strained to keep my eyes open. I internally fought the effects, feeling my mind fog over. It wasn't entirely unpleasant, but I didn't want to fall to the drug.

"You really should have listened."

EUPHORIA ENVELOPED MY SENSES. I touched my cheek. Why was it wet? Had I been crying? Captain Devland stood over me, and I was so angry at him...but why? I shook my head. My thoughts were cloudy, but surely Devland and I weren't fighting. I gave him a smile. There was a soft glow around him.

"Devland, you look like a god." My mouth felt thick, my tongue too big. I laughed, trying to roll my tongue in my mouth. Everything felt fuzzy and warm. Loose giggles left my mouth when two arms braced under mine, lifting me up. My head lolled, and I couldn't put any weight on my legs or feet. It was silly; I felt like a sea anemone drifting along the ocean's current.

"I'm no god, sweetheart." He dragged me through doors and out into the open. The cool sea air met my skin like a kiss. I drew in a deep breath, basking in the breeze. Devland moved me into a small boat that was tied along the hull of the ship. I sat, wobbling back and forth, trying to keep myself upright. Devland swung his legs over and boarded. A funny-looking man with a seriously impressive mustache lowered us into the water.

"Captain!" another voice called, and I looked up. There was one of Devland's pirates, or was it two? They looked the same...I shook my head, and there was only one. "Captain! He's gone! The men guarding him are dead!"

Devland growled at the pirate. "He can't have gone far. Go. Find. Him."

"Why are you so mad?" I gave him pleading eyes.

"Shut the fuck up, Leoni."

I crossed my arms over my chest and huffed and looked out at the horizon. The horizon was stunning, and the moon lit up the vast ocean. It was glossy and black, reflecting the night sky.

Devland rowed us to shore, parking the boat on the soft golden sands. My only desire was to touch the sand, let my hands run through it, let it fall over my face. I wanted to feel every pebble run down and sift over my skin. I stared at that sand for what felt like eons until rough hands picked me up.

The sky was lightening now, early morning rays turning the sky into a pale blue in the east. Aurum would sleep for another few hours. If I could only get control over my limbs, then I could run. I wanted to skip, I wanted to feel the wind against my skin.

Devland carried me cradled to his chest. I leaned into him, inhaling the familiar scent of tobacco and the sea breeze that clung to his clothes. He made no notice of my contact and kept a steady pace to the main docks. Devland stiffened and stopped. I peered over his shoulder. Not a soul was loitering along the wooden planks.

"Put her here," a low voice directed at Devland. I blinked. Dread encompassed me. I felt like I had heard that voice before, but I couldn't quite place it. My head was swimming, and my body started aching.

Devland slowly put me on the hard wooden planks and propped me up against barrels. His face shifted in front of me, and I started to remember how he shoved me and broke me.

Those crates on his ship... My eyes shot to my wrist, the magical shackle still attached. He frowned as he dug something out of his pocket. I tried to shift away, to scoot back, but my limbs were still numb and I had nowhere to go.

"You nearly destroyed my entire operation, Leoni. And I am not a forgiving man." Devland looked away, and his hand slammed over my mouth. I coughed, blue powder puffing from between his fingers. Devland's hand was firm against my face, and I let in an involuntary swallow.

"This will send a message to your darling General. Don't mess with Captain James Devland." His hand fell from my face, and the universe turned, spiraling. I fell heavily against the planks below me. A hooded figure stepped forward and crouched in front of me.

The hood over him still covered his features, but I thought I saw a flash of green eyes. Those were the eyes that had given me kindness when no one else had. He frowned at me, his face pulled in the wrong direction. He should have been smiling, he was always smiling. My eyelids grew heavy, and I struggled to commit what I saw to memory. My mind was hazy. I couldn't latch onto my own thoughts. But I could have sworn that was Chefren looking down at me.

My mouth was thick. I couldn't form words and the world tilted again. Sharp, stabbing pains in my stomach made me wretch. The drug Devland had given me was too much. Bile rose in the back of my throat, but I couldn't get my muscles to work well enough to vomit.

The men walked away, leaving me here to choke on my own vomit or overdose. My body was too hot and too cold at the same time. I reluctantly tore my eyes from their forms and looked at the sky above me.

Tears streamed down my cheeks. I felt like I was dying. I tried to hold on, to think about anything to keep me going, but I struggled to remember the faces of those I loved. Tala, the children. Their faces muddled and blurry in my mind. Is this how Seraph felt in his last moments? Poor Seraph, he didn't deserve his fate. And it was Devland's fault.

Pain lanced through my body, but I had given up all fight. I wasn't enough. Tala would have to figure out how to run the orphanage without me. The sky above me swirled with its purple clusters.

Pinks and light blues melded in with the darker blues. My pain became pleasure, and I couldn't feel the sharp stabs any longer. Tangible thoughts faded as soon as I thought them. I rolled on my side, expelling all the contents of my stomach. I didn't even feel it.

Riel's face drifted into my vision, and I laughed. What would he think? I betrayed him. He gave me his heart, and I wasted no time in doing exactly what he trusted me not to do. He would hate me in death, and I deserved it.

How I wished I told him that as much as I inspired and challenged him, he did the same thing for me. I yearned to start over—I was going to start over. I wanted him, I wanted it all.

Why had it taken me this long to realize? And now, it was too late. Riel's face stayed in front of me, hazy and swirling with the stars above—a drug-induced hallucination. I should have never denied the pull I felt toward him, and it seemed like the gods above were taunting me for it.

He had the most beautiful honey eyes. Had I told him that before? I wanted to reach out and touch him, even if he wasn't real. Tears streamed down my face. I couldn't move my arms.

I was floating. Pinks and purples and blues and Riel. I was on a soft cloud. Blues and pinks turned into golds and rainbow fragments. I thought I heard a commotion, but I didn't pay attention. I couldn't grasp my thoughts clearly enough to understand.

Only the thoughts in my head and the colors in my vision mattered. Something warm trickled through me, and my vision darkened.

Chapter 17

I PRIED MY EYES open. My body wasn't in pain, but I was beyond exhaustion. My bones felt heavy and laden.

Riel sat across from me, his posture rigid and features tense with anger, hurt, and betrayal. Embarrassment, shame, and a coil of mixed emotions tightened in my chest. I peeled my eyes away from Riel, instead focusing on a loose thread on the bedsheet.

"You're lucky I found you in time," he ground out through his teeth. Palpable tension rolled off of him, threatening my shoulders to buckle under his gaze. Gone was the Riel that had bedded me the night before. The sliver of openness that he had allowed me to see was once again locked tight. I swallowed thickly. My body felt sluggish, but I needed to face Riel. I would not run from him. I would not hide.

"Riel—" I started, but he shot me a glare so sharp it could have cut glass. Slowly, he steepled his hands on his knees and leaned forward, locking his eyes on me. They were burning with the need to understand.

"Why did you do it?" he asked flatly. "And no bullshit. Give me the truth, or you will not walk out of this house. Not unless it's to the underground dungeons, where you will wait for your verdict for betraying Aurum."

I took a deep breath and steadied myself as tears pricked the back of my eyes. Nothing could have prepared me for the anguish that shot through my chest from Riel's threat. It wasn't fear that struck through me, it was heartbreak. After all we had shared, would he really put me back in those dungeons?

"And if you don't like the truth?" I asked. My voice was scratchy and weak. "What happens then?"

Riel leaned back, every bit of him as imposing as if he were towering over me. "That's for me to decide," he said.

I rubbed my palms against the sheets of the bed and blew out a long-winded exhale. I bid my time, choosing my next words carefully.

Riel only stared at me with unblinking eyes as I gathered myself. Not being able to read his facial expressions had me reeling. I had grown accustomed to his small tells, and now they were gone. His face was a blank slate. My heart crumbled, and I inhaled a shaky breath, willing the tears to not fall from my eyes.

"I went to the docks. I overheard Kasiel talking to someone, asking where the drugs were coming from, and I followed." Wringing my hands in my lap, I paused, waiting to gauge Riel's reaction. But he barely even moved.

"I wanted to warn Devland, because I didn't believe he could have been involved with the drugs. I was wrong. So wrong." Riel widened his eyes, but otherwise stayed as still as a statue. "I was trying to protect myself. I didn't want him to think I was the one that sold him out."

Riel stood abruptly. "When I told you I would protect you, in what world did you think I couldn't or wouldn't? Why is it so hard for you to trust me?" He was shouting, unable to keep his rage under wraps. "I am the godsdamned general of Aurum—do you know what that means?"

I met his gaze. What was so cold before now burned with fury.

"It means that no matter what that damned captain did, you would not be laying in the streets awaiting death. Do you think your life is dispensable? Did you even consider the people you would leave behind?"

Tears threatened to escape my eyes. Riel grasped the back of the chair and gripped it so tight that his knuckles were white. He looked down, refusing to meet my gaze.

"You went out knowing full well how dangerous it would be. You followed a deadly assassin to a ship in the middle of the sea that was potentially harboring illegal drugs. Devland was a suspect, and you knew that. And instead of immediately coming back to make a plan, you jumped ahead, nearly getting yourself killed." Riel threw his arms out, his features wild with fury. "You're lucky Kasiel came and woke me up."

"The assassin?" I sat up straight. "Why?"

"Kasiel is brutal, but he still works for the people. He may be an assassin for the Seaside Cliffs, but his true loyalty is to all of Ambrose, and that includes Aurum. Since he already knew we were working together, he came to me as soon as he had escaped." His eyes were wild with betrayal.

"Why did you leave, Leoni? Didn't you trust my word? Everything I said to keep you here wasn't to lock you in, it was to protect you—" he choked on his own words. "To protect you from this exact situation."

I cleared my throat, and this time I couldn't stop the tears from rolling down my cheeks.

"It's not that I don't trust you, Riel." He scoffed, but I barreled on.

"If he was innocent, and you came knocking on his door, he would have blamed me, and hit me where it hurt the worst. He would have gone after the orphanage." I choked back a sob. "While I've never seen him kill children, I have seen him do horrible things. And after last night, I wouldn't put child murder past him." Riel let loose a low growl and stalked around the bed. "I had to see for myself, and I had to reason with him.

"Turns out you were right, though. He has the drugs, Riel. Boxes and boxes of them. And once I found them, he didn't even deny his role. He was happy to poison our people for the sake of making a spare coin—"

A quick knock on the bedroom door interrupted, and Riel strode over and cracked it open. Whoever was on the other side was hushed, and I couldn't make out what they were saying. The door clicked shut and Riel made his way back to me.

"I have some things I need to tend to," he said. "I have to meet with Kasiel and see if there is a way we can find Devland. Now that we know he is the culprit, I have to take action." He turned to leave, but I grasped his wrist just as he was turning. He glanced down at my hand, but he didn't pull away.

"Riel—" I shuddered out a breath, "Chefren is working with him." Riel's eyes widened, but he didn't say a word. "I saw him on the docks. I know it was him."

"Are you sure?" Riel asked, not bothering to hide the shock from his face.

I nodded. "It was. He was telling Devland where to leave me."

Riel stood above me, assessing my words, and frowned. "I need to relay this information. Masika will be here while I'm gone. Otherwise, let your body heal, and please...don't leave."

"I won't," I said, pushing every regretful emotion into my eyes, hoping he would see it. "I promise."

"What's going on?" I asked through sleepy eyes as I padded down the stairs and into the common room. Frantic shouting and crying woke me up from light sleep. I hurriedly put on a robe and darted to see what the commotion was.

Riel and Masika stood face-to-face with each other. Riel wore a deep frown, on the verge of anger, while Masika was clearly upset, tears drying on her cheeks and her chest heaving. My heart broke for her.

"Why would he do this?" she cried. Her long black hair flowed freely around her face, as though she had torn her braid apart in frustration.

"Clearly we never knew Chefren for who he was." Riel shot me a sideways glance, and I was unsure if I was intruding or if I could be of some help.

I wrapped my robe tighter as I took tentative steps toward them. Masika wrapped her arms around her middle, squeezing tight until her knuckles turned white. I reached out toward her, grasping at her shoulders and guiding her down to one of the plush chairs. They must have gotten some sort of confirmation that Chefren was indeed the one I saw on the docks while I was asleep.

"Can you go put on some tea?" I asked Riel with pleading eyes, and he gave me a curt nod before exiting to the kitchen.

"I am so sorry," I told Masika as I kneeled down and gripped her hand in mine. Her eyes were red and puffy, and she bit her lip and shuddered out a deep breath. She wouldn't meet my eye, but she didn't pull away.

"I want to hate you," she said. "It's not fair that you come into our lives and upended everything. I was happy. Chefren and I—" She shook her head. "We were supposed to make things official soon. He said he wanted me to move in with him, and...it was all a lie."

Her puffy eyes met mine, fresh tears lining the edges. "It was all a lie...and I know that isn't your fault, but it doesn't make it any easier. It feels like I should blame somebody, anyone, other than myself for being such a fool." I squeezed her hand in reassurance. Riel came back with a cup of tea for Masika. He handed it to her, and she let go of my grip before sighing and reclining back into the chair.

"You aren't a fool," I told her. "Chefren could read your mind. He knows what people are thinking, and what they want to hear. Don't blame yourself, but if you need to hate me, then hate me. I can take it."

She let out a strained chuckle, and I gave her a sad smile. I couldn't imagine the heartbreak that she was going through. As a product of the South District, and a life of crime, betrayal had been something I had learned to expect. I hated Devland for what he was doing to my people, but I refused to let my heart break for him. I never even let him through my barriers enough to let himself wedge into my heart like that.

Sure, I was grateful for the life he had given me. The opportunity to snag stability for myself, but I wasn't beholden to him. And his wrongs definitely outweighed any loyalty I held to him. He was attacking my city, my people, and I wanted vengeance, not repentance.

"Everything makes sense now, though." Riel muttered. He was lost in thought, his hands clasped in between his knees.

"What do you mean?" I asked, but I felt like I knew what Riel was about to say. Chefren was a spy—a good one. One that had direct insight into the city's toughest security.

"Chefren is how the drugs got into the city. I let him spearhead security protocols until recently."

"How recently?" I asked, straightening my posture with intrigue.

"Until you mentioned the drugs in the South District." Riel sighed with exhaustion. "And he was also the one that had the insider information on you. I didn't question how he knew you would be interested in the Lord's estate or the diadem, but it seems like he heard it from Devland—who wanted you out of his way."

I cursed under my breath. Devland had been working against me this entire time. Rage burned under my skin, but I wouldn't lose my head. No, I needed to remain vigilant. I thought about our last night together. He seemed...normal.

Except for when he discouraged me from getting the diadem. Did that mean he was having second thoughts about turning me in? Or did he think telling me not to do something would only push me further to do it? I gritted my teeth together. It wasn't enough. I still got caught, I was still used, and my people were still dying.

I spoke through a clenched jaw. "If I had to guess, the drugs were going into circulation two moons ago, when I left for the summer. After Devland had picked me up. Because I never noticed those crates while I was with him. Then again, I wouldn't have looked, nor would I have tried to open them."

I ran my hands down my face, trying to wrack my brain on how I could have prevented this, and I was coming up short. Devland was playing the long game, and he was damn good at it.

Riel sighed. "I'm going to look into it. There is a lot of work to be done, and I'm going to need to spend the next few days reconciling the damage from Chefren. Masika," he looked at her with eyes full of sympathy, "I know it's a lot to ask, but I could use your help. I'll give you as much time off as I can, but I need you by my side."

She sniffled and straightened her shoulders. "Whatever you need from me, I can do. Don't worry about it."

Riel walked me back upstairs after Masika insisted on going home for the night. We had tried to reason with her to stay, but she wasn't having any of it. Instead, she rolled her shoulders and walked straight out the front door.

Riel and I stopped in front of the guest room door. He didn't meet my gaze, and his body was not nearly close enough for my liking.

"How are you feeling?" His words were cold and unfeeling, and my heart sank as he said them.

"I feel fine. Thank you." I held my breath, but Riel only nodded in acknowledgment. Silence filled the hallway, and neither one of us could look at each other.

"I'm so sorry, Riel," I pleaded. He glanced at me, but his lips remained in a thin line. Riel had trusted me, and I betrayed him as much as Chefren did.

"I shouldn't have left. It was a mistake." He didn't say a word, but his eyes grazed over me, angry and sad and guarded. "I hope you can find it in yourself to forgive me."

I turned away from him, pushing the door open before gently tugging it closed behind me. A sob wracked through my chest and tears cascaded down my cheeks. Riel was right. I shouldn't have left. He was only asking me to trust him, and I shattered every shot of building the bridge to a better Aurum. An Aurum where we would be together.

When Riel didn't knock or make a move to come back in, the crack in my heart widened, and I didn't know how to mend this pain. Maybe this was a sign, though. A sign that Riel and I were never truly meant for each other. Was this how Masika felt over Chefren? If so, I understood her anguish.

FOUR DAYS PASSED, AND Riel didn't return to the house. I would have worried about his safety if Masika wasn't consistently checking in and letting me know of any updates. I had recounted to her multiple times of what happened on the ship, and she reassured me that Riel was being diligent.

She was here frequently, and I assumed it was him trying to give her space to mourn Chefren without sacrificing her duty. Riel never said that I was under any sort of watch, but I knew he probably wanted eyes on me all the same, so it worked out. Whether it was for my protection, his peace of mind, or both, I didn't really care. I just wanted to get this over with and see my family. I wanted to see Devland suffer. And I really wanted to feel Riel's arms around me.

Day after day, I fought off the feeling of loneliness, and my thoughts often warred about my feelings for Riel. How could he go from wanting me with every fiber of his being to not even showing his face? Maybe I didn't deserve an explanation, though. I had betrayed his trust, and he had every right to be angry with me.

I found myself in the courtyard, pacing around the sanded yard. Every tear I had was shed, and instead I sought to get some blood pumping through my veins. Working out seemed like a great way to vent my frustrations.

"He's been busy." Masika sat on a shaded spot and watched while I pushed my arms to their limit with what felt like my hundredth pushup. I wasn't counting though, only going until my arms gave out. "But I'm afraid I can't divulge any details."

I sat on the heels of my feet, shaking out my arms, and nodded. "He's avoiding me."

Masika sighed in confirmation. "He saw you running off as a betrayal. Riel lets his guard down for very few people, and you were one of them. You hurt him deeply. But to be fair, he has been very busy." She sounded exhausted. Dark circles lined her eyes, and I hadn't even felt her magic in a while. Two days ago, she had been using it to calm me down, but now I felt nothing.

"I know, it was a mistake. One that I wish I could take back." I stared into the sky, blinking back more tears. "How are you doing?" I hedged. "I know the last place you want to be is stuck in this house."

Masika laughed, and I raised an eyebrow.

"Actually, working so much has been a good distraction. Riel has been...demanding to put it lightly." She averted her gaze for a moment and bit her cheek. "I'm not supposed to tell you this, but we found out that the teahouse incident was planned by Chefren, too," she cleared her throat, "I hate he did this. I hate that I thought I knew him, and yet he was a monster all along."

"I'm sorry, Masika. You don't deserve that. You deserve better than him," I said apologetically.

"It's not your fault. The man is a psychopath. He hid his emotions from me. Which is pretty hard to do, I might add." She flashed me a soft smile. "It's the same way I can feel your intentions. I knew as soon as you recounted your experience, you weren't trying to betray Aurum or Riel."

I gave her a quizzical look. She sighed and tapped her chest. "Guilt for getting caught feels different from guilt for trying to do the right thing. You worked in the best interest for everyone. I tried telling him, but," her face fell, "he isn't listening right now."

My chest ached. I had done that. I created his anguish. Riel wasn't the type of person to trust easily, but he had trusted me. He trusted me, and I chewed it up and spit it out. Tears I didn't know I had were flowing and dripping on the dirt below me.

"Stop." Masika's sharp voice cut through my inner turmoil. She crouched in front of me and grasped my shoulders.

"No more tears, Leoni." She pinched my chin with her fingers and forced me to give her my full eye contact. "You did what you thought was right, right?"

I nodded.

"Good. There is no changing the past. Thanks to you, we found out that we had a traitor."

Masika's eyes flashed with sadness, but it was gone before she let it settle. "And now we have the upper hand. If you hadn't found out about Chefren, then we would forever be one step behind."

I sniffled back my tears. I had helped. No matter my personal consequences, I had helped Aurum, and gotten closer to protecting those I loved. And that was my personal motto, was it not?

"Riel will get over himself eventually, but he doesn't deserve your tears, and Chefren doesn't deserve mine. Now is the time to take the next step. Figure out what you're going to do to fight back." She grasped my hand with firm resolve, and I felt my broken heart mending. Was she talking about me and Riel, or were these the words she told herself, too? She sighed and gave me a wry smile.

"Come on. Let's go get some tea."

I followed Masika to the kitchen, where she poured a steaming cup of tea and set it in front of me. Herbal and floral scents embraced and calmed me. Masika was right. Now wasn't the time to cry; it was time to figure out where I would go from here. But I needed to speak with Riel. If he didn't want me anymore, I would understand, but I still wanted to help.

A door clicked and footsteps echoed toward us. I expected it to be the guard to reprieve Masika from her duties, but when a broad frame, dark skin, and hair with the slightest curl strode in, I leaped from my chair, sending it skidding across the floor.

Riel's lips were tight as he nodded in greeting. "Masika, Leoni."

My heart beat faster, and I wanted to cry, but I remembered what Masika had told me.

He doesn't deserve my tears.

He looked worse for wear. Scruff had grown into nearly a full beard, and shadows lined his features. I knew I had hurt him, but to see him so disheveled tore a piece of the hardness I closed around my heart.

"I need to talk to Leoni." His voice was stern. Masika nodded and took that as a queue for her leave.

She brushed her shoulder against mine as she left and whispered in my ear, "You know what to do." I nodded at her as she departed.

The air was thick. Riel refused to look at me directly, and I could see his jaw clenching. I settled back into the chair and took a deep breath. Attempting to convey strength and resolve, I straightened my back and steeled myself.

"I'm going to help Aurum. Tell me what I need to do. If I need to stay in this house under lock and key, so be it, but please tell me if there is something, anything, that I can do."

Riel pulled out a chair and sat across from me. He laid his arms on the table, and his shoulders caved in.

"I spoke to Kasiel." He grunted. "He told me everything that happened that night."

My pulse beat so wildly that I thought Riel could hear it across the table.

"What did he say?" I couldn't meet Riel's gaze. I didn't think that I could take looking at him while he told me that he wanted nothing to do with me anymore. If he wanted to execute me, or throw me back in the dungeons, he would have already done so. But I was learning that there were plenty of things worse than death. Heartbreak might be one of them.

"He reached out to me once again. He said he thought I ought to know the truth, as if he knew I would assume the worst." Riel let out a breath, crossing his arms. "He also really wants that bastard dead, and I can't say I blame him." I finally chanced a glance at Riel and caught onto his topaz eyes that lit with a fire behind them.

"I'm coming with you," I said. I wanted to deliver Devland's punishment myself. I needed to look him in the eye and make him pay for his wrongdoings.

"No."

"Riel, I know you don't trust me right now, but—"

"No, you aren't going, and not because I don't trust you." Riel blew out a long breath. "After I spoke with Kasiel, he told me how hard you fought. That you had a drive to find the truth, and I can't exactly blame you for that."

He buried his head in his hands. "I should have listened to Masika."

I reached my hand out and grazed it along his arm.

"It was never my intention to hurt you. I truly thought I was doing the right thing. It was a mistake. One that I am prepared to pay for. I understand if you don't want me—"

Riel leaped up from his chair and barreled into me. He took me in his arms, crushing me against him.

"Of course I want you," his voice broke. "I am sorry, Leoni." I pulled away from him, confused.

"Why? You didn't do anything wrong. I'm the one that snuck out. I made my own decisions."

Riel shook his head and leaned into the crook of my neck. His words were soft against my skin.

"Because I didn't give you enough reason to think you were safe with me. Because I didn't listen to what you were saying when you so clearly had reservations about Devland. I reacted with my hurt, when I should have been listening the whole time.

"Instead of listening to what my heart wanted, which was to be right here with you, I ran. I was so scared to lose you, I thought distancing myself would make it easier, but I was wrong. I couldn't keep my mind off of you, and I'm so, so, sorry if I hurt you in that process."

And just like that, the walls around my heart shattered. I wrapped my arms around his shoulders and held him tight.

"You promised me a better city. A better city made by the both of us. Together. I want to be with you, by your side, fighting on the same team." I choked back a sob.

My soul was aching to be near him. It was a deep call that only his embrace could answer. I needed him by my side; the two of us, together, regardless of our differences.

"I can't lose you, Leoni." His face was still buried in my neck and his skin felt hot against mine. I squeezed him tighter and peppered a kiss along his shoulder. All of my anger and sadness were swept away as he held me. I never wanted to let Riel go. I wanted to bask in him forever.

Riel picked me up in a flourish and sat me on the kitchen table. I ran my hands along his chest. He grasped my wrists tight enough to stop their movement.

"I can't let you come along to find Devland." He muttered the words, and I had to take a second to register what he was saying.

"Why not?" I leaned away from him, searching his eyes for answers.

"Because you are safer here. I will not have a repeat of the nightmare from the other night." He shifted his gaze to the floor.

"I will not become a captive in this house. If we are going to work together on this, I need to be an active participant. I'm not a prize to be kept in a locked box."

"Of course not. I never want to hold you captive again, but—"

"You're afraid of something happening to me."

"Yes!" He grabbed me tighter, and I pushed back.

"Riel." I ran hands down his arms, feeling the corded muscles underneath. "What I did that night was foolish. I was defenseless and ignorant about the situation. I have been in many risky situations and caught by only two people. And one of them was a setup by you. Let me do this. I'm loyal to the right person now. Let me prove it."

Riel pulled away from me. His features were pulled tight. "If anything were to happen to you—" I cut him off with a finger to his lips.

"You can't keep me locked in a cage forever. Today it's Devland; tomorrow it will be something else. I want to fight. I have a duty to this city and its people. The moment Devland poisoned my people was the moment he decided his fate."

Riel nodded. "Fine." He rolled his head back and sighed. "You can come with us, but there are rules."

"That sounds good," I agreed. "What are my rules?"

He nuzzled into me again, pressing his lips along my collarbone, and I nearly melted. I was so glad to have him back in my arms, so glad that we could finally find an understanding between us.

"The rules, Riel." He pulled back and looked at me with a small smile playing on his lips.

"You'll use your magic," he said, and I grinned, loving how he allowed me to embrace myself. I would be his most valuable asset.

Riel moved out of my arms and went into the hall where I couldn't see. I waited until he came back with a black box. "And you'll have this with you. At all times."

My hands trembled as I took the box and opened it. Inside sat my black diamond dagger.

"I thought you got rid of this..." My fingers trailed over the stones and I lifted it from the box. It was unharmed and perfect. The black diamonds warmed in my hands as I held it. I looked back up at Riel. He was giving me my weapon back—he truly was giving me freedom.

"No," he shook his head, "I knew you would earn your way back to freedom, and so I kept it safe until you did."

"I thought you didn't want me to go with you. Why did you bring this today? You could have kept it until you got back."

"I still don't want you to come along," he murmured, but there was a playfulness in his eyes. "But I had a feeling you would insist."

I threw him a vicious smile. The dagger in my hand was itching for use.

"Devland will pay for his crimes. He poisoned my people. He attempted to murder me, and I will pay him back with the same ferocity." The black diamonds gleamed as a lifted it up to the light. "Devland will die by my hand, I swear it."

Riel lifted a brow. "Who is Aurum's Executioner now?"

I grinned. "Still you, but now you have a teammate."

I placed the dagger back into the box and clasped it in my hands. Riel pulled me back into his chest, his entire being embracing me, and I felt my shoulders relax and my lungs released a breath that melted my body into his.

"We'll have guests tonight. I hope you don't mind." Riel released me and I stared up into his eyes, his face tired and worried.

"Who?"

Riel rubbed the back of his neck and sighed. "Kasiel. We need to work with him. I have to tell him about our discoveries. He has a friend who thinks can help, too."

"I suppose I should thank him for sending you to save my life, and also for speaking to you afterward. Kasiel is the last person I would have thought to get through your stubborn head," I muttered with a small laugh.

Although I wasn't exactly eager to see Kasiel again, I was relieved he was on our side. Riel grimaced, and his cheeks grew red.

"I am sorry, I..." his words trailed off, his eyes glazing over to his thoughts as he struggled to find his next words. "It's difficult for me to trust, and feeling this connection with you..." He ran his thumb along my chin, forcing me to meet his eyes. "I know I'm not the best at communicating, but I am terrified. I fear opening up to you so fully and then losing you. My heart would shatter, and I don't think I could recover."

"Oh, Riel," I sighed, pulling him close to me so that my head fit into his chest. His arms wrapped around me, encasing me in his warmth, and the smell of incense filled my nose.

It was what home smelled like, my true home. We shared no more words, but I put every ounce of my emotions into my arms that embraced him, and I felt him tighten his hold on me, as if he already understood.

I hopped off the table and went back to my room. I needed to bathe and do something with the tangled mess of my hair. Riel followed close behind me, his hands brushing against me any moment he could manage. Our shoulders touched as we walked together, and I had to bite back a smile at the contact. I stopped in front of my door, pressing my back against it while gripping the handle.

"I need to get ready," I breathed as Riel placed his hands in his pockets and pinned me with his gaze.

"I'll see you when you're done, then." Riel gave me a sad smile. "I can't apologize enough for leaving you here for so long. I shouldn't have stayed away—"

"It's fine, Riel." I grasped for his hand, pulling it out of his pocket and into mine, feeling his warm palm against my cooled skin. "I can't pretend that it didn't hurt me, but I understand why you did it."

Riel sighed and grasped my chin with his free hand.

"You are too good for me, Leoni."

His amber eyes held all the pain, forgiveness, and apologies between us. I reached on my tip toes and pressed my lips to his for a brief moment and then pulled back and stepped into my room.

"Don't speak too soon, Riel. I'm still a thief, after all." He gave me a questioning look, and I laughed and held up two coins I had lifted from his pocket.

"Oh, Leoni, you are asking for trouble."

He stalked into the room and I squealed as he wrapped his arms around me and lifted me from the ground. I laughed along with him as he snatched the coins from my hand. He placed me down, and I put my palm on his chest, giving him a gentle shove.

Instead of leaving, he wrapped his arms around my middle, and I swatted at him while laughing. He only held on tighter, his arms caging me in and holding me hostage.

He splayed one hand on my back, immobilizing me, while his other hand reached up and tucked a strand of hair behind my ear. I bit my lip and looked at him through my eyelashes, unable to hide my feelings from him. He leaned toward me, placing his lips against mine, and I grasped his tunic in my hands, pulling him further into me. I felt his lips quirk against mine, and I smiled back, only to give him a half-hearted shove to push him away from me. No matter how much Riel made my body sing, we had bigger priorities that we had to deal with, and soon.

I expected Riel to look disappointed as I shoved him away, but he was smirking, a heat in his eyes that made me shiver.

"Just wait, Leoni, this isn't over," he said, thick with dark promises. "I have a lot to make up for." My face heated under his scrutiny, my body eager for those promises to be fulfilled.

"I have no doubts that you'll finish what you started. Now, get out. I need to clean up." Riel shook his head as he walked out, still chuckling at the two coins he held in his hand. I pushed the door closed behind him and breathed a contented sigh. My delight was short-lived though, because as I settled in the tub, I knew we would only be walking into a much larger problem tonight—Devland, and how to defeat him.

Chapter 18

Masika had returned with her arms full of provisions for tonight's dinner. I followed her lead, chopping vegetables and slicing meat to go over the fire. We cooked the food, and the familiar aroma of Aurum spices filled the air. I sat back in a chair while Masika monitored the food and helped myself to a bottle of wine that she had brought along.

"Here you go. This one is for you." I handed her a glass that was filled to the brim, and she chuckled.

"Thanks, I needed this," she said, and I lifted my glass to clink to hers. Masika went back to the stove in the warm kitchen. The open windows in the Quarters let in a cool breeze, which saved us from the sweltering heat.

"How are you and Riel?" Masika asked, and I felt a wave of her magic fall over me. A gentle sense of calming and trust settled through my mind, not enough to make me divulge anything I didn't want to, but enough to set me at ease.

I gave her a grin and tucked a curl behind my ear.

"We are fine. Good, even." I sighed, dreamily thinking of Riel, and bit my lip. "I don't know what it is about him," I confessed. "There's a million reasons we shouldn't be together, why we shouldn't work, but I can't even begin to shake how I feel about him. Like there's a pull that no matter what happens, we will always find each other."

She shot me a knowing smile. "I can feel it, you know. Through you—through the both of you, actually."

"Feel what?" I laughed into my glass, feeling my cheeks get hot with embarrassment.

"Love." She shrugged. As if that wasn't a terrifying and enormous prospect.

"Love?" I nearly spat out my wine. "Bah. We don't know each other well enough for it to be love. Attraction—yes, definitely attraction. But love is a big word."

Masika only shrugged, but she didn't say any more about it when footsteps came from outside of the kitchen and I heard male voices talking through the walls.

I peeked my head around the corner of the kitchen, seeing Riel usher Kasiel and a man with dark hair into the living space. All the books and parchments that sat strewn around the room before he had been cleaned and put away. The living space was exactly as I had seen it when I came into the Quarters for the first time. Cozy, clean, and inviting.

"Who's that?" I whispered to Masika, who had come up next to me to see our guests walk in. She sucked in a sharp breath.

"It's Galen." She stared and smirked, wide-eyed.

"Do you know him?" I raised an eyebrow at her.

Masika nodded. "We've met a few times." She looked at me, her olive cheeks tinging pink. "I knew him before..." Her voice trailed off.

"Before what?" I prodded with a smirk on my face.

Masika shook her head. "Go out there and introduce yourself. The food's almost ready. I'll bring it out."

I was inching my way out of the kitchen when Riel caught my eye and beckoned me forward. With a determined look, I strode forward. Kasiel nodded to me in greeting.

"Hello, I'm Leoni. It's a pleasure." I said to Kasiel and the stranger Masika had called Galen. Riel came up behind me, his own mask reaffirmed on his face. The heat and compassion locked away, only for me to see.

"You know Kasiel, of course." Riel nodded to Kasiel, who was peering around the room like he was admiring the way Riel had furnished it.

I bit back a laugh at an image that popped into my head. One that had Riel and Kasiel sitting around a desk, murmuring to each other about what drapery would look better on what window. Then another about them bickering about what shade the table coverings needed to be.

"Yes, I do."

Kasiel turned at the sound of his name. His bottomless black eyes stared right back at me; the smirk that stretched the scar on his face was unsettling.

"Thank you for retrieving Riel the other night," I said. "He saved my life because of you, so you saved my life, too."

His smirk turned down.

"I don't save lives often, so think of it as a one-time moment of weakness." I held back a shiver from his bitter words and gave him a smile that I could only muster into a grimace.

Riel shifted and gestured to the other man. His dark hair was cropped and unkempt, and the tan across his skin told me he spent a lot of time in the sun. He gave me a friendly smile and held out his hand to shake it. I grasped it in return.

"I'm Galen. It's nice to meet you, Leoni." His blue eyes looked eager and excitable. We sat down, and Masika brought out a platter of our prepared food. Riel gathered glasses and passed them out before filling each one with wine. Masika sat next to Galen, who gave her his thanks and a nod of recognition.

"Leoni, Galen is a Dragon Rider." Riel grinned at me while he said it, a little snippet of the man underneath before he put his mask back on.

I gaped. "Are you serious?" I bounced my eyes between Riel and Galen, seeing him in a whole new light as I drank in that little fact.

Galen laughed and brushed his hand on the nape of his neck. "It's true. The only known one in Ambrose, actually."

I gasped. "Wh-why are you here?"

"He owes me a favor," Kasiel growled, clearly unhappy with Galen receiving the extra attention. Galen narrowed his eyes on Kasiel, and I got a feeling that whatever their pasts may have entailed, they didn't necessarily like working together.

"I would have come regardless, if I had known." He looked over at Masika, whose face was slowly tinging pink. "Why didn't you send a message? A drug ring in Aurum is reason enough for me to investigate."

Masika opened her mouth to say something, but Riel cut in. "I wouldn't have allowed it. We didn't have the information. Now, it looks like this may pertain to our country's security from Tantal, which is why I felt it necessary that we take further precautions." The General's commanding voice rang through the room with such an authority that the entire group sobered.

Galen shifted in his seat. His smile was wiped from his face, realizing the seriousness of the turn of conversation. Kasiel looked bored, rotating the rings around his fingers as he waited for Riel to continue.

"We started our investigation because of some missing artifacts."

Riel admitted to being unaware of their importance or drug association in Aurum while pacing with clasped hands.

"Leoni figured out that each relic that has gone missing contains historical use of magic. Only after her confrontation with Devland did we learn about his transfer of the relics to the mortal King." There was a glimmer of pride in his eyes, and I couldn't help but melt a little on the inside. Galen grimaced, and I swore I heard him hiss.

"But why would the King want relics from our gods? With our magic?" I asked.

Kasiel leaned his elbows on his knees and peered at me through the sides of his eyes. "The 'why' doesn't matter. What matters most right now is destroying the supply."

"No, Kasiel. We need to recover those relics. If the King of Tantal wants them, they must be important." Galen's voice was hard as he spoke. "Furthermore, if the King gets his hands on them, he will be taking our history. He's looking for power. His pursuit of the relics is motivated by something."

Unease sank between the five of us. Whatever the King was planning didn't seem like it could be anything good. For Ambrose or for Magi. The implications weighed on my chest and I blew out a heavy breath because I needed to focus on what was right in front of me. I looked around at the others. Their faces showed the same worries as mine.

Masika sighed with melancholy. "Devland has Chefren on his side. It will be even more difficult to find and capture him with a mind reader doing his bidding. He will hear us approaching before we get the chance to attack."

"I have a potion that will help, but I only have one, so we can only use it when the time is right." Kasiel frowned and looked at Riel, who nodded back at him.

I reclined back into my chair as they continued to talk about logistics of how and when we were going to make our move. I barely put any input in of my own, knowing that this was outside of my realm of expertise, but I listened intently.

The longer we gave Devland the chance to run, the harder it would get for us to catch and find him. Galen said that he had scoured the skies on his dragon and found his ship heading toward the Towering Isles. The cluster of islands that reached to the skies weren't too far away, but getting there in time would be difficult.

"What kind of technology can you get your hands on?" Kasiel directed his question to Riel, who pressed his lips together in a thin line.

"I can get whatever you need." His rigid posture told me he didn't want to give the assassin anything, but I knew he would do almost anything to find Devland.

"How about a transporter?"

Riel groaned and rubbed his palms against his chin. "I should be able to get one." He folded his arms against his chest. "You would want one of the most rare and complex forms of technology, wouldn't you?"

Kasiel grinned viciously. "If it helps with a quick getaway, then what exactly is the issue?"

Tension crackled between the two of them.

"Fine," Riel relented, and Kasiel sat with a smug smile. I poured more wine into my glass, hoping that this evening would be over soon.

As the night went on, the tensity of what we were up against grew. Masika would use her magic to remove cloistering stress from the air, and we would all sigh a breath of relief until it inevitably rose once again.

"We have an early morning tomorrow, so I better get going. Casimir is no doubt waiting for my return." Galen said as he rose from his chair. He stretched his arms over his head and shook out his legs before making his way through the house to the front door.

"Who is Casimir?" I asked, wondering if we would have yet another person joining us on our journey tomorrow.

Galen smiled widely, his teeth gleaming. "Casimir is the dragon I'm bonded to."

Anticipation flooded through me, sending my stomach into little swoops.

"Will I get to meet him?" I asked, and Galen nodded.

"I rarely go anywhere without him." He threw the door open, and night air drifted in the house, leaving goosebumps on my flesh. Galen clasped his hand with Riel and reached out for mine as well. I shook it with a firm hand, and he walked out toward the city.

"Can you get the transporter before the morning?" Kasiel called from behind us. Riel pursed his lips.

"I'll have it."

Kasiel glared at Riel for a few long moments and then strode out the door, giving me nothing more than a curt nod. Masika left shortly after, and I blew out a breath of relief that the night was finally over. I turned to Riel in the empty and quiet house. He opened his arms, begging for my embrace. I wrapped my arms around him and let myself bask in the comforting feel of his body around mine.

My relief was short-lived, as I thought about how close we were to capturing Devland, and the prospect of finding myself in his presence once again.

"Do you need to leave to get the transporter?" I asked Riel and looked up into his brown eyes, taking in the sharp angles of his cheekbones and the stubble on his jaw. Riel smirked at me, his gaze dipping to my lips, and I wet them with my tongue in reaction.

Riel's grip tightened around me, and I felt a low rumble in his chest as his eyes turned hungry.

"I won't take too long," he said as he sighed and loosened his grip on me. "I just need to retrieve one from my office in the spire."

He placed a soft kiss on my cheek, his hair tickling against my skin. Riel moved away from me, and I was suddenly cold with his absence. As soon as he left, I went back upstairs to my bedroom and waited quietly in the dark for his return.

I fell asleep soon after, only waking when I felt Riel's large body slide under the covers next to me. He reached out his hand and brushed my hair away from my face before placing a kiss on my cheek and curling around me.

His strong arms embraced me, making me feel secure. Riel trailed his fingers over my stomach, and I shivered under each touch. I arched back into him, the lazy touches making my body feel awake. Riel smirked against my cheek as his hand traveled my body, sliding my nightgown up, each of his fingers running along my thigh.

He lifted my leg over his, giving him access to run his hand over my already wet center. He made a satisfied hum in my ear, and I arched into him further as he brushed his knuckles across my thighs, his fingers toying with my clit as I grew slick with need.

"Stop playing with me, Riel," I muttered, sleep and need making my voice rough.

"But it's my favorite game to play." Riel's lips met mine, his tongue delving in and tenderly savoring me. I met him in stride, wrapping my arms behind me around his neck, trying to pull him closer, but we were already as close as we could get.

His hard erection pressed into my backside, but he made no move to ease himself into me, pressing in one of his fingers instead. I moaned in Riel's mouth, and that encouraged him more. He added another finger and pumped into me in slow strokes.

When he curved his fingers, I bucked my hips, grinding his palm over my most sensitive spot. Riel's other hand kept roaming my torso until he found my breast, kneading it and running his thumb over my nipple. Riel's embrace and skilled hands were the only place I wanted to be, making my body hum.

My orgasm came easily, a rolling tide of endorphins coursing through my body. I heaved a deep breath as I broke away from Riel's kiss. My body flushed and relaxed.

Riel notched himself at my entrance, my core pulsing around the tip of his cock. He groaned, his breath fluttering over my ear as he pushed into me and I molded around him. I could feel every ridge, every part of his hardness filling me, taking me, using me for his own pleasure. Riel gripped my thigh, his fingers biting into my flesh as he pumped, and another shockwave overcame me.

He was slow and sure with his movements, and he peppered my neck with gentle nips, tiny little bites that didn't hurt, but added to the overwhelming feeling of Riel. Letting me know exactly who was at whose mercy. One look down and it set me on the course of another orgasm. His cock was shiny with my release, and with every thrust he pulled out almost completely, letting me see his hard length in full. I undulated my hips, matching his pace, and he groaned in my ear.

"Don't stop," he growled, sensing his own release. I ground against him and Riel cursed, his arms tightening around me, nearly suffocating me around my chest as he tensed behind me and found release for himself.

"My gods, Leoni," he huffed in my ear. We both laughed roughly, and he grinned wider than I'd ever seen. If he hadn't already satisfied me, that would have been enough.

Riel rose from the bed, and I propped myself on my elbows.

"Where are you going?" Surely he wasn't about to leave after that. Panic gripped my chest. Was this revenge for when I left to Devland's ship? Surely Riel wouldn't be that cruel?

He only chuckled as he went into the bathroom and emerged with a wet towel. "I should probably clean up the mess I made."

The panic inside of me shattered, replaced instead with gratitude. I watched intently as Riel wiped the towel over my thighs, carefully wiping away the evidence of our love making. He looked like he wanted to begin another round. I could see it in the spark in his eyes, and the way he bit his lip. But he only ran the towel over my pussy, before discarding it and sliding back to bed. He pulled me close to his chest, his heart thumping in my ear.

"Sleep well, Leoni." He placed his lips on my cheek and blew out the candle that was still burning on the nightstand.

THE SUN WAS BARELY cresting over the ocean when Riel and I stood inside a small unoccupied cove a few miles from Aurum's bustling city. Here, the air was quiet, with only the soft tide rushing over golden sands. From this distance, Aurum's spires stood out starkly against the pale sky, reaching to their tips to the heavens.

I inhaled the dry air, heating steadily with the rising sun. Riel stood next to me, his posture rigid, his face hard with anticipation. Rolling my neck and shaking out my arms, I expelled the last bit of nerves from my body.

I would face Devland, I would destroy the drugs, and if I had to kill him, I would. I thirsted for his blood. He needed to pay for the pain he caused me, for the betrayal to me, the betrayal to my family. He needed to pay for Seraph's death, and for all the other deaths he had caused.

"Are you sure you're up for this?" Riel's voice was filled with concern. His eyes trailed along my body, assessing me, trying to find any reason to dismiss me back to the house.

"Yes." There was no second guessing, and nothing but resolve in my answer. "Where's Masika?"

"Greeting our guest," Riel nodded towards the dune closest to us. Two people walked toward us, their figures distorting in the climbing desert heat. They arrived as the sun broke over the dune, the sky's clear blue offsetting the orange-gold sand beneath our feet. Masika greeted me with a firm handshake. As usual, she kept up her stern demeanor, but I caught the way her gaze caught on mine and smiled.

Kasiel stared out at the horizon, his jaw set. He didn't even acknowledge my presence. Instead, he just stared, squinting his eyes like he was looking for something. I followed his gaze, but all that I saw was the endless sky and ocean.

Before I could ask what we were looking for, a small speck in the sky emerged. It looked to be getting closer, the speck becoming larger with each passing second. I squinted my eyes at what looked to be a glimmering red bird.

Riel bristled next to me. The bird grew closer and kept getting larger and larger. Red scales gleamed in the sunlight as a massive dragon headed straight toward us.

I looked up in disbelief, raising my hands to my mouth. I glanced at Riel, blinking to make sure that this wasn't a hallucination. The dragon was the one that belonged to Galen, who was surely riding on its back.

He gave me a small, reassuring smile before reapplying his mask of indifference. The dragon and his rider approached quickly, and the dragon let out a mighty roar that had me shaking from head to toe.

Red, mighty wings flapped above us, blowing sand in every direction. The dragon, Casimir, landed in front of us with a loud, reverberating thump. I stumbled, but Riel grasped my arm, righting me before I had the chance to fall. I drank in the dragon's scales and teeth. A large and dangerous creature that could eat me whole if it felt the need. I swallowed thickly and tried to wipe the sweat from my palms.

Galen unstrapped himself from the large saddle that sat atop the creature. His dark hair looked wilder and blue eyes burned brighter as he approached with a friendly smile. He beamed at the sight of Riel and Masika. I caught Riel's eye, and he gave me a tight smile. I couldn't believe that I stood in front of one of the most powerful creatures in existence. My cheeks warmed and there was nothing that could prevent the smile that crossed my face so wide that it hurt.

"Devland is still on the Isles." Galen slid off his dragon. The creature huffed out a warm breath as Galen caressed his snout, rubbing the red scales in a back-and-forth motion. "I don't suspect they will leave at least for another day, but it looks like they are prepared to sail off at any time."

Kasiel turned, peeling his gaze away from the horizon. His jaw was set, his black eyes vicious.

"Let's burn him down." Kasiel said, radiating lethal resolve. I narrowed my eyes and nodded to Riel in agreement.

"Masika will ride over with Galen while we will meet at the rendezvous point with Kasiel," Riel directed.

Masika strode over to Galen with revered apprehension and bowed in front of the dragon, who huffed his approval at her sign of respect. My heart swelled at the interaction. I couldn't wipe the smile off of my face at seeing a dragon this close, with his gleaming scales and sharp teeth alongside a Rider. It was unreal, and I pinched myself to make sure I wasn't dreaming. I watched closely as Galen strapped Masika into the saddle before he sat behind her.

"Why aren't we going with them?" I asked Riel. My jealousy was apparent. I wanted to be on the back of the dragon, soaring over the clear skies. Riel's eyes narrowed at me as the dragon lifted his head and shook his wings, and I sighed. It would have to be enough to just watch.

"It's better if we separate for the approach in case somebody gets accosted," Riel said.

"Won't people notice a giant red dragon approaching the Isles?"

"They might, but it's not unheard of to see a dragon once in a while. Let's just hope they don't see the riders on top."

GALEN AND MASIKA FLEW away, growing smaller and smaller until they became a dot on the horizon. Riel crossed over to Kasiel and handed him a small circular device made of bronze. The black-haired man fidgeted with it with deft fingers. He twisted a knob on the side, and I peered over his shoulder to get a closer look.

"That would have been handy when Devland captured us last time," I observed. He only nodded in response, his jaw clenched.

"Yes, well," he hissed through gritted teeth, "last time I got lucky. This time, we will be more prepared." He made one final click and looked up. "Alright. Both of you place your hands on mine."

We formed a stack with our hands layered on each other, and Kasiel pressed a knob on the device. Darkness enveloped me as we spun, and it felt like someone had sucked all the air out of my lungs. We spun and spun, and when we stopped, I lost my balance as we hit solid ground.

I opened my eyes and shielded myself against the bright sunlight. Green grass hit my knees as I fell forward with an *oof*. Aurum's golden sands were gone; no desert to be seen. I breathed in, meeting the salty humidity of the Towering Isles.

I stood up, slightly dizzy from the transporter, and peered over a tall cliff. Far below, the ocean crashed against a wall of black rocks. A fall would most definitely be lethal. The Isles were small sets of land, all connected with wooden bridges suspended over the water. Surrounding those smaller lands stood gargantuan rock formations. One of which we were currently on top of.

My stomach turned at the sight. I had only ever seen the pillars from below. The city from this distance was small, and my heart skipped as I took in the bird's-eye view. From here, I could map out the city's docks and taverns and homes. We could see everything from this hidden, high vantage point. I took a large step back from the edge, my back bumping into a broad chest.

Arms wrapped around my torso.

"Afraid of heights?" Riel's voice whispered in my ear. My stomach flipped at his voice. I relaxed into his embrace.

"Not unless you plan on pushing me over." I let myself bask in his warmth. His arms pinned me close to him. The smell of incense washed over me. I would have given anything to stay in his arms for eternity. Between the loud crashing of the ocean meeting rocks below and the gentle salty breeze, it was almost too easy to forget why we came here.

We stood in comfortable silence for a few moments. Kasiel was busy working on his transporter, no doubt prepping it for the next jump. He turned away from us, not paying us any attention.

"Riel," I turned to face him, and he looked down at me with a kind smile playing on his lips. His arms loosened and braced me on my shoulders. His thumbs rubbing small circles on my biceps. I wrapped my arms around his back. I let my hands linger, tracing his muscles, and Riel responded with a low hum, tightening his grip around me.

He lifted my chin towards him and bent down. His soft lips met mine, and my world tilted. The waves seemed louder. The wind seemed warmer. I wrapped my hands around Riel's neck, and he embraced my waist. His hands fisted my shirt as the kiss became more urgent, more passionate. I never wanted to let him go.

Pursuing Devland was risky, and I feared Riel falling into a trap and losing him. Riel filled my heart, and I wasn't sure if I could bear the emptiness if something happened. His tight embrace told me he felt the same.

We broke apart, and he leaned close to me. I heard him breathe me in, marking my scent to his memory.

"This is not goodbye, Leoni. We will fight, and we will conquer. I refuse to let us come together now and be torn apart before we get the chance to know the future we deserve. Together." His words hung between us. Fire burned in those brown eyes of his, and I was sure it reflected in mine.

Chapter 19

OFF IN THE DISTANCE, I spotted the red-winged creature making its way toward our little group. The dragon landed on the soft grasses with a whoosh of wings and a huff of hot breath that blew my hair away from my face.

The riders dismounted, Galen offering Masika a hand. Her braid, which had been tight before they left, was now loose, black stray hairs flying in different directions. She stumbled off the dragon, a hue of green tinting her skin. Galen braced her, laughing while she shot him daggers with her eyes, her hands bracing her knees as she took in deep breaths.

I jogged over to meet them, skirting around the dragon's immediate area.

"Masika! Are you alright?" She moved her vicious gaze to me, and I stopped in my tracks.

"I'm fine." The color was returning to her face, but her scowl and heavy breaths remained. "I'm never riding one of those again." The dragon growled low, and Masika stepped back with wide eyes.

Riel came up behind me. He frowned at Masika but said no words about her condition.

"We need to talk about the plan." He turned to me. "You know Devland the best. Where do you think we can find him?"

I racked my brain, thinking about his normal habits when we arrived and stayed on the Isles. There would be no doubt that he would be working with other tradespeople, trying to get them to buy and distribute his goods. But with the drugs, his strategies could change.

"There's a market away from the main docks. That's where he goes for information. If he needs recruits to hire, then he would go there." I looked up in the sky, the morning sun still low on the horizon. "It's worth starting there, and then we can track his movements from there."

Kasiel moved beside me, and I turned to see him place the transporter in his pocket. He shook his head.

"We don't need to make guesses. I can have eyes on him if you give me a few moments."

I looked at Riel, confused since Kasiel's magic was wind.

"Do it," he commanded.

"I'll find him," Kasiel said with a clenched jaw. He crouched down on the ground and placed his hands on the grass.

I watched closely as Kasiel took a deep breath and looked to be in some sort of trance. His eyes flashed with a gold brightness and I peered to get a closer look, but it was gone so fast I thought I could have imagined it.

We all waited, the sun creeping higher in the sky. Kasiel remained in his crouched position. I started pacing in the grass. The dragon followed me with one eye, although his head rested on the ground. Masika and Galen had stepped aside and fell into soft conversation.

Riel walked next to me in my pacing and looked down at me, taking in my rigid posture and my hands that shook with anticipation.

"It just takes time. Try to calm yourself."

I scowled at him. "It's taking too long. I just need to get down there. He is poisoning this town just like he is Aurum."

Riel stopped in front of me.

"Sit." A soft command. I plopped down on the ground, brushing my fingers against the soft grass. Riel sat next to me, crossing his legs in front of him. I glanced over to Galen and Masika, both still in conversation, but I noticed Masika shift in her stance as she watched us out of the corner of her eye. Soft wind rustled through the grass and pulled on loose strands of my curls.

Riel's knees grazed mine, and he laid his hand on my knee. His face was serious, his honey eyes full of thought.

"I want you to stay away from Devland, Leoni."

"He is mine," I protested, but my will softened as I looked into his eyes, which crinkled in a sad smile.

"I can't allow you to be in the same situation with him again, even though I understand how you feel." He tucked one loose strand of hair behind my ear.

"It won't happen, Riel. He caught me by surprise last time. This time will be different." And it would. I steeled my heart against the man that betrayed me, clenching my fists in determination.

"You have nearly died in my care already, and I refuse to watch it happen again." Riel's face was a mask of cold steel, but I could read the anxiety on his shoulders. I placed my hand on his knee, rubbing small circles over his kneecap.

"Once we have a plan, I will stick to it," I swallowed, "but you can't ask me not to risk myself. You have to trust me."

Riel nodded slowly. He let out a long breath, giving up his argument. He knew that this was something I had to do. For myself, for my family, for Aurum.

Finally, Kasiel unwound himself from his crouch, stretching his limbs as he stood. He cracked his neck, his black hair fluttering in the breeze behind him. His head was tilted, as if he was listening to something.

"He's planning on meeting someone. Jasper. Does that ring any bells?"

I scowled at Kasiel. I nearly kicked myself for not thinking of him sooner. Of course, fucking Jasper. The smarmy man was no doubt kissing up to Devland and bragging about how glad he was that I'm not part of his crew anymore.

I sighed. "Yes, I know who he is. I could find him and talk to him. We have a… working relationship."

Riel scowled. "No, that won't work. You're supposed to be dead, according to Devland. And if he has told anyone about your death, it could blow our mission."

Fair point. But I didn't see another way to get past Devland's guards.

Galen stepped forward. "If we can find him and you can show me his face, then I can go in his stead." I gasped as Galen's aura shimmered, and I was looking at another Riel.

"You're a shapeshifter," Riel growled. Galen removed his magic, but he shook his head.

"Sort of, it's more of a glamor. I can shift into a person, but nothing else. Although shapeshifting would have its own perks." Galen grinned, but Riel's eyes narrowed. He clearly didn't trust Galen, and I wondered if that was how he regarded most people he didn't know very well.

"He's difficult to find," I countered. "But it could be done. I would just have to walk through the city with my shadows." I looked up at the bright sky. Only a few wispy clouds drifted above. Not enough to block out sunlight. Hiding in my shadows would be difficult, but not impossible.

"This Jasper"—I shuddered at Kasiel's gaze as he pinned me with his black eyes—"he's hiding out in the sewers. Seems like he's taking his time before heading to the cave."

Through the Isles was an intricate system of sewers that doubled as a meeting spot for criminals and thieves. I nodded, well-versed in the tunnel system, and could pretty much guess exactly where he was.

"How did you find him?" I wasn't sure how Kaisel even knew what he looked like.

"All I needed to do was listen. Even whispers can be heard if you listen carefully enough."

I waited for him to elaborate, but once I realized he would not say any more, I turned to Galen.

"I'm familiar with the tunnel systems. If I can get you down there, do you think you will be able to glamor into him?"

Galen flashed me a wicked grin. "I don't think. I know I can."

I LED GALEN THROUGH the winding bridges and wooden spirals of the Isles. Galen changed his appearance to make himself look like an unidentifiable mortal. I admired the hold that he had on his magic. His changes were subtle. His skin was duller, he increased wrinkles and grey hairs, looking much more like a mortal in their brief old age. The amount of magic he was using was pinpointed and highly controlled. It was a matter of many decades of practice versus my measly twenty.

I dodged and weaved through the city effortlessly, sticking to paths that went underneath awnings and overhead bridges. Wood creaked and bent under my feet, but I was confident no one would give it a second glance. My body hummed with pleasure as I cruised through the homes and buildings built on the sides of cliffs overlooking the water. My shadows danced over my skin, caressing me. The magic settled exactly where it belonged.

I shook off my magic as I skipped up to a side entrance to the sewers. The gate was rusty from the salty air. Galen's eyes tracked my every movement as I reached in my pocket for my lock pick—one of many items that Riel had retrieved for me that morning.

The lock released with a satisfying click, and the gate swung on creaky hinges. Cold metal met my hands when I reached out. Galen looked behind his back in apprehension, and I grinned. No one would bother to look here. This entrance was tucked away and not used often due to patrol officers that were normally spotted close by. But, even without my shadows, I never had any issues. Galen followed me into the tunnel. Darkness and a cool, damp smell of stagnant water filled my senses as we passed through.

I let my magic flow over me, the darkness in the tunnel aiding me in complete invisibility. I moved through the tunnels on light feet, narrowly avoiding stepping into puddles of mystery liquid that collected in dips of the sewers.

We turned through the tunnels until we reached a large round room that flickered with candlelight, low chatter echoing around the stone walls. I sidled up to the entrance wall and peered at the inhabitants.

Jasper was sitting at a small round table, reading over what looked to be ledgers. He had one leg propped up on his knee as chatted with a hooded figure across from him, both unaware of our presence. I swept my eyes across the room, recognizing familiar thieves that were in simple company, chatting and laughing amongst themselves.

I tugged on my shadows, pulling them closer to me. Galen confidently strolled through the room, and I raised my brows at how impressively casual he was. The others didn't even acknowledge him. Galen sat at a table facing Jasper.

I held my breath, but Jasper didn't even glance at Galen. Galen sat with the swagger of a regular thief, embodying the entire facade. I wondered how many faces Galen had portrayed in his life, but appearance wasn't the only factor. He was able to mimic mannerisms, too. Of course he would be worthy of a dragon—they didn't choose weak riders.

I kept shifting my gaze to the hooded man speaking with Jasper. His presence made my skin itch, and I was eager to leave the sewers. I bit my lip. How long did Galen need to memorize Jasper's features? I suppressed a groan.

I paced around the room on light feet while I watched Galen. Without any urgency, he got up and made his way back to our starting point. I followed on his heels, keeping to the shadows of the rounded walls just in case. We weaved through the tunnels once again before returning to the gate. I removed my magic with a sigh.

"Did you get everything you needed?" I asked once we were close to the exit.

"Yes, I'm ready." Galen's face shifted into a replica of Jasper, down to the small freckle below his left eye. I shivered at the change. Seeing a different man that wasn't Galen was unnerving, but seeing him as Jasper was grotesque.

"Alright," I pulled on the gate, "let's go meet our friends." Galen shifted back to the unnamed mortal, and I opened the gate, letting light spill into the tunnels.

"If it isn't the dead coming back to life," a cold, smooth voice drawled from the shadows beyond the gate.

I donned my magic instantly, absorbing the shadows and melding into the world around me, but it wasn't fast enough. Rough hands grabbed my shoulders, gripping tight enough to bruise. I wriggled and fought Devland's hands as he grappled at me, his beefy arms wrapping around my invisible body.

"Run!" I shouted at Galen. Devland pinned my arms close to my body, and as much as I kicked and pulled, he was too strong. Galen sprinted along the wooden path, up to the stairs that would allow him to disappear into the hustle of the interlocking islands above. He took two steps at a time, and I sighed a breath of relief as I watched him disappear above me.

"How did you know I was here?" I gritted out between my teeth, still kicking and wrangling.

"I have a friend who notified me of you and your friend's entrance. As soon as you waltzed into the Thief's Den, he knew," he laughed. Devland's arms banded around me. The man in the hood. He knew and somehow notified Devland. I had two guesses as to who that man was, and I was willing to bet it was the same man that was no longer a Watchman.

"You won't get away with this, Devland." My arms burned from my struggle. A cold laugh brushed across my ear.

"Behave yourself, Leoni." His voice made my stomach turn. "If you don't fight me, I may let you live this time." Sweat broke out over my forehead. How many times would I meet death's brink because of this man? I gritted my teeth together.

"I'll go willingly if you don't drug me this time," I spat. Wriggling and thrashing out of his grip was no use. He only squeezed me tighter. His hands, which had once touched me with intimacy, now held me with the force of a brute.

Devland laughed again, low and cruel. He removed an arm, the other one keeping me in a tight hold. A pinch of a sharp knife pointed at my lower back, and I stood still.

"Give me your knife," he said, and I cringed and slowly removed my dagger from its sheath. I dropped it on the ground and stood still while I watched Devland tuck it into his own sheath. The black diamonds looked wrong against his brown garb.

"You'll come with me, and if you try to run, I will slice you open and dump you into the depths of the waters so you'll never get another breath of air again."

His threat was a cold promise, his knife etching into my back. I stumbled alongside Devland through the maze of wooden pathways, up sets of stairs, across the gaps of the ocean flowing underneath, and back down more stairs. His tight grip on my arm never loosened. Splotches of purple and blue would surely show in their wake.

His knife point never left my body. I scanned the skies and across the bridges for any signs of Galen, Riel, Masika, or even the dragon. There were only passersby who gave us no attention. I kept my chin up, unwilling to let Devland see the fear that pulsed through my veins. My fingers tingled, and my hands quivered.

Whatever Devland had planned, I knew my fate was hanging on by a thin string. We walked to the end of a bridge, greeted by a discrete rock path. The path was small, and we followed it up and up and up, spiraling around one of the Isle's pillars until we emerged near a small cave. Devland pushed me in, only the light from the sunny sky pouring through the entrance.

I stared out of the opening, only to be greeted with an empty sky and wind whipping through my hair. No sign of the dragon, and too far from straying pedestrians. I barely had time to appreciate the view before Devland shoved me into the darker part of the alcove.

"No shadow business, Leoni," Devland growled. He shoved me further in and let go of my arm. I stumbled, catching my breath now that I no longer had the threat of a knife on my back. I blinked repeatedly, making my eyes adjust to the dim cave light. Crates lined the back of the cave. So much more than what I had seen on his ship. I turned to find Devland watching me.

"I could just walk out and leave." I pointed my nose toward the outside of the cave.

"You won't." Devland turned his back and gave me a dismissive wave.

"Why not?" I sneered. His arrogance made my blood boil. Rage contorted my face, and I clenched my fists. I took a deep breath, careful not to let my heightened emotions fog my actions. Instead, I brushed my hand along the cave wall, reaching for anything to ground myself at the moment.

The cave was large and smooth, like someone had cut out the usual shards of rock that grew on the ceilings and floors of caves. As many times as I had been to the Isles, I didn't know this place even existed. It definitely made for a good hideout for what Devland intended it for—a base for his illegal goods.

I weighed my odds for escape. If I could skirt past Devland, I could make a break for it, but there were pirates that guarded the cave. And I would have to be careful not to be overthrown into the deadly ocean below.

Devland snapped his fingers twice, the quick pings echoing off the cave walls. The hooded man in the Thief's Den stepped toward me, peeling away his hood and revealing sharp green eyes. Chefren. I grimaced at the smug smile he wore. He was in the Thief's Den and likely heard my and Galen's thoughts. I wasn't sure of the full extent of his powers, but I had seen enough of him around Masika and Riel to assume he could communicate telepathically, too.

"If you even think of running, I'll know and catch you before you even take your first step," Chefren smiled. It was cold and menacing, and held none of the humor I had grown used to from him. Trying to avoid thoughts of my companions and our plan, I attempted to clear my mind.

Mind reading bastard.

Chefren chuckled, and I narrowed my eyes. Devland moved around Chefren and exited the cave, leaving us without a word. I tracked him until he moved out of my line of sight.

"How does it feel to betray your city, Chefren?" I sneered. "How does it feel to know that you are actively killing innocent citizens?" I met his cold stare with my arms crossed over my chest. "How does it feel"—I let every bitter and pent up emotion lace my words—"to betray the people that trusted you the most?" I pointed my finger at him, jabbing him in his chest.

Chefren wrapped his hand around my extended arm and pulled. I lost my balance, and he pounced, tackling me to the ground. I struggled against him, my fingers scraping and clawing his arms, but it was useless.

Chefren's knee sank into my stomach, and he shifted his weight so the air squeezed out of my lungs. He pinned my arms above my head. I writhed beneath him, but his hold was too strong.

"Betrayal implies there was something to be betrayed," he hissed in my ear. I tried to distance myself from him by turning away.

"Aurum has become a fallen society. No longer do we live in a world where the strong survive and thrive. Instead, we are beholden to the weak. They hold us back." Chefren pressed his knee in further, making me gasp for air. "I am not betraying Aurum. I am feeding it." Poison laced his every word. "The poor and weak muddle our city. They clog the streets with filth. Whatever happens to them is well deserved. Once they are thinned out, we can rid the city of their stench. I am doing Aurum a favor."

Chefren pressed his knee further into my gut and I let out a cry in protest. My lungs seized and my eyes watered from his hold. He freed one hand and pulled out a pair of stone cuffs from his pocket. He slapped them on my wrists and my magic dissipated once again.

Chapter 20

CHEFREN REMOVED HIMSELF FROM me, and I stood on shaky limbs. I tried to reign in my anger. My hands shook, my throat bobbed. Chefren was precisely what was wrong with Aurum, and exactly why I stole and robbed to provide for my family. For my city. People like him could never understand.

"You think you're doing Aurum a favor?" I scoffed, "And I'm sure you are getting compensated for it handsomely."

Chefren's lips curved into a smirk. I forced all of my rage at that smirk in the back of my mind. Whatever it took to make it seem like I was calm and collected.

I didn't know if Chefren bought my act, but I wouldn't allow him any reason to harm me or put the bigger plan at risk.

"For someone who can read minds, you sure don't grasp the importance of life." I stepped away from him, rolling my shoulders and breathing out my anger.

"The importance of life?" Chefren stalked around me with the gait of a mighty predator, limber legs that crossed the cave floor gracefully with a deadly glimmer in his eye. "How about the life of misery those people have to live in? The squalor? Living each day in fear of making it to the next day? What sort of way is that to live?"

"You don't get to decide who lives and dies because of their status, Chefren." I kept my voice even, but I was seeing red. He would never understand the joy, love, and compassion experienced in the South District. As much as those people in that small, poor district suffered, there was life. Authentic life that no amount of money could purchase.

I sagged against the wall. I didn't have time to react before the back of his hand struck my cheek with a loud slap. My ears rang and pain reverberated against my skull. Chefren's hit was so hard I saw stars. His rings left cuts along my cheekbone, and I could feel the sting of air and the drip of blood on my face.

I begged the shadows to wrap around my arms and legs, to hide me, let me escape, but my magic was gone. I pulled and tugged at that now empty well inside of me. *Please*, I cried to the skies, to anyone who would listen. *Let me get out of here.* I crumpled to the floor.

Chefren wasn't done. He kicked his boot against my ribs, and a powerful crunch reverberated inside me. I groaned, unable to do anything against the pain that throbbed throughout my body.

He bent over my broken body, casting a shadow over me, and for the first time, the shadows scared me. I couldn't move. I wheezed and looked into his eyes, finding hardened evil lurking behind the glimmering green.

"You're wrong, Leoni. I do get to decide who lives and dies. I will create a world where only the strong live, and right now you look awfully weak." He smirked, my name leaving his lips with lethal promise.

My fear morphed back into anger. I was broken, my magic was gone. I should have been terrified, but as I stared into the face of my impending death, I saw red.

Devland stepped back into the cave and glanced between us. "Take her to the ship. I'll be there shortly."

Chefren pulled me up in a rough grasp and shuffled me out of the cave. I was limp and weak as he yanked me along. I blinked in the bright onslaught of light from the sun as Chefren dragged my mostly limp body down the path toward the docks. We were still high above the town, and my legs protested at the thought of the long trek to the ship.

I knew that as soon as I got on that ship, it would be my death sentence. If we left port, Riel wouldn't be able to save me. Devland would drug me and then throw me into the depths of the sea.

But I wasn't scared; I was angry. Angry that I once again found myself at Devland's mercy. Angry that I had broken my promise to Riel.

We walked down the trail, and I stared out at the ocean below. Rocks and waves clashed far below. The path was narrow, and I stuck to the inside, leaning toward the towering stone wall next to us, even though Chefren gripped my arm. I took a deep, rattling breath. Walking had eased some of my muscles into a dulling burn rather than a sharp pain. I opened and closed my fists, testing my mobility. I silently cursed myself, wishing I had spent more time sparring with Riel.

Once we were far enough away from Devland, I mustered up as much strength as possible and gave Chefren a large shove. We were close enough to the bottom that I hoped I could at least stumble my way to the safety of the crowded town. He took an involuntary step back, and I held my breath, hoping for him to fall, but I wasn't so lucky. I cursed as he righted himself.

"Nice try," Chefren shoved me back. My feet slipped out from underneath me, and I fell on the path. Loose rocks dug into the palm of my hands. My arms buckled from under me. I kicked my feet, trying to scuttle as far back from Chefren as I could until my back hit the stone behind me.

Chefren lumbered toward me. The wind picked up, blowing my hair loose from my braid. My pulse quickened at his menacing grin as he strode toward me. I pressed myself as far back as I could. My fingers grasped for hand holds, anything to grip onto so he couldn't pick me up and pitch me over the side of the cliff.

An enormous shadow passed over us, and Chefren's eyes widened. Red scales, gleaming and powerful, flew over our heads. I let out a sigh of relief, but the fight wasn't over.

Rocks fell, and the stone tower above us shook as the large, red dragon perched itself alongside the pillar. Talons scraped and dug into the stone, clawing and screeching. I covered my head from the debris, my body still weak and unable to get up. Galen swung from the dragon's back. He forwent his disguise, snarling and leaping towards Chefren. He landed on the path gracefully, his legs forming a wide squat to brace himself.

Chefren slid out of Galen's trajectory, snagging the two knives he had tucked in his boots. He crouched low and assumed a defensive stance. The dragon's wings buffeted against the air, sending debris skittering. I let out a nervous laugh—I was saved.

The stone groaned under the dragon's weight. I watched with my mouth agape as the dragon released an earth-shattering roar. He then flew around the pillar, out of sight. Galen held a sword at his side. He stalked towards Chefren with his shoulders back and chin high.

Galen looked like a warrior. Gone was his casual demeanor, and I blinked at the subtle changes in his posture. Even his features looked sharper, more lethal.

Chefren lunged. Galen met each of his swings with a block of his sword, metal pinging against metal in a flurry of up-kicked dirt. They fought evenly, a hardened dragon warrior against Aurum's trained guard. I swallowed thickly. Surely a trained Dragon Rider could defeat a city's third-in-command officer? But as I watched, I realized they were too evenly matched. Galen would push Chefren close to the edge, but then Chefren would whirl and gain footing. They met each other's hits with a loud, echoing clang over and over.

I sat next to the stone pillar, the shackles on my hands heavy. I needed to get them off at any cost. Pain ricocheted through me as I slammed them against the wall, grimacing with rage and conviction.

These cuffs were not the same as the metal bracelets I had worn. They were made of hardened stone, and with each bash, each bang against my bones, the manacles chipped away. Each cling of Chefren's knives and Galen's sword echoed with the crack of me banging stone against stone. I smashed my hands against the wall over and over, feeling the cuffs cut into my skin.

My broken rib pounded with each hit. My breath wheezed and sputtered as I tried to get more oxygen, more energy, to break the stone. Tears streamed down my face and I screamed when I felt the snap of bones in my wrists. The cuffs finally shattered, the pain in my body sharpened as the heavy cuffs fell off.

My magic rushed back to me in a wave. The rush of power pushed itself through my veins, and I breathed through each pulse of magic.

I took deep, steadying breaths and tried to block out the surrounding noise. A loud shout pulled me out of my panic. Galen had swept Chefren out from under his feet. He was near the ledge. All Galen would have to do was give him one swift kick, and he would be at the mercy of the ocean below.

Instead, Galen ran toward me. I tried shouting at him. He needed to turn back. Chefren was still very much alive and very much still able to fight. What was he doing? He grasped me around my middle, his arm striking the air out of my lungs. I screamed from the pressure and black dots blurred my vision.

He jumped. My heart leaped into my throat. The water below was all I could see, and my heart skipped several beats as it grew closer. Rock formations, jagged and sharp, became larger and larger. Wind rushed past my face, blowing my hair back, giving me a clear view of the death that awaited us.

I closed my eyes, waiting to be impaled by the rocks below, or drown in the icy embrace of churning waters. Instead, I collapsed on a hard surface. Galen was tugging on my legs and arms. He adjusted my legs to where I was straddling something large. I opened my eyes to find that I sat in front of Galen on top of a wide saddle.

We landed on top of the dragon. Large black spikes protruded on the dragon's neck in front of me. Galen wrapped his arms around me, and the dragon pumped his mighty wings. Once, twice, three times, and we soared into the sky. I peered over the dragon's wing just in time to see a small Chefren glaring at us.

I breathed a sigh of relief, realizing that I was safe. For now. My bones were throbbing in my wrist, I was gasping for breaths that I couldn't quite make, and my body was weak. Sharp pain pulsed through me. But I was alive. I leaned into Galen's hold as we rose into the sky, drifting through wispy clouds that left a cool moisture on my skin.

The Isles looked small from this view. Tiny dots of people ran around the small, bridge-webbed city. I expected to feel a creeping fear rising from our ascent in the sky, but it never came. Instead, I found solace.

Up this high, it was easy not to think about the peril that I had just endured. Easy to forget about Devland and Chefren, and all the reasons I had found myself in the predicament I was in now. I let my mind wander. I allowed myself to breathe in the fresh air.

The dragon circled over the city. No doubt, the people on the Isles were aware of the dragon and its mysterious rider. Eventually, we landed at the top of the column of stone we had met initially. However, Kasiel was the only one standing there. Riel and Masika were nowhere to be seen.

Galen slid down and helped me dismount from the dragon's back. I looked at the beast, whose head was twice the size of my body. He let out a loose growl, and I gave him a quick bow in thanks, wincing as pain ricocheted through me. I wasn't really sure about dragon etiquette, but that last thing I needed was an angry dragon willing to eat me for plopping on his backside. When the dragon removed its yellow eyes away from me, I dared to turn and head towards Kasiel.

"Where are they?" I demanded. I cradled my wrists to my chest, aching and pounding from the broken bones. My head was light, and I felt myself stumble before Galen caught me. My body wasn't healing fast enough, the injuries were too severe.

Kasiel barely gave Galen a second glance as he strode toward me. He assessed me with calculation, his piercing eyes so dark they didn't even reflect the sun. His eyes dipped as he noted my wrists and the slight tilt in my body. Rummaging in his satchel, he pulled out a small vial of yellow liquid.

"Drink this." He unstoppered the vial and tipped it towards me. I took a step back.

"What is that?" I spat at him. I knew I could trust him, but my mind was unwilling to allow any more strange substances into my body.

"It's a healing potion. Your magic won't be able to heal you fast enough on its own." He stepped toward me and gently laid a hand on the nape of my neck. Healing potions were rare and expensive. The ingredients—much like the one Jyran's wife needed—were obtained in other parts of the world. He coaxed my head back, and I opened my mouth and let him pour it in.

"My sister is a witch. She never lets me leave without supplying me with valuable potions and medicines. I carry several healing potions, just in case. One of these is strong enough to save someone on the brink of death." The liquid slid down my throat. It tingled against my tongue, sending sparks down my body. It wasn't unpleasant. "I rarely have to use them, but it seems this time it came in handy." Once the vial was empty, Kasiel placed it back into his satchel. "Sit."

I didn't even have time to heed his command. My knees buckled, and if it weren't for Galen's arms already around me, I would have collapsed on the ground.

The medicine made its way through my bloodstream. It tingled, and then it burned. I clenched my jaw from the pain. Broken bones in my body snapped and melded back together. I bit back a scream. Each second that passed felt like minutes.

The tendons and skin that I had torn stitched itself back together. Rocks embedded into my skin pushed their way out, tumbling on the grass below me. My ribs cracked back into place and I yelled. Tears flowed freely, coating my cheeks and dropping to the grass below. As soon as the healing was done, the pain receded.

I felt a warmth trickle over my body, and I opened my eyes. Galen crouched beside me with his hand on my shoulder. I could breathe again. Full deep breaths feeding oxygen into my lungs. The black spots that blurred my vision faded, and I felt whole.

"You alright?" Galen's face pinched with worry, but I nodded. He stood up, blowing out a breath. The healing potion not only mended my body, but also gave me a much-needed energy boost. Kasiel's sister's creation was potent. I didn't want to know the cost of such a medicine.

"Where are Riel and Masika?" I scanned below, looking past the crashing waves and jutting rocks for any sign of them.

Kasiel peered down with his hands in his pockets. He located Jasper before, could he locate Riel? What kind of magic did Kasiel even have? He seemed to do more than just manipulate the air. For a simple assassin, he was powerful. Magi never contained two magical powers.

Then again, I didn't know many Dragon Riders either. A shiver went down my spine, recognizing how much power the people I stood next to could wield. I was glad I was on their side.

"They went to the ship," he said simply.

"What?" A rushing sound filled my ears. If they had gone to the ship, regardless of their intentions, they would encounter Devland directly. If he caught them unaware...

"We need to go get them. It's too dangerous. Devland was making his move to go back to the ship when Galen rescued me. He's probably there now." My words came out too fast. My mind reeled. I saw too clearly the image of Riel and Masika lying dead at the bottom of the ocean. "We can't let him get away."

Kasiel grimaced, but Galen stepped in. "I agree. We may have caused Devland to become unpredictable. He'll know of Casimir's involvement, if he doesn't already. Chefren is still alive, and we can assume he has told Devland about our interruption. He will expect us."

Kasiel turned on his heel and marched toward Casimir. He checked the straps on his sword, tightening the buckles against him. He unbuckled a dagger from his thigh and handed it to me.

"Take this in case you get caught again." Kasiel thrust the dagger toward me. "And actually use it this time."

I strapped the dagger to my thigh, its weight lighter than my own. I missed my dagger, and I was determined to get it back.

"And there's one more thing." Kasiel rummaged through his satchel. Bottles clanked against one another. He pulled out another small vial. It was the same silver liquid I had seen the men in the tea shop use.

"This should help block Chefren's mental capabilities. I only have one, so I'm giving it to you."

"We should share it," I countered. Kasiel stroked his chin in thought.

"It will decrease the potency. You won't have as much time, and I'm positive I can keep myself hidden—"

I raised my hand in protest. "I'm not willing to take that risk. We share it and I'll kill him before it wears off," I stated. Kasiel raised his eyebrow at me and nodded. He tipped back the vial and drank half and handed the rest to me. I swallowed down the rest of the liquid and winced at the sour taste.

Galen offered a helping hand to Kasiel when he approached Casimir's wing, but Kasiel brushed his hand away. He climbed up with impressive grace.

"You're next." Galen held out his hand to me as I clambered on. Casimir shook his head in irritation, but he wasn't hostile. Galen climbed up, causing me to be sandwiched between the two men in the cramped saddle.

We took off abruptly. The docks weren't far, and my stomach dropped with the sudden decline toward the city. As we made our approach, the people of the islands scattered and screamed. They ran away from the dragon and his talon-tipped feet, leaving a wide berth around us.

I slid off the saddle after Kasiel. He didn't even say a word before he took off toward *The Devil's Serpent*. I headed after him, but I stopped when I realized Galen wasn't following. I turned and saw he still sat atop Casimir.

"You go ahead! I'm going to destroy the drugs here and I'll catch up after." Casimir shot up to the sky in a single swoop of his wings. The wind knocked me back as I watched in awe as they climbed higher and higher. I spared them one last glance before I turned and ran toward the ship.

WITH MY MAGIC FULLY restored, I camouflaged myself in the shadows of the ship's hull. The sun was still high, so I carefully trod next to the ropes hooked on the belaying pins for shade. The deck was empty. All the pirates vacated to shore for whatever degenerate activities they wanted to be involved in.

I stayed crouched in the shade, invisible, listening carefully for any sounds of Riel, Masika, or even Devland. With renewed strength, I pumped my legs to a run across the deck, wincing at the creaks the wood made beneath each step. I aimed myself at another shady spot on the deck next to the door that led down to the lower decks. I reached for the door, but as my hand brushed to the wooden handle, it swung open violently, and I yanked my hand back to my chest, holding in a hiss of surprise.

"Tie them up, and keep your swords to their throats!" Devland stomped onto the deck in front of me. His face was red, and his hair disheveled. Four figures followed him out, and I gasped.

Chefren and another pirate had Riel and Masika bound and chained in the magic suppressant cuffs. I couldn't blink, couldn't move, as I watched Chefren tie Riel and Masika to a mast. The other pirate held a sword at their throats. Riel and Masika both sported blooming bruises and cuts. Blood trickled down Riel's face and his cheeks were swelling.

I stood, frozen in place, trying to take in every detail. Riel was strong and fast. How did he get caught so quickly? My heart beat out of my chest, and I fully expected to grab Chefren's attention, but it appeared the potion split between Kasiel and me was working.

A tendril of wind wrapped around my right bicep; a warning. I hadn't even realized I was making my way toward them, disregarding the patterns of the sunlight on the ship. Kasiel's magic stopped me before I stepped into the sun, revealing myself in full form. I turned around to whisper a thanks, but I didn't see him anywhere.

I turned my attention back to Devland. He was making his way to the captain's cabin. The room that he had nearly killed me in just a few days ago. I wondered if he held any remorse for the way he betrayed me when memories of us were etched into the desk in his cabin. Could a monster even feel guilt?

On swift and quiet feet, I danced past Riel and Masika, silently promising that I would get them out of here. I ached to go to them and unbind their shackles, but I kept reminding myself to be patient.

I followed behind Devland. He didn't notice when I slid my foot in the door to keep it from closing, nor when I slipped inside the cabin and allowed myself to stand. My heart pounded in my ears, and I took quiet breaths to calm myself. I squeezed against the far wall, watching as Devland lost himself in anger. He couldn't see me, but I flinched just the same.

Devland was irate. I watched as he slammed his fist against his desk, scattering maps and parchment across the floor. He took his decanter of expensive wine and threw it at the wall. Glass shattered, leaving a dripping red stain on the wall.

He stormed through the cabin, shedding his belt with his weapons and tossing it on the ground. A glimmer caught my eye—a set of keys was on the belt next to the sheathed sword he was normally so careful with.

He stormed into his small bedchamber, slamming the door behind him, and I pounced at the opportunity. In the dim light of the cabin, my shadows firmly clung to my skin. I approached the keyring with practiced hands that had so many times unlocked doors and chests.

The familiar adrenaline of a high-stakes robbery coursed through my veins. My hands shook violently. People's lives were on the line, people I loved. I silently placed the keys into my pockets, but with the way Devland was slamming chest drawers and throwing his belongings around in his room, it was doubtful that he would have heard me, anyway.

Chapter 21

I slipped back out onto the deck. Devland wouldn't leave himself wallowing in anger for too long, so I had to work quickly. Along the port side of the ship, I spotted a quick movement. Hoping it was Kasiel, I dodged ropes and booms toward whatever caught my eye. A figure shrouded in a cape stood across from me, crouching and watching the deck. A tendril of air brushed against my calf. Kasiel's eyes shot to my invisible body, and even though I knew he couldn't see me, he beckoned me toward him.

"I have the keys to the cuffs," I whispered, keeping my eye on the door to the captain's cabin. "Do you think you can take those two out while I free Riel and Masika?" Chefren stood next to Riel, grimacing.

Riel gave him a similar glare to the one he had given me when I was arrested. Chefren was as good as dead to Riel. But his eyes were colder and sharper than I had ever seen. Pure hatred lined his features. Riel had never looked at me with those eyes, and I hoped he never would. Kasiel nodded and sank further to the ground. I felt the air whirl and the pressure thicken. Kasiel's brows creased with concentration.

Two streams of air, so dense I could see them, shot from Kasiel's hands toward Chefren and the other pirate. The air wrapped around them, trapping their arms to their sides and slithered up around their throats, coating their faces and suffocating them. I stared, horrified, watching their faces turn red, then purple.

A slam of the door to the captain's cabin made me jump. Devland, still red with rage, stormed out.

"What the fuck is going on here?" he roared. I scurried toward a shaded part of the ship, even though I was confident he hadn't spotted me. The lingering sunlight made everything so much trickier. His eyes trailed the winding tendrils of air straight to Kasiel.

Devland sprinted to Kasiel before he got away. Devland grappled against Kasiel and pitched one well-aimed blow to his ribs. Kasiel crumpled on the spot. I bit my lip in panic, my eyes roaming around, trying to figure a way to get everyone off the ship. Kasiel's magic faltered, leaving Chefren and the pirate on the ground, gasping for air.

"Get the others. We set sail immediately."

"But, sir," the pirate protested, "the hostages! Shouldn't we at least put them in the brig?"

Devland turned slowly, his eyes wild, his aura deadly. "Are you questioning my authority?"

The pirate recoiled. "N-no, sir. It just might be best for the safety of the crew—"

Devland's face turned purple. "Go get the others. That is an OR-DER!" His voice echoed off the tall spires of stone around us.

The pirate and Chefren clamored up and ran off the deck. It was just us now. I swallowed thickly.

"I know you're there, Leoni." Devland's taunt sent dread down my spine. "Who else would have stolen my keys!?" He twisted about as if he could lock eyes with me and make me visible.

I almost didn't recognize the Devland in front of me. His eyes were so wide the whites surrounded his irises, and he wore a crazed smile that showed all of his teeth.

I crept across the deck, trying to keep my feet light and make no noise as I edged my way across. Devland kept pacing back and forth, not taking his eyes too far from his prisoners.

The sun crested over a pillar and cast the ship in a long shadow, and I breathed a sigh of relief. With the newfound freedom of movement, I found myself behind Riel. His hands were bruised and bloody, tightly bound in those magical manacles.

Devland continued to prowl the ship, throwing taunts and threats. "Leoni, where are you, you invisible sneak?"

Riel's shoulders tightened at his insult, and my heart warmed at his defensiveness. I grabbed two of his fingers, letting him know I was there. He wrapped his bloody hand around mine with a tight grip that was almost painful. I could have sworn I saw him shudder at my touch. I pried my hand out of his slowly, but gave him a reassuring squeeze on his forearm before reaching for the keys.

My hands shook. There were several keys on the ring. Careful not to make any noise, I fumbled for a key that looked small enough to fit the lock on the cuffs. A tiny silver key in the middle of the ring looked like a good fit, and I slid it into the lock.

Please, please, please work, I begged.

The key fit the lock, and I sighed, but I needed it to open quietly. I turned the lock, and with a small click, the cuffs unlocked. I lifted the cuffs off of Riel, carefully avoiding the cuts around his wrists, and pocketed them in my satchel.

Riel kept his hands behind him and kept his face forward. I moved over to Masika and repeated the process. She jolted when I touched her, but I got the cuffs off with ease.

A thundering of footsteps cascaded from the docks and onto the deck of *The Devil's Serpent*. Pirates flooded the ship, moving to their posts, weaving through each other, releasing ropes and sails. Men stormed around me, shouting orders and adhering to the standard cluster of activities to set sail.

I edged my back against the pole Riel was tied to and grabbed his hand. He squeezed me back in reassurance. If we made a move now, we would surely be dead. Devland remained standing, staring daggers at Riel and Masika, as if he could tell we were making plans to escape.

"Wait until we are on the high seas," I whispered to Riel. "Things will calm and people will go below deck once we're out."

I saw Kasiel being dragged to the lower decks by three men while Devland scowled at his captors. I bit back a curse before squeezing Riel's hand. I lurched forward as the ship was setting its sail. It must have been a record time to get the ship out of docks, but Devland knew how to make a quick exit.

"I'm going below. Don't do anything without me back here first."

Riel tensed, and I was sure if he could protest, he would. I sliced the ropes that bound them to the ship with Kasiel's dagger and ran to the lower decks.

Jumping over the ladder, my feet landed with a loud thud. Luckily, it didn't draw any attention. There were men bantering loudly.

Three men threw Kasiel into the small brig and slammed the bars shut.

"You two stay here. I'll go back up and tell the Captain we locked up the bilge rat," said one pirate with dark oily hair, his face scarred and leathery from the sun. He wore an eyepatch. His name was Benji, or Benny, or something like that. I couldn't remember, and it didn't matter, anyway.

"Hang on, Buckey," the one next to him protested, his long dusty blond hair tied in a loose bun at the back of his head. "Why do you get to go up? I ain't no prison guard." He crossed his burly arms over his chest.

The last man stood silently, observing the arguing pirates while cleaning his nails with a knife.

"Because I'm on crow's nest!" Buckey scowled.

"You were on crow's nest last night! It's my turn!"

Two men argued while the third smirked and leaned on the cell bars. I rolled my eyes, used to the constant pirate banter from my time on the ship. I stood in my shadows and watched, hoping they would break out into a fight and knock each other out.

While the men argued, I observed the room. There were fewer drug boxes in the room compared to my previous visit a few days ago. Devland was clearly busy. The artifacts weren't here either, and I wondered if Devland still kept them in his cabin above.

I crept around the cases, searching for a blunt weapon. I held Kasiel's dagger, but didn't want to use it unnecessarily. Along one side of stacked boxes sat a metal crowbar. I wrapped my hand around the cold steel and absorbed it in my shadows.

"You're stronger!" Buckey shouted. "you have ta' stay here."

I crept towards the men, keeping my feet wide, hoping that I could swing with enough strength to knock the bigger one out first. They continued to argue while the third just watched with amusement written on his features. He was thin, but his arms corded with muscle. He would be quick. I just needed to be quicker.

"Fine! I'll stay here with the prisoner, if anything, to get ya outta my face!"

Buckey walked out confidently with a smirk while the burly man stood next to the cell. I inched myself closer and held my breath. I swung. My aim hit my mark with a loud crack.

He crumpled on the floor. I exhaled but didn't linger my eyes on him as the skinny man shot up, his eyes wild in confusion and fear. I reared my arms back and swung again.

My hit missed and hit the outside of his arm instead. I was right. He was fast. He sidestepped, and I stumbled, catching myself before I fell. My feet thudded against the wood, hard and loud.

"Show yourself!" He lunged toward me. I scrambled back and hit the burly unmoving man's body. My legs gave out, and I hit the deck with such force that it knocked the wind out of my lungs.

The man jumped at me, pulling me underneath him. I squirmed and kicked, the large body underneath preventing my feet from getting traction.

The man pinned down my legs, and I writhed beneath him, desperate to get out. Despite his lithe frame, his body was heavy and I couldn't drag in enough breath. I shifted my arms to my sides, grasping for the small dagger on my thigh. He braced his arms around my head, locking me in place.

With all the strength I could muster, I unsheathed the knife and shoved it up into his chest. I stared wide-eyed with shallow breaths as the man gasped and shuddered. I pulled the knife out and blood sprayed over my face, my chest, and my legs.

Warm, sticky blood pooled over me, dripping into my mouth, the coppery tang hitting my taste buds. I strained to shove the dead man, heavier now with his complete weight on me, to the side so I could free myself. My legs shook and my hands trembled as I wrestled him off me. Releasing my shadows, I dropped the dagger with a soft clang against the wooden floorboards.

I knew I needed to move fast, but I couldn't stop staring. My hands wouldn't stop shaking. I had never killed a man before. From how I heard it described from Devland, it was supposed to be exciting. A bloodlust is what Devland had called it.

No. I didn't relish this at all. I emptied my stomach on the floor, gagging and heaving until nothing remained. With my hands braced on my knees, I gave the dead and unconscious men another look.

Shouts and screams echoed from the top of the ship. Shit. Riel and Masika had made their move. I must have taken too long. Of course Riel wouldn't be patient.

Luckily, the key to the brig was on Devland's keyring I stole. Even though I couldn't stop my hands from shaking, I fit the key into the lock and the door swung open. Kasiel was still on the ground, and I sat him up.

"Come on, Kasiel," I urged. Despite his closed eyes, he breathed and had color in his cheeks. His eyes fluttered, but it was too slow. Shouts rang out, and it sounded an awful lot like swords clanging above us.

I smacked Kasiel across the face. My fingers stung at the contact, but I sighed a relieved breath when his eyes flashed open. Those black eyes filled with anger and confusion.

"Kasiel," I breathed his name. "Get up. We have problems we need to attend to." I gestured to the noises above. He grimaced and rolled his neck. They had put no cuffs on him. "Do you still have your magic?"

Kasiel didn't answer and instead took out another vial with a light purple liquid. He downed it in one swig. "I'm fine. Let's go."

Kasiel and I grabbed weapons from the two prostrate pirates, and I sheathed Kasiel's bloodied dagger back to my thigh. I had little practice with the thin sword I stole from the smaller pirate, but it would be better than nothing.

As we stepped onto the dimly lit deck, I slid my magic over me. The sunset cast golden hues across the shining, glittering open sea. The Towering Isles were but a speck on the horizon. I grazed my sight over the deck. The entire ship was in chaos. Blood and sea water coated the wooden slats.

Riel and Masika stood back to back, each holding their own against the onslaught of pirates. Masika would swing, cutting them down one by one, while Riel skipped between pirates, slaughtering four or five at a time. He was using his time magic.

I froze in place as I marveled. It was no wonder why he was considered lethal, and the sight was equally terrifying and fascinating.

I held my breath. Riel was slashing and stabbing, hitting every one of his targets. His muscles strained with each powerful thrust. Blood splattered across his body and face, sweat beading and dripping in rivulets tainted red. I let out an involuntary gasp when a pirate appeared behind him, his sword raised and poised to strike.

As he swung, Riel disappeared and reappeared behind the pirate. With a battle cry that rang out across the ship, Riel carved through the pirate, and innards spilled onto the deck with a slashing spray of blood that arced high in the air.

Masika sliced through another pirate and faced off with Chefren. They scowled at each other, but I could have sworn I saw a tear glisten on Masika's face. They met each other strike for strike, clinging and reverberating across the ship.

I stepped through the bloodbath of the ship. Countless bodies lay prostrate, bleeding out or already dead. Masika and Chefren inched toward me. Tears streaked through blood, dirt, and sweat along her cheeks.

"Why?!" she screamed and lurched toward Chefren. "We trusted you! How could you betray us—how could you betray me?" A vein pulsed at her temple when Chefren only laughed and slid away from her attack.

"You are a fool, Masika. You like your tough facade, but your heart is weak." He met her strike for strike. "Aurum is a cesspool. I just joined the winning side."

He swung for her, and as she parried, I couldn't remove my gaze from Masika's shaking hands.

"I was going to spare you, but you also got involved with that shadow-shifting bitch. I heard your thoughts, Masika. You really think she could save Aurum?" Chefren threw his head back and laughed a full-bellied laugh. He spread out his arms in a mocking posture. I gritted my teeth, my vision slowly turning red.

"The only way Aurum needs to be saved is by going back to the old ways, when the strong fought for what they wanted and the weak died trying."

I didn't dare blink. Masika's eyes went from hurt and betrayal to cold steeled resolve. Chefren was still laughing when Masika charged. His eyes went wide when he realized that Masika's thoughts had shifted.

With his arms still outstretched, Masika thrust her blade into his chest. She pushed it deeper and pierced his heart until the tip was protruding from his back. Blood slowly stained his tunic around the puncture wound. He gasped and fell to his knees. Masika twisted the sword with a resounding shout, and scarlet blood dribbled out of Chefren's mouth. Masika bent toward him, her face level with his as she gritted her teeth.

"The weak are the ones that refuse to change when the opportunity grants a better option. Weakness is reverting to barbaric systems for the comfort of yourself." Masika withdrew the sword slowly. The squish of flesh and blood was louder in my ears than the clinging of swords behind them.

Chefren's eyes rolled into the back of his head and he collapsed. Masika stood tall, and the noise of the ongoing battle behind her came back to me.

I made my way through the crowd, slicing my dagger along any still-standing pirates' calves and ankles. One by one, they would scream and fall. The mixture of copper and salt in the air made bile rise in my throat. Kasiel thrust his wind magic at pirates, throwing them overboard and choking whomever his magic could reach.

The Devil's Serpent became a vessel for the writhing and dying. Devland stood on the bridge, scowling at the slaughter. He gripped the banister in front of him with white knuckles.

My focus narrowed in on him, and I charged. He was responsible for all of this. I saw his face and truly understood the bloodlust term now. I wanted to plunge my fist into his chest and feel his dying heartbeat.

I ran past Riel, who was still fighting off a surly pirate. I ran past Masika. Tears poured down her face as she held her own against the more surviving pirates that crossed her path. I ran past the dead bodies. I ran straight up to Devland and gripped my short sword with a death grip.

With a flick of my wrist, I dismissed my shadows. I wanted Devland to see me while I killed him. I wanted him to see exactly the lengths of what I would do to protect my town, my city, my family.

Devland turned to me. A flash of shock crossed his face and then into a scowl. Time seemed to slow down as I swung my sword. I lifted it over my head, my arms burning with the energy I focused on them. I locked eyes with Devland. His death was mine. Five more steps. Four. Three.

Broad shoulders and dark hair that curled on the ends appeared in front of me, and I gasped. Riel's back was toward me and I watched in horror as he grunted and stumbled forward. A dagger protruded from his chest, the black diamonds gleaming. Devland stabbed Riel and used *my* dagger to do it.

I screamed as Devland grinned with vicious darkness. My heart felt like it was being sliced straight down the middle. I grabbed Riel quickly, keeping him from slamming onto the ground and gentling his fall. Devland seemed to be slower, his hands outstretched, reaching for me in slow-motion. I glanced at Riel to see him grimacing as he held onto the fabric of time.

Devland, grinning like a madman, stood still as a statue with his hands attempting to grab me from Riel, but he was no match against Riel's magic. I glanced down, seeing that he used my dagger to try and kill me, aiming right for my chest. He used my most prized possession, and I didn't even see him do it.

I looked at Riel with disbelief, tears streaming down my face. Everything around us was still and quiet. Not even the wind or sails moved.

The pain from seeing Riel's stab wound fed into the boiling rage I felt. I held onto Riel, blood covering my hands as I tried to stop the bleeding. Devland was in my grasp. I was going to make him pay, and instead, Riel got a knife to the chest because I had been naive to Devland's preparedness.

"Why...?" I pleaded through clenched teeth. "Why would you jump in front of me like that?"

"Leoni," Riel held me in his arms, his golden eyes meeting mine with grave emotion. "He was ready to stab you the moment he saw you."

I tried to blink my tears away as I stared down at Riel, trying to recall every moment from the time I stepped out onto the deck. Riel's hands wrapped around my arms.

"I saw him ready for his attack. And when you removed yourself from your shadows, he was quicker than you were. I'm sorry." Riel had been watching. While fighting, he had never let his mind wander too far away from me. And I had been too overcome with rage to see anything other than Devland's death by my hand to see him ready for his attack.

I crouched over Riel and shuddered. I put my hands on his face. My fingers tingled as I helplessly watched the stab wound leaking onto *The Devil's Serpent*. I spread my hands across his skin, memorizing each crease in his face, memorizing each piece of stubble.

I could find a way to save him—I needed to save him. He was supposed to stay with me. We had so much to do, to achieve together. He promised me we would. Tears fell, beading and dripping down my cheeks as I felt my pain. My chest was caving in, and I couldn't get enough air to breathe.

Without warning, Riel pulled the knife out of his chest. I screamed while he grunted. Blood pooled through his shirt. He coughed, blood spurting out of his mouth, his breaths coming in brief spurts.

"What are you doing?" I demanded, my hands pushing down as hard as I could over the wound. I never let my eyes stray from Riel's beautiful brown eyes. Death had his grip on him. His heart rate was slowing, his healing not working fast enough. Tears flowed freely down my cheeks, and I shook my head. I wasn't ready to lose him.

"Don't cry for me, Leoni." He shoved the dagger into my palm and gave me a hard look. "You know what to do."

I wailed as his eyes fluttered closed and I felt time start to revert. What was I going to do without him? We had only just started to get to know each other. The gods didn't even give us a chance.

Anger and rage pulsed through me. At Devland, at the gods, at this whole situation. Riel held on to his magic as long as he could and I laid him down carefully before dragging my feet underneath me and turned toward Devland's still frozen body.

I stared straight into the eyes of the man that had given me everything and then took it all away.

It was unforgivable, and I was unshakeable.

I HELD THE DAGGER tightly in my palm, the black diamonds warm in my hand. I didn't think twice before rounding behind Devland, placing the tip of my blade on his neck. I gave Riel one last glance and I let my resolve and bitterness and anger flow through me, strengthen me, when Riel's magic faded completely.

The wind picked back up, shouts rang out as the fighting resumed. Devland stiffened under my hold. There was no nausea, no dread when I shoved the dagger into his neck. Devland gurgled and tried to say something, but only spat blood and incoherent sounds.

"This is a message from me," I hissed in his ear, using the same mocking words he had said to me on the docks when he tried to poison me, tried to kill me. "I will stop at nothing to protect the people of Aurum."

I yanked the dagger from his neck and watched in bitter triumph. Devland was my mentor, my partner. But as I watched him kneel on the ground, his own blood flowing and merging with the rest on the deck, I saw him for who he really was. A greedy, power-hungry son of a bitch who could never find it within his cold, nearly dead heart to find something worth living for other than himself.

How wrong I had been. I had once thought the people in Aurum as cold and non-feeling when it was the man who stood beside me all along.

Devland's face slackened, and he collapsed. His lifeless, un-staring eyes were directed at the sky above. I turned to Riel, who lay on the deck next to him, unseeing and gone from this life. I fell to my knees and let my grief overtake me. My hands shook, my sight blurred from my sorrow.

I barely noticed as Kasiel rushed toward me, shoving me aside. My mind and body were numb, and I didn't really care what happened from now on. Devland was dead, but at what cost?

Chapter 22

I STARED AT RIEL while Kasiel rummaged through his bag. He knocked my hand away from Riel, and I growled at him. Placing his head over Riel's chest, he seemed to sigh a breath of relief.

How dare he push me away from Riel? The man that sacrificed himself so I could have my vengeance. I was supposed to be the one curled on top of him. Who did he think he was?

I reached out to shove Kasiel off of Riel. I needed to hold Riel in my arms. He was gone–and my heart was with him. I needed to feel his skin against mine one last time. Kasiel tipped the potion into Riel's too-still mouth and cursed, and I stopped in my tracks.

"Come on, General." Kasiel's black eyes met mine, and a flicker of panic gleamed from them. But that wasn't right. Kasiel never panicked.

I held my breath in false hope. I had seen Riel die, watched his life fade away right before my eyes. Bringing the dead back to life was impossible. But as I was talking myself out of feeling any sort of hope,

I saw Riel's chest move the tiniest amount and gasped. He coughed a wracking, wet cough, blood spewing from his lips, but he was alive.

I cried out, flinging myself over Riel, burying my face in his neck. Relief, confusion, gratitude filled my heart.

"You should be grateful I packed extra healing potions," Kasiel growled at Riel. "I got to you just in time. A minute later and your heart would have stopped beating and there would be nothing I could do."

"You saved him," I blabbered through my tears. My arms wrapped around Riel. I would never let him go again. His steady beating heart thumped against me, and I sobbed in relief.

"It's nothing," he muttered under his breath before he walked away.

I turned to Riel who was taking healthy deep breaths. I ripped his tunic apart, revealing the hole in his chest that had already stitched together.

"Thank the gods," I said to him through wet eyes.

"Did you kill him?" Riel asked, his eyes sparkling with hope. I nodded my head rapidly.

"I did." I gave him a smile that had nothing to do with the dead pirate lord. My smile was only for the very much alive eyes that drank me in.

Riel's breaths were becoming steadier, his chest rising and falling, and the color and warmth returned to his skin. I clutched his hand, my fingers tingling and biting into his skin.

He is alive.

I kept repeating it to myself, like if I blinked for one second, he would be gone again. Riel sighed, and let his eyes flutter closed, utter exhaustion wracking through his body. I squeezed his hand tighter until he peeked his eyes open at me.

"Don't ever do that again," I demanded of him. "My life is not worth the cost of your own, ever." I was relieved he was alive, but anger settled through my veins. I didn't deserve to be saved. My soul was tainted, and Riel's was pure. He was a good, honest man, and I was a lying thief.

"Leoni," Riel's raspy voice jolted me out of my thoughts. "Your life is worth everything."

My throat tightened and more tears cascaded down my cheeks. I smiled back down at him, but he was wrong, so very wrong.

WITH DEVLAND AND HIS pirates dead, only Riel, Masika, Kasiel, and I remained on the blood-stained ship. We were all worn out. No one said any words. The breeze billowed through the sails, making them flap against each other. I propped Riel up against the side of the ship, color finally returning to his face. The blood on his shirt only reminded me of how close I had come to losing him, and how desperate I was to keep him.

The cloth slapping against ropes sounded like a bell toll for the dead among us. Masika was next to Chefren's lifeless body, her sword forgotten next to her as she buried her head in her hands. Kasiel slung his arm around her, turning her away from Chefren's corpse. He pulled out his transporter and whisked them back to Aurum.

Riel stood up, his legs gaining strength, and I thanked the gods for Kasiel and his witch sister. We stared at each other, both covered in blood, our chests heaving. I twisted toward Devland's cabin.

"The relics!" I shouted, my voice too loud for the quiet of the dead. "Devland kept them in his cabin." I raced to the cabin, Riel slowly following behind me, our footsteps heavy over the silent deck.

I flung open the door to find nothing but the wine stain on the wall and Devland's personal artifacts and cursed. There was only the same vase sitting amongst other relics that Devland kept for his own personal inventory. Ones that I now knew had to have priceless worth, but weren't the ones that the King wanted.

"They're gone," I breathed. I didn't notice them missing when I stole his keys, too preoccupied with the dire need for survival. Riel stalked over to his private bedchambers and threw the door open, also revealing an empty room.

Riel made a noise that sounded like a growl.

"Where could they have gone?" I asked in horror. If the King of the mortal lands already had the artifacts, the chances of us getting them back were slim to none.

"They weren't down below?" he asked while he limped around Devland's empty space.

I shook my head. "No, and most of the drugs were gone, too."

Riel cursed and raked his hands through his hair in frustration. In the distance, Casimir roared. I breathed a sigh of relief. The cavalry had arrived.

"Time to go, Leoni," Riel warned. I grabbed his hand and pulled him back onto the main deck. We climbed onto the side of the ship, the vast ocean smooth and glittering beyond us. An infinite sea for infinite possibilities. I breathed in the salty air, silently saying goodbye to this ship, to the life that I had once lived.

Riel jumped first, but I waited until I saw brown hair emerge from the water before reassuring myself he was okay.

With one deep breath of finality, I launched myself off the side of *The Devil's Serpent*. For one fleeting moment, I embraced the sea air and the feeling of falling before I crashed into the sea. I allowed myself to sink in the warm water. It invited and enveloped me.

Red stained the clear water around me. I let the water wash away the blood and death that had surrounded me on this day. I would emerge from the surf a new woman with a new life to look forward to.

Fresh sea air filled my lungs as I broke through the water, and I blinked the salt water out of my eyes. The ship had drifted further away from us, the white sails puffed and billowing in a current of air.

Riel was next to me, treading water. I swam up to him and clung to him, feeling his face, his shoulders. He touched his brow to mine, and I smiled and embraced him in return. I pressed my lips to his, and he wrapped his arms around me, holding me tight, but a booming roar from the sky cut our kiss short.

Casimir flew above us, circling the ship. Red scales radiated in the orange sunset. Hot, bright flames shot from the dragon's mouth and engulfed *The Devil's Serpent*. The ship never even stood a chance against the dragon's flames. Sails deteriorated, the masts cracked and fell. The hull was fully ablaze, and with it, my lifetime's work as a thief. The ship that had provided me with so much temporary shelter was no more.

Casimir swung low and sank into the sea next to us. Water sprayed and doused me and Riel. We swam toward the magnificent beast, the blazing ship at our backs. We didn't say a word as Galen held out his hand and helped us climb on top of Casimir's back, both of us eager to put the day behind us.

Kasiel and Masika were waiting for us back at the beach we used as our rendezvous point before leaving for the Isles. The sun had completely set, and the stars were twinkling against the increasing darkness. I slid off Casimir's back as soon as he landed. The sand under my feet never felt so good.

I ran to Masika and met her with a hard embrace. Her face was puffy and red. My heart squeezed for her. The betrayal that she was feeling. She would need some time to reconcile with it. She leaned into me and sobbed into my neck.

I squeezed my arms around her and whispered, "Someone very wise told me he doesn't deserve any more of your tears. It's time to focus on how to fight what's next." She nodded into my neck and took a shuddering breath. "But, I think it's okay to let yourself feel, Masika." She pulled away from my embrace and grasped my hands in hers. "I'm here for you whenever you need to talk, if you want to."

Masika nodded and stepped away. She blinked back her tears and stood up straight.

Kasiel turned to us, his black hair now loose and fluttering in the seaside breeze. There were no signs of the ship. We were too far away. A part of me had wished I could see the billowing smoke on the horizon, if only to confirm the reality of Devland's death.

Kasiel stood with an unnatural calm, considering our situation. "Well, if that's all, I will express my gratitude and be taking my leave."

"What about the rest of the drugs?" Riel's hand rested on the small of my back as he approached from behind.

I glanced between Kasiel and Riel, but it was Galen who answered, "I burned the drugs in the cave, but we don't know where else Devland may have distributed them."

"We cut the snake's head off," Kasiel replied, "we just need to suck the venom out where we can. Or we can let the drugs dissipate in their own time. They will run out eventually."

Riel rubbed a hand against his chin. "And what about the missing relics?"

Galen stepped forward with his head high. "I will keep an eye out for them as I trek my way back to the mortal lands. If the King wants them, there must be a reason, and I have a duty to find out why."

Riel nodded. "In the meantime, I'll have to bolster security. And even then, I think I'll have to give more incentive to our guards to perform their jobs correctly." Riel glanced down at me with a twinkle in his eye. "I believe you might be of some help with that, Leoni. As our District Liaison, you have more insight into the inner workings of our working men and women and what they need."

My face reddened. I wasn't sure I was exactly qualified to answer his request, but I had hope that I could at least ease relations between districts.

Galen offered to use Casimir to drop us off in the city, but Riel had dismissed the idea. A dragon sighting in the city would cause panic. So, despite our exhaustion, we trudged through the sand that eventually turned into stone and dirt.

I sighed at the sight of the tall golden spires that towered over the city. Those strong, tall towers that held through storms of sand and wind. Pillars of hope for a future. A future with promises of self-improvement and sheer will to thrive. That is what Aurum stood for, what it had overcome. It is what I would do for Aurum in return.

Masika bid us goodnight even though I had insisted she come back to the house with us. Despite the pain she was in, Riel reassured me she would be fine for one night. I made a point of remembering to visit her in the morning.

"How are you dealing with Chefren's betrayal?" I asked Riel.

He looked up at the moon thoughtfully before he answered.

"I won't lie and tell you it doesn't sting, but I don't suppose I'm too surprised, to be honest."

"Why? Wasn't he your friend?"

"He was, but—" Riel sighed. "I was still his superior. He was beholden to my orders. Masika and Chefren were in similar ranks, so I imagine they bonded that way. But we were never such companions. If I'm being honest, it wasn't the first time I've been betrayed, and it won't be the last." He let out a frustrated breath of air. "You already know I find it hard to trust, and so I often prepare for such instances."

"Don't get too close to the fire, lest you get burned," I muttered, and he nodded. My life was lived in a similar way. Perhaps that's why, even when Devland's betrayal hurt, I didn't feel the same grief that Masika did.

We walked the rest of the way to the house in silence. When we arrived at the gate, I stopped. The house was beautiful as always, with a clean pathway to the door lined with native desert plants of dusty reds and light greens. Under the light of the low-hanging moon, they almost looked silver.

"What is it, Leoni?" Riel stopped a few steps ahead of me.

I gazed at the Quarters and realized I was no longer a prisoner or bound by a bargain. The perfectly carved walls and the solid wood-framed door—they no longer held me. My duties were finished. I could walk away entirely if I wanted to. I was a free woman.

My feet were planted on the solid ground, but the world seemed to move underneath me. My breath hitched. I couldn't stay here. If I remained, I would be falling into the same pattern as those I despised. I couldn't enjoy luxury while my family and people lived in squalor.

Riel had risked his life because of me, and I truly wasn't deserving. He offered me his home, his life, his partnership, but what had I even offered him in return? A sinking feeling gripped my soul. I wasn't worthy of his forgiveness or his sacrifice. I wasn't worthy of him.

Tears pricked the back of my eyes, and my chest heaved. I promised Riel I would stay, build a new Aurum together, but I just didn't know how it could be feasible. I was a thief, born and raised. He was Aurum's General.

Now that the mission was over, surely we would be, too. No matter what we felt for each other now, our lives were too different, our futures holding different fates. Shadows danced along my fingertips, pulsing in the same rhythm as my cracking heart.

"Leoni?" Riel turned and his brow pinched in confusion. His gaze tracked to where a single tear had rolled down the side of my cheek.

"I-I don't belong here, Riel. This isn't my life." My heart started beating so fast I thought it would burst from my chest. I thought I could become something that I knew in my heart I wasn't.

Doubts that whispered in the back of my mind were now a raging, blaring shout. I played a fun little game of detective and deliverer of justice, but now I was back in the real world. One where a Lord and the other high-standing citizens would never see me as an equal.

I would have to fight front and center to get what I needed for my people. My shadows could no longer hide me. I would have to step forward into the light. I breathed heavily, the weight of the prospect terrifying me into my bones. Riel rushed over and grasped my face between his palms, forcing me to look into his eyes.

"What is it? Tell me what you're thinking." His face was creased with worry, his hands comforting but strong against my cheeks.

"I want to keep my promise, but I can't keep the promise I made to my family, the people in the South District, and keep the one I made to you at the same time. I want to help, but I can't live here while my family suffers—I need to go back home." My heart raced, and my head hummed with a lightheadedness that I desperately needed to clear.

"I really appreciate everything you have done for me. I can't express how much I hurt when I thought you died, but I just can't picture myself walking into this life as a true equal..."

"You're just tired, and we went through a lot today. Let's rest and we can talk about it in the morning." Riel grazed his thumb against my cheekbone and wiped away my tears.

Everything felt like all too much and not enough at the same time. My thoughts were incoherent. I couldn't think straight. I stepped back from Riel, unsure of what I even wanted anymore.

I willed my shadows up my arms, but they were reluctant. My magic was my heart and soul, and it warred with my mind. My shadows nor my heart never cared for logic. Riel zeroed in on my arms, slowly disappearing into nothingness.

"Wait! Leoni!" he growled. He stalked toward me, and it took everything in my soul to turn my head away from his golden-brown eyes.

"I'm sorry. I just need my home right now," I whispered. My voice cracked. I flung my arms over my head and disappeared. I didn't glance back and started running. His steps behind me got fainter with each beat of my heart.

I didn't stop running. My legs burned, my lungs ached, and my magic waned, but I did not stop. My feet slammed against the cobblestone of the city center until they met the wood of the docks. Ships and buildings rushed past me in a watery blur. It didn't matter how many times I wiped across my face, the tears refused to cease. When I slowed, utterly spent, I found myself staring up at the orphanage. My home.

It was dark and quiet. Everyone inside was asleep, laughter and shrieking children resting until the rise of the sun. I would disrupt the rare peace in the orphanage by going in. But it was all I had. This was my home, where I needed to be.

I was meant to be in the South District, protecting everyone I know here. Where I would hide in the shadows for them. Where I would take the fall for them. I would put myself in the line of their fire so they might all have a better life.

I tried to slide through the cloth, but found a new door instead. Hard wood slid under my palms. I jiggled the knob, but it was locked. My heart ached even though they finally had some semblance of safety. I was locked out of my home—the one place I would never lock pick my way inside.

My knees buckled and the emotions I was half attempting to hold in poured out. I held my face in my palms as sobs wracked through my chest. For the first time since I could remember, I felt lonely. I left a piece of my soul on that property of the General's Quarters.

I just needed some normalcy. Instead, there was a stupid door that kept me away from the only comfort I could have. I was truly Leoni of No One.

"Leoni?" Tala's soft voice pulled me from my thoughts. "What are you doing here?" She pulled me off the ground, her warm arms wrapping around me. My sobs grew harder, tears staining the soft nightdress she wore.

"I'm sorry," I sputtered. "I just wanted to come home." She led me into the house and sat me down at the kitchen table. Someone replaced the table. What was a rickety piece of wood before was now new and sturdy.

Tala gave my shoulders a squeeze. "Let me pull you a cot for tonight. You look terrible."

I let out a laugh through my tears. Tala was never one to shy away from the brutal truth.

I squeezed her hand in thanks, and she looked at me with knowing eyes.

"You always have a place here, Leoni."

She left me by myself, fetching items for me to rest on, and I took in the surroundings of the orphanage's kitchen. Shelves that were crooked or crumbling were replaced and fixed. Pots and pans shined in newness against the flickering lanterns. Lanterns...

Gone were the mostly melted candles that threatened to burn the orphanage down. A new stone oven lined one side of the kitchen, big enough to make large batches of food. The entire kitchen looked like it had been renovated.

Tala returned with her arms full of linens, blankets, and even a fluffy pillow. She placed them in my arms, and I inspected them. There were no holes, no signs of wear. I frowned.

"Where did you get all of this?" The money I had provided before my arrest was substantial, but to afford all of this...I estimated it would have cost at least three or four times the amount. My heart beat faster.

I stole and robbed so that no other child would have to. If someone else had taken up my mantle, if my arrest had sparked illicit behavior in another child...I wouldn't know what to do. My stomach turned.

"Your general friend came to us shortly after your arrest. He offered to fix up the orphanage for free." She gave me a small smile and patted my wrist. I snapped my mouth closed. Riel had done this? Blood rushed through my ears. He had done all of this, and I just left him in the dark as I ran away. A tear slid down my cheek.

"Of course," she continued, "I turned him down at first. The government never cared about us and I thought he had ulterior motives. Wanting information about you or something else, I didn't know.

"He stopped by here every day, insisting that he only wanted to help. He said that he had a good friend that enlightened him about our needs." She sighed. It was a satisfied sound, one that released ages of worry and fatigue.

"After he stopped by the third time, I ran into Jyran and his wife. She was healthy—glowing, even. Jyran told me about The General, how he saw you two together, how he saved her life. I let him in to help the next day."

While I had been stuck in the Quarters, crying over Riel's absence, fearing what the next day might bring, Riel was feeding and providing for my family. New tears stung my eyes.

"Why?" I asked.

"Because I care more for you than I have cared about another person since I can remember. Because I want to make you happy. I want to make your life easier, no matter what happens in our future." I whirled to find Riel leaning against the wall. His hair was disheveled, and his eyes crinkled in a worried smirk. I longed to run to him, to feel his embrace. Instead, I sat still with my heart in my throat.

Riel peeled himself from the doorway and made his way to me. Tala quietly removed herself from the kitchen but shot me a knowing look over her shoulder before disappearing around the corner.

Riel dropped to his knees in front of me and I followed. We sat on the floor, staring at each other. He held my hands tightly, unsure if he should pull me closer.

"I meant it when I said I couldn't lose you," he whispered. His hands slightly trembled in mine.

"Why did you follow me?" I asked.

"Leoni, I would traverse the world to find you. I would scour every corner of Ambrose, dive into the depths of the ocean, and raze through the mortal lands if it meant I would find you and bring you home."

"Home?" Tears welled in my eyes. "I'm not sure I have a home right now." I looked around, noting all the changes. The orphanage certainly didn't feel like my home anymore.

"Your home is with me." Riel lifted his hand and stroked his thumb across my cheek. His fingers wrapped around the back of my head, cradling it, and I leaned into his touch.

"I belong here, with my family. I need to take care of them." I breathed in his earthy scent and it quieted my pounding heart.

"Look around, Leoni. Does it look like your family is struggling right now? They are safe, they are resting peacefully, and they aren't going hungry. I meant every word I said to you. But we need to do this together. I need you with me. We can achieve more, but not from the South District alone."

I chewed on my bottom lip while I let myself absorb the changes he made to the orphanage. The children could have normal childhoods with the money he put in this place. Even Tala looked more well-rested than usual.

"You set the plan into motion, and I have the resources. We are a team—if you want to be." Riel's eyes were pleading with me, and I wiped the frown away between his brows.

I heard tiny footsteps approaching me from behind, and when I turned around, I saw Seth with bleary eyes. I quickly wiped my tear-tracked cheeks with my sleeve, blinking back any more that willed to fall.

"What are you doing awake?" I asked and reached for the child. He crawled into my lap. He weighed heavier in my lap than he did months ago, but I loved that he still was young enough to feel comfortable piling onto me.

"I thought I heard you and Riel, and I wanted to say hi." He yawned into my neck and I patted his back. I couldn't help the chuckle I let out.

"You two are on a first-name basis?" I asked, and Seth nodded sleepily.

Riel shifted, reaching for something in his pocket. "I was going to give this to Tala to give to you later, but since you're here now—" Riel pulled out a shiny purple and blue sea shell. "It's supposed to be a shell from the belt of a mermaid."

Seth gasped and scrambled from my arms to Riel. I raised my eyebrow at Riel. I mouthed the word 'mermaid' in a question and he shrugged with a smirk. "I may have lifted it from a certain ship. That's what the plaque said next to it." Red tinged Riel's cheeks.

I widened my eyes. Riel had stolen one of Devland's artifacts. If Seth wasn't clamoring and asking Riel demanding questions, I would have kissed him right then. He spent weeks renovating the orphanage and getting to know the children. Tears spilled onto my filthy tunic.

Riel looked up at me. "Leoni, you are my family. Your family is my family. I take care of my family, and I want to take care of you, too."

I gave him a grin and curled myself around Seth while he protested and squealed in my arms.

"Time to go back to bed, Seth." I nudged Seth back towards the hallway and he giggled, clutching the shell in his small hands. "I won't tell Tala that you've been sneaking out of bed, either." He gave me one last hug, and then wrapped his arms around Riel's neck and scurried away.

I stood up, still smiling, and reached my hand out to Riel. "Let's go home."

I WOKE UP THE next morning fully awake from a restful sleep. We had returned from the orphanage, bathed, and piled into bed, falling asleep almost instantly. I couldn't remember the last time I had slept so well.

Riel held me in his arms, and he tightened his hold when I stretched. He pulled me closer to him, his very obvious erection pressing into my back. I leaned into him and let out a groggy moan. I could stay in his arms forever. My heart swelled as I brushed my fingers over his dark skin, tracing lines along his forearm.

Riel pressed kisses along my neck, gentle and smooth, with my skin pebbling under each breath he took in between. His hand drifted lower, and my thighs moistened under his gentle touch, but it was too gentle, too soft. I needed him. My body called for him.

I pressed my hand on his hardened cock, and he hissed in pleasure, but grabbed my wrist and pushed it away. Riel rolled us over, pinning me underneath him, his arms caged around my head. He looked into my eyes and then dropped his gaze to my lips. "Do you trust me?"

I nodded. "With my life." Riel gave me a wicked grin, and I raised my eyebrow. I clenched my thighs at the sight. He could get me off with that look alone.

I blinked. Riel was no longer caging me in, and instead, at the end of the bed and in his hands, he held the large tunic I was using as sleepwear. He chuckled darkly, biting his lip as he took in my now nearly naked body still lying on the bed. I hadn't felt a thing until the cool air brushed along my skin, leaving pebbles in its wake. I gasped, but then I blinked again.

He was now on the side of the bed, the undergarment covering my breasts removed.

"Riel!" I squealed with laughter. Riel was grinning mischievously, his eyes hooded. I could hardly keep up with Riel using his time magic, but my body sang as he removed more clothing. This was wild and nothing like I could have imagined. My heart beat erratically, not knowing what Riel's next move would be, and my body tingled with anticipation.

I blinked again, and he was back on top of me, my nipple wet and taught and he stroked his thumb along my other breast. Pleasure crashed through me suddenly. When Riel stopped time, my body collected every feeling, every nerve that was touched, and released at once.

He leaned in, his hot breath caressing the shell of my ear as he spoke. "I'm going to give you so much pleasure that your body won't know how to process it. I'm going to make you come before you even know you're there and then I won't stop. I want to see you shaking. I want to see you so weak from my tongue that you can't form words."

I nodded, giving him a wicked grin. "Do it."

Riel chuckled as his hand drifted lower. His fingers toyed with my clit. Gentle, soft circles that had me writhing for more. He dipped his finger into me, and my hips bucked at the sensation. I felt his smile against my cheek. "You're so wet already, Leoni. How messy can I make you by the time I'm done?"

"Let's find out," I whispered in a husky voice filled with lust. I was already breathless, heat rising through my body. My hips undulated under him, begging for friction, begging for more than those gentle swirls of his fingertips.

Riel shifted and moved down my body, his lips and tongue dancing across my skin. He chuckled and licked my center. I was on fire. One of his hands pressed my thigh down, and the other continued kneading my breast. I moaned.

"More."

"Your wish is my command," he purred against me.

An overwhelming orgasm nearly sent my hips through the roof. My thighs shook, and my breaths were raw and haggard. I didn't have time to process what happened. My limbs tingled as wave after wave of pleasure was wrung from my body. So much sensation moved through me at once, and I screamed until my throat turned raw. I was positive that Riel had just sent me into another realm. My body was practically floating.

My limbs sagged, and no matter how much I wanted to move, I couldn't. Pleasure coursed through me and I looked down to see Riel gripping my thighs. Wet evidence of my pleasure coated his chin. My body struggled against his grip involuntarily. I panted and shook, Riel's eyes gleaming with wickedness.

He pressed two fingers into me, and I moaned. I was sensitive and sated. I didn't know how, but I was on the verge of another orgasm. He pumped in and out slowly and I uttered incoherent words as he pressed on the spot that made me roll into his hand. He groaned as he felt my walls tighten around his fingers. I was on the edge of the cliff, ready to fall. He leaned over me once again, his fingers pumping into me with one hand, fisting his cock with another.

"Look at you," he murmured. "Untamed and wild and blushing. Utter perfection."

I whimpered as he removed his fingers, leaving me empty and wanting. He dug his hand into my thigh, lifting it as he pressed into me. His cock stretched and filled me and I couldn't help the cry I let out. Inch by inch, I took him and he slid in painfully slowly until he filled me to the hilt. He smirked down at me, his eyes closed, and I could feel his cock twitch inside me.

"Fuck," he hissed. "You feel incredible, Leoni," he groaned. "You make me come undone." I basked in his compliments and arched into him.

Riel thrust into me over and over, hard and concise. My breasts bounced from the force. I couldn't think, could barely breathe, as he took and claimed me over and over. I was free-falling into the pleasure and sensations that Riel had played so expertly through my body.

Sweat beaded over the both of us, the only sound was our panting and skin slapping skin as our bodies collided. Riel moaned as he came—his arms collapsing from under him. His weight pressed into my body as he released, and we lay there for moments, catching our breath, and I lifted my arms around him.

I was Riel's, and he was mine.

Chapter 23

"Leoni, we can't get rid of every item in the household." Riel came up behind me, wrapping his arms around me and prying a very expensive, very fragile lamp from my hands.

"The easiest way to get quick money to the South District is if we sell the items we don't need," I countered with exasperation. The weeks following the destruction of *The Devil's Serpent* were filled with countless meetings and stuffy politics.

There were promises from Aurum's leaders to find funds to funnel into the poorer areas of the city, but it was all so political. And it took far too long.

The Lord fought us on every proposal we made, so I was determined to find other ways to send money to the orphanage and get medicine to that part of town. Determined to do it legally. Which meant selling items that I now considered mine, since Riel had declared that I was to be his wife at the end of the season. So as far as I was concerned, what was his was now mine, and if we didn't need it, I was going to sell it.

I turned to him and melted at the sight of him. He wore a sideways smile, something that I had never imagined he could wear so easily. He smiled down at me, pressing his lips to mine, and I kissed him back. I let out a small moan, and he grinned against my lips.

I soon forgot the lamp as he swept me off my feet, carrying me down the hall toward the bedroom. He laid me on our bed, still plush and messy, since neither one of us cared to make it after we woke up. He trailed kisses down my neck, his hands roaming under my shirt and working their way around my breasts.

"I love seeing you this way," he muttered against my skin, sending shivers down my spine and heat through my core.

"And how is that?" I laughed, "selling all of your frivolous items?"

"I was going to say 'healthy and happy in my arms'. But also completely at my disposal," he joked back. But it wasn't a joke, not really. He had me at his complete mercy, and I met his touch, tearing away his shirt, and exposing those defined muscles and smooth skin.

His lips met mine, and it sent a shockwave through me. Something that felt like an invisible thread wrapped around me, around us. Our shared love had always felt like a deep connection, but today there was something more, something urgent. I opened my eyes to see not an invisible thread, but a shining golden cord weaving around the both of us.

"What the fuck?" I gasped.

He lifted his eyes and sucked in a breath. He stood, pulling me up with him, his hand firmly clasping my own. The thread weaved around our hands, swirling and twirling and binding. He shook his head in awe.

"Soulmates..." his words trailed off, but he met my gaze with a burning desire. My heart raced, and the thread pulsed around us, waiting. The pages of the history book in Riel's personal study flooded my mind. I read those pages an embarrassing amount after I settled into Riel's house. But those were stories from before the gods disappeared. How was this possible? Riel licked his lips as he traced the thread with his eyes.

"We have to either accept it or deny it—they say it's a bond that will bind us together forever," I said. I looked up at Riel, who was staring down at me. His lips were parted and a look of wonder held his features.

I watched the thread binding around us. I had already planned to spend forever with Riel, but this was The Divine. The gods had been gone for ages, but there was no denying they were very much alive right now. The golden thread around us hummed and sang an ethereal tune, and I couldn't help myself from wondering why?

Why would the gods choose now, and why would they choose us for this bond? Plenty of people fell in love, but as far as I knew, Riel and I weren't any different from any other couple in Ambrose.

"What happens when we do?" I peered up at Riel, whose face was blank. The General mask had taken over, assessing everything.

"I don't know," he responded.

"What happens if we don't?" A flash of concern passed over his features, but he quickly schooled back into his mask. His hands tightened on mine, but I gave him a wide smile.

"You don't have to worry." I leaned into him, stepping on my toes to whisper in his ear. "I love you, Riel." I didn't know what would happen after we accepted the bond, but I was all in with Riel, whether he liked it or not.

"For all the good and bad. I would never leave you, even if the gods tried to force us apart themselves." The gold thread crackled at my words. "If that means I have to accept this call to be yours forever, I choose so willingly." The threads hummed, and Riel's eyes lit up with desire, excitement, and what I could only describe as pure adoration. He swiped a thumb over my lips and pulled my chin toward him.

"By the gods, Leoni, I love you. I will allow nothing to come between us, and if we are bonded, then I accept it with honor."

The golden thread intertwined and circled us. It spun around us and wrapped around our limbs. The thread brushed against our skin, and I shivered from the contact. The entire room was bathed in gold. It kept wrapping around us, and then it sank into our skin, and I felt it.

I felt my heartbeat synchronize with Riel's. I felt the gasps of breath he took. A small entwining line of gold sank onto my skin, on my wrist—the same one that I wore the bracelet all those months ago. It marked my skin in continuous lines and patterns. It was subtle, but in the light, it shimmered. Riel held his arm next to mine. He had the same markings, a mirror image. The thread had tied our souls together, and our hearts beat as one.

Seven Years Later

"Eduard Magnus, you have been negligent to Aurum's citizens, citing the use of city funding for your own personal gain. As a result, Aurum's health and morale has depleted from the once-known thriving city in Ambrose. We propose for the removal of your title, stripping away your privileges of command. All of whom are in favor say 'aye'."

A stout man with hair white as the snow-capped mountains declared in our small circle of Aurum's council. Riel and I worked hard to join the Council and fulfill our duties to Aurum. Theo, the oldest council member, grew on me over the past few years.

He was a vital piece of the reformation of Aurum and I found that our values were often aligned. He was the first to persuade the councilors to invest in all citizens' welfare. Our work was far from over, but we had made incredible strides.

The sound of the majority of the council's "Aye" reverberated against the pillars in the shiny gold central room in Aurum's largest spire. My heart swelled, knowing that half the battle was won. Lord Eduard's face was red with anger as he started sputtering.

"This is preposterous! You have no right to do this!" He pointed his long finger at me. "That half-witted criminal scum is at fault for all the problems in Aurum! She has no right to be here!"

Riel stiffened next to me, his arms banded across his chest.

"Watch what you say about my wife," he snarled at the Lord. The golden mark on Riel's wrist pulsed with his heartbeat. I placed my hand on his forearm.

"It's okay, Riel," I whispered. He leaned back in his chair, his shoulders relaxing slightly, but he didn't take his eyes off of the renounced Lord.

"Eduard, you are dismissed," Theo waved him off as Eduard seethed.

Riel signaled his guards to remove Eduard from the building.

"Now," Theo commanded the room easily, "we must vote for the next person who will take up the mantle of Eduard's previous position. Please place your votes on the parchment in front of you and hand them to me."

The noise of scratching quills and rustling parchment filled the air. I wrote Theo's name, as I thought of him being the only one on the council that properly deserved the Lordship. I glanced over at Riel, who covered his parchment too quickly for me to see what he wrote, and he smirked at me.

We placed our parchment in the middle on top of the other votes. Once all the votes were in, Theo waved his hand in the air, making the parchment float toward him.

He counted the votes in front of him, each nomination stacked in their own pile. One pile was larger than the rest, and I was curious about who was the obvious victor.

"I don't think this comes as any surprise." Theo smiled. "But our new Lady will be Leoni Valor. Former District Liaison, current Lady of Aurum."

I sat, shocked, and glanced at Riel, who looked at me with a shit-eating grin on his face.

"You knew this would happen?" I asked with wide eyes, my mouth hanging open. He only shrugged and grasped my hand.

"You are the best person for the job." He placed a small peck on my cheek, and I rose from my chair and regarded all the councilors of Aurum with an awkward smile. I truly wasn't prepared for this, but I would embrace my new title. I had to.

"I don't know what to say." I glanced down at Theo, who was beaming.

Extra attention always felt awkward, no matter how many times I spoke. I never desired to be a Lady in my past, but now…it felt like the right decision. I was the gatekeeper for Aurum's needs.

There would be no more hoops to jump through, because I would be the hoop. I would make all the final decisions. I had every confidence that when I didn't know what to do, I had Riel and those around us to help. The responsibility terrified me, but I had learned that I could use and harness that fear, rather than run from it.

I didn't call my shadows to hide, instead I stood proudly in front of these peering eyes, ready to take Aurum to the next level. I took a deep breath.

"Thank you for your faith, and I will do my best to represent the best for and of Aurum. This city isn't just a place to live. It represents hope, and a future for everyone who enters our gates. As one of the wealthiest cities in Ambrose, our children deserve to get the best education and chances of life. There's still work to do, but I vow to make Aurum the city we deserve."

The council clapped softly as I took my seat once more. I grinned at Riel, my hands shaking with the shock and sudden nerves.

"Will you and Riel be moving into the Lord's—or Lady's—estate?" Theo asked with a twinkle in his eye. I laughed nervously. He knew what I would do with the estate given the chance. Riel placed his hand in mine once again and gave it a squeeze of support. I cleared my throat.

"Riel and I will be remaining at the General's Quarters. We will continue our duties to Aurum as we normally would. I will remodel the estate into a school. Anyone who wishes to receive a proper education can attend for free."

Saphira scoffed. The councilor wore her brown hair back in an intricate style that swept it over her right shoulder. She frowned as she looked over at me with skeptical eyes. Her green dress sparkled with gemstones sewn into elaborate designs. I argued with her the most. We had never grown to like or respect each other.

"Where do you think you're going to get the money? We can't just upend our daily lives to make a school," she spat at me.

I stared at her, unblinking. "I am the elected Lady, am I not?"

She averted her gaze and clenched her jaw. "Yes."

"Then let me make this clear for you." I leaned over the table and sneered. "The last Lord wasted precious resources on keeping his life comfortable. You will not find that from me. I fight for the people, and I win.

"If you have an issue with the way I create a better system for this city, then I suggest you give up your seat right now. Because vapid gossip and petty words from a weak-willed woman will not dissuade me."

She grimaced, but said no more. I looked over at Riel, who gave me a supporting nod. I would not back down from this responsibility.

The council was dismissed, and I let out a breath of relief, and a sort of surreal feeling came over me. I was nervous and terrified, but I was also ready.

I turned around, ready to make my way back to the Quarters, back home. I needed a large glass of wine, and Riel probably wanted to celebrate, pride emanating from the look he gave me as we exited the council room.

Masika stood right outside the entrance, and I couldn't wait to tell her about my nomination and election. My excitement faded when I saw her speaking to a brawny man—one of Riel's guards. Her eyes met mine, wide with shock. I nudged Riel's shoulder, and he nodded, concern flashing over his face as we made our way over to them.

"Riel, Leoni." The man greeted us with a quick bow of his head.

"It's Lady, now," Riel corrected, and the guard started mumbling apologies. I shoved my elbow into Riel's ribs, making him grunt a low oof.

"There's no need for formal titles," I said. Riel frowned at me, but I just rolled my eyes instead. "What's going on?"

The guard straightened his back and looked at me directly in the eye. I raised my eyebrow. Typically, guards would report to Riel, but I guessed I was higher on the food chain now. The thought made my skin tingle, questioning the reality of the promotion. I would have to pinch myself later.

"There was a sighting, a Dragon Rider, in the northern region."

"Was it Galen?" I asked, the prospect of seeing our old friend lighting an excitement in me. The guard shook his head. My blood turned to ice.

"Are you sure? Was it one of the Tantal riders?" I asked. Galen was the only known rider in Ambrose, but in Tantal, the mortals bred dragons for their army. If they crossed the border, it could mean war, and it would be messy and bloody, and that was something I never even wanted to entertain for the future of my people. He shook his head again.

"Reports don't believe so. I'm still garnering information, but so far it's looking like another Ambrosian Dragon Rider. A Magi. There are rumors it's Lady Halcyon of Dolan."

Riel cursed under his breath, and I shared the sentiment. Galen was a fluke, an anomaly. What did it mean that there was another Rider in our lands? My mind flashed to the mating bond that Riel and I shared. I glanced down at my wrist, the gold band shining against my skin. After we bonded, we discovered that Dragon Bonds were like Mating Bonds—both considered Divine and godly gifts. Both leaving gold bands on the arms. Ours around our wrists, Galen's around his forearm.

How the mortals were getting the bonds in their magic-less land was the whole reason Galen was currently under cover in their army. He thought that the stolen relics could be connected and wanted to investigate. And now the gods had once again given a Magi a piece of their power and demanded their presence known. I took in a deep breath as I realized my duties as Lady would surpass my predecessors.

Acknowledgements

WOW! It has been my dream to write and publish a fantasy novel, and I can't believe it actually happened. I would not have been able to do it without the support of my husband, who always encouraging me to find my joy. I truly don't know where I would be without you, my love.

To my best friends, Keli, Sarah, and Jasmine who have heard the highest of highs, and lowest of lows. Thank you for listening to me scream in joy, and cry in panic. Without you I would be lost. To my wonderful Beta Readers- you are the ones that truly took a wimpy draft and helped me take it to leg day. Thank you, Kate, Sara M., Meagan, Melanie P, Sarah B., Mel S., Keli and Ashley.

Thank you to my discord buddies who have been an amazing sound board to bounce ideas off of, and give an insurmountable amount of advice, support, and encouragement.

A MASSIVE thank you to Julie the YarnWyvern who helped with a much needed polish and gave me many laughs along the way!

Cheers, to Shadows in the Golden City and the rest of the Chronicles of Ambrose.

Afterword

If you enjoyed Shadows in the Golden City, please leave a review on Goodreads and Amazon. As an indie author, every review is crucial to a book's success.

Sign up for my newsletter to get sneak peeks and bonus content at www.authorjenniferkay.com

You can find me on TikTok and Instagram @jenniferkayauthor